WILL GOTHARD

OPERATION TRACER

A NOVEL

Bow Bell Books

AUTHOR'S NOTE

The real-life Operation Tracer mission, although never activated, remained top secret after World War II. Rumours of its existence were commonplace in Gibraltar and beyond until its public discovery in 1997.

This story is fiction. As for the real people involved, some being public figures, their histories recorded, appear here under their own names. Others have been fictionalised, their names changed along with their fates.

Will Gothard

For Grandad and Granny

SPAIN

Seville

SPAIN

Malaga

Algeciras   Rock of Gibraltar

ATLANTIC
OCEAN   Tangier   MEDITERRANEAN SEA

MOROCCO

Casablanca

AIRFIELD

RUNWAY

Waterport Road

Devil's Tower Road

5

11

BAY of GIBRALTAR

Queensway

Main Street

Gibraltar Harbour

2

4 1   8

Signal Hill
387m

The Rock

3

Dry Docks

Rose Road

Europa Road

Queen's Road

Summit 426m

9

10

Dudley Ward Way

7

1 The Angry Friar Pub

2 John Mackintosh Square

3 The Rock Hotel

4 Governor's Residence

5 Commercial Mole

6 German Prisoner of War (POW) Camp

7 Windmill Hill, Prisoner Cells

8 The Battery at Devil's Gap

9 Lord Airey's Battery Tunnel & Shelter

10 O'Hara's Battery

11 Hays Level Gate

12 Harley Street Tunnels

13 Little Bay Tunnels

Mediterranean Sea

12

13

6

Europa Point

0	0.5	1	1.5	2 km
0	1/2		1mi	

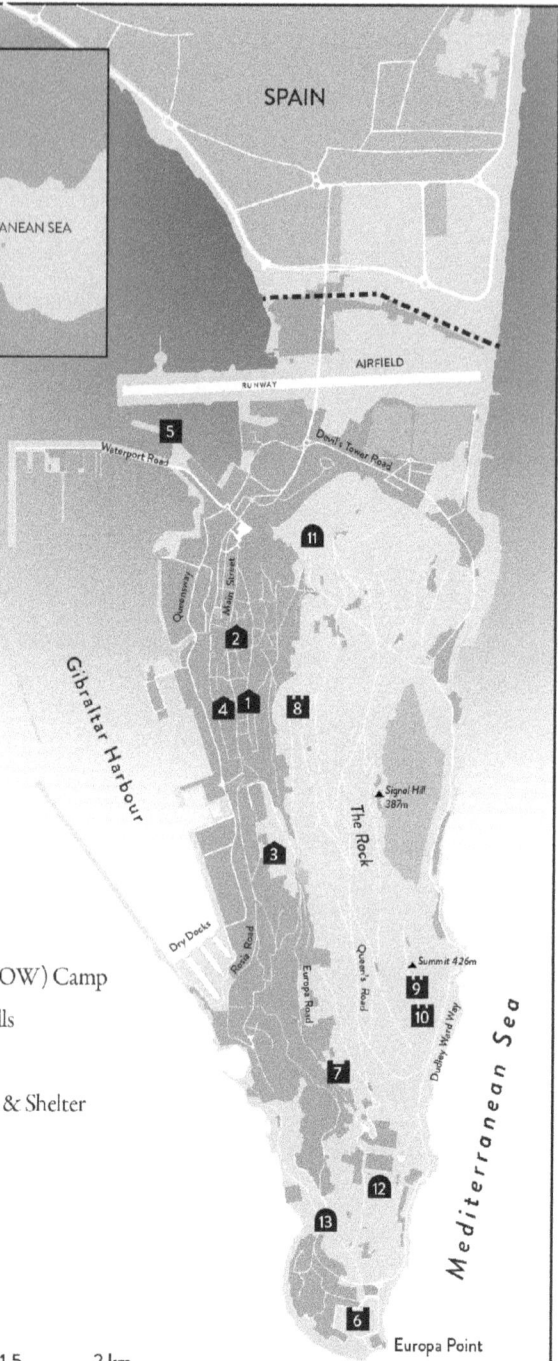

STRAIT of GIBRALTAR

1

JACKBOOTS ON THE ROCK

1942, September 10 (13:52h)
Turnbull's Lane, Rock of Gibraltar

A secret you keep from yourself isn't a secret at all. It's a lie. Lying was the only way Commander Frederick 'Windy' Gale could get the job done. We're all going to make it, he thought, ducking down a narrow street to avoid a hail of enemy bullets. Backs pressed to a wall, the commander and two of his men listened intently as the jackboots crossed the cobbled streets of the British overseas territory.

Constant gunfire and the pungent smell of sulphur told Windy all he needed to know. The Germans and Spanish had invaded the Rock. How they'd managed it with the element of surprise was a matter for later discussion if they weren't shot dead in the next ten minutes.

Windy knew they were exposed, with no chance of defending a position even if they wanted to, and they didn't. They needed to get to the top of the Rock as quickly as possible or Operation Tracer was over before it had begun. The clock was ticking; everything had been planned to the final detail for every eventuality, everything except this, a surprise attack. The Admiralty had deemed it impossible, but here they were, with thousands of Wehrmacht swarming the Rock. The longer they stood there, the less likely they'd get out of town alive. Windy looked along the wall at his comrades, African rifleman Hubert "Hoop" Fundi and Staff Surgeon Doctor "Syd" Milburn. He'd trained with Hoop and Doctor Milburn for months, but he'd never seen their

1

eyes looking at him the way they were right now. Electrified. Fear, yes, but determination too. He was proud of them, and the mission hadn't even begun. Their faces, one dark-skinned, one light, both had 'that' expression. The one most men have the first time the bullets start to fly. He'd seen it all too often in his short but active Naval Intelligence career. The "What now?" look. Getting them out of this one alive was going to be difficult, but he wasn't going to let that thought show on his face. Steady the buffs, he told himself. You know what you're doing. Secure your position. No fuss, quickly and quietly out of town.

"Ready, chaps?" Windy flashed his best smile.

The commander led the way. Turnbull's Lane ran parallel to Main Street, joined up with Lynch's Lane, and from there a steep staircase led out of town. Get to the top of the staircase and they had a chance to disappear up the Rock. The others wouldn't wait for them more than an hour, probably less if they followed protocol. There was no playing hide-and-seek and waiting for the cover of darkness – the mission would have been compromised by then and with it the war effort. Crikey, thought Windy. The stakes are so much higher than our lives. He put the thought out of his mind and replaced it with just get to the next corner alive. Windy, Hoop, and Doctor Milburn hit the wall at the corner of Turnbull's Lane. Windy peered around: the street was empty. Gun barrels poked through the shutters on the first floor of the building across the street. British for sure.

"Hopefully our chaps won't shoot us," he said optimistically as he set off up the lane. Hoop and Doctor Milburn hung back as the commander ran, his heart racing, his eyes and his Sten machine gun bouncing as he tried to keep them fixed on the corner in front of him. If the Germans appeared, that was it. There was nowhere to take cover in the street. Nothing came around the corner. This was easier than he'd expected. Narrow Lynch's Lane crossed Main Street at the bottom; Windy peered around the next corner. Grey-green uniforms, those distinct curve-shaped helmets and short black boots, unfamiliar silhouettes, German Wehrmacht, more than out of place on Main

Street, Gibraltar. A scout car pulled up and the officers inside looked straight at him. Windy pulled his head back as Hoop and Doctor Milburn joined him at the corner. Snatching a second look, Windy saw that the car was gone.

"Secure the top," he ordered. Hoop shot up the stone staircase three steps at a time, clutching his rifle as gunfire rang out behind him. The protruding barrels rattled the shutters of the upstairs windows, filling Turnbull's Lane with smoke and that rich smell of sulphur. One Wehrmacht infantryman twisted in agony and moaned on the ground; another crawled slowly back the way he'd come; three others lay perfectly still, killed instantly, thick crimson blood seeping out of them and filling the cracks in the cobblestones.

"Go!" Windy shouted at Doctor Milburn, a frozen spectator. The doctor snapped back to his reality and did his best to copy Hoop, taking multiple steep steps at a time, although the older and heavier-set man made hard work of the challenge. More Wehrmacht ran up Lynch's Lane towards Windy, who spun his Sten gun towards them and rattled off enough rounds to hit two, the others taking cover as the commander ran for the stairs.

Bullets hit the walls on both sides of Windy as he ran from side to side up the steps, making himself a difficult target. Brick shavings flew off the walls, getting into his eyes, and he could taste the wall in his mouth. He tried to blink out the dust, no time to rub his eyes. Windy kept pumping his legs, propelling himself up the staircase as fast as he could. At the top, Hoop and Doctor Milburn poked their heads out from the corner and then the barrels of their guns. Windy saw the flash of Hoop's weapon discharging at the enemy behind him. The bullet must have come close to him because he heard it whistle past. He certainly wasn't going to stop and check if Hoop had hit his target; he put his head down and kept taking the steps as fast as he could. Windy had seen Staff Surgeon Milburn shoot on the firing range during training for the mission. It wasn't pretty. The doctor would hit him for sure.

Gasping for air to fill his lungs quickly enough to keep up the pace, Windy felt his legs burn. But he was almost there. Just a few steps remained and he'd made it. The bullet that struck him in the back wasn't the cause of his fall. He felt a heavy tap like a stone hitting him above the hip. No pain, but it took his mind off the steps for a moment: he knew he'd been hit and missed his footing. He caught the top of a step with the toe of his boot and it sent him crashing forward. Not good, he thought as his head hit a step and his knee cracked into another. At any moment he expected to feel the thud of a second round, but before he knew it two powerful hands wrapped around his forearms and he was back on his feet. He surprised himself with how quickly he stood. It was Hoop out there on the steps with him. The incoming fire hit the step next to them, the wall to the side, and Windy heard at least one other round whistle overhead, but it was the voice of Doctor Milburn that he'd remember.

"Damn you blasted bloody Nazis." As Hoop and Windy made for the shelter of the corner, the doctor drew the German fire. He stood out on the steps in the open, shooting indiscriminately down the staircase at an unseen enemy. "Go to hell," he shouted as the first bullet passed through his chest and ricocheted off some part of his skeleton, diverting its bloodstained trajectory onto one of the whitewashed walls. Two more bullets took the doctor's breath and with it the words out of his mouth before he hit the steps hard. The two or three further bullets that hit him were overkill – he wasn't getting up. Hoop dropped Windy safely around the corner at the top, but as he did so he lost his footing. Windy saw Hoop begin to fall backwards. The rifleman's sound of surprise and dread matched the look on his face. It happened too fast for Windy to help. He watched helplessly from the corner as Hoop tumbled down the steps at breakneck speed, head over heels, like a marble out of control. Windy shut his eyes, this wasn't happening. He'd lost them both.

He took one calming deep breath, picked up Hoop's rifle, and steadied himself. He was next. They were coming, he was bleeding;

he couldn't outrun them, he couldn't outshoot them, and surrender wasn't an option. The next few minutes would be the difference between escape, capture, or killing. He felt the burn. Having been shot before, he knew what came next. The pain would intensify steadily. It was going to get a lot worse. There was no time to lose while he still had the benefit of adrenaline.

He looked up at the top of the Rock, then down at the hole in his uniform leaking blood. I don't have a cat in hell's chance of getting to the top alive. It was over, but what choice did he have but to try? Spilling blood, Windy ran across the road, hopped a low garden fence, shuffled up the short path to a back door, and tried the handle. It was open. Overwhelmed with relief, he entered the house, leaving a trail of blood behind him.

2

KILL OR BE KILLED

Windy walked quickly through the house. There were dishes in the kitchen sink and a book open on the living-room table, a cigarette in the ashtray, burnt out as if left there after first lighting. The front door was open – whoever lived there had left as quickly as he'd arrived. He exited the front door onto the street. Gunfire large calibre and small punctuated by explosions rang out in all directions. Two men, one in civvies, the other uniformed, darted across the street holding two weapons each. Flattening his hand over the bullet's exit wound at the front of his hip, Windy tried to restrict the drip of blood as he crossed the road and tested more door handles. He couldn't prevent a trail of red dots leading to him but he could make them few and far between and so hard to follow. One after another, all the doors were locked. The fifth one was open. Snatching a look back down the street Windy quickly stepped inside, closed the door, and locked it.

The living room was empty; the carpet, burgundy – *Lucky for the owner,* Windy thought as the blood began to drip through his fingers. There were two small sofas and a sideboard with a bottle of whisky on a silver tray. He grabbed the bottle and walked quickly through to the kitchen as the sound of rapid fire filled the street outside.

The kitchen was a compact space with a sink, a little table, and cupboards. As quickly as he could, Windy removed his jacket and dropped it to the floor. His shirt was soaked with blood above his hip. The wound was still leaking but not dramatically. *You're one lucky blighter,* he told himself. It was a flesh wound and if he was going to get shot, he couldn't have been shot in a better place. He wouldn't bleed excessively in that location, although every twist brought an intensified stinging burn, like a swarm of bees each taking their turn to attack him in the same spot repeatedly. The adrenaline that had dulled his senses on the street had worn off; he knew that was when the real pain would start. The bleeding had slowed, although he already had nausea; he'd black out for sure if he lost too much blood, so he had to plug the holes. Right now.

Buttons were ripped off as Windy removed his shirt. Gripping the cloth with his teeth, he tore two strips from it. Popping the cork from the bottle he poured whisky over both. The gunfire on the street outside stopped. The two brave men outside had been silenced. He needed to work fast.

He took a shot of the whisky. It burnt his throat. A momentary distraction. He picked up a kitchen knife and stuck the wooden-handle in his mouth before pouring whisky on the open wound. He felt his teeth sink into the wood as the alcohol settled on his raw flesh. His legs gave way and he was suddenly down on the floor with bent knees. The burn was unbearable, then finally numbness, like his body was no longer his. On the second attempt he managed to lift himself up to lean on the sink.

Windy located the bullet hole, grabbed one of the whisky-drenched pieces of his shirt and pushed it and his finger deep into the hole. His nerve endings fizzed with electricity; he saw the ceiling for a moment and almost lost consciousness. His knees gave way again and Windy was back on the floor but he kept pushing until the fabric wouldn't go any deeper into the wound. The entrance wound at the back was harder to plug but – *one way or another this is going in* – harder and harder, faster and faster, until the cloth was deep inside the hole. Windy puked on himself, all over the Lucky Strike cigarette packet still in his breast pocket. Dropping his head, he lay exhausted on the kitchen floor.

I'm not going to make it, am I? He looked at Hoop's rifle pitched up against the kitchen door. He couldn't take it up the Rock with him. It was too heavy. He wouldn't make it with the rifle. *I won't make it either way, let's be honest, and capture isn't an option.* It wouldn't take them long to establish his identity. It was highly likely that the Abwehr, the German intelligence service, had a file on him, just as MI6 did on many German spies. He wouldn't become the weakest link in the operation. He couldn't risk that. There was too much at stake. Too many lives. The mission had to go on with or without him. He knew he should put the barrel of the gun in his mouth and pull the trigger – it was the only sure way to protect the mission – but something inside him said, *Hang on, you're not done yet.* Windy stopped talking to himself and dragged his frame up on one knee, tied what was left of his bloodstained shirt around his wound. Windy took another swig of whisky, picked up the kitchen knife, left Hoop's rifle, and put his head up against the back-door window.

The terraced house had a small garden with high walls on all sides, a little lawn area with flowerbeds and a tall gate that led onto a back street. Just over the top of the wall he could see the first of the bushes and trees that led to greater cover and a path up the Rock. Windy opened the back door and stepped out into the garden. He needed to get out of town. Get into the trees, unseen. It was his only chance of making it to the top of the Rock. Windy looked at his watch: he was running out of time. The others wouldn't wait. He crossed the garden, took hold of the circular handle of the gate, and pulled. The latch slipped but the gate didn't open. There was a large rusty keyhole but no key. The wall was too high to climb in his current state. Going back out the front door held greater risk. It was then he saw the bolt. The gate was locked with a bolt. He hadn't noticed it at first, he wasn't thinking straight, but he now heard shouts in Spanish. That was unmistakable. Looking through the open back door, through to the living room, he could see the window that looked out onto the street, veiled by lace curtains. A Spanish uniform was standing in front of the window. They'd found him.

His adrenaline kicked in again. Windy slipped the bolt and pulled again on the garden gate. It didn't open but the front door of the house did, hit by the butt of a gun or kicked in. He dropped to his knees on the lawn. He could see Hoop's rifle where he'd left it in the kitchen. He wouldn't make it to the gun in time. The four high walls that provided such needed security moments ago closed in on him. There was nowhere to run or hide. Trapped. He had a knife and no idea how many were coming, or how experienced they were. He knew in an instant what he had to do. Shot, bleeding, burning from the pain, without a gun, he was going to have to fight.

Windy took a firm grip on the knife and dropped to the lawn face down, making sure that the wound could be easily seen, then scrambled his legs in an awkward-looking position and put his arm holding the knife, also awkwardly, under his side, hiding the blade. They'd be through the back door at any moment. He took a deep breath and concentrated on shallowing his breathing. If they saw his chest rising and falling, he was dead. If he moved, he was dead; any sign of life and he was dead. Even if they were convinced by his act, he had no idea how many there would be. More than two and he was dead. He would have a moment, a fraction of a second. His only hope was that they would be inexperienced and overconfident.

You've had a good run, he told himself as he listened intently. His breathing soon became so light that it was like he was trying not to drown. He desperately wanted a full intake of breath, to fill his lungs. He couldn't keep this up much longer. *For God's sake, hurry up.* Then they were upon him. He heard the name Juan, one Spaniard addressing the other. He wished he hadn't. He didn't want to know the name of a man he had to try to kill.

Windy remained perfectly still, with almost no breath, not even an eyelid twitch.

The barrel of a gun was forced into his chest, triggering his reaction: one arm swung out, hitting the rifle. The gun went off and Windy felt the bullet burn his arm. All in one movement he brought the knife across the leg of the Spaniard closest to him. The man fell. Windy, now wide-eyed, could see his partner: a thick-set Spaniard with a bushy black moustache. He was too far away to reach with the knife but that wasn't what crossed Windy's mind first. The man was wearing a British Army warrant officer's uniform!

The Spaniard panicked, caught off guard by Windy's sudden attack. He fired his gun before pointing it. Windy rolled and threw himself forward with his arm outstretched. The tip of the knife found the Spaniard's knee. It didn't embed far but deep enough to bring him down. One scramble later and Windy was upon him. This time the knife entered the Spaniard's chest. Windy had aimed for his heart but it went in around his gut. He let go of the knife and grabbed the gun, turning it on the second man. He was smaller, without facial hair, bleeding from the wound on his leg and in panic mode, pulling frantically at the trigger of his weapon. Windy steadied himself. He knew the best way to hit a target under extreme emotional circumstances was to pause and take aim. He fired. The headshot thrust the man back and removed some of his skull, splattering brains on the locked garden gate.

Windy spun back around to the moustachioed Spaniard still lying next to him, the knife protruding from his gut. He was close enough to put the barrel of the gun against the man's head, who wiggled and moaned from the knife wound. Windy positioned the barrel under the Spaniard's neck, pushed it up hard into the soft skin, and pulled the trigger. The man's bushy moustache stretched across his top lip as the muffled sound of a discharged weapon made Windy blink. The splatter of flesh and bone left a smell in the air and a remnant on Windy's face. It had a memorable butcher's shop odour of fresh meat.

With both Spaniards dead, Windy fell panting onto the lawn. The hole above his hip was leaking blood again and he had a new burning sensation. His arm was now bleeding too – the bullet had clearly nicked him and left a channel down his arm where the flesh had been removed. If it hurts now, which it did, that was nothing compared with what it would feel like later. He was tired of being shot. *Hell, I'm still alive though!* He knew that it would be twice as hard to move and twice as painful very soon. He needed to take advantage of the endorphins racing through his body. Go before another comes. He couldn't take another fight for his life. Not here and now. *Get up.* Windy took the Nagant revolver from the Spaniard's holster, picked up the Italian-made rifle, and emptied the four remaining bullets of the magazine into the lock on the garden gate. *What blithering idiot locks their garden gate with a key?*

Bleeding and exhausted, Operation Tracer team leader Frederick 'Windy' Gale exited the gate, putting one foot in front of the other, and continued to drag himself up towards the top of the Rock. Destination: Lord Airey's Battery.

3

PSST!

1942, September 10 (16:02h)
Queen's Road, Rock of Gibraltar

The crackle of small-arms was a permanent echo as Windy dragged himself steadily up the Rock. He could hear the Germans and Spaniards below, taking Gibraltar street by street, but there was also a serious battle above him at the top of the Rock. The chaos was punctuated by the rare discharge of an artillery battery. Not nearly as many shots were being fired in defence of the Rock as he would have expected. *Why aren't the big guns firing?* He'd anticipated a barrage of artillery shelling to protect British positions from the invaders, but that wasn't happening. Windy stopped for a moment and looked back out over the harbour: he was more than halfway up. Twenty minutes earlier, the skies above the Rock had been full of parachutes. German paratroopers, maybe a thousand of them or more, had dropped in nearly every part of the British overseas territory, except for the steep sides of the Rock. They were clearly aware of the danger posed by the escarpments that were his route to the top. Thankfully for him – although he knew he'd encounter the enemy again before the Tracer team. *If the Tracer team is there at all.*

Another loud explosion sent seawater jetting into the air. It must have been the tenth ship he'd seen disabled in as many minutes. It looked like HMS *Capetown* this time. The harbour was full of burning British vessels. The *Nelson*, the *Formidable*, and HMS *Furious* were all sinking. He could see a convoy of German artillery streaming over the frontier border and heading into town. He recognised Panzer tanks but there were also larger versions: *Are they Tigers? Could a Tiger tank cross the short concrete-block dragon's teeth constructed along the neutral zone? What about the defences at Calatan Bay and Sandy Bay, had they been breached too?* The Germans owned the skies above the Rock. Stukas and Messerschmitt aircraft zigzagged, firing indiscriminately at British-held positions while the airfield to his right was littered with burning RAF planes. They'd never even got off the ground. Any British aircraft still on the runway were static target practice for their German counterparts. It was depressing.

How on earth had they managed it? The Italians were responsible for the ship sinking; there was no question about that. They'd failed for months to sink a ship in the Gibraltar harbour but not for lack of trying. The game of cat-and-mouse had become notorious. Italian frogmen had been riding their torpedoes into British waters almost weekly, but their missions only resulted in the two-man crews being fished out of the water by the coastguard. He had a grudging respect for those who risked their lives underwater on what were nothing less than bizarre attempts at causing damage to the naval fleet – though that respect was fast becoming hatred as he watched in horror at the Italians' newfound success. The Germans had come by land, sea, and air and done the impossible. Surprised them. How had he been happily drinking a pint and reading the *Times* at the entrance to the Star Bar an hour before? "A great nation was getting into its war stride." That's what Mister Churchill had told the House of Commons before the sirens had brought Windy to his feet. He'd been sure the gunfire was a training operation. The Germans were supposed to be focused on the Russian front and Stalingrad. They'd made a mistake to relax.

As he'd stepped into the street, Hoop and Syd arrived at speed, fully armed.

"Tracer," said the doctor. Windy dropped his paper and all three had run in the direction of the Rock Hotel.

The burn from both his gunshot wounds put away thoughts of what no longer mattered. Execute the mission at all costs, get the job done, that's what he'd been told, but was there even a mission left? *I've lost two of my team. What about the others? Are they dead or captured too?* He felt light-headed as he approached the southern end of the upper Rock: the tunnel entrance to Lord Airey's Battery. O'Hara's Battery beyond it must have been the last big gun still firing in anger.

He'd done his best to stop the hole in his hip from bleeding, surprised by how little blood there had been considering the calibre of the round that had entered and exited on the other side. The struggle up the Rock had drained him mentally more than the blood from the holes. He'd expected at any moment to be ended by a German bullet – it had been impossible to put it out of his mind for long. What a disastrous situation! But crouching in the trees by the small stone wall on Ohara's Road, opposite the entrance to the lower end of Lord Airey's Battery tunnel system, the belief that he'd make it to the others was now unshakable in him.

The entrance was unguarded. Up the hill to his right, Windy could see the backs of German and Spanish uniforms, laying siege to the big gun at O'Hara's Battery. The loud boom of shells propelling into the straits had all but stopped. A single gun, no matter how big, wouldn't save the Rock now. It was just a matter of time before those brave men holding Lord Airey's Battery were killed or captured. Only the British secured inside the tunnels would be able to put up a sustainable resistance. *For how long? A year, maybe two?* What good would they be to the war effort trapped like rats if Jerry owned the straits and the airfield? Never had his Tracer mission felt more important than right then. His mind was clear, crystal-clear. He'd execute Tracer, on his own if he had to, or die trying. His knee wobbled. *Focus, man,* he told himself. *You're almost there.*

Windy took a firm grip on the revolver, hopped over the small stone wall, and ran across the road to the tunnel entrance. He skipped between the two concrete walls that dovetailed the access with no idea what he would find on the other side. The heart rate he'd been working to keep down was pumping off the scale now. The blood loss, albeit smaller than expected, was taking its toll: he felt light-headed. Once inside the tunnel, Windy stood perfectly still and listened. It was dark, the power had been cut, but he knew the way. He waited for his pupils to dilate, although the deeper he went inside the darker it would get. When he was sure he hadn't been followed, Windy limped on, dragging his hand along the wall. He turned left and then right through the narrow channels, past the NCO office and then out into Lord Airey's Shelter. Using the wall as his guide, he walked slowly and quietly deeper inside. Paranoia or a sixth sense for some inexplicable reason made him feel like he wasn't alone. He could hear the battle outside and voices. Whispers in the darkness. *There.* Then nothing.

Never letting go of the wall, Windy began to limp fast. He'd been inside that cave hundreds of times, day and night, training for this moment. It was twenty-three strides along the wall to the doorway at the other end. He'd counted twenty-two as the torches came on and illuminated the space. Gunshots rang out, hitting the plaster on the wall in front of him, peppering him with dust. The flashes lit the whole shelter momentarily. A drape curtain covered one of the walls opposite and Spanish uniforms filled the entrance. Windy turned the corner and ran down the long narrow tunnel on the other side of the cave, away from the Spanish intruders. It was dark too, but he knew this tunnel as well. Standard in its construction, similar to if not the same as ninety per cent of the honeycomb network of tunnels that crisscrossed the Rock on the inside. Narrow but wide enough for two men to walk side by side, mostly high enough for a six-footer to walk standing up straight. Corrugated iron panels covered both walls and the ceiling, which was curved in a large U shape. Low to the ground on each side were two-foot-high concrete walls running the tunnel's full length. A tube that contained electrical cables ran throughout, secured to the roof like drainage guttering.

Arm outstretched and hand guiding the way in the pitch black,

Windy hoped that nothing had been abandoned on the floor in front of him – he'd know by the fall before he saw it. *I've lost count of my steps!* The Spanish were coming, but he had the upper hand, or so he thought until the bend in the tunnel in front of him lit up. The voices echoed off the corrugated metal sheets. *They're German.* Spanish behind him, Germans in front. *Blast!* He'd come so far and got so close. Windy stopped dead, panting for breath as torches approached from both sides.

"Psst!" came a sound from behind the corrugated panel wall.

4

FOUR OUT OF SIX

1942, September 10 (16:43h)
Upper Lord Airey's Battery Tunnel, Rock of Gibraltar

Windy heard the Germans reach the Spanish in the middle of the narrow tunnel.

Commander Windy Gale was nowhere to be seen. The phantom wounded British soldier had disappeared "as if by magic", according to the German-Franco alliance's report later. Having crawled behind one of the corrugated iron panels that lined the tunnel walls, Windy sat as silent as a mouse, subduing the pant in his breath, not moving a muscle just a few feet away from them.

He continued to hear Spanish and German voices as, bewildered by his disappearance, the soldiers moved back up the tunnel to where he'd entered. Finally, there was silence. The tunnel was empty once more. Windy sat, taking long quiet slow breaths, trying to lower his heart rate: the beats were irregular but their pumps were powerful. Finally, he thought it was safe to move. He reached into his breast pocket and felt past his cigarettes to his box of matches. He struck a match and the space behind the corrugated iron panel burst into view. Sitting waiting for him, also hiding in the small space, were three men: Doctor Tom Carter, and signalmen 'Bunny' Stuart and 'Young Albert' Hamilton. All that was left of his Operation Tracer team.

The four men stood up and walked away from the corrugated iron access, down a roughly carved-out entrance channel with raw rock walls. The channel was short but wide, the floor uneven, made of large stones and rubble mixed with household bricks. Twenty or more bags of cement were stacked to one side next to a bucket. The men moved in almost pitch darkness with practised ease. Bunny Stuart, a short, thick-set, muscular Scot with curly hair and freckles, led the way, as Doctor Carter and lean teenager Albert Hamilton continued to assist Windy. The Scotsman reached a whitewashed wooden doorway and turned the well-oiled handle. The silent door swung open outwards. The four men passed through the door and Bunny closed it behind them.

At the flick of a switch, the single light bulb at the centre of a rectangular chamber cast low light around the room. All four walls, like the door, were whitewashed. Bunny struck another match to light a fat-powered lamp, which shed more light into the chamber, which was approximately forty feet in length and fifteen feet wide with a low ceiling, packed to its roof with cardboard boxes lining all four walls, three rows deep. An Aladdin's cave. A stationary exercise bicycle was snug between two rows of boxes on one side. Instead of a chain and cables, it had a leather strap running into the wall from a small box attached to its crank. The walls were approximately eight feet high and created a barracks-like space around the three thick-legged bunk beds, two beds per bunk. The floor was tiled with cork; as the men walked across it, there was no sound. A six-feet-square solid table placed at the centre of the chamber was quickly cleared of boxes by the now worried-looking Albert Hamilton. The youngster had the beginnings of facial hair, black in colour to match his short-cropped skull. Doctor Carter, square-jawed and in his mid-thirties, with a furrowed intellectual brow, laid Windy down on the table. He handed his team leader a bottle of whisky, removed Windy's jacket, and pulled the torn shirt pieces from the bloody entry and exit wounds on his hip. Windy was relieved to be finally in the hands of Doctor Carter.

"Let's put some blood in you," said the doctor as he pulled various tubes, needles, and pumps from his extensive and well-organised medical kit. He rolled up his sleeve.

"Syd?" asked the doctor.

"Didn't make it," said Windy soberly.

Carter continued preparing a blood transfusion without looking at Windy. "Hoop?" Windy shook his head.

Carter pushed a needle into his commanding officer's arm. "Can it be done with just four?" He continued to fiddle with rubber tubes, plugging them into a steel apparatus. He knew the answer to his own question. Operation Tracer was going to be tough with six men but impossible with four.

"What choice do we have?" replied Windy, now almost white as a sheet. Bunny looked nervously at Carter and Albert. Windy could see what they were all thinking. It looked like they might be down to just three men soon. He wanted to vomit but fought against it. He needed to get them sealed in before he let go. The mission was seriously compromised. Lives would be lost as a result. *How many lives?* Even if they worked around the clock without sleep, they couldn't now execute the mission as planned. They all knew it, but what did it change? Nothing. What choice did they have but to go on?

"Brick it up!" said Windy.

Bunny nodded as Doctor Carter started pumping blood into his commanding officer. Windy drifted as the blood hit his veins.

5

FLEMING AND GODFREY

1941, May 21 (15:00h)
36 Curzon Street, home of John Henry Godfrey,
Director of Naval Intelligence, Mayfair, London,
England, United Kingdom

Nearly a year and a half before Windy was having blood pumped into him on the Rock of Gibraltar, he took a packet of Camel cigarettes out of his tweed jacket pocket on a London street and turned them over. The address written on the back was 36 Curzon Street, Mayfair.

Wearing brogue shoes and chino trousers, Windy blended in, just another chap on the street, exactly the image he'd been told to portray for this meeting. No uniform, no taxi to share the address with. He'd walked from Regent Street, taken side roads, double-backed on himself, and mingled outside the new Lansdowne Club to make sure he hadn't been followed. He struck a Swan Vesta match and lit a cigarette standing across the road from the home of John Henry Godfrey, Director of Naval Intelligence.

He casually eyed the street. A baker's van and delivery boy, a couple having a heated discussion on a bench, a smartly dressed young woman walking with purpose, watched by a couple of sailors sharing a private joke. He hadn't been followed; he was sure of it. He'd been told to be over-cautious and that's exactly what he was being. Almost all of his previous Naval Intelligence meetings had been held at the chambers of Admiralty House in Whitehall, so when he had been invited to the private home of John Henry Godfrey and asked to arrive dressed as a civilian with the utmost care not to be followed, he knew something was afoot beyond the usual. He was downright intrigued, although a bit nervous. He'd played a little fast and loose with Admiralty regulations on more than one occasion. Always in the pursuit of getting the job done, of course. But he'd broken quite a few rules in recent years and the Admiralty was, under normal circumstances, sticklers for the regulations.

He hadn't exactly lied on official documents after the Duke of Windsor incident, but he hadn't told the truth either. The truth would have ended his career, and who would it have helped? Nobody. Not his country. He'd been warned to watch his step privately, but no public admonishment had come his way so far. *Is that what this is?* They wanted another 'chat' about Windsor. Or was this a more serious 'talking-to', maybe? If it was, why the cloak-and-dagger? The assassination attempt on the former King and all that had followed was old news since the outbreak of war; it was behind him and that's where he wanted it to stay.

Windy took a last draw on the cigarette and dropped it on the street. He looked at his watch. Fifteen hundred hours. It was time. He didn't want to be early or late – neither scenario carried the image he wanted to associate with his career. Windy stepped up to the front door and rang the bell, wiping his feet on the mat outside at precisely the top of the hour. As he stepped back from the glossy blue panelled door, he saw the curtains inside the window to the side of him twitch, only slightly, but enough for him to know he was being observed. Windy ignored whomever it was watching him – it was a superior officer for sure and he didn't want to make them feel uncomfortable by exposing their lack of stealth. He remembered the only other time he'd met Director Rear Admiral Godfrey. He'd been in a briefing for a mission at the Admiralty. The director had come into the meeting and introduced himself to each member of the team individually before taking up a seat in the corner of the room with one leg crossed over the other and sitting silently until they left. He'd seen the admiral in the corridors, usually flanked by a secretary and various uniformed officers but nearly always Commander Ian Fleming, his assistant. It was Commander Fleming who had asked him to attend today.

Finally, the front door was opened by a rotund lady in her fifties.

"Commander Gale, madam," said Windy quietly. She reminded him of his boyhood nanny: kind eyes, a round face, and a warm demeanour. Windy stepped inside.

The highly polished floorboards creaked as he stepped onto them. The director's house smelt of wood polish and flowers, although nothing from the garden was on show. A set of double doors opened and out stepped Commander Fleming.

"Windy! How the devil?" said Fleming with a big smile. "Thank you for coming." He was wearing his naval uniform so whatever this was about it was strictly Admiralty business, not a smoke, a whisky, and a word in the ear. Windy stood up and shaped to give a salute that Fleming waved away before he had a chance to complete it. He shared the rank of lieutenant commander with Fleming, but Ian's proximity to Rear Admiral Godfrey and the missions he was assigned always seemed to require recognition.

"Not needed, old boy, please come on in."

Windy liked Fleming. He had an easy way about him, although he maintained a professional distance personally. He'd always found him to be a man of his word, which made him easy to trust. There was nothing more important than trust on a mission. Trust of the men on the team and trust in those running the mission.

The director was sitting behind a leather-bound desk. A small reading lamp illuminated the smoke rising from an ashtray, and the curtains were closed. Windy pulled his shoes together and saluted the director. It felt odd, such formality in civilian clothing, but he'd rather be told it wasn't necessary than feel later that he should have done it.

"Commander Gale reporting, sir." Windy tried not to shout.

"At ease, Commander," said Admiral Godfrey.

"Thank you, sir." Windy stood at the centre of the room, uneasy.

"Commander Fleming tells me that you have a capacity for using creativity on missions to get results." Windy felt hot under the collar – it was the Duke of Windsor again. It had finally caught up with him.

"Yes, sir. Well, sir, sort of, sir." He'd been naive to think he could walk away from what he knew, or what he thought he knew. It was time to come clean.

"We have a mission that requires that creativity, Commander." The words were music to his ears. It wasn't about Windsor. That wasn't why he was there.

"You're probably wondering why we're not having this meeting at the Admiralty and why Commander Fleming requested that you arrive dressed as a civilian?"

"Yes, sir." Whatever it was, so long as it wasn't the Windsor affair. That was all that mattered.

"Simple, Commander. The mission we would like to talk to you about doesn't exist. The mission we would like you to undertake will not be run out of the Admiralty. No one at the Admiralty building, outside of myself and Commander Fleming here, will have knowledge of the mission. All mission briefings will take place here in this room and this room alone." Windy looked over at Commander Fleming, who lit a cigarette and looked back at his boss. "Under normal circumstances, you would be assigned this mission, but due to the extraordinary" – the director paused and searched for the correct word – "requirement, we want you to volunteer." Windy wasn't sure he'd heard the director correctly. *Did Admiral Godfrey ask me, not order me, to take on a mission?* Godfrey's next words confirmed it. "You'll need to agree to lead the team before we can brief you." *Golly,* thought Windy. Whatever was going on was downright bonkers.

"I accept the mission, sir. Jolly good of you to think of me." Windy saluted Godfrey.

"Good show," said the director, acknowledging Fleming for his selection of team leader for Operation Tracer.

6

MARIA & LOGAN

1942, September 10 (17:05h)
Main Chamber, Stay Behind Cave, Rock of Gibraltar

Back in the cave on the day of the invasion, Windy was ripped from thoughts of Mayfair, Godfrey, and Fleming as Doctor Carter pulled the sharp metal intravenous drip out of his own arm. The small amount of the doctor's blood that splattered Windy's biceps quickly smudged against Carter's jacket as he began to dress his commanding officer's gunshot graze.

Meanwhile, outside the cave entrance, up the dark tunnel in Lord Airey's Shelter, the larger space that Windy had traversed at speed and under fire, the continuous distant sound of gunfire could be heard. The large drape that spanned one wall of the shelter twitched and then twitched again before a man's hand, inside the cuff of a British Army-issue tunic, came out from behind it.

Twenty-three-year-old Petty Officer Maria Bona of the Women's Royal Naval Service couldn't see her boyfriend, Major Logan Warlock, standing beside her, but she knew he was peering around the drape in the shelter. The coarse material had stayed perfectly still, in line with them, since they had climbed in behind it – although Maria felt it shift now, sideways, against her nose. She'd heard the Spanish return to the hut they were in with the Wehrmacht Germans but without the injured British officer they'd been chasing. She didn't know the tunnels well, but she did speak both languages: "The phantom British officer was bleeding and wouldn't get far," she'd heard in her native Spanish. The torches and voices, both Spanish and German, had left the shelter some time ago.

Staying behind the safety of the draped curtain was preferable to the alcove they'd found themselves trapped in half an hour earlier up the hill next to Lord Airey's Battery. Maria had introduced Logan to the small space more than a month ago. It was the perfect place for their romantic encounters and to wait out the dangers of the invasion, or so she'd thought. How wrong she'd been. The alcove had fallen into the realm of 'no man's land' between the positions the Germans had taken up and the defences the British had put in place to hold Lord Airey's Battery and O'Hara's Battery beyond it from the invaders.

When the fighting started – it had been Logan's idea to stay put – neither of them could have guessed that the battle for the big gun would have turned out to be so fierce. A German stick grenade had missed its target and skittled into the alcove entrance. Maria had frozen at its appearance. Thank God Logan hadn't. He'd managed to kick it out before it exploded, sending stone and brick fragments everywhere. How disappointed she was with herself. Considering what she'd overcome, what she'd achieved. Now like a frightened mouse, she'd become so fragile and it was Logan's fault. She hated herself for being afraid, but she was. Fearful for both of them. Had the shooting not stopped for clearing the dead and rescuing the wounded, they might still be stuck there.

Maria ran her hand along the draped curtain: it was sack-like material. The fact that it extended from the roof of the shelter to the floor, with just enough space to squeeze behind it, made it silk to the touch, though: it was keeping them safe.

"We can't stay here," whispered Logan. Not what she wanted to hear. "They'll be back and put the lights on eventually. We need to take one of the tunnels." She didn't mind getting caught so long as they didn't shoot her, but she wasn't going to tell Logan that; she didn't want to go deeper into the tunnels.

"What if we give ourselves up?" asked Maria. Logan ignored the question, his head peeking out of the drape again, listening. She couldn't see much of him, but she could smell him: his aftershave was sweet but also dry. It was a comfort there in the darkness, with the distant sound of chaos outside. She felt the little hole she'd ripped into her sleeve somehow during the past hour. Maria liked to keep her Wren uniform spotless; it didn't bear thinking about what it looked like right now. *What does it matter?* She wouldn't be back in the typing pool for anyone to see.

"Come on." Logan stepped out from behind the drape. She didn't want to follow him, but she needed to listen to him: *this wasn't the time to tell him what to do, he'd kept them alive so far.*

Maria very slowly stepped out into the open shelter space. Logan took her hand firmly, and she followed him in the same direction as the injured man. Usually when she let Logan lead, he was doing her bidding, unwittingly or otherwise. She'd convinced him to claim he was sick and skip his shift at the frontier gate. She wanted him up there with her and she got what she wanted. She always had everything planned, down to the last detail, but look at her now: she was a mess, being pulled through the darkness to who knew where, like a frightened little girl.

"Wait, *tranquilo.*" She pulled her hand out of Logan's and stopped at the entrance to the narrow tunnel. She didn't want to go down there. She hated confined spaces. She wanted to be caught.

"What if we just wait here?" she whispered.

"You want to get shot?" asked Logan, frustrated. He tried to take her hand, but she wouldn't give it to him.

"Wait!" She raised her voice again.

"Shh…" was Logan's reply.

He didn't understand. She wasn't going into that narrow tunnel.

"Maria, it's dark in here. If they come back, they're very likely to shoot first and ask questions later. Listen." They could hear the ongoing chaos of war outside. "No one is taking prisoners right now.

They'll kill us." She knew he was right, but she felt sick at the thought of going deep into the tunnelled belly of the Rock. She hated it. She couldn't get out quick enough when sent on assignments inside. It was torture for her, but she couldn't do her job if she wouldn't enter the Rock. Her work was everything to her so she'd found a way. The walls closed in on her as she gave Logan back her hand and inched silently down the narrow tunnel towards the Operation Tracer team.

7

INVITED GUESTS

1942, September 10 (17:10h)
Stay Behind Cave cave entrance channel, Rock of Gibraltar

Bunny Stuart had mixed the cement he needed and stacked the bricks next to the entrance inside the cave, on the other side of the corrugated iron panel. He'd been trained in bricklaying for this eventuality. The original plan was that they would be bricked in from the outside and then the wall behind the metal sheet would be made to look like any other part of the tunnel. Windy, however, had insisted that one of the team be trained to bricklay in the dark, just in case something went wrong. Bunny respected his commanding officer, although he had thought it was pointless at the time. How wrong he'd been! The challenge had been learning to lay bricks quietly. They'd moved the noisy business of mixing cement in buckets into the main chamber, which was Albert's job. For Bunny, it was mostly about not hitting bricks together – with just the low light from the main chamber that was a challenge. Pressing them down into place rather than tapping them with the trowel was also a new skill. Bunny had laid the first two lines when he heard the light footsteps and whispering of somebody approaching.

Albert stepped through from the main chamber into the passageway holding a heavy bucket. The Scotsman put his finger to his lips and Albert froze. Seconds later Windy and Doctor Carter were also back at the entrance, Windy with revolver in hand and a look of trepidation. He was uncomfortable holding the gun. The plan had been for no weapons in the cave and for them all to be wearing a uniform, even if not their own, at all times. As Commander Fleming had made clear, if the cave were to be discovered, that was considered their best bet for being captured alive and not shot as spies.

Discharging the weapon, whoever was on the outside, would likely get them all killed. The four men sat silently and listened in the darkness. Bunny had his ear pressed against the corrugated iron panel. He held up two fingers in the low light to symbolise two people on the other side.

Bunny continued his charades, this time one finger up and his other hand down by his crotch, moving it around like the sign of a swinging dick. Replacing one finger with two, he used his other hand to create the shape of a breast.

Windy, feeling twice as nauseous now, knew what he was going to do, and the others weren't going to like it. He didn't like it either, but the mission required it. Nothing else mattered. He was sure of that. He'd been picked for the mission because the Admiralty believed he would get it done at all costs. This was all costs.

Windy handed his revolver to Bunny and gestured to bring them in.

Bunny repeated the sign language back to his team leader to make sure he understood. The doctor tapped Windy on the arm. They were close enough to exchange eye contact – the doctor clearly wanted to speak but Windy didn't have the time or inclination to include the others in his decision, not even his doctor. It was for him and him alone to make, and he'd made it. Windy knew he was breaking every rule the mission had laid down. He was recklessly endangering Operation Tracer. Opening the corrugated iron access again was a huge risk, but six bodies were the number they needed to successfully execute this mission – they were only four but there were two more outside. There was no doubt in his mind that this was a risk worth taking. One was a woman. That was a problem, but he couldn't take just the man. It was both or neither.

Windy repeated his silent order. Bunny gave a thumbs up, took a firm grip on the Nagant revolver in one hand, put his other on the corrugated iron panel, and prepared to push.

8

HOBSON'S CHOICE

"Don't pull me, Logan, or I'll fall!" Maria said, raising her voice in irritation. She was as deep down the tunnel as she was prepared to go. Every step she took was one more than she wanted to take. She was ready to turn and walk back up the way she had come, alone if necessary. *If she was caught?* All the better but she couldn't tell Logan that, Logan wouldn't understand, but she couldn't stay in this suffocating rat hole a minute longer.

The wall in front of her opened like the mouth of a great beast ready to swallow her whole. The walls had come alive and they were going to eat her. Maria screamed; stepping backwards, she used the corrugated iron panels to steady herself. She was hallucinating, the stress had got the better of her and she'd snapped. There was no other explanation. Out of the monster wall's mouth came a devil, with bright red hair.

"Move a muscle and I'll shoot yous," said the devil in a Scottish accent.

The monster had puked a Scotsman at her. Maria returned to logic as Logan stepped in front of her. The Scotsman was holding the mouth of the beast open with one hand and a revolver in the other.

"Bring the lassie, you need to get in!" said the Scotsman, this time speaking more aggressively. Maria looked up and down the tunnel: silence and darkness at both ends.

"Who the hell are you?" demanded Logan. Maria knew his voice well: it broke somewhere in the middle of the question like she'd never heard it before.

"Now," repeated the Scot. "No questions or I promise I'll shoot yous. It's nae personal, but you enter here or you die here. It's your choice."

Something turned over in Maria's stomach, she wanted to be sick. The space in the wall was smaller than the tunnel. She tried to catch her breath. In the little light that emanated from the monster's mouth, she could see both men looking at her. She was hyperventilating. Her hands were shaking and her legs seemed to give way. Her physical state appeared to decide for Logan. It wasn't what she wanted, but what choice did she have, she couldn't even speak. Logan helped her climb slowly through the narrow hole in behind the corrugated iron panels. Into the mouth of the monster, away from the freedom she longed for back up the tunnel. At that moment she would rather have been shot by accident trying to give herself up to the Germans than follow the Scotsman into that cramped hellhole in the wall.

The Scotsman stood alone in the tunnel for a moment, staring into the darkness of both ends, listening intently. There was silence but for the distant sound of an invasion taking place outside. He quietly stepped back behind the corrugated iron panel and secured it into position, leaving it indistinguishable again from the hundreds of others that lined that tunnel wall.

9

SURPRISE PACKAGE

Windy watched from his chair. He needed to sit. He didn't feel well. He could hear Bunny, Young Albert, and the mission's newest recruits as they crossed the rubble in the darkness of the entrance channel on the other side of the main chamber door. It was no time to start second-guessing himself. The decision was made. They were already inside and they could never leave, not while Operation Tracer was active. They were part of the team now, like it or not. He was taking a huge risk. Of course, he didn't want them. Whatever their previous experience, they'd need considerable on-the-job training. He had no idea of their temperament, which would be a factor. He was forcing them into the most difficult of circumstances and living conditions; they weren't prepared for it and they weren't going to thank him. This wasn't going to be easy for them, for the others on the team, or for him, but the Tracer mission was back up to six personnel, even if one of them was a woman. Six bodies were all that mattered. The mission was to be executed at all costs. He'd do whatever it took to get the job done. If that meant a woman, so be it.

The well-oiled handle of the door turned as it silently and slowly swung open. Doctor Carter stepped forward into his peripheral vision. Windy saw the army man first, a major: they shared rank. He was physically fit, clean-shaven but for the sharp pencil moustache, no hair on the philtrum under his nose, just two well-manicured dark sharp stripes. A mirror of his eyebrows. With his hair creamed tight to his head, he was a ladies' man for sure. There was something 'Clark Gable' in his look. Windy wasn't going to like him, although it was the girl who was going to be the problem.

She was a Wren, a petty officer in the Women's Royal Naval Service, and Windy knew her; or at least he knew of her, everybody did. How could he have been so unlucky? There were no women on the Rock like her. The moment she stepped out from behind the major, into the main chamber, Windy realised what a huge mistake he'd just made. Petty Officer Bona had one hand held by the major, the other clutched her large football-shaped stomach. She was heavily pregnant.

* * *

Young Albert's eyes were wide and his mouth frozen open in disbelief. He closed the door behind Bunny, who still had the revolver pointed at the recruits. Windy shut his eyes tightly, squeezed them closed, and reopened them. He couldn't make her disappear. She was still standing in front of him.

What have I done? Not just pregnant but shaking with fear, shoulders forward, hunched, her legs wobbly and ready to give way.

"What the bally hell's going on?" asked the major, clearly angry at the revolver still pointed at them. "Are you going to shoot us? Put that gun away!"

"I couldn't shoot the wee lassie there, no, but you? Aye. Maybe," replied Bunny also provocatively.

"Please keep your voices down," requested Doctor Carter politely.

"Name and rank?" interrupted Windy. He needed to get a hold of the situation and himself.

"Major Logan Warlock." Logan didn't salute.

"Army laddy," replied Bunny, clearly irritated by the lack of respect being shown to his commanding officer.

"What were you doing in the tunnel?" demanded Windy, feeling sicker than ever.

"Hiding," stated Logan.

Doctor Carter stepped forward. "How far gone are you?" He addressed the woman, although his tone was aimed, with his glance, at Windy.

"Eight months," came the reply in a whimper.

"Your name's Maria, yes? Staff Surgeon Milburn's patient?" Carter undoubtedly knew the girl too.

"Yes, sir. Petty Officer Maria Bona."

Windy remembered her name. Admiral Somerville himself, the commander of the British forces on the Rock, had given her permission to remain in Gibraltar. It had seemed a strange decision, but life on the Rock was full of the odd. And after Somerville sank friendly French ships in the port of Mers-el-Kébir, second-guessing the admiral was a waste of valuable energy. *Warlock?* thought Windy. *Major Warlock,* that name rang a bell too.

Carter swung to face Windy. "She can't stay here!" Windy ignored his doctor's advice.

"Why are you up here?" Windy asked. "What are your orders?"

Maria's leg gave way momentarily. Carter ran for a chair.

"Why were you up here in your condition?" Windy asked again, this time more forcefully.

Maria threw a nervous glance at her boyfriend.

"Windy, please." Doctor Carter, clearly distressed, placed the chair under the woman and Logan eased her down into it.

It was the first time Windy had seen his doctor lose his cool. He knew there would be hell to pay, but pregnant or not this petty officer wasn't leaving the hut.

Windy wasn't a ladies' man, but he put the story together on his own. He gestured for Bunny to lower the revolver. *The child is Logan's and there were no orders to be in the tunnel.*

"We have to let her out, Windy," repeated Doctor Carter. This time his statement sounded more like a plea.

They all looked at Windy. The chair suddenly felt smaller to him and was shrinking fast. He felt awful. Not just for what he was going to do but sick too. Nauseous and his hip wound burnt, like a blazing fire in his side. His doctor was over-emotional, Young Albert was confused, and the Scotsman was preparing to shoot his superior officer. Windy felt the burn in his arm too, which made focusing his mind a challenge. *Defuse the situation,* he told himself. *Bring everybody down a notch.* This was going to be difficult enough without tensions running high, and he certainly didn't want Major Logan shot. They'd be a man down.

"Cup of tea?" said Windy, pointing at the pot on the table. His change in tack seemed to catch them all off guard.

Logan looked over at Bunny, who finally put the revolver in his pocket, without letting go of its handle.

"Earl Grey, I believe. Is that right, Doc?" asked Windy.

Doctor Carter nodded.

Windy pointed at the empty chairs around the table. "Let's have a cuppa and a natter, shall we?" It was what his nanny used to say when he was angry or upset as a boy. It was low class but always a good icebreaker. "I'll explain everything." He put on his best show of courtesy, although he knew tea wouldn't solve this one.

Logan moved first, leading Maria tentatively over to the table. Doctor Carter tapped the tin containing the tea leaves on the tabletop twice: it was the only way to release the tight lid. He emptied tea leaves into the pot and Albert lit the small Benghazi cooker.

"If it's not too much trouble. We'd awfully appreciate you telling us what the hell's going on?" Logan's tone was lower, more conciliatory but still adamant.

They hadn't yet poured a cup and it was working.

Windy liked to plan for difficult situations that he knew were coming his way. Having plans and executing them had held him in good stead over the years, but he was flying blind here. The lovers sitting across the table weren't going to take his explanation of Operation Tracer well.

Carter put a small bag of sugar on the table with a spoon. Windy was going to give it to them straight; it was the only way he knew how. They were about to embark upon what was sure to be the most painful experience of their military service and they might not make it out alive. There was no way of sugar-coating it.

10

JURASSIC LIMESTONE

1941, August 17 (13:24h)
Operation Tracer Training Facility, Shortly,
East Anglia, England, United Kingdom

Assistant to the Director of Naval Intelligence Ian Fleming stood in front of the Operation Tracer team at their training facility outside the East Anglian town of Shortly.

"Chaps," he said, and the low rumble of conversations inside the little whitewashed room came to an abrupt silence. "I'm delighted to introduce to you Commander Fred 'Windy' Gale. Windy will be your team leader."

Hoop Fundi, Bunny Stuart, Young Albert, and Doctors Carter and Milburn each nodded an informal hello.

Windy was happy to be in the room. Very little information had been forthcoming in the weeks since agreeing to lead the mission, although the cloak-and-dagger had continued. Under normal circumstances, he, as team leader, would help pick and brief the men he would command; that hadn't happened.

He'd been given a membership to the Lansdowne Club and told to attend the Wednesday night blackjack game. One of the waitresses had slipped a jack of hearts into his pocket. It wasn't the first time he'd received instructions from a playing card. He knew to rip off the front. The message was concealed in the centre of the card. No briefing notes, no schedule, just the time, date, and address. The message did, however, state 'team meeting': finally, an introduction to the men he would command. *With any luck, they'll be good chaps.* The train from London had been late. Windy was the last to arrive.

"Leaves on the track?" said Commander Fleming with his usual enthusiasm.

Windy smiled.

"Look on the bright side, sir. If Jerry invades, they won't be expecting our leaves!" said Young Albert, introducing himself to Windy and the others followed suit. There was an informality Commander Fleming had fostered.

Of the two doctors and three signalmen, one of them, Hoop Fundi, stood out. Windy had never seen a Black person included in any Admiralty mission he'd served on – yet another surprise.

Commander Fleming continued, "We're delighted to finally have you all in the same room and you're long overdue for a briefing." He pointed at the maps on the wall: one of Europe, which included North Africa, and the other a crude illustration of Gibraltar. "Our intelligence tells us that Adolf Hitler and General Francisco Franco, the Spanish dictator, are close to agreeing to an alliance. If this takes place, German and Spanish forces will undoubtedly invade the Rock of Gibraltar. Defences are, as we speak, being beefed up to best repel an invasion, but realistically we can't guarantee continued ownership of the Rock." The room remained silent. "The British overseas territory is a crucial strategic outpost. Our command of the Rock, located at the gateway to the Mediterranean, provides us with an aircraft, ship, and submarine base but also, most importantly, control of the Straits of Gibraltar." Fleming put his finger on the map and looked back over his shoulder at the team. "Ships entering here, from the Atlantic theatre of war into the Mediterranean, must pass the Rock. The Rock also provides a crucial strategic airfield for the RAF." He removed his finger and turned to face the room again.

"As you can see, gentlemen, the loss of Gibraltar to Jerry will cripple our war effort across the Mediterranean. Malta becomes isolated, so does Alexandria, the Eighth Army loses its supply route, we lose North Africa."

Windy scanned the map of Europe and the small Strait of Gibraltar entrance to the large blue area marked the Mediterranean, then the five faces; one of them, Albert, just a boy.

Fleming continued, "Losing the Rock would also mean losing the intelligence we currently receive from the Straits of Gibraltar." He paused, either for dramatic effect or to consider his next words. "If we don't know what's coming in and out of the straits, it could cost us the war."

The air in the room seemed thicker to Windy, a little harder to breathe.

"That's where you chaps come in." Fleming's tone and posture switched to upbeat. "You six chaps are our backup plan," he said with enthusiasm. "For those of you unfamiliar with the geology of Gibraltar, it's a 465-yard piece of Jurassic limestone. That's a sedimentary rock. In short, Gibraltar is a Swiss cheese, full of natural holes, crevasses, and, thanks to our digging since the eighteenth century, tunnels!"

The mission became clear to Windy in an instant.

"If Jerry takes Gibraltar, we will be sealing you six inside a purpose-built cave at the very top of the Rock. You'll observe ship movements through the Strait of Gibraltar from specially carved-out vantage points and relay this crucial ship movement intelligence back to us here in Blighty via a specially designed radio system."

Windy felt the briefing room become smaller.

"As you can see, Operation Tracer is more than top secret. The mission's success depends on you, the Tracer team, remaining undiscovered at the top of the Rock. Were you to be discovered by the Germans, you'll likely be shot as spies."

Windy eyed the faces of his men. They shared the strain of this new information but, to their credit, remained silent.

"You will wear your uniform, and no weapons will be sealed inside the cave with you. If you're discovered, they won't do you much good anyway; and of course, we want to avoid the chances of you shooting each other." Fleming offered a wry smile and received a flutter of ironic laughter in return. "If the worst comes to the worst and you are discovered, let's hope the Germans turn out to be gentlemen, shall we?"

The group shared another nervous laugh.

"Have you ever met a Nazi gentleman, sir?" asked Young Albert.

"No, I can't say I have, Albert." Commander Fleming continued, "I think you now understand our caution in the planning and dissemination of detail for this mission."

Windy and the others nodded.

"Your lives, the success of the mission, and the dire consequences of failure hinge on one hundred per cent stealth." Fleming straightened his uniform. "Questions?"

Bunny Stuart raised his arm and was given the go-ahead to speak. "Just a wee one. Do ya know how long we might be in the cave for, sir?"

Commander Fleming must've expected the question, but Windy saw in his body language that he was unnerved by the answer.

"Anything up to three years."

11

BRICK IT UP

1942, September 10 (17:46h)
Main Chamber, Stay Behind Cave, Rock of Gibraltar

"Three years!" shouted Logan, jumping to his feet, causing his chair to fall backwards onto the cork-tiled floor.

"Aye, but keep your voice down," hissed Bunny, still standing in the doorway, his hand on the revolver in his pocket.

Maria made a low wailing noise. As her shoulders sank, so did the wail to a whimper.

"You're seriously telling me that you're going to imprison us here in this room for three years?" Logan stood tall and indignant.

"It might not come to that," said Windy.

"But it might?" replied Logan.

Windy pursed his lips before speaking. "Yes, it might." He wouldn't lie to the man. It was better, everything out in the open, here and now, so they could start coming to terms with reality. They had time to do so, plenty of it.

"You can't make us stay here. You're downright bonkers if you think you can." Logan's voice was again raised. "You don't have the authority." Carter shushed Logan this time as the major lifted his girlfriend from her chair. "We're leaving!"

Bunny pulled Windy's revolver from his pocket as Logan ushered a tearful Maria back towards the door. The Scotman's formidable stocky frame filled the space, the revolver now pointed hip-high and

41

squarely at Logan. Maria stepped away from her boyfriend and wilted like a flower denied water.

"Away with ya. Show a little backbone, man." Bunny seemed to be almost enjoying the major's emotions. He cast a glance at Windy for permission to shoot if necessary.

"Please take a seat, Major," said Windy. "It doesn't benefit us to shoot you and I'm sure you don't want to be shot. Surely you can see our predicament? The mission must come first."

"Shoot me and the Germans will hear it," said Logan, shoulders back and defiant.

Bunny shook his head. "With all that's going on outside? Another wee gunshot? I don't think so, but it'll get yous attention for sure."

"Look, Logan, old chap, we simply can't sustain the intelligence gathering around the clock with only four men. We need your help," Windy, changing tack again, implored. *Appeal to his sense of patriotism,* he thought. "Your sacrifice here will have a direct impact on the outcome of the war." He also played to the man's vanity. The Brylcreemed hair and dapper touches to his self-presentation were clear indications that the young officer cared about his image.

Logan's shape softened, and his stance sagged slightly.

"Get me out of here, Logan, *por favor,*" whimpered Maria, and Windy's work was undone in an instant. Then Maria raised her voice. "*Por favor,* Logan. Get me out of here!"

Logan's frame puffed larger than before, like a beach ball pumped with breath. He stepped towards Bunny with renewed determination to leave. Eyes glued to the Scotsman and ready to fight, his words were for Windy. "I'm sorry, Commander, but you're going to have to darn well shoot me."

Windy dropped his head in disappointment. "Shoot him in the leg," he said.

"No!" Carter said, rushing forward. "Stop this. It's insane. No one needs to be shot." The doctor stood next to Logan. "I don't want to be patching up another gunshot wound today, or worse, burying you in the rubble outside that door tomorrow!"

Windy gave Carter the space he needed to try something new. He'd failed to calm the situation. Maybe the doctor would have better luck. Either way, no one was leaving.

"Look. Think it through for a moment." Carter addressed both Logan and Maria. "What's on the outside for you? There's a battle raging for the Rock. Chances are you might both get killed if you go back out there. Agreed?"

Logan and Maria said nothing, so Doctor Carter kept going: "The Germans are here on the Rock, but that doesn't mean they will hold the Rock, does it?"

Logan's eyebrow appeared to accept the possibility that the Rock could be taken back.

"Right now, this is the safest place to be for all of us." Carter didn't mention the fact that if discovered they might be shot as spies and Windy certainly wasn't going to bring it up.

"We all might be out in a month, a week, even days from now. The Admiralty knows we're here. If the Rock is taken back, and I can assure you every effort will be taken by our chaps to do so, then we could be out before you know it."

Windy was impressed by the doctor's storytelling abilities.

"And hey, look on the bright side." Carter turned his hands, open palm. "You're now a member of MI6. The secret service. You're working for Naval Intelligence. They'll probably give you a medal when it's all over and a promotion. Logan, you might make colonel by the end of the year!" Windy watched the doctor force the best smile he could muster. It wasn't his natural smile, but they didn't know that.

Maria used her sleeve to wipe the tears from her face.

"Tea's getting cold." Carter put his hands in his pockets in a relaxed manner. "We're not going to waste it, are we?"

The doctor almost had Windy convinced they'd be out of there by next week if he didn't know better.

"One of these boxes has some digestive biscuits, shall I root them out?" Carter's slow advance, back across the room, was a clear indication for Logan and Maria to follow.

Logan deflated some, looked to Maria for a sign. She nodded reluctantly. She'd regained some composure but the look on her face was hateful. Carter led them both back to the table and Windy shuffled out of the way to give them some space. Carter put the biscuits on the table. Their tentative movements towards the sugary snacks reminded Windy of feeding squirrels in Hyde Park. He reached Bunny at the door and took the revolver from him. "Brick it up, Bunny," he whispered. "Quick as you can." Windy had appreciated the skills of Doctor Carter from the early days of training, but never more than now. If he ever gave up his medical profession, he'd fit right in at the diplomatic corps. Windy turned the Nagant revolver over in his hand. He recognised the weapon. Shiny silver steel with a brown wooden handle. It was a .22 calibre, gas seal, and held seven shots in the cylinder. He checked inside; there were just five bullets. The Spaniard he'd killed for it had almost certainly done the same to acquire it. It was Russian-made. Windy put the weapon in his pocket, pulled up a chair, and sat in the doorway as Bunny Stuart sealed all six of them inside Gibraltar's Stay Behind Cave.

12

NORTH MOLE

1941, October 2 (12:37h)
Commericial Mole, Gibraltar Harbour Gangplank,
Rock of Gibraltar

Almost a year before the Germans had invaded the Rock, Windy, and most of the Tracer Team, arrived in Gibraltar by boat. He walked the wobbly gangplank and stepped onto the dockside, happy to be on dry land. It was ironic that he worked for the Admiralty but never liked being at sea. He'd kept quiet about it because the perks of working for Naval Intelligence far outweighed his dislike of bobbing up and down in the water.

Windy felt a bump from behind and turned to see Young Albert also holding a leather suitcase.

"Beg your pardon, sir," said Albert with a wry smile.

Always the joker, thought Windy. Albert was going to be good for morale if things got tough.

Doctor Carter came down the gangplank and walked right by him, ignoring him completely. That was the protocol: they didn't know each other as far as anyone was concerned. They'd been ordered to avoid each other on the trip down. To wait a couple of weeks before 'getting to know each other'. Windy had spent most of the voyage in his cabin. He'd taken an evening walk along the ship's deck every night after dinner for a smoke and it was difficult not to bump into Carter, who also liked a tote on his pipe at that time. They'd implemented an unspoken rule to stay on separate sides of the ship. It had seemed over the top, being that the ship was populated only by British servicemen, plus the odd military businessman, but with this particular mission no precaution was too much. Only 'essential' contact and conversations were to be had aboard ship, and even those were to be conducted in the utmost secrecy.

Windy followed the rest of the passengers as they made their way along Commercial Mole dockside towards the doorway marked *Immigration*. A line formed. Looking along the people in front and behind him, he could see all the Tracer team, except Doctor Milburn, who'd been allowed to fly. Apparently, the doctor hated the sea even more than he did and had only agreed to be part of the mission if there was no sailing involved. They needed two doctors and one with experience in command. Doctor Milburn was primed to take up the reins if anything happened to Windy. That had swung the flight for him, and it was right on time.

Windy watched the Armstrong Whitworth Atlanta passenger plane as it descended around the Rock, banked, and lumbered in to land. He recognised the Armstrong immediately; he'd flown in one down to Casablanca only last year. He hadn't expected to see another. The steward had told him theirs was the last flight the old girl would make – her and all her sisters had been decommissioned. Well, one of the sisters clearly wasn't going quietly. It was a nifty little piece of kit; it could be put down on both sea and land. Commander Fleming had taken a great interest in Windy's knowledge of Allied and particularly German aircraft at their first meeting. He'd been sure the Tracer mission would involve aircraft of some kind. Strange if it didn't. If the Germans took the Rock, surely information on flights in and out would be as crucial as ship movements? Particularly since the airfield extension and the increased traffic. He would have preferred looking out on the airfield and watching German planes fan clouds of screed and dust than trying to guess the names of enemy ships. Windy eyed the other men in the queue he didn't know. *What are they doing here? Is there a second team? Another six men, primed and ready to spy on the Gibraltar airfield?*

* * *

The rotors of the Armstrong plane were still slowly spinning to a halt as Major Logan Warlock stepped onto the tarmac to collect his suitcase in front of Staff Surgeon Doctor Milburn. Newly arrived passengers headed for the series of small huts just off the airfield. An officer in khaki shorts sat under a canopy of shade outside the largest of the huts at a simple wooden desk and checked documentation. Logan also noticed the armed guard off and to the side. Logan stepped up to the wooden desk and handed the officer in khaki shorts his passport.

"Major Logan Warlock reporting for duty." Logan was excited to be on the Rock. He'd waited a long time for this moment: finally, he was here.

A man in plain clothes stepped out of the hut and joined them at the desk. The seated officer flicked through Logan's passport, page by page, before looking up at Logan stone-faced. Logan grew nervous. The officer handed Logan's passport to the man in plain clothes. He was a silver-haired man wearing a short-sleeved shirt open at the neck. He studied Logan's passport, from the back to the front.

"Major Warlock?" he asked. "Where're your orders?"

Logan hadn't expected to be asked for that document, but luckily he had the piece of paper at hand. He reached into the button-down pocket of his jacket and pulled out the folded paper that contained his orders. He was to present them to Colonel Fielding on his arrival at Casemates Square. Logan handed them over.

"Is there a problem?"

"Just formality, sir," said the man in the shirt sleeves. Though Logan knew the operational procedures for the frontier well. He'd studied them as part of his training. They didn't know it, but he was coming to take charge of the frontier. If there was a problem, he could only imagine it was one thing. Now he was worried.

Everything had been in order, he was sure of it. He'd checked and double-checked. What had he missed? What had they spotted that he hadn't, or what did they know that he didn't?

"Come with me please, sir." The civilian in the short-sleeved shirt gestured to be followed. An armed guard followed close behind Logan as the immigration officer at the desk continued to process those entering Gibraltar who had waited impatiently for their turn. The civilian led Logan towards the largest hut, up three steps, and in through a door. Logan was aware of the armed guard who kept his distance but followed them.

The room, with plain wooden floors and walls, had a table and two chairs at its centre, one on either side, and a doorway identical to the one they'd come through on the opposite side. No windows.

The man in the short-sleeved shirt dropped Logan's passport onto the table and with it his orders.

"Sit, please." The request sounded more like an order. "Your port of embarkation was Biggin Hill?"

Logan's hand began to shake. They clearly knew something, but he needed to hold his nerve. *How much do they know?* As the plane left Biggin Hill, he thought he was home and dry.

"Yes, that's right, Biggin Hill," he replied as confidently as he could.

"And before that, Major Warlock, where were you stationed?"

They knew. Somebody somewhere had put it all together. He'd been so careful but clearly not careful enough. He crossed his fingers mainly to stop his hands from shaking.

"Aldershot, South-Eastern, under the command of GOC, General Dill. Is there a problem?"

The man in the short-sleeved shirt nodded knowingly.

"Do you know why we've detained you, Major Warlock?"

He did. *This was it, the end of the road.* He was suddenly very aware of the armed guard standing behind him. There was no running away.

"Guard!" shouted the man in the short-sleeved shirt. Logan jumped with fright in his chair and before he knew it the guard was at his side, pointing the barrel of the weapon directly at him. It was over.

The guard pulled the trigger. The chamber was empty. The guard had a big smile on his face, as did the man in the short-sleeved shirt.

"Welcome to frontier control, Major Warlock. Delighted to have you aboard."

Both doors flew open and the room was suddenly full of laughing, smiling faces, many of the men holding tin cups and others bottles of whisky.

"Sorry, old chap, but it's a bit of a tradition for new arrivals, even majors! You understand." The man in the short-sleeved shirt slapped Logan on the back hard enough to rattle him in his seat. Logan cracked a nervous smile; he'd just died a little inside. The smiling faces were all around him and he was being touched, greeted continuously. He downed, in one gulp, the contents of the tin cup that had been thrust into his hand. How close he'd come to exposing himself. The cup was refilled immediately.

"That's the spirit," said somebody.

"Should have seen your face," said another.

"White as a sheet, wasn't he, chaps?" They all laughed.

"Looked like you were about to confess to being a German spy." Logan joined the laughter. *Now that was funny.*

"Come, let me introduce you to the team." The man in the short-sleeved shirt led Logan into the large section of the hut.

There were tables and chairs scattered around the room, taped windows, a few shelves with miniature aircraft models, a bank of filing cabinets, and schematic drawings pinned to the walls. These were mostly maps of the Rock, with defences marked in red, green, and blue. There were too many names to remember, and most of them soon dispersed back to their stations and responsibilities, men close to his age, still chuckling at his unknown near confession. The final introduction was to a woman. She had her back to him in the corner of the room and was tapping away on a typewriter. As Logan approached her from behind, she stopped and turned in her chair to face them.

"Saving the best to last, of course." Maria stood up and gave a huge smile.

"Logan, please meet our Spanish rose among the thorns, Petty Officer Maria Bona of the Women's Royal Naval Service. Maria, my pleasure to introduce Major Logan Warlock."

13

PHASE ONE

1942, September 10 (17:49h)
Main Street, Rock of Gibraltar

Sergeant Hoop Fundi's fall, away from Windy and back down the steps towards the Germans and Turnbull's Lane, was so dramatic and uncontrolled it took him past several Wehrmacht who'd positioned themselves halfway up the staircase. They simply watched the African rifleman plunge head over heels while trying his best to slow the fall with his arms and legs as he went. Any one of them could've let off a round at the moving target, but the spectacle of the fall had obviously caught everybody by surprise. Hoop finally came to a halt close to the bottom of the staircase, sprawled across the steps, ringed by German and Spanish gun barrels.

After being marched to Main Street at gunpoint, Hoop Fundi was placed on his knees with his hands on his head along with more than ten others, surrounded by German Wehrmacht. The mission was safe so long as he didn't let anything slip. He wouldn't. They knew nothing, he was just a negro in the British Army.

Gunfire still punctuated the soundscape as lines of British prisoners were being herded in all directions. The invasion had obviously been a success, short of the resistance inside the Rock. *How many?* he wondered. There was space to house a whole garrison in the honeycombs, but the surprise attack would have reduced considerably the numbers of who'd made it inside. Hoop looked along the lines of captured men, expecting to see Windy. He couldn't have made it up to the cave in the state he was in. *Or is he dead? Shot trying to escape?* That would leave just three in the cave: Carter, Young Albert, and Bunny. If they even made it. *Was there an operation at all?*

The Germans holding the prisoners at gunpoint stood to attention as Standartenführer Wolfgang Richter approached. The SS Assault Unit officer in charge of the invasion was flanked by two SS guards. He removed his grey service-uniform cap to wipe the sweat from his brow. Thin light-brown hair, long on top, cropped short at the back and sides, saw the sun briefly. Young to have achieved the equivalent rank of colonel, not quite thirty years of age, fresh-faced Richter looked up at the Rock and then down at the British on their knees.

The SS officer was more than pleased. *Phase one complete,* he thought. He walked with a certain sense of satisfaction, having managed what many of his superiors had privately thought was impossible. He'd taken the Rock by surprise. He'd been warned that his reputation and career would not survive failure. He'd been advised by his closest friends in the SS to duck the responsibility of Operation Felix, the plan to invade the Rock of Gibraltar. He'd been warned that any mission to invade the Rock was doomed to failure and the officer in charge of that failure would end up commanding forces at the Russian front, if he was lucky. Operation Felix had been considered a poisoned chalice; nobody wanted the mission. But Richter hadn't seen it that way. Difficult, yes, it was always going to be that; but Operation Felix was also an opportunity. An ambitious officer could fast-track himself up the chain of command by taking the Rock. Perfect planning, stealth, and clinical execution were his specialty. He hadn't doubted for a moment that he could do it. As he walked on, he knew that Herr Himmler would already have been informed of his achievement – that meant his name was now known to the Reichsführer of the SS and maybe even to the Führer himself! Richter had earned that spring in his step.

Taking the Rock was phase one. Routing the British rats out of their tunnels inside the Rock was phase two. There had been no way of preventing them from retreating into their tunnels. He knew all about the network they had built inside the Rock. He had full access to the secret Abwehr files on Gibraltar to prepare for the mission. Abwehr agents had been watching and listening to activities on the Rock from across the bay in the town of Algeciras for years, long before war had broken out. The British had created substantial defences inside the Rock even though he'd given orders for his men, and those Spaniards put under his command, to kill as many British as possible trying to enter the tunnels. He'd wanted to reduce the numbers remaining inside. No one had believed phase one was possible, at least not at the speed at which he'd achieved it. Phase two would take a little longer and require some local intelligence. By taking the Rock, he'd bought himself some time for phase two.

The Third Reich was now in command of the Strait of Gibraltar, which meant no access to or exit from the Mediterranean for the Allies, but Berlin wouldn't wait forever for full control of Gibraltar. Failure to complete phase two would surely result in his replacement and negative reports to his superiors – that one-way ticket to the Russian front was still a real threat, as was a counterattack by the British. He needed information on the tunnels and he needed it quickly.

"Hello, chaps," said Richter sarcastically as he walked along the line of men that included Hoop. "My name is Standartenführer Wolfgang Richter. Gibraltar, as you can see, has been taken and is now the property of the Third Reich."

"Not for long." A small stocky corporal on his knees next to Hoop provided the solitary dissenting voice. Richter ignored him and continued.

"I want to make this as quick and painless as possible for all of you. So help me help you. Small pockets of your countrymen have taken up refuge inside the Rock. This we expected." Richter raised his voice to make sure that as many of the captured British standing around could hear. "The resistance of your comrades in their tunnels and caves is futile. They will run out of ammunition and food, they will be forced to surrender. Many unnecessary lives will be lost in that process. This, however, can be avoided. It's in everybody's mutual interest that we quickly resolve this situation. I want to give you the opportunity to save your comrades' lives. I want to work with you to see a sensible resolution here. I believe that one of you here today will be remembered as the man who saved hundreds of lives. Lives that will otherwise be lost needlessly." Richter stopped at the end of the line of men but continued to address them all. "So, work with me. I need to know the access points to the tunnels inside the Rock. I need schematic drawings of the tunnel systems. I need your help to bring a sensible conclusion to this untenable situation."

"Are you bonkers?" The stocky corporal's left eyebrow rose high up his youthful forehead. Those fellow British in earshot laughed. "Go ahead. Bang ya head against the Rock, ya won't get in, mate."

Richter smiled. He smiled because he knew men. Their strengths and their weaknesses.

"A Third Reich reward of five thousand British pounds will be paid to the man who saves his comrades' lives by providing information leading to access to the tunnels." This wasn't the first time Richter had tried such a tactic, and successfully too. He wanted the offer out there early – word of mouth would carry the story quickly through the ranks of the prisoners. Of course, they would laugh publicly at the audacity to think a British soldier would sell out his comrades for any amount of money. Privately, however, the right man might well be bought.

"Have you flipped your wig, Fritz?" said the stocky young corporal. Eyeing his comrades excitedly, he clearly enjoyed being the centre of attention, leading the charge of dissent. He embodied the British spirit that Richter needed to break in the coming weeks.

"Despite what you may have been told," Richter continued, "we're not here to kill as many of you as possible. Quite the opposite. I want to save lives, not take them. Hundreds of lives will be saved by avoiding a long, drawn-out siege. The pounds will be payment for your act of patriotism."

"Bollocks!" shouted the corporal as Richter arrived in front of him.

Hoop observed the SS officer as he looked down at the overconfident youngster next to him. The Nazi's steely blue eyes were cold, unblinking. His demeanour and posture screamed killer. Hoop had been around Germans enough to sense when their rigid and organised control had reached its breaking point. He looked at the Luger pistol in its polished leather holster and his boots. The Standartenführer's jackboots were spotlessly clean, unlike the boots of the men around him. They were polished to the point of reflection, with shiny stitching, but the heels had been raised, an extra sole or maybe two had been added. He didn't want to engage the bastard, but if he didn't the boy who couldn't shut up would get himself killed for sure.

Hoop spoke.

"There's one way in and one way out. I'm afraid you're wasting your time," said Hoop in German. His African accent always exposed his heritage quickly. The Standartenführer's body stayed facing the stocky, cocky corporal, but his head turned, almost mechanically, to look at Hoop. The German never said a word, just stared. His eyes scanned Hoop's whole body, slowly and methodically. Hoop felt like he was being X-rayed, not as a man for his physicality but more as a species. Like a scientist might study a minuscule creature under a microscope.

14

CLEVER NEGRO

It took Richter a moment to register that the negro was speaking his language. He knew the British Army had enlisted plenty of negroes from the West Indies and Africa. *African,* thought Richter. He could see the one in front of him was physically fit, with broad shoulders and striking facial features. High cheekbones. Tight, oily dark skin, glistening wet with perspiration. *The protruding jaw, definitely African.* He knew coloureds to be simple-minded by nature, but the British had harnessed them as a resource. Tall and strong-backed, they clearly had their uses. This one's accent, with clicks and pop sounds, suggested to him that it wasn't born in the Fatherland. *Curious.*

He turned his head slowly back to the boy. Unlike some of his colleagues in the SS, Richter didn't enjoy killing. It was a messy business. He liked to keep his uniform and particularly his boots clean. Blood spatter was an unavoidable consequence of discharging his weapon at close range; however, there were times when public shows of brutality served a purpose and boots could always be cleaned. This wasn't one of those times. Public executions created fear and right now he wanted to harness the opposite. Richter had not found fear to be a particularly good producer of results when it came to intelligence gathering. Killing too quickly or indiscriminately didn't loosen tongues; there were better methods. Of course, fear of being shot broke some men who would say anything to avoid being next, although the information generated was often found to be useless. He'd been experimenting with more cerebral approaches. Good treatment of prisoners wasn't seen by many in the SS or Gestapo as a viable form of intelligence gathering, but he'd seen it work successfully on captured British RAF pilots.

He'd done all he could publicly for now. The bait was in the water and he'd projected the image of himself that would best serve his needs going forward. They'd take a look at the British individually to identify potential targets for interrogation, but first they needed to secure them. Work had already begun on a camp at the south side of the Rock. The plans for it had been drawn up weeks ago.

Without another word, Richter ordered the prisoners incarcerated. The cocky boy would have to die, of course.

He watched the negro as he was led across the road. *What is his story?* He wanted to see him again. A quick debrief at his staff car and two orders later, he and two guards were stepping around the corner of Market Lane to the sound of small-arms fire from the ongoing siege of the tunnels. Richter's stomach rumbled. He took a packet of Juno cigarettes from his inside pocket and lit one. Breakfast had been light and very early. He'd need something to tide him over. They headed along Irish Town Street and into John Mackintosh Square. The cocky corporal was waiting there for him on his knees against a wall, flanked by two SS guards. Richter flipped the leather loop that secured his P08 ordnance model Luger pistol in its holster on his hip. He took a last draw on his cigarette and dropped it to the ground, then put the weapon calmly against the forehead of the stocky corporal, pushing the boy's head backwards with the barrel, leaving a circular mark. He wanted to see his face. They shared eye contact for a moment. It was clear to the cocky Brit what the Standartenführer was about to do, but there was no fear in his eyes. Only defiance. Richter paused before pulling on the trigger. Nothing happened. He flicked the safety catch and tried again. He expected to see fear in the boy's face but it wasn't there. He wasn't brave, only young and stupid. He didn't need to die today. Courage he respected, he had no time for the rest. The boy opened his mouth to speak, but his breath was taken away as a piece of his skull slapped against the wall, painting it and the gutter a gooey blood red.

Killing today was nothing like the early days of Richter's time in the SS: the adrenaline and excitement of a kill had been a rush. Now the emotion was gone.

The first time he'd killed was imprinted on the back of his eye. He remembered everything about it. The click sound from the trigger, the recoil, that little leap backwards of his Luger pistol in his hand on discharge. The puff of smoke, brief whiff of sulphur. The shell casing spinning away from him and the shock of ending a living, breathing life. The first kill had preyed on his mind. Had it not been a Jew it might have been harder to reconcile. He'd wake up in the night with the grotesque images, though he couldn't say he had nightmares because the dreams didn't disturb him. He hadn't killed anybody who hadn't given him a reason in the course of his duties. There was less rush and more of an inquisitive reaction these days. The shape the human body took with its central decision-making function deactivated was a curiosity. How it relaxed completely and flopped to the ground, no bounce, sometimes landing awkwardly, as in this case. The smell of urine was in the air, the boy's bladder having released itself.

Richter turned his focus on the guard who had let go of the boy as his head had come apart. Times like these were also helpful for showing him whom he could trust most among his own men. Those who enjoyed the spectacle. It showed on their faces. Those who disapproved of his action but said nothing – like this one – it showed on their faces too.

Richter removed the clip from his Lugar pistol. The Luger held seven bullets in a clip and one in the chamber. He was obsessive in counting the eight rounds as he used the weapon, convinced that knowing exactly how many rounds were in his weapon at any one time could potentially save his life one day. It was second nature to him. He'd used three at the frontier border crossing, two on the way to Main Street, and one more just now. He replaced the clip and turned his thoughts to dinner.

15

ADMIRAL HIPPER

1941, August 17 (16:10h)
Operation Tracer Training Facility,
Shortly, East Anglia, England, United Kingdom

"I've seen the clock," said Commander Fleming. "Well past tea and tiffin time, but before you tuck in I want to introduce your next challenge and, more importantly, illustrate the competence level you'll need to be aiming for. Hoop?"

Commander Fleming singled out the African rifleman, who stood up. The commander pinned a series of enlarged photographs to the board behind him. Approximately ten ships. Of varying quality and size, some of the pictures were darker than others, having been taken late at night. Commander Fleming pointed a short stick at one of the ships.

"Deutschland class, sir," said Hoop. Fleming selected another ship at random.

"Bismarck battleship." Then came another, this time one of the dark photographs. Hoop squinted at the image before answering. "A heavy cruiser, I think, sir. *Admiral Hipper* class. Actually, I think that is the *Admiral Hipper* itself, sir."

Commander Fleming leaned in to read the small handwritten title next to the photo.

"Fourteen thousand tons, sir," continued the African. "Eight 203mm guns."

"Thank you, Hoop."

"The *Admiral Hipper* was built at the Blohm and Voss shipyard in Hamburg, sir, and launched in February 1937."

"That's great, thank you, Hoop. No need to tell us who was leaning against the clipper bow at launch."

"Actually no one was leaning against the clipper bow, sir. She was built with a straight stem; the clipper bow was only added later, sir."

The room erupted in laughter. Hoop smiled at them.

"Now you all know why Hoop Fundi here of the King's African Rifles was selected for the mission," Fleming said. Hoop acknowledged the room politely. "We don't expect you to learn the encyclopaedia of the German Navy to match Hoop, but we'd like you each to be able to distinguish a battleship from a hipper before the end of your training. Hoop will be your instructor. Sergeant Fundi is also fluent in German, but let's hope his language skills won't be required."

Fleming spoke on. "Living in close quarters with each other for an inordinate amount of time will bring its own set of problems. I'm guessing none of you has been lost in the wilderness for excessively long periods and forced to adapt to your environment to survive?" Fleming looked out over the group. "If you have, please make yourself known."

Scotsman Bunny Stuart stepped forward and grinned.

"Gentlemen, Bunny here has been sent to us by George Murray Levick," Fleming said. "Levick, for those of you who don't read the papers, was part of Captain Scott's *Terra Nova* expedition. Bunny not only has a wealth of experience surviving hostile environments, he's also a trained signalman so he hits the ground running on this mission from two fronts. Bunny will be providing you with priceless insights on how to survive the challenge of incarceration over a long period both mentally and physically. Bunny recently spent eight months of winter in an ice cave and survived eating seal blubber. Correct, Bunny?"

"Aye, and penguins too." Bunny grinned.

"Please share your invaluable experience with all the chaps." Fleming eyed the group again. "You've all met with Doctors Milburn and Carter for your medicals earlier today. I believe we have two operations for the removal of tonsils and an appendix already scheduled." The doctors concurred. "Windy, you'll get your poking and prodding this evening."

Windy acknowledged the two doctors on the team.

"Finally, spotting German vessels and staying alive won't be of much use to us if you can't transmit what you see back to us here in Blighty. Albert?" Fleming said. Young Albert put down his cup of tea and stood up. "Now don't be fooled by those boyish looks, gentlemen." Albert gave an embarrassed smile. "Young Albert here may look like he's yet to leave the classroom at Eton College" – the group laughed again and so did Albert – "but I can assure you there is nobody with more high-technology radio communications experience than Albert, who I'm told can take apart an 1155 receiver and put it back together with his eyes closed. Albert was Brigadier Sir Richard Gambier-Parry's pick for the mission. Dicky is controller of Special Communications, so our radios couldn't be in better hands. Albert will be giving you each a crash course in the operational system of the revolutionary communications we'll be using for the mission and how we plan to power it."

"Bicycle clips provided," quipped Young Albert before Commander Fleming's tone changed to end the briefing.

"The new faces you see around you today will become very familiar to you over the next two weeks. You were each selected for this mission for a reason. You each possess special skills that, we believe, are key to a successful mission." Commander Fleming paused. "Director Godfrey wanted me to impress upon you the importance of this mission that you have been selected for. I hope that I have done that already. Without wanting to sound dramatic, I'd like to finally say this."

Fleming's voice dropped an octave.

"There are approximately a million men and women currently serving in the European and North African theatres of operations. We would expect to lose half that number in a defeat to Jerry, and a defeat to Jerry is highly likely if we lose our intelligence from the Rock of

Gibraltar. We're counting on you chaps to prepare for this mission to the best of your abilities. To keep Operation Tracer top secret and to execute it. This mission must succeed." He paused again. "At all costs." The room fell silent and the men nodded. "And with that, it's my pleasure to hand you over to Bunny here for some inhuman torture training. After a spot of tea, of course."

16

THE CAPTAIN

1942, September 11 (09:43h)

Windmill Hill, Prisoner Cell, Rock of Gibraltar

"What were your plans for entering the Rock?"

Hoop was tied to a chair. The German guard shouted at him again. "How many access points are there into the tunnel system?" The guard struck him across the cheek.

Hoop had lost count of the number of blows he'd taken. The first few hurt, but either the guard was getting tired or he was getting numb to the pain. Blood dripped from his nose and above his left eye. It had run and was clouding his vision; he wanted to wipe it away but couldn't. His head felt hot, puffed, and swollen, but his wrists annoyed him the most. The knot the guard had tied was digging into his skin. It was the most irritating part of his interrogation. The truth was he had stopped listening to the questions. They'd become repetitive, monotonous. He knew far more than the guard could have imagined, but he was taking what he knew to the grave no matter what. He wasn't going to give these Nazi bastards anything. The lives that would be saved by his silence far outnumbered the loss of his life. The maths was simple. He smiled at the guard with his bloodstained teeth. The guard was wasting his time and he didn't even know it.

"Who were the men you were escaping with, what were their names, their rank?" The guard struck Hoop again, this time in the stomach. He gasped for air, but there wasn't any. The guard hit him again in the same place, and he started to suffocate. He couldn't catch his breath. Starved of oxygen, he felt the room sway; he could smell the body odour of the sweaty guard but no longer saw him.

Hoop blacked out.

* * *

He was back in his Namibian homeland. He'd had such love for everything German as a teenager. He couldn't learn the language fast enough. Their culture fascinated him.

The world he knew was happy but basic before he'd met the captain. He'd heard about Europe and how these white people had everything. He feared white people mostly because they had power – power to give but, more importantly, power to take away. They could beat any of his Herero people they wanted to without reason. Retired German sea captain Otto Beckerman of the Reichsmarine, the Imperial Navy of the Weimar Republic, was a white man too but different.

His mother had picked up a cleaner's job at one of the big houses. She was particularly happy and told him, "Tomorrow you will go to work with me." She'd made him wear his Sunday-best clothes, the ones she washed once a week and kept laid out for church. His shoes too, the ones his mother made him polish until he could see his face in them. They'd walk the two miles his mother walked every day to go to work and back. He wasn't sure why he had to go with her; he hadn't wanted to on the first occasion. Meeting new people wasn't his thing and meeting old white people certainly wasn't, particularly if he had to dress up for it.

The captain's house was set back from the road behind a large fence. The secret garden was lush and green, with palm trees lining the path up to the front gate and mangos littering the wet lawn. The front door was thick dark wood, with black painted bolts, and had a giant knocker in the shape of a lion's head. He'd been so nervous standing next to his mother that first day waiting for the door to open.

When it did, his life changed.

Hoop's head hit the concrete floor of the cell hard.

It brought him crashing back to reality. The guard stood over him in the shadow of the single light bulb. The chair was on its side and he was still tied to it. He felt a kick, which connected only partially with him but also with the hardwood of the chair.

"*Scheisse*," shouted the guard, limping out of the cell. Hoop smiled. *God's punishment,* his mother used to say.

17

AGENT A-54

1942, September 11 (09:51h)
Ohara's Road, Lord Airey's Battery, Rock of Gibraltar

Meanwhile, Standartenführer Wolfgang Richter stood at the entrance to Lord Airey's Battery. The blood splatter on the walls and the puddles on the concrete floors, now dry, illustrated the battle that had taken place for the big gun at O'Hara's Battery. Piles of dead British were stacked three high by the side of the road. He'd ordered them burnt, but his order hadn't yet been carried out. The smell of urine and shit hung in the air. He could taste it on his tongue; it used to make him want to vomit but it didn't anymore. Dark eyes stared at him, set back in pale sockets without facial features. Men from every nation looked the same when they were dead. But Richter hadn't come to the top of the Rock to see the dead. He eyed the trees and the road down the hill, then he studied the handwritten map he was holding. It was a crude illustration of his current location. Lord Airey's Battery was marked, as was O'Hara's Battery. Breakneck Battery tunnel was shown as a thin pencil line that ran away from the gun back along the Rock to join up with Lord Airey's Shelter. The trees were marked and the road ran away towards the Spanish mainland, and then there was the *X* that marked the spot. As far as he could tell, he was standing on the *X*. He'd expected the map to be enough the first time he'd seen it, but now it was proving insufficient. Its bottom corner was signed with a letter and two numbers: A-54.

A guard ran up and stood to attention, his face nervous. That's how Richter liked to keep his men, on their toes, although this also told him immediately that the news he was about to receive wasn't what he'd hoped for.

"Nothing, Herr Standartenführer."

"You're sure?"

"Yes, Herr Standartenführer." *Where is A-54?* thought Richter. The Operation Felix invasion had not been a success by accident. Agent-54 had provided all the intelligence that he needed. The truth was, their surprise attack had only been possible due to the unique information of Agent-54.

Richter had coordinated one of the most audacious missions from a small whitewashed terraced house just across the Gibraltar frontier border, in the town of La Linea, thanks only to Agent-54.

He remembered back as the three Tiger tanks crashed through the border gates. Almost three hundred miles along the Spanish coast, east of the Rock, Vichy French and German aircraft took to the skies heavily loaded with German paratroopers. Aircraft also departed from Seville in the north, Casablanca in the south, and Sardinia in the Italian east. Thousands of German SS and Wehrmacht revealed themselves from civilian and Spanish military disguises to converge on the frontier border. His armoured vehicles, the Tigers, and artillery had been brought in by Spanish train, camouflaged and transported separately, exactly as Agent-54 had suggested. His men, too, had made their way south and sat for weeks scattered across the region in quiet villages, uniforms hidden away. His superior officers had given him everything he'd asked for: motorised infantry and Panzer divisions, twenty-six heavy artillery battalions, not to mention the new remotely controlled mine-clearing vehicles. The detail and subterfuge in Agent-54's plan, most of which Richter had passed off as his own, had been exceptional. When the moment came for his battalions to line up alongside their Spanish allies, they had overwhelmed the British at the frontier gate. As for coordination with those Gibraltarians sympathetic to his cause and Falange saboteurs already on the Rock, dressed as British, without their attacks from within on battery positions the full-frontal assault would not have been a success. Princess Caroline's Tovey high up on the Rock and the gun at Montague Bastion were both silenced almost immediately.

Agent-54's men had watched the Rock from the Spanish coast for almost a year. Observation posts with telescopes monitored the Rock's northern cliff face day and night. Every puff of dust from the blasting of a new defence, every hole the British engineers made in the rockface, they knew about it as soon as the drill came through the limestone. All thanks to Agent-54.

Richter looked again at the piece of paper. The agent had been adamant that this must be the rendezvous location. His information was always so specific. It had to be this location and no other. *Why here? What was special about this particular spot on the Rock that made it imperative for our first meeting to take place here? And why had Agent-54 failed to make himself known now that his German forces controlled the Rock? Had he been killed during the invasion?* It seemed the most logical answer. That would explain why he hadn't appeared. There had been radio silence since the night before the invasion. No communications from A-54 at all. If he had been killed, then his identity might remain secret forever. Those members of Abwehr who had put him and the SS in contact with their top spy on the Rock were more than a little secretive about their asset. They might never share his identity. He had been looking forward to meeting the man who had single-handedly undone the British hold on the Rock. His extraordinary intel had seriously contributed to Richter's current SS status, in Berlin, of most favoured. His eye wandered over the bloodstained rocks onto a single flower, somehow managing to survive, even flourishing, growing up through a small crack in a rock. Wind escaped a corpse on the pile of dead. He'd smelt something similar before; it was time to leave.

"Burn the dead, don't make me tell you again," said Richter.

He looked out from the Rock towards Morocco in the distance, before his eye drifted back towards the Spanish city of Algeciras just across the bay. One American ship was visible; he'd been told there were now others. Then another spectator, much closer, grabbed his attention. An ape sat on a flat rock just feet away, picking its nose and eating what it found. It stared at him. Richter stared back. The ape's eyes were dark pools of judgement. He waved his hand rapidly towards the creature. The ape didn't move an inch. It just kept staring.

18

FALANGIST

1942, September 10 (08:21h)
Frontier Gate, Rock of Gibraltar

A few hours before the German-Spanish invasion of the Rock, a thick-set Spaniard with a bushy moustache had passed through the British frontier gate at Gibraltar with his bicycle and a bag – as he'd done every day for the past month. Today, however, was different. This time, he was hiding a disassembled German-made MP38 submachine gun in the false bottom of his bag. He told himself not to be nervous, but he was. The crossing should go smoothly, as it had done so every other day. He had his contact at the border gate. *Act normally,* he told himself as he pushed his bicycle toward the British. He was just one of over six thousand Spaniards crossing the frontier to enter Gibraltar daily. *There was nothing to worry about.*

The frontier had a central column with the design of a wrought-iron crown atop. There were two double gates on both sides: one for entering and one for exiting. Usually, like today, only one half of the two was open. Dark grey, almost black, the gates were rectangular, approximately fifteen feet high, with around twenty individual vertical railings per gate. The top of each split into two and sharpened to a point. Impossible to climb. The huge gates were affixed at each end to heavy, thick iron columns about twenty feet in height. A German Tiger tank at full speed would almost certainly pull one off its hinges, or at least that had been the topic of discussion last night when he and the others had received their orders. However, the weakest link of the invasion plan wasn't the fortitude of the Gibraltar frontier gates. The greatest risk to the planned Gibraltar attack was intelligence. *Will it be kept a secret long enough for me and the other Falange members to take out the most substantial defences?* Loose lips sink ships, as he'd seen an American poster say. The Falangists placed under his command were told only what they needed to know. That didn't include the word *invasion*. As far as they knew, they were taking out an artillery position and leaving the Rock. Itself an audacious plan, only as the day developed would the men realise the significance of their actions. In truth, they were about to become heroes of the Falangist movement and their nation. Libertadores.

He reached the frontier and waited in line. His heart was pounding faster than usual. *Relax,* he told himself, although he couldn't convince himself. He was next in line. He reached in his pocket for his papers. He knew the drill: hand over papers, open the bag, they'd see a sandwich and jumper. He'd close the bag, mount his bicycle, and before he knew it the gate would be in his tail feathers.

"Papers, please," said one of the British guards, the one not holding a machine gun.

The moustachioed Spaniard passed them over. His hand was shaking and he was struggling to hold eye contact. He opened the bag and the guard looked inside. He closed it again. *Now give me the walk-on-through signal,* but it didn't come.

"How long will you be staying in Gibraltar?" asked the guard. The Spaniard hadn't been ready for that question. No one had ever asked him that question, not in the month he'd been crossing the frontier. He thought hard. *Permanently* was the right answer.

"Days," he said. He meant to say *just today* but it came out confused.

"Days?" repeated the guard.

"I mean, a day, just today." He knew the rules – he had to be out by 18:00 hours local time.

"What's your business here on the Rock, sir?"

He began to panic. *Business? What is my business?*

"Stevedore?" said the Spaniard, but it came out as a question, not an answer.

The guard, unconvinced, frowned and took a step away. The machine-gun holder now took an interest. Adrenaline pumped into the Spaniard's system, standing the hairs on the back of his neck on end.

"I'm afraid I'm going to have to ask you to come with me." The guard pointed towards the hut.

"Big man. You're early!" said Major Logan Warlock, walking up quickly and slapping the Spaniard on his back. "Is this one causing trouble?" Logan questioned the guard.

"Er, no, sir." The guard handed him back his papers. The Spaniard hoped the relief he was feeling wasn't written on his face. The guard with the machine gun turned his attention elsewhere and the one questioning waved him through.

"Slowing down traffic at the gate, big man? That's a bag of lemons fine for you tomorrow," shouted Logan as the Spaniard mounted his bicycle.

"Yes, Major Warlock. Sorry, Major Warlock." The Spaniard forced a smile before hurriedly pedalling away.

Logan tracked the bicycle as the moustachioed Spaniard crossed the airfield, then looked at his watch. It was almost time. Maria would be there any moment. He had arranged for a car to take them both up the Rock. As she'd requested.

The effort of the ride into town gave the Spaniard's heart something else to pump about as he turned off Line Wall Road. There were plenty of British troops on the streets, none of them with any idea how their lives were about to change. He pedalled up to Prince Edward's Road. How often he'd made this trip, but only carrying Lucky Strike cigarettes or other contraband for delivery to his contact. Today was different, and if all went well nothing on the Rock would ever be the same again.

The Spaniard stopped on Bastion Road and propped his bicycle against the whitewashed wall of house number 46. The blue door was surrounded on both sides by fake pillars that arched at the top above a semicircular window. It was a double door with four frames rectangular in shape.

He glanced towards Devil's Gap Battery across the road. His target. The battery was perched on the eastern side of the Rock towards the bottom of the sharp incline. The Spaniard had heard that Devil's Gap was a popular British duty to work, mainly because of its secluded nature, allowing for on-duty British gunners to behave more casually throughout the day. Devil's Gap was also close to town but not in town. The gun installation was only fifty feet from the door of 48 Bastion Road.

The Spaniard knocked three times and waited, stroking his bushy moustache. He heard movement on the other side of the closed green shutters before one of the two doors opened inwards. The man on the other side nodded without speaking. Letting the Spaniard pass, he stepped outside onto the street and lit a cigarette. Two puffs and a scan of Bastion Road and he was back inside, closing the blue door.

The smoking man led the Spaniard down a short corridor. He pushed a blanket aside to expose a room full of heavily armed Falange operatives and saboteurs. At the centre of the room was a pile of weapons and explosives. The Spaniard's moves were practised, focused, and unblinking. His Franco-aligned Falange compatriots in the room were all wearing British Army-issue uniforms. The Spaniard's was laid out on a chair for him. It was that of a warrant officer, first class.

19

HOLD IT TOGETHER

1942, September 11 (10:58h)
Westwall Lookout, Stay Behind Cave, Rock of Gibraltar

In the Stay Behind Cave, Maria stood back from the west wall lookout as Logan examined the letterbox-shaped rectangle cut into the Rock. *I won't make it.* She couldn't be trapped in this cave, like an animal in a cage.

Light streamed in through the lookout. It was dark behind them. She looked nervously back up the tunnel from where they'd come. Then the walls closed in on her. *Madre mia. Hold it together.* They didn't understand – confined spaces, she couldn't do confined spaces. Maria closed her eyes and remembered back when she was a seventeen-year-old, trapped inside a trunk, knees up to her chin. She could barely breathe. The space was so small and hot, sweat dripped from her cheeks, mixed with tears. How she'd suffered during the Civil War. Hiding from Republicans. Light sneaked its way into the box where the trunk's seal didn't quite fit. She could see the patterned interior of the trunk's stripes and squares; it smelt dry, like an old carpet. She was afraid, so afraid. Maria opened her eyes again. She was still in the Stay Behind Cave and Logan was looking at her. His eyes asked the question and the answer was *No! I'm not okay. Far from it, damn you.*

Logan was taking it so bloody well. *Why hadn't he pushed back more?* If not for himself, then for her. *Had he done all he could?* She wasn't sure. She didn't want him to get shot trying, or maybe she did. She couldn't think straight. The walls moved towards her again. They tried to stop her breathing. *Breathe!* she told herself. *Tranquilo, just breathe.* She was powerless, that was the part she hated most. She was only half listening to Young Albert talking. He couldn't have been much older than eighteen. He had the appearance of a boy who should still be at school. The light through the lookout silhouetted his head, exposing the tufts of hair beginning to appear on his face that was currently passing as maturity.

"Take a peek?" There was a long silence. He was talking to her.

"*Si,*" she said finally, "sorry." She meant to say *yes.* She found herself defaulting to her mother tongue. Maria stepped forward and peered out. The cracks of gunfire continued below. She'd been frightened outside but at least she'd been outside.

"You observe the vessels from here. Identify them with the help of these." He pointed at three charts full of German ship drawings and names, heavily taped to the corrugated iron panels. "Note down what you see" – he picked up a piece of paper – "on one of our very swanky intelligence gathering sheets. Then comes the clever bit. Follow me."

Is the boy still speaking? Pushing her nose as far through the lookout as she could, Maria took the deepest breath of freedom that her lungs would allow. It calmed her, slightly. She took another. She'd been nervous the moment the invasion had started. She hadn't expected to react that way when the fighting started. She'd been visibly shaking, even her teeth had been chattering. Logan had made light of it, but she was embarrassed. The reality of so much gunfire, of whistling bullets overhead, was bad, but this was worse.

"Ria?" Logan's voice was soft. He and the boy were waiting for her. She didn't want to follow them back into the darkness. She wanted to scream. The panic ran up and down her back as she took the steps back down towards the east wall lookout, back into the dark confines of her new hell. This wasn't going to get any better for her as the days and weeks rolled on. She had to get out of here. She just had to.

The boy stood pointing at a pipe running along the steps.

"We can't spy at night, of course, we won't see the buggers." The boy was so cheerful. Strangely, he took the edge off her suffering. "So that's when we push our well-greased flexible pole here, concealed in 'that-there' pipe, out of the hole in the wall. High-frequency Morse code to the Admiralty building in London, if you're interested in state-of-the-art communication systems."

The boy kept talking, but she'd tuned out again. She couldn't give birth, here, in this place. Entombed with five unwashed men. The commander was hoping for a stillborn child, she could see it in his eyes. They couldn't have a screaming baby in here, they all knew it. So what was the plan for her if she carried to term and gave birth a month from now or before? Kill her baby? Smother it? That was a job for her. She couldn't help herself, she burst into tears.

Real ones this time.

* * *

"And then what happened?" Windy spoke in a low whisper sitting next to Young Albert in the radio room. Albert looked down at his cup of tea, turning the cup around twice in a thoughtful manner.

"She kept crying, sir."

Windy sat back in his chair and looked up at the whitewashed ceiling. Every space inside the cave needed a roof to keep the rain out. The limestone was porous, he'd been surprised when he's been told it. When it rained outside, it rained inside the cave too. The radio room was rectangular, just about large enough to swing a cat, with a fitted desk against one of the walls and cupboards below it. Shelves covered the walls, full of cables, wires, and rubber-covered leads, technical parts Windy had no idea the purpose of. There were three large square 12-volt batteries under the desk connected to multiple cables, some running out of the small room via a hole in the wall. Windy knew that those came out on the other side, in the main chamber, and connected to the exercise bicycle. Pedalling the bicycle with its leather strap, instead of a chain, powered up the batteries. Windy knew that from training.

Logan would be fine, he thought, even an asset to the mission if dealt with correctly. It was Maria who was going to be the problem. There were no upsides to the woman. The moment she'd walked in the door the mission had been at risk, but he couldn't put her back out either. *Could I?* She wasn't made of the right stuff, she could let something slip. The stakes were too high. He needed his doctor's help; he was out of his depth when it came to managing mental weakness. There were no good options for Maria. He'd decided to bring her inside. It was all on him. He did it to protect the mission, but that wasn't how it had worked out. The Tracer mission was at greater risk with pregnant Maria inside than it had been with just four team members. *Protect the mission at all costs,* he told himself again. That was still his goal and all that mattered. The obvious solution was unthinkable. Inhumane, barbaric even, but he couldn't ignore it.

Windy looked at the innocent young face of Albert waiting for his next words. The burn from the hole in his hip was excruciatingly painful and getting worse, not to mention nausea and shortness of breath. He wanted to lie down, but there was still work to be done.

"When the Admiralty communication comes back, bring it to me directly. Only to me, understood?" Albert nodded. "There's a good lad."

Windy tapped Young Albert on the shoulder but winced as he stood up to leave the radio room. All his waist area was now in trauma. The burning sensation was like a red-hot poker being jabbed at his hip over and over. He'd expected it to be painful, but this was debilitating and getting worse.

"Golly, are you okay, sir?" Albert's brow was furrowed in concern.

He was a good lad. "Never better, m'boy." Windy shuffled out of the radio room with a smile. He felt awful, light-headed, and nauseous, but he needed to stay focused on the tasks at hand. He could trust Albert to be discreet. Logan and Maria were unknown. A vetting was standard procedure. Asking for an Admiralty background check was in order, although he didn't want it to get out that he was delving into their personal lives. It wouldn't be good for morale. If he found something? *What then?* They were sealed in so no one was leaving. The intelligence might come in handy, leverage if he needed it, but, more importantly, he didn't want any surprises. Neither did the Admiralty, and now they'd been informed.

As for Hoop, *is he dead or alive?* Alive and there was a risk, considering what he knew of the Tracer mission. *Could the Germans make him talk?* Sure. But why would they single out a Black man for special interrogation? They weren't looking for a secret cave at the top of the Rock. They'd take no interest in African Sergeant "Hoop" Fundi, and Hoop could be trusted to stay silent about what he knew. Windy was sure of it.

Operation Tracer

Stay Behind Cave

Rock of Gibraltar

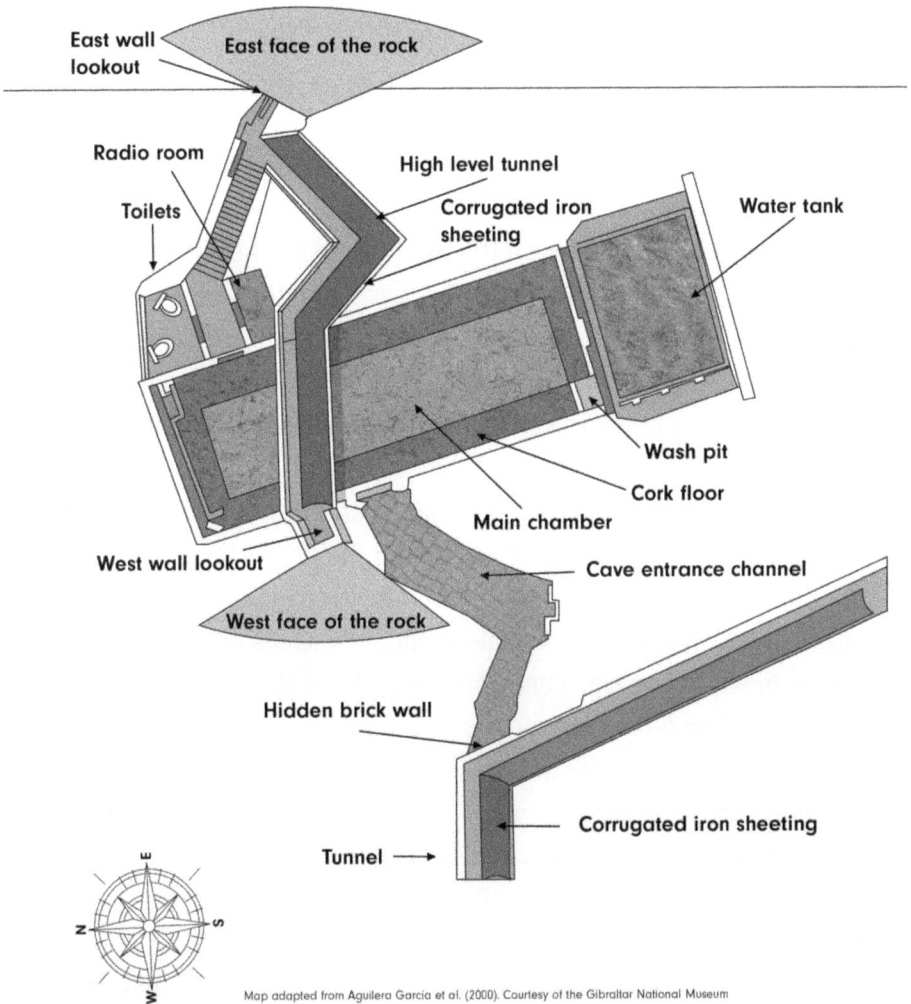

East wall lookout

East face of the rock

Radio room

High level tunnel

Toilets

Corrugated iron sheeting

Water tank

Wash pit

Cork floor

Main chamber

West wall lookout

Cave entrance channel

West face of the rock

Hidden brick wall

Corrugated iron sheeting

Tunnel →

Map adapted from Aguilera Garcia et al. (2000). Courtesy of the Gibraltar National Museum

20

MAJOR BLACKTOOTH

1942, September 16 (13:17h)
Windmill Hill Prisoner Cell, Rock of Gibraltar

Hoop lay on his pillowless, sheetless bunk, listening to the wailing and screeching. *Is that in my mind or is it really a siren?* He'd never heard the same in his short time on the Rock. He was staring at the wall in the low light, the same old shapes appearing on the wall to haunt him. He saw the shape of a mountain and those demons rising beyond, shadow monsters ready to swallow him whole. He reached out his finger and ran it along the line of the silhouette; the wall was bumpy to the touch. Dragon's skin.

Hoop's eye twitched when the flap at the bottom of the cell door opened. A tray was pushed through onto the floor. He knew what was on the tray. It had been the same for… he didn't know how long. A tin cup of water, two-thirds full, stale bread, two slices of cured ham, and a piece of white cheese. The same came through the flap every day.

What do they think I know? Is it Tracer? How could it be? If it is, why aren't they asking specific questions relating to the mission? Have they caught Windy? Is Windy or one of the other Tracer team members in a cell down the hall? Have they broken, given the game away? And what did it matter if they have? He still wasn't going to tell these bastards anything! *I'll die first.*

The small flap on his cell door slammed shut as the door to the captain's home back in Namibia opened.

* * *

Captain Otto Beckerman was tall, over six feet, with a manicured moustache and white beard. He wore, almost exclusively, a black double-breasted jacket and a white shirt with a collar, even in the heat of the day, which he rarely ventured out into. He'd sit in the shade, usually under a fan, drinking tonic with ice. He would either read in the afternoon or play chess against himself, spinning the board around continuously and even playing backwards.

It had been the captain who had taught Hoop how to play chess, the German language, and all about the navy. He retired to Namibia from the Imperial Navy in 1920, after having lost an arm. The accident happened aboard his last command, an S90-class torpedo boat that had foundered off the coast of the German town of Wilhelmshaven on March 13 of the same year.

As the captain told it, they had been forced to abandon ship. They took to lifeboats, one of which broke free and trapped his arm, crushing it. According to the captain, he trailed his bleeding arm over the edge of the lifeboat into the salty sea, but when he'd tried to bring it back out it had gone. "Taken by a shark," the captain would say. Hoop would ask him to tell the story every time he'd go to the house. The story seemed to change each time he told it, but Hoop liked the story anyway. There were others too, like the time he was shipwrecked on a Caribbean island, with just a bottle of Schnapps, a newspaper from 1912, and a Cuban cigar but no matches to light it. It ended with him being rescued by a native girl in a grass skirt while sitting by a fire. "How had he lit the fire without matches?" Hoop had asked. His mother had laughed out loud when he'd asked the captain to explain the *Inkongruenz*, the inaccuracy. That was the day the captain gave him his first book. It had a green binding and a silver cover, with only a few words on the front: *Learn to Speak German*. He took it from the room he called the library. Shelf on shelf of books. The room had a smell of musk; how he loved that smell. He read for hours in that room, mostly about ships, while his mother and the captain *cleaned* upstairs. The house had five bedrooms, but the captain lived alone. He'd never experienced such kindness from a white man. He was funny too and he listened. He asked questions and then didn't nod and change the subject like other white people; instead, he asked more questions. He was interested in what Hoop had to say. That was unusual for old people, and unheard of for white ones.

His mother liked him too. She was excited to go to work; he'd never seen that before.

Squeak! The bolt to Hoop's Gibraltar cell door screeched and his drifting mind jumped back, fully present, between those four stone walls. The door swung on its hinges and a German major entered enthusiastically. He removed his jacket quickly and smiled at Hoop; one of his two front teeth was black and rotten.

As if possessed, the black-toothed major attacked. He leapt like a large cat at Hoop and rained frenzied blows down upon him. The explosive approach was punctuated by a loud panting sound as the major tried to maintain his ferocious level of assault. Like a rag doll, Hoop bounced from blow to blow. His head hit the wall of dragon's skin before he was pulled from his bunk by one leg. His back hit the floor of the cell, knocking the wind out of him. He heard the crack of a rib as the major kicked violently at him multiple times before standing over him, trying to catch his breath. For a long moment, Hoop lay on the floor, rolling from side to side in pain. *My ribs!* He tried to breathe through the blood flowing from his nose. It tasted metallic. *Where am I cut?* A bead of sweat dropped from the major's forehead and landed on Hoop's cheek. He looked up at the major grinning down at him, the German's crystal-blue eyes blazing with excitement. Hoop saw the devil.

* * *

The black-toothed major showed up at all hours of the day and night. Sometimes he'd hit Hoop with his fists, but he also used a wet sock with small stones. Hoop could hear the stones jangle together; they reminded him of pebbles on a beach. Pebbles that cut his skin open. He knew the major's smell too. The major liked to get in close and whisper his interrogation questions slowly, articulating every syllable as if the words held personal meaning to him alone.

The major smelt British – he was using the British Army-issue soap, the same lavender-smelling one they'd all been using before the invasion – but his breath was stale, like rotten meat. His name was Major Haas.

"The tunnels, where to enter?" The major didn't wait for a reply before swinging his next blow.

"The officer in charge of the tunnels, the name, you have the name?" He hit Hoop again.

"The tunnels, how many men inside, what supplies they have?" Like soothing lines of a whispered poem, they needed no answer. Major Haas sang them in a low tone in time to his beating.

Hoop let his head fall backwards, his eyes rolling up into his head again.

21

HANKY-PANKY

1942, September 16 (16:38h)
Main Chamber, Stay Behind Cave, Rock of Gibraltar

Back in the Stay Behind Cave, a fresh pot of tea was on the table. Having come for a cup, Windy stood in the doorway as Logan kissed and embraced Maria. It was time to have *that* conversation. Albert was where Albert always was, in the radio room, while Bunny and Carter were on duty at the lookouts. There wouldn't be a better moment than this.

It was the hardest job of the day. Windy hated personal stuff. He'd gone over the options in his head. *Logan, you can't touch your girlfriend in here* – too direct. *No nooky, please, the two of you* – too light-hearted. There was no good way to say this to them, but it had to be said. He invited them to the table with a cup of tea in front of each. "Now don't get in a tizzy, but I have to ask you to put your relationship on hold." Windy adjusted his legs to get more comfortable in his seat. It didn't help.

Logan folded his arms. "I say, begging your pardon, but I'm not sure that's any of your affair."

"He's right, Logan," said Maria.

Windy's mouth dropped open slightly before he snatched at Maria's unexpected support. "It's a bit of a nuisance, I know, but it's a confined space and the mission must come first. Thank you, my dear." His target already achieved, it was time to stop speaking, stand up, and walk away – but he didn't. His mouth moved again and more words came out. None of them was planned. "We don't want any..."

Embarrassment prevented Windy from finishing his sentence. "Well, you know." He wasn't sure how best to describe the delicate subject; he wasn't one for talking about such things. "Quite frankly, that sort of thing, it impacts the morale of the chaps." He was still speaking when Logan interrupted.

"You drag us in here at gunpoint and now you're getting ballywell personal. You've got a nerve."

"The commander's right, Logan," Maria repeated. "We can't just carry on as normal. I don't want to."

The rejection twisted Logan's handsome face and slumped his shoulders. "If that's the way you want it." He stood up. "Relationship on hold." The major stepped away from the table, clearly frustrated. Maria stood up unaided, with remarkable ease and more mobility than Windy had seen her exhibit to date.

"The mission must come first. Thank you for your understanding, my dear," said Windy.

Maria didn't answer. If looks could kill, he would've been a dead man for sure. He watched Maria walk after Logan.

Bloody awkward, he thought, and it wasn't going to solve the Maria problem. She was a distraction, disruptive, and her predicament presented a serious threat to the mission. She'd already changed the attitude of his team towards each other, but short of shooting her in the head and burying her in the rubble, there was nothing he could do about it right now. Windy turned his thoughts to furniture.

There were three double bunk beds in the cave: a bunk for each of the men, but no privacy for a woman. Six swinging dicks didn't need space of their own, but Maria did. If not for herself, then to keep her out of sight of the rest of the team. Maria on parade would lead to problems for sure. They needed to rearrange the storage boxes to create a space inside the cave to house her separately. Section her off with one of the bunks, and there was no time like the present.

Windy pulled on the leg of a bunk bed with his good arm. It moved, but the bunks had been solidly made and he knew it was a job for two hands. He tried to use his other hand, but the pain of his hip stopped him in his tracks. He grimaced and saw Doctor Carter watching him.

"If you rip those stitches, it will start bleeding again. If you don't listen to me, I've got a good mind to let you bleed to death."

A bead of sweat rolled down Windy's forehead. The truth was he was okay to be told to take it easy. He felt hot under the collar and still nauseous. He pulled up a chair and sat back down at the table.

Windy and Carter had the room. Windy knew he didn't have to explain himself to the doctor but he wanted to.

"We were unlucky," Windy said.

Carter lifted Windy's shirt to one side and began to undo the bandage but he didn't answer.

"Six bodies is what we need," Windy added.

Carter clearly disapproved of his decision to bring them aboard and Windy knew it. He respected the fact that the doctor hadn't questioned the order. Windy had made the call in the moment: *did I make a mistake?* Maybe.

"Six bodies is the minimum that it's going to take to deliver as planned," he continued. "Okay, so one is now a woman. We'll adjust, we'll manage." He could tell his doctor didn't agree.

Carter unwrapped the bloodstained cloth but still said nothing. Windy could see that the doctor was disappointed with his wound as well.

Males only in training had allowed for a completely relaxed environment. Showering, use of the toilets – there was a locker room atmosphere. He'd seen that dynamic change in the few days Maria had been with them. The men had all altered the way they were behaving, including him. The pressure to keep up appearances in front of her was going to take its toll.

"It'll work itself out, these things usually do." Windy looked at the doctor for a reaction. The slight lift of an eyebrow was the only sign of disagreement with his superior officer but still not a word. Windy, already hot under the collar, became frustrated with the man.

He rubbed his sleeve over his forehead to clear the beads of sweat. "We'll keep her womanliness under wraps, create a wall of boxes to hide the water pit and her bunk. Let's establish a protocol and a schedule for her."

He winced as Carter put pressure on his stitches with a clean swab. "Say something," Windy blurted, "for God's sake, man!"

The doctor looked at his commanding officer.

Windy waited. He could see Carter working on his word selection. He finally spoke.

"You better hide that gun of yours," he said.

They shared a worried look of agreement as Young Albert came into the main chamber.

"Cup of rosy lea for ya, guv'nor?" he asked in a comic East End of London accent.

Windy smiled at Carter. He'd been right about Albert: the boy would provide the ray of sunshine they were all going to so desperately need to prevent them from shooting each other.

"Rest," was the doctor's advice. "You need to get on that bunk and not get off it until I tell you."

Windy was almost relieved to be ordered to his bed. He could see Doctor Carter was serious and he wasn't going to argue.

"Let's stack some of the boxes in front of the faucet. It will give Maria some privacy," said Windy.

"Bed," repeated Doctor Carter. "And I don't want to see you for twenty-four hours. We'll bring you what you need."

"Right you are, sir," jested Windy, saluting the doctor as he climbed onto his bunk, rolled over, and closed his eyes. He didn't feel well, not at all.

22

MORNING IS BROKEN

1942, September 17 (02:05h)
Main Chamber, Stay Behind Cave, Rock of Gibraltar

Windy was having a dream.

The knock on the double doors was firm and confident. Six-year-old Frederick 'Windy' Gale stood outside the drawing-room door next to his nanny. Nanny was a formidable size and shape and more than a match for the children in her care when they played up, which in Windy's case was pretty much all the time. There were few occasions that subdued young Frederick, but this was always one of them. Being presented to his parents. It was the worst part of his day. Nanny would go through the list of do's and don'ts; there were so many, they became muddled. By the time he was standing at the double door waiting to go in, he couldn't think straight. Life was so much easier on the first-floor nursery. When he did something wrong, Nanny would just tell him; sometimes she'd be angry and other times she'd just ask him if he understood. He always said he did, even if he didn't. It was different from his parents. When he got something wrong they didn't say anything, just asked Nanny to stay behind and he'd be led upstairs. He'd cry. What had he done? He knew he'd been bad. Nanny would stroke his head, then tell him what he got wrong. He wanted to please his parents, really he did, particularly his mother. He'd seen her take hold of his sister once, pull her close and kiss her. He longed for her to do the same to him, but he couldn't remember Nanny's list. Some nights he was sure he'd got everything perfect, but his mother would just sit there on the side of the patterned fabric chair with its shiny carved arms and smile at him. Her long dress puffed out over most of the space around her, making it difficult to get close to her even if Nanny would have allowed it. Nanny didn't want him or his sister to get too close. He'd tried to sit on his mother's knee once, but it hadn't gone well. His father, too, would stand with his arms firmly behind his back and ask him questions. "What did you learn today, son?" He never knew what to say. His father didn't know anything, he just had questions.

This particular evening, however, was different. It had been almost two weeks since he'd been standing at the double door. He'd been in bed for most of that time. He'd had, what they were all calling, 'the sickness'. He'd felt ill after returning from a day out to the park with his sister. Nanny had put him to bed. He'd become very hot and wet and then cold, North Pole cold. Nanny had brought him soup for the first few days. A doctor had come and poked him. He'd slept a lot and his sister wasn't allowed in his room.

He'd seen more of his mother in that week than ever before. Instead of Nanny, it was she who would feed him soup. His mother had also come when it was dark, or at least he thought it was her. Standing by his bed as he drifted in and out of sleep. Each day had slipped into the next and then suddenly he'd felt well again.

That was yesterday.

This was the first day back to the drawing room. He was more nervous than usual because Nanny had forgotten to go through the list. Stand up straight, only speak when spoken to, and don't fidget. He remembered those. The double doors opened, he and Nanny entered. His father wasn't standing by the fireplace, maybe because the fire was raging as he'd never seen it before. Flames were racing up the chimney and the room was not just warm but hot. His father was standing behind his mother in her usual seat. He had his hand on her shoulder; he'd never seen his father touch his mother before.

Nanny had positioned herself back near the door as he walked up to the spot he usually took up, a few feet from his mother. He said nothing, stood as straight as he could, and didn't fidget. He was waiting for somebody to say something, but nobody did. Finally, his mother put out her arms and beckoned to him. He looked to Nanny for guidance but got none. Tentatively, he stepped towards his mother until he was in touching distance. She took his arm and pulled him off his feet. Right onto her dress, his feet were on her dress, then his feet were on the chair and she gripped him so tight he lost his breath for a moment. Next thing he knew, she was swinging him from side to side and repeating his name continuously. She started to cry. It was what he'd always wanted but now that it was happening, it wasn't that great. Nanny had both hands up at her face. Probably in shock. Then his father touched his neck. His father never touched him, ever! It was all rather weird, he thought. Having been kissed all over his head, Windy left the drawing room, ran across the entrance hall and up the staircase. It was the happiest moment of his life.

* * *

The sun crested on the horizon in the east as the first of its rays chased across the waters of the Mediterranean and twinkled on the overnight Gibraltar dew.

Hoop Fundi stared at the ceiling of his cell at the same moment Standartenführer Wolfgang Richter swung his legs out of the four-poster bed at the Governor's residence. He walked over to the window and looked up at the Rock framed by the sun.

Meanwhile, inside the Stay Behind Cave, the morning light moved slowly along the inside of the wall in the shape of an ever more stretched letterbox at the east lookout. It provided just a touch of brightness in the corridor tunnel. The glare of a new day forced a tired-looking, on-duty Young Albert to turn his back on the lookout.

Bunny was manning the west wall, wrapped tightly in a blanket. He could see the same morning sun on the other side of the Rock, far off in the distance as it painted the Spanish coast.

Down in the main chamber there was only the sound of the heavy-duty brass faucet at the wash pit in the corner, running water, then a squeak of it turning, then nothing. Maria was behind the boxes of salted fish, boiled sweets, and dried fruit, trying to get herself clean.

The rest of the room was quiet, with only the light sound of Carter snoring. Logan was in his bunk facing the wall as Windy's arm fell from his bunk and hung pale and limp. As Maria dressed behind the barrier of boxes, the commander's arm swayed ever so slightly as his forearm pivoted on the edge of the wooden bed frame. Windy's eyes were open but lifeless, fixed on a point in the ceiling he'd never see again. His lips were blue and his bed wet. Operation Tracer team leader Commander Frederick 'Windy' Gale was dead.

23

COLD TEA

Maria stepped out from behind the boxes. She picked up the teapot and took it back behind the storage box wall to the faucet. The pot filled with water slowly. Maria listened impassively to the vigorous sound of liquid hitting pot turn to that deeper water into water noise. Returning to the table, she took two spoonfuls of tea leaves from the tin on the makeshift shelf and put them in the teapot. She sat looking at the pot. Then at the clock on the cave wall. Finally, Maria poured a cup of cold tea and took a sip. Taking a deep breath, she looked at the mirror on the wall and then directly at Windy's pale arm. Quickly but calmly, she ran to Carter and shook him.

"It's Commander Gale!" she said urgently.

Carter jumped from his bunk. He had no idea what was happening but he was on his feet if not clear-headed.

"The commander!" said Maria.

The room was still a blur for Doctor Carter. Something was wrong, that much he understood from Maria's tone. He took her arm and steadied himself. She was pointing. Carter saw Windy's arm and ran for his bunk. He knew the commander was dead before he got close. He'd seen enough cadavers to recognise that limp pale lifelessness when he saw it, even from a distance. Windy was gone. Long gone. Carter put his fingers on the commander's cold neck and felt for the pulse he knew wasn't there.

"He's dead, isn't he?" said Maria, backing away.

"What's going on?" Logan joined them at Windy's bunk. Commander Gale was white against the dark-green sheets of his bed.

"Tell me he's not dead. He can't be..." said Maria, starting to cry and still backing away.

Carter dropped to the cork floor. *This isn't happening,* he thought, *he can't be dead. Not Windy.*

Logan stood stone-faced, staring at the commander's corpse. "We need to get him under the rubble right away." His words were more of an order than an observation.

The door to the tunnel lookouts opened and Bunny stepped through, followed by a yawning Young Albert holding an empty teacup.

"Have you buggers drunk all the cold tea already?" said Albert with a big smile.

24

WHAT NOW?

1942, September 17 (16:05h)
Main Chamber, Stay Behind Cave, Rock of Gibraltar

Sitting alone in the main chamber, Carter could hear the distant sound of Logan and Bunny moving bricks and rubble in the entrance channel on the other side of the door. Although he wasn't a drinker, right now Carter could have done with a stiff one. 'Consideration' had been given to providing each team member with a ration of alcohol and cigarettes. Commander Fleming had left that decision up to him and Doctor Milburn. They'd agreed over a glass of Scotch not to take either, much to the disdain of their team leader. Windy had a twenty-a-day habit. The Benghazi stove and the fat-burning lamps were already a fire hazard without men lighting matches willy-nilly about the place. Smoking also caused men to cough, sometimes loudly.

He stared, eyes transfixed on the open box of corned beef cans. The tops of the cans were identical. Circular shapes row on row, but three tins were missing. *Maria?* thought Carter. She'd been rifling through the stores looking for fruit juice and salted fish. The missing ones would turn up somewhere. He closed the lid of the box and dropped his head, wishing that a few unaccounted-for tins of corned beef were his only problem.

The plan for a death and a burial in the rubble deliberately left loose between the cave entrance channel and the door to the cave had been little more than a contingency plan. Carter had considered what he might do if death occurred, but it seemed unlikely at the time. They were six healthy men with little chance of an accident occurring between their bunks, the lookout holes in the wall, and the toilets. If Jerry came crashing in, they wouldn't be burying anyone there and no one would have died of old age even if the mission had lasted years. So he hadn't expected to be preparing a body.

"What now?" Carter asked Windy's corpse, which was currently bound, ready for burial, lying in the centre of the main chamber. How much everyone had relied upon Windy. He made the decisions, calculated the risks, and gave the orders. Firmly adjusted anything that needed adjusting in the way of attitude and behaviour. Always with that gentlemanly touch, but if needed with the threat of more forceful means. Everyone knew where they stood with Windy. He was straight as an arrow. *What now?*

Young Albert, who had aimed all his questions at Windy, now aimed them at him, even though Logan had become the ranking officer in the cave. He not only outranked him but Logan had real experience commanding men and running missions. Bunny, too, was asking, *What now?* Logan had taken the lead in the logistics to get Windy buried. Carter, Bunny, and Albert had all trained with Windy, and he could tell they were all still in shock. Logan didn't have that encumbrance. The major was just being pragmatic. The dynamic in the cave had shifted too. Albert had withdrawn, his light-hearted attitude slipping away, albeit temporarily. Carter was no sociologist, but he knew the new dynamic would develop into problems sooner rather than later. Taking over as team leader made him nervous. He could lead in a controlled environment, he'd proved that aboard ship many times; but they weren't aboard ship, they were spies sealed in a cave, two of whom didn't want to be there. Orders wouldn't be followed without question. This was going to be a battle of wills. Personalities. And the ranking officer, Logan, knew little of the mission. Windy's death had changed everything inside the cave, except the stakes. The success or failure of the Tracer mission would still have a drastic impact on hundreds of thousands of servicemen and -women, maybe even millions of lives, if not the outcome of the war itself. He dropped his head, which felt heavy with the thought. *Am I even officially in charge now?* Staff Surgeon Milburn was the senior medical officer, and as such he was supposed to have picked up that job if anything had happened to Windy. Syd had far more experience leading teams. It was never discussed what would happen if both of them died.

Instinctively, Logan had already started to give unofficial directions. He was a natural leader – no one could argue with that, it was obvious – but Albert didn't want to take orders from him and Bunny wouldn't. Were they to allow him to take the reins and replace Windy, what would be Logan's first order? Open the cave and let's all go our separate ways? He wanted out after all, so did Maria: that was no secret. And what about training? He hadn't had any. The mission detail was unknown to him in so many ways. God knows, he didn't want the job, but as Windy never stopped repeating, *the mission was everything.* Sitting there with Windy's body he was unsure about so much, but one thing was crystal clear: the mission. He would do whatever it took to complete what Windy had started.

"Whatever it takes, my friend." No one heard Doctor Carter's whisper.

Maria and Albert had happily taken up the intelligence-gathering jobs while he prepared Windy for the ground. Bunny and Logan had set about mixing the concrete and digging the hole between the cave entrance channel and the cave main door. He'd wrapped Windy in his bedding but rigor had already started to set in, the tightening of the sheet in small areas showing its onset. He'd been dead for at least five hours before they'd found him. It had been Maria who'd asked the big question, the one he couldn't answer. What killed Windy? He had a few ideas, but without cutting him up here on the cave table and putting his organs in the bowls they were using for meals there was no way of knowing for sure. Heart failure? Cardiac arrest? Heart disease was the biggest killer of men Windy's age and he died quietly, that was for sure, without knowing it was coming or he would've called out for help.

Carter's thoughts were broken by the sound of raised voices in the cave entrance channel. He moved quickly to the main door and ran through the doorway.

"You lying bastard," said Bunny as he grappled with Logan, rolling around inside the hole they'd dug for Windy, wrestling and throwing punches.

25

LAID OUT TO REST

Carter grabbed Bunny's belt and pulled him off Logan, who touched his lip looking for blood. The droplets came from his nose. Bunny struggled to break free, but Carter wrapped his arms around the Scot.

"He did it!" Bunny's voice was again too loud and Carter shook him, replying in a passionate whisper as close to his ear as possible.

"Quiet."

"Aye, it was him!"

Carter tightened his grip.

"For God's sake, think." Carter had his mouth up against the back of Bunny's head. "You're gonna get us all killed." The message got through and Bunny relaxed against the restraint and Carter let go, rolling him to the side.

Logan sat on the edge of the grave, letting the blood drip into his hand and gripping the bridge of his nose.

"Striking a superior officer, that's a court-martial offence, old chap," Logan said. "You're done when this is over, you're bloody done!"

Bunny nodded at Logan's threat as he tried to catch his breath. Then he launched himself at the major with arms flailing. Carter grabbed Bunny a second time as Logan swung in his defence. All three were now entangled. Carter held Bunny as Logan backed away.

"Enough!" whispered Carter emphatically. "Go!" He'd aimed his words at Logan, who was happy to oblige.

"Try it again, I dare you. Next time it won't go well for you, pal," said Logan. Carter noticed something different about the major's accent as he backed away through the main chamber doorway.

"What the hell are you doing, Bunny?" Exasperated, Carter snatched a worried glance at the cave entrance.

"Aye, he did it, he killed Windy." Bunny pushed Carter off him and sat in the grave, his head lowered, his forearms rested on his knees.

"Get a hold of yourself, man." Carter sat opposite the Scotsman. "What if Jerry was in the tunnel? The game would be up. Christ, Bunny, what were you thinking?" He shook his head. "Like we don't have enough to deal with."

"Killed him, he did! What would ya have me do?" Bunny's voice was still emotionally high.

"Lower your voice. I'm serious, Bunny. I'm not going to ask you again." Although the truth was, Carter had no idea what he would do if Bunny didn't lower his voice. It was an empty threat but all he had. They exchanged eye contact of unspoken agreement and Bunny continued in an impassioned whisper.

"Do you not be hearing me? Logan killed Windy."

Carter put his hand on Bunny's shoulder. "Okay, tell me, but for God's sake quietly."

"It was his only way out, get rid of Windy," Bunny said. Carter hoped there was more; that couldn't be all. "I asked him where he was last night at two a.m. and what do you think he told me?" Carter waited for the answer. "Asleep!" Bunny scoffed at the idea. "'Never got up all night,' he said, and what was 'I' insinuating?" Bunny was wide-eyed at the brazenness of Logan's defence.

Carter upturned his hand, raised both his eyebrows, and waited.

"I know that was a lie. Couldn't sleep last night so I took a wee stroll up to the east wall lookout. It was a half-moon and more light than I'd expected so I came back down to fetch a set of binoculars from the radio room. Exactly two a.m. Looked at my watch." Bunny leaned in as if sharing a secret. "Door to the main chamber was open, wasn't it? Had a wee look inside, I did. There was only one of you up. Logan, bold as ya like, standing at Windy's bed." Carter leaned back to take in the story. "He didn't sleep through like he said he did. I never thought much of it at the time, but it's been preying on my mind since." Bunny paused. "So I asked him outright, and he lied by no mistake. The lie says it all. He lied because he killed Windy."

Carter stood up and paced the small space without speaking. Bunny just watched him, waiting for a reaction.

"You're sure it was Logan standing at Windy's bed?"

"Aye. I saw what I saw." Bunny was adamant.

Carter continued to pace. What was Logan doing at Windy's bed in the middle of the night and why hadn't he mentioned it? Although it didn't mean he'd killed him, and he wasn't about to add to the mayhem by encouraging Bunny, especially not with Windy lying dead in the other room.

"So he didn't tell the truth." Carter stopped pacing. "We need to ask him about that."

Bunny jumped to his feet. "Smashing! You ask him, I'll hold him." He was raring to go.

Carter wasn't about to bring them together for round two. "We're not going to have another punch-up, Bunny. I want to hear what he has to say. We're not going to accuse anyone of anything right off the bat."

"He lied, it's as simple as that."

"Being a liar doesn't automatically make him a killer, Bunny. Think what you're saying. Logan, one of our own, would kill his superior officer because he doesn't like the orders he's giving?" Bunny didn't answer. "What you're saying is that Logan murdered his superior officer with no guarantee of getting out of this place by doing so." Carter stood squarely facing Bunny. "There are no obvious signs of a fight on Windy's body – he wasn't strangled, suffocated, he didn't have his throat cut, or any other major artery severed." Bunny looked up at Carter, less confident now. "So how exactly did Logan standing by Windy's bed kill him?"

Bunny searched for an answer but one wasn't forthcoming. "I don't know how he did it. You're the doctor."

Carter could see Bunny's accusation crumbling. "That's right. I'm the doctor and I'm telling you that Windy died of natural causes." Carter had no proof that was the case. The truth was he had no idea what killed Windy. He'd certainly died quietly. *Could I say there was no foul play?* No, he couldn't. Logan wanted out, yes, but that surely wasn't motive enough to kill. It was madness to think of it, wasn't it? Ridiculous. Windy had lost a lot of blood and his heart gave out and that was that.

"You're sure?" Bunny's brow furrowed and his shoulders dropped.

"Yes, I'm sure." It was what Windy would have said. They needed to move forward and they couldn't do that with Bunny believing Logan killed Windy. Besides, he was as sure as he could be, so it wasn't a lie. "You're gonna have to take his hand, you know that?"

Bunny's face contorted. "No way."

Carter could see Bunny's disdain for his new Tracer teammate ran deeper than just this accusation.

"I won't shake that bastard's hand."

Was this it for the next God knows how many weeks, months, years? Carter's heart sank. Was he to spend the rest of the mission playing peacemaker? He felt like a schoolteacher. It would have been funny had Windy's body not been lying in the other room with them standing in his grave. He was barely cold and the mission was falling apart.

"We all have to live here, Bunny, together. That means you and Logan too." Carter knew he sounded irritated but he couldn't help it. Bunny was being unreasonable. "We're going to have an atmosphere between you two for how long?" Carter put both hands on his hips. "A month? Six months? Three years? I don't expect you to kiss and make up, but you damn well need to put this to bed."

Bunny looked at the floor.

It was embarrassing and Carter felt himself lose his patience. "Quite frankly, Bunny, you're being bloody selfish. Damn it, man, think of the mission. What's more important: our mission or a bloody handshake?"

Bunny's resolve cracked. It rippled through his posture, onto his face, and in his tone. "Aye, all right. I'll do me part. I'll take his hand. Ya mother curse ya if ya wrong."

Carter was relieved this conversation was over.

"One condition," Bunny added.

Condition? What did the bloody Scotsman think this was? A negotiation for following orders? Carter surprised himself. He was taking charge. Giving orders without thinking.

"What do you want, Bunny?" Carter was direct and his intonation was enough to convey his irritation.

"Ask him why he lied? A wee question, nothing more."

It was a reasonable request. He also wanted to know why Logan had lied.

"Agreed."

Carter led the way back into the main chamber. Logan was sitting at the table. He stood up as if prepared for another attack. Windy's body lay between them. Carter looked at Bunny to speak. He could see that it was curdling his insides to do it, but the Scot spoke.

"I did my nut. I shouldn't have. You have my apology. If you'll take it?" Bunny's apology was more convincing than Carter had expected, but he needed him to complete the job. Bunny continued, "I don't think you killed Windy." Bunny paused. "I made a mistake and I'm man enough to say so." Bunny stepped forward and offered his hand.

Logan relaxed and Carter felt a small sense of achievement. Preventing the Tracer team from ripping each other apart was an early victory for his leadership. Maybe he could do this after all.

"We're all a little frayed. No hard feelings, old chap." The upper-class plum in Logan's mouth had returned. The major stepped over

Windy's body rather than walk around it on his way to Bunny's hand. There was something in his movement that conveyed immense disrespect.

As he reached Bunny and went to take his hand, the Scotsman's left fist came around, haymaker-style, and cracked Logan on the side of the head, knocking him sideways. Major Logan Warlock never saw it coming and the connection was perfect. His legs turned to jelly and his eyes rolled back in his head as he hit the cork floor. The top half of his body bounced slightly before it was lights out. Logan lay motionless a few feet from Windy. Carter looked at Bunny with immense disappointment. There was nothing left to say. Bunny simply shrugged his shoulders, in no way of an apology, went over to his bunk, and lay down.

26

FROM A GREAT HEIGHT

1941, April 4 (14:22h)

Hart Warren Beach, Hartlepool, England, United Kingdom

Yet to hear of a top-secret Admiralty mission called "Tracer", Doctor Tom Carter was on leave. He'd been excited about the trip home for weeks. He'd had letters from his girlfriend Joan before he went to sea. She'd been all he could think about in the sweltering Gambian heat as the ship sailed down the west coast of Africa. He'd missed her desperately. All those hours looking at the crumpled photo of her in that white blouse and now here she was sitting right opposite him in the flesh. Her perfect skin, the perfume. He was high on her charms and trying not to stare. He longed to be touching her but it wouldn't be proper. His feelings were intoxicating, but there was a time and place for that sort of thing and they weren't quite there yet. Sitting on a square concrete anti-tank block on the crest of the sand dunes, they looked down over the beach. The sea was choppier than usual for that time of the year and the wind had a chill. Neither bothered Carter; he would've sat there in a blizzard and wouldn't have batted an eyelid – as long as Joan was with him.

Joan, however, had her coat buttoned high up her neck and her arms and legs crossed. The sandy walk over the footbridge had lacked their usual banter, but he wasn't about to let a little thing like the weather spoil the encounter he'd waited so long for.

Joan stared out over the rolling seas. "Life is short, isn't it, Tom?"

Her intonation was rhetorical. "We really can't afford to waste a second of it." She nodded to herself.

Apparently German bombing had hit Hartlepool quite badly in his absence; he wondered if that was the cause of his girlfriend's reticence?

"We can't. I missed you," he replied enthusiastically. She was clearly cold on the outside, but he wanted and needed to feel that warmth he knew she had inside her. He'd dreamt about this moment for months, and it wasn't quite living up to his expectations.

Joan's stare finally left the sea where it was and came back to shore fully sober. As she held his gaze, he saw it. It hit him like a lightning bolt. He'd been so wrapped up in his feelings for her; she'd been his stabiliser when he'd closed his door at night. Her letters, with the faded scent of her perfume, had sustained him, given meaning to everything. She didn't need to speak the words. Everything she wanted to say was etched on the face he knew so well. Their relationship was ending. Here. Now. On these cold hard concrete squares. Her eyes said, *I want out.* Her lips said, *I don't want to hurt you,* and her chin said, *I must do what needs doing.* Carter had no idea what his face said in reply. Joan broke the silence.

"I'm sorry, Tom."

He wanted to take her in his arms and have her say it wasn't so. What if he told her how much he loved her, that he couldn't live without her? That he would change – whatever it was that he needed to do to make himself into the man she would want. He opened his mouth to speak. The words came out but not the ones he'd expected.

"It's okay, Joan." A weight visibly lifted from her shoulders. She reached out and touched his hand. He wished she hadn't. The touch broke his heart.

The conversation back to the car was mostly about the weather, cordial and polite. It lacked all intimacy, they were acquaintances again in an instant. She couldn't get away quick enough. The drive back to town was littered with silences. Carter wanted to ask what had happened, but what difference did it make? A dam of steadfast etiquette and gentlemanly reserve came to his aid. He didn't want their last moments together to be ugly or for her to remember him as weak.

He stopped the car outside her home, stepped out as she waited, walked around the front of the motor wishing for it to run him over. Carter opened the car door and Joan stepped out. He saw the shape of her firm thighs beneath her dress.

"Keep in touch, Tom."

Did she mean it? She wanted him to call her? *Of course she doesn't.*

"I will," Carter lied.

"Stay safe," were the last words she ever spoke to him.

He couldn't promise that. If a German bomb dropped on him right now, he would've welcomed it.

"You too," he replied. Carter watched Joan push a key into her front door, enter, and close the door on him and their relationship, without looking back. Tears in his eyes and a lump in his throat, Carter drove his black Austin 8 home. As he turned into Holdforth Road and pulled up outside the family house, his brother was waiting outside. There was nothing unusual about that; it was the two men in naval uniforms standing behind him that surprised Carter. As he stepped out of his Austin, one of the naval men approached him and reached out a hand.

"Commander Ian Fleming, assistant to the Director of Naval Intelligence. May I have a word?"

27

KILLING HIM SOFTLY

1942, September 19 (08:31h)
Windmill Hill, Prisoner Cell, Rock of Gibraltar

Hoop could still feel the sharp pain in his rib, although the swelling around his face had reduced and the open wounds had scabbed.

"They're using the temporary barracks at Europa Point," said the young British medic. He sat opposite Hoop with a bright red spot on his nose. He was speaking English, *which is nice after so much German.*

"Jerry erected two lines of barbed-wire fence right around the barracks, couple of watchtowers, and hey presto: POW camp." He'd bunked in one of the wooden huts at Europa Point on arrival at the Rock. They all had. There were no creature comforts. The facilities were basic.

"Crammed in, thousands of us," said the medic. He couldn't have been more than eighteen years of age; the army-issue uniform barely fitted him but his tone was indignant, that of a cynic twice his age. He pulled the bandage tight around Hoop's ribs, *too tight*: a nervous system electrical current shot around his hip and down his leg.

"Jerry's furious with all the escapes too." The medic grinned, a naughty schoolboy grin. It suited him perfectly. Prison camp sirens had been the sound to blight Hoop's sleep: the signal of a British escape. Every time that he'd been harshly woken by them was automatically excused. It was good to hear news from the outside but he was jealous of the young medic. Green with envy. The boy was about to leave Hoop's cell but he wasn't. He was getting to the point where he'd do almost anything to get out of that cell.

"... and the shitter, my God, it's the worst you've ever seen, they can probably smell it from here!" The boy lifted his nose and gave a sniff, followed by another cheeky grin. Hoop couldn't find it inside himself to laugh. He knew it would hurt if he did.

The hours after the medic's departure were worse than Hoop had feared. The walls of his cell crept in on him. He could hear the individual stones mumbling threats and actuations towards him. *You're going to hell, you know that, don't you?* said the largest of them with the purple streak. *Don't be afraid, I won't hurt you,* claimed another in tenderness. *The stones aren't talking!* He closed his eyes and put his hands over his ears.

It was the beginning of the end for Hoop. The end came without warning.

His eyes were red and tired, his rib still ached, and finding a comfortable position on his side was difficult. He'd just managed to drop off to sleep, something he'd struggled to do at night, when the light of his cell came on. Then it went off again. On then off, again and again. He could hear the guards laughing in the corridor. Every hour now they'd play their little game with him. On then off went that bulb. He'd become so tired that he couldn't think straight, couldn't concentrate. He needed to sleep. He had to sleep.

Hoop covered his eyes with his arm to blank out the light. What if he told them something, he thought, anything? *Maybe there isn't a Tracer mission anymore; maybe they've all been killed or captured?* Windy was shot and bleeding and the Rock was so steep. He couldn't have made it to the top. They were sure to have caught or killed him. Maybe Windy was in the cell next door being given the same treatment. Would Windy crack? Without sleep? Maybe. Any man would. So who was up there if not Windy? Just the three of them – Bunny, Carter, and Albert? They wouldn't be collecting much intelligence with just three team members. Hoop turned over on his other side. The pain in his rib returned. If there were just three of them, then what was lost by giving away the location? Operation Tracer was pointless with three. *Isn't it?*

Hoop was suddenly wide-eyed and up off the bunk. The room spun, he hadn't been on his feet all day. He limped quickly, circling the room, trying not to faint as the blood rushed from his head. *Get a grip of yourself.* Never had the room felt so small and claustrophobic. He was done. He was ready to talk.

Hoop panicked. His mind swirled and he lost control of it. The room spun double time and his heart raced. He was beaten, broken. He put out a hand and held on to the wall before dropping to his knees. They'd won.

"No-no-no." Each word brought with it a resolution. It didn't matter if Windy was dead and there were only three of them up there or the Stay Behind Cave was empty. He wouldn't say a word to the enemy, but he couldn't take any more of this either. That left just one option. In that moment, the fog of his mind lifted. The fear left him in an instant. The Lord was his saviour.

He was calm, almost serene.

Hoop pushed himself up with a long deep breath. He felt every moment of it enter his nostrils until his lungs could take no more; the breath was black in colour, full of filth, putrid, the very essence of this war and his state of mind. As he exhaled, the same breath exited his nostrils, this time pure and white, cleaned from the stench of the cell and the fear he harboured there. The small room filled with light and seemed even spacious. Hoop lay down on his bunk and watched the clouds in the bright blue morning sky drift along beyond that dirty ceiling. His eyes were bloodshot but his mind was clear. He asked himself how? *How am I going to kill myself?*

28

A GENTLEMAN

1942, September 19 (09:23h)
Main Chamber, Stay Behind Cave, Rock of Gibraltar

Carter could feel that rigor had now taken a firm hold of Windy's body as he and Bunny carried the commander onto the rubble between the main chamber and the cave entrance. Logan was on the far side of the shallow grave with a cut to his cheek and a lump on his head. One had been caused by Bunny's left, the other by the cork floor that didn't have the give of a traditional boxing ring. Maria stood next to Logan, both arms supporting her stomach. Young Albert was on cement-mixing duty. He'd used the three buckets they had available for the mixing, although by the look of him Carter thought the boy had rolled in it rather than mixed it. They laid Windy's body to rest in the grey wet stuff.

Despite not having yet been formally established as the new team leader, Carter had suggested that they all attend the burial and that the east and west wall lookouts would have to remain unmanned for the short time it took to pay their respects. They'd all agreed. Even Bunny and Logan. It was probably the only thing they had agreed on to date.

The grave had been dug and the body wrapped, in line with the description provided in the Tracer Operation manual. It had text and photos explaining pretty much everything in the cave. Photos and sketches to illustrate operational use where necessary. The manual had been invaluable in training and they, the team, played a considerable part in its creation. Training had provided some priceless insights that had been included in the manual, although the burial page was one of those few pages underdeveloped. No one was supposed to die.

Carter had added lime to help with decomposition as instructed. What the manual had not mentioned was a eulogy. It was clear somebody should speak. They all looked at him, maybe because he was the one holding the King James bible.

"What can I say about Commander Frederick Gale? I didn't know Windy for long, but I think I knew him well." He paused. "Commander Gale was an exemplary soldier and a man of principle. Windy believed in integrity, honour, and honesty."

Carter watched Bunny glance over at Logan, who hadn't taken his eyes off the Scot for a moment.

"Commander Gale was a natural leader," Carter continued. "Windy led by example. In the short time, I knew him..." Carter paused and looked at Bunny and Young Albert. "In the short time *we* knew Windy, we never once heard him unfairly criticise or discipline a man under his command. He was a fair-minded leader. Always professional, always a gentleman, a loyal patriot of the King and his country, and a trusted friend. We'll miss you, Windy."

Doctor Carter knew he would miss him more than anyone. He looked at Bunny, then Logan. "We promise," he added, "to honour you by putting our very best foot forward and completing your mission to the best of our abilities." Carter saluted and held his salute, allowing the others to catch up. "God speed, Frederick. See you on the other side."

Young Albert's eyes were fixed on the corpse, a worried look as if he'd lost the rudder to his boat and a storm was coming. Maria snivelled, took a handkerchief from up her sleeve, and blew her nose. Logan, next to her, continued to glare at Bunny. If looks could kill, the Scotsman would've been lying in the rubble next to Windy. For his part, Bunny just nodded at Carter, a respectful sign of approval. It brought the ceremony to a close. He and Young Albert began to cover Windy's body with bricks and stones as Logan and Maria made their way back into the main chamber.

"Kind words," said Maria as Carter joined them, putting her hand on his arm. She had a tear welling up under her long curved lashes. Carter couldn't help noticing the tight skin around her eyes, smooth and blemish-free. It was hard for him to ignore her beauty. Maria was radiant, more so in sorrow than ever. Somehow shared sadness only deepened his connection to her. It was a connection he didn't want. He knew it was a bad idea. But he felt it all the same.

There was no good time for the questions he had for Logan. With respect in the air, now was as good as any. He hoped Logan wouldn't cause a scene.

"Logan, may I have a quick word?" Carter said. He figured if he stayed polite and respectful throughout, he could get this done without too much fuss.

Logan gestured to the door opposite, almost as if he'd expected the request. They crossed the main chamber and entered the stairway next to the radio room and toilets. Carter closed the door behind them. They were standing in the exact spot from which Bunny had claimed to have seen Logan on the night Windy died.

"It would be amiss of me not to ask this question of you, Logan. It requires an answer, but let me assure you that, in no way am I making any kind of accusation or insinuation of wrongdoing." Carter could see from Logan's nod of the head that he already had an idea what was coming.

"The night Commander Gale died?" Logan said, to Carter's relief. "Why did I lie to the Scotsman about never leaving my bunk?"

Logan was going to make it easy for him. Thank God. "Yes, that's really what I'd like to know. Why did you say you were in your bunk the whole time when you weren't?"

"I lied because I saw no reason to share the incident."

"What incident?" said Carter.

112

"Were it me in the same situation, I wouldn't want this shared with the other chaps."

"We've just buried our commanding officer and you were the last person seen with him before he suddenly died. With the greatest of respect, Logan" – Carter folded his arms – "as team doctor, I'm going to have to insist you tell me everything that happened."

"He was crying," said Logan.

The words caught Carter by surprise. "What do you mean, crying?"

"Commander Gale was crying. I got out of bed to see what was happening, I thought the noises were coming from Maria but they weren't. It was Commander Gale. He'd kicked off his blanket and he was crying. *Whimpering* might be a better term. I replaced the blanket back over him and returned to my bunk. It's as simple as that." Logan put his hands on his hips, like he was done. "Now, if you believe that the commander died from the extra heat of the blanket that I placed back on top of him, then, yes, I killed him. Maybe he cried himself to death. I don't know, but I see no reason to shame a dead gentleman by sharing this story."

Carter didn't know what to say. Windy was crying? Was that even possible?

"Are we done here?" asked Logan.

"Yes, of course," Carter answered, still trying to process the information.

"With the greatest of respect, Doctor, I'm afraid that neither you nor the Scotsman could ever understand why one gentleman would defend the honour of another. I lied. Yes. Given the same set of circumstances, I would do the same again."

Logan almost pushed past Carter on his way out of the door and back into the main chamber.

Carter had not known what to expect from Logan. A lie to cover the previous one would have come as no surprise to him, but Windy crying! Was he going to share that with Bunny? Would Bunny even believe it? Did *he* believe it? It was so bizarre that it had to be true.

Didn't it? He knew many men of title and rank, many good men, but did he understand the rules that governed that world of landed gentry? No, he couldn't say he did, but that wasn't the thought he was struggling with right now. The answer to the questions he had been intent on getting an answer to had only led to another, more curious question: why was Windy crying?

29

DELICATE EQUIPMENT

No sooner was Carter back in the main chamber at the table than Albert came storming out of the radio room.

"Who was in my room last?" Albert's voice was an octave higher than its usual pitch, and his eyes were flaming. *What happened to the light-hearted happy-go-lucky lad who had joined the team?* Carter didn't recognise the boy: humour had left him and now apparently reason too. The screeched question illustrated a problem of its own. The radio room wasn't actually 'Albert's' room.

"What's the problem, Albert?" Carter deliberately spoke the words slowly and in the softest tone he could find.

"The problem is this." Albert was still high key as he raised a small piece of odd-shaped metal into the air. It had two parallel silver rods that made a T-shape.

"What is it?" asked Logan, putting down his cup of tea while maintaining his aloof posture.

"It's only our ability to receive communication with the outside world, that's all, and it's broken." Albert suddenly had Carter's full attention.. "I left it on the radio room table this morning. It's been snapped."

Carter stepped forward to get a closer look at the two metal rods swinging in Albert's hand.

"It wasn't broken when I left it this morning and now it is, so somebody has done it." Albert raised his voice again.

"Easy, old chap," Logan said, joining Carter in front of the boy. Logan's experience of command seeped out of his demeanour. The doctor felt overshadowed.

"Show me where you left it?" continued Logan. Albert turned and stomped back towards the radio room, followed by Logan, trailed by Carter.

Albert entered the radio room. "I told you, I left it here on the desk this morning and it was in perfect working order."

Carter hadn't been in the radio room for more than forty-eight hours. Albert had scattered everything across the desks. The drawers and cupboards had been moved around, the equipment had been pulled off the shelves, notes had been posted with explanations, and warnings had been written in large black letters. The two posters on the wall – one of Katharine Hepburn; the other, Ingrid Bergman – had the radio room resembling a sixth-form study room at Eton College.

"There." Albert pointed at the pieces of technical radio equipment laid out on the bench next to his cup of tea. "I left it there on the desk, so somebody has been playing with the damn thing and now it's broken." Albert tossed it back onto the desk. "This equipment is extremely sensitive and needs to be treated with the utmost care. People can't just wander in and mess about with it." Albert breathed out in a heavy manner through his nose, the way a boxer might before starting his next round.

"What does it do, Albert?" asked Logan.

"We can't receive incoming messages without it." Albert cut to the chase and Carter couldn't believe his ears. Their communications with the outside world had hinged on a single piece of delicate equipment?

Albert could see the shock without words. "That's right, we can no longer receive transmissions. We can send but we can't receive."

Logan wanted confirmation. "We can't receive messages from the Admiralty?"

"No incoming messages. None. Zero," replied Albert, picking up his empty cup of tea and putting it down again immediately.

"We don't have a replacement part for this?" Carter asked, confused.

"It's missing," replied Albert.

"What do you mean *missing*?" Carter was dumbfounded. Why hadn't Albert mentioned this crucial piece of information until asked?

"I can't find it." The youngster looked more than a little embarrassed. "I mean, it isn't in the drawer where I put it." Albert stood, arms crossed.

First some tins of corned beef, then a crucial radio part.

"Well, you better look again," said Logan.

"I told you, I've looked and it's not here!" Albert stormed out of the room in a sulk.

Carter looked at Logan, speechless.

"Golly gumdrops," said Logan, poking fun at Albert's teenage antics. "Let's all look again when he's calmed down." Sounding like a father, Logan left the radio room.

Carter was alone. He scanned the desks and shelves. Albert had pulled everything out looking for the replacement part. Bits of technology were scattered everywhere, most of which Carter had no idea what they were for. People were up and down the stairs between the radio room and the east and west wall lookouts all day and in and out of the toilet opposite. Anyone could have stepped in there, but that wasn't really the question, was it? If somebody had broken something in the radio room, by accident, they'd have mentioned it. Not just put it back on the table and waited for it to be discovered. *Wouldn't they?*

Maybe the person who broke it didn't know they'd broken it? That was what Carter wanted to believe.

Windy was dead, Bunny was a bull in a china shop, they'd lost communication with London, and Albert was having a breakdown. They'd been in the cave just over a week. Things couldn't be worse, thought Carter. Then he remembered: there was a woman next door about to have a baby.

30

OLD ELGIN

1942, September 20 (11:34h)

Windmill Hill, Prisoner Cell, Rock of Gibraltar

Hoop lay on his bunk, looking up at the bare light bulb hanging from a very short cord connected to the ceiling of his cell. His belt and bootlaces had been taken from him on day one and the blanket was too thick for the job. Even wound around his neck, it wouldn't pull tight enough to restrict his breathing. The bed below his thin mattress was of a wooden construction, held together with screws rather than nails. Extracting one was impossible without a tool. There were no other sharp objects in the cell. Hitting his head repeatedly against the wall would only bring the guards to save him and it was unlikely to get the job done anyway. He didn't want them reviving him. Deciding to kill himself was easier than actually doing it. His eyes came to rest on his trousers. Maybe he could tie one leg into a noose? He looked up at the small window with two bars. Could he hang himself with his trousers?

Clack. It was a sound always followed by the screech of metal on metal – *the cell door!* Hoop's heart missed a beat, his breath slowed dramatically. His shoulders lifted as his body instinctively withdrew a little. Hoop's pupils dilated and his eyes moved rapidly as he listened intently. His nose twitched for a hint of lavender and he drew his legs up slightly for protection. If an attack came, he needed to protect his rib. The door began to open and Hoop heard himself almost growl under his breath, like a feral animal.

The door swung open but no Major Haas. Two German SS guards entered. Hoop didn't recognise them. One carried a chair and small table, the other a square wooden chequered board. Hoop watched in silence as they put the board on the table and placed chess pieces upon the board. Neither man looked at him while doing so, not once. Then, without a word, the two Germans left as quickly as they'd entered.

Hoop swung his legs off his bunk and peered around the still-open door. The guards were gone and there was an eerie silence on the other side. He looked down at the chessboard. One of the pawns was out of place: he couldn't help himself, he moved it back to regimental order as the sound of a shoe scuffing the floor brought his eyes back to the doorway of his cell.

A German officer came into view, clutching a bottle. Caught in a trance of the bizarre, Hoop didn't immediately recognise him. Third Reich insignia; two Iron Crosses, one on his breast pocket and the other at the centre of his neck, were highly polished. The white stitching of his shoulder marks was immaculate, as were those of a leaf on his collar, and Hoop could practically see his own reflection in the mirror-like jackboots. It was the boots he recognised, from their first meeting. The raised heels made them unmistakable.

His visitor spoke. "My name is—"

"Standartenführer Wolfgang Richter," said Hoop, interrupting. The German's eyes were blue, his hair thin, light brown, combed and creamed to his head. He had that air of an officer who didn't do the fighting.

"I'm flattered," replied the Standartenführer.

"Don't be," shot Hoop in return.

The German moved in slow motion, like a cat. The bottle in his hand was whisky. Putting it on the table next to the chessboard, he sat down, pulled a packet of Juno cigarettes from his pocket, and lit one. He was almost in touching distance.

"Your treatment has been unfortunate," he said.

Hoop eyed the pistol on the Standartenführer's hip; there was no guard in the doorway watching. Although he'd need to act fast.

"Maybe you can take it from me?" said the Standartenführer. Hoop recoiled.

The German opened the leather holster to expose his pistol. "Maybe you can get off a shot before my guards out there get in?"

Hoop eased the thought from his mind. Maybe he could, but the Nazi bastard wanted him to try so he wasn't going to give him the satisfaction.

"No?" asked the Standartenführer.

Hoop pushed himself back onto his bunk, his back against the wall, his bare feet up on the mattress. "What do you want?"

The Standartenführer closed the holster and tossed the bottle of whisky. Hoop caught it.

"A drink, a chat, a game of chess maybe?"

Hoop looked down at the bottle. The label read: *Old Elgin, Highland Malt Scotch Whisky*. The bottle was full of golden yellow-coloured liquid and the cap was still sealed. "You like a little now and again, don't you, Hubert?" The Standartenführer raised one eyebrow.

"Took you this long to find my name?" Hoop could see what was going on. Major Haas had failed to get anything out of him with the beatings so they'd changed tack. Get him drunk, maybe then he'll talk. Did they really think he was that stupid? They thought because he was a Black man he would be easy to outsmart. This wasn't the first time a white man had underestimated him. He'd got used to killing white men who did that.

The truth was, he wanted a sip from the bottle. He decided to take one. Play along. *Why not?* He didn't want to be alone again. It couldn't hurt to listen to the Standartenführer for a while. A sip of whisky wouldn't change anything.

Hoop twisted the top of the bottle and heard that little opened-for-the-first-time clicking sound. He put it under his nose. The scent almost caused him to faint. It was potent, rich, smooth – the whisky assaulted his nasal cavity. He put the bottle to his lips and lifted it. The whisky hit his tongue and he shivered. It rolled around his mouth like the devil his churchgoing mother said it was. The devil leapt from taste bud to taste bud, soaking his mouth with reckless warm rich flavours. Hoop closed his eyes. The liquor slipped off his tongue, burning a soft channel down his throat and into his belly, where it pooled in malevolence.

* * *

Richter watched the Negro drink from the bottle. He'd taken a guess with the whisky and it appeared he was right. They'd found only one medical record for a Negro stationed on the Rock. An African rifleman, Sergeant Hubert Fundi, Ordnance Survey Department, Royal Engineers. Fundi was a map maker. On the medical questionnaire, the Negro's answer to the question of alcohol consumption had been 'sometimes'. This was one of those times.

Richter could see the scars on the Negro's face. Major Haas had failed to get any information at all from this one, although in his job as a map maker on the Rock he obviously knew something. How to get into the tunnels, almost certainly. The Standartenführer didn't need Berlin to tell him that his men were exposed on the outside of the Rock. He needed to get them inside.

During his time in the SS, Richter had seen the failures of interrogations that involved violence and torture. Yes, of course, they had seen some success too, when used on weak-minded subjects, but if a man was prepared to give up his life to stay silent then torture was not the best method for intelligence gathering, although he'd allowed the beatings anyway. Beatings followed by stretches of solitude and sleep deprivation effectively broke down a subject physically and mentally. Weakening their resolve.

The Negro was a fine physical specimen: large firm thighs, muscular torso. With youth on his side, he'd recovered from his injuries quickly with visits from the British medics but not so quickly from the lack of sleep. He'd stopped exercising and was spending most of his time on his bunk. The whisky was perfectly timed. To a man, they never refused the whisky at this moment – in that respect, this Negro was no different from a white man.

* * *

Hoop saw the Standartenführer's smirk. It killed the moment. He swallowed what he had left in his mouth, screwed the top on the bottle, and threw it back. Disappointment hit the Standartenführer's face as he caught the bottle; Hoop enjoyed that too. He watched the Nazi put the bottle down by his chair and gestured at the chessboard. Hoop nonchalantly accepted the invitation with his eyebrows.

"I'd offer you a cigarette, but I know you don't smoke," said the Standartenführer as he picked up a white pawn and moved it two spaces forward towards Hoop.

Medical file! The recollection hit Hoop. They'd seen his medical file. Slipping forward on his bed to move a black pawn forward, he didn't remember mentioning his love of chess to the doctor but the game, even with this Nazi, was welcome. When the door of the cell closed again, his demons would return.

The Standartenführer moved a knight. "Humour me," said the Nazi.

As Hoop moved another pawn, he smelt the Standartenführer. He was that close. He didn't smell of lavender like Major Haas but more of a spiced aftershave.

"I'm guessing a man such as yourself knows how your East African homeland became populated by my German people?"

Not a question Hoop had expected. He knew the answer, but his mind was suddenly focused on the Standartenführer's pale neck.

"Heligoland, the Anglo-German Agreement of 1890?" replied Hoop casually. He needed to hide what he was thinking. The Standartenführer was so close, but the attack would need to be a complete surprise to have any chance of success in his current physical condition.

The Standartenführer captured one of Hoop's pawns. "That's right! The agreement gave Germany control of the Caprivi Strip and the Zambezi River."

Both arms around his neck and a full forced twist before the guard got in would do the job, thought Hoop, moving another piece on the chessboard and trying not to look at his target.

"The English gave your homeland to us over a cup of tea." The Standartenführer smiled. "What do they pay you?" Hoop could see where this was leading. It was embarrassingly obvious. "What is the wage of an African rifleman? As opposed to a white man with a rifle?" asked the German.

It was true that his wages of five shillings a month as a sergeant were considerably less than the sixteen shillings paid to his white counterpart here in Europe. He rolled his tongue around the inside of his mouth, looking for the reminisce of the beverage for Dutch courage.

The Standartenführer waited for an answer. Hoop didn't give one.

"Just one of many examples where your English masters remind you of their superiority?" This time the Standartenführer didn't wait for a reply. "Am I right in thinking that sergeant is the highest rank a Negro is allowed to achieve?"

Hoop adjusted his seated position to find a firmer grip under his feet.

"Coloured soldiers, fighting for the King, are also required to salute all white men no matter their rank," said Hoop, trying to put the Nazi at ease by agreeing with him.

"So you admit it. Coloureds, like you, are second-class citizens even under British rule?" The Standartenführer captured another of Hoop's pieces on the chessboard with glee. "I hear that Negroes are snatched from their homeland and forced to fight for the British." The Standartenführer was now removing Hoop's pieces from the chessboard at will.

"Yes, that's right, and it's okay to publicly beat a coloured man in the British Army too. But where else can a Negro like me kill a white man like you and get a medal for it?" Hoop couldn't resist. His adrenaline was up and he was almost ready to leap at the bastard.

The Standartenführer leaned back in his chair and forgot the chess game for a moment. His face was serious as he eyed Hoop. Then, without warning, the German cracked a wide grin and slapped his leg in jest. "There! My Nubian friend, that's the spark I like about you."

Hoop tipped his weight forward on his toes. "What do you want?" He needed to keep him talking – "Are you here to save me?" – keep him distracted.

"No, of course not," said the Standartenführer. "You're too sharp to believe that. I'm not selling utopia in the Fatherland. I'm afraid that you and your people are destined to serve no matter the outcome of our white man's war."

Hoop agreed. It was probably the first thing the German had said that wasn't trying to manipulate him.

"Then what are you selling?" It was the last question Hoop was going to ask. It was now or never.

He pulled his feet in. He'd need some spring to launch himself. His adrenaline spiked. He threw a final glance at the guard in the cell window – he was smoking.

"Careful..." The Standartenführer's voice was firm. Under new stiff serious eyebrows, his crystal-blue eyes had lost their shine, sunk back into the sockets of the Nazi's skull, and now glared out at Hoop from deep inside his head. The German's hand was on his holster. "We don't want you to join Captain Beckerman, just yet."

The mention of the captain floored Hoop. Snapped him out of the moment. His legs stayed static and his blood ran cold. They knew of the captain. If they knew about the captain, they knew where to find his mother.

"Brakwater South Road, Brakwater, Windhoek, Namibia."

The Standartenführer held Hoop's gaze. They didn't need to speak. The Nazi had his mother's address.

The Standartenführer had just changed the game. It was no longer just about his life and keeping the Tracer mission concealed. It was personal. They could get to his mother.

Hoop's shoulders dropped as he slumped back against the wall of his bunk. He needed time to think. The Standartenführer didn't give him any.

"I need information on accessing the tunnels. You're a map maker here on the Rock," said Richter, standing and methodically placing his chair to one side.

"What do you think I know?" asked Hoop. "I just drew maps."

"I think you know how I get my men into the tunnel system without being seen."

"I don't."

Picking up the bottle of whisky but leaving the chessboard, the Standartenführer kicked the cell door. The guard opened it with another smirk for Hoop.

"Sleep on it," said the Standartenführer as the door was closed and bolted behind him.

Crestfallen, Hoop took a look at the chessboard. The Standartenführer's bishop stood next to his king.

* * *

SS Standartenführer Wolfgang Richter walked away from the cell of Sergeant Hubert Fundi, confident his time had been well spent. He didn't *think* the Negro knew his way around the tunnels inside the Rock. Richter *knew* he did. It was there in black and white on his medical record. Signed by Dr. Tom Carter. It read: "Seconded to the Ordnance Survey Department of the Royal Engineers..." He had to know the Rock, its entrances, exits, and weaknesses better than most. Although something was bothering the Standartenführer.

A question occurred to him and it wouldn't go away: *Why was there only one Negro soldier on the Rock of Gibraltar?*

31

OUTVOTED

1942, September 20 (11:44h)
Main Chamber, Stay Behind Cave, Rock of Gibraltar

Carter closed the top of the box that contained tins of corned beef. The sound of Maria vomiting came from the double toilets. With a furrowed brow the doctor took a seat at the table with Bunny, Albert, and Logan. One of the lookouts was unmanned again for another hour of a second day, but it was unavoidable. Carter had called the meeting. He needed to establish officially what they all seemed to accept: that he would take on the responsibility of team leader. Although not particularly comfortable with the position, Carter was coming to terms with the reality that he was getting the job, like it or not. His first decision had already been made and taken care of while the others were asleep. Carter had wrapped Windy's pistol in a piece of his torn bedding and buried it along with him shallowly under the loose rubble. Commander Fleming had been very clear that the mission was to be conducted without weapons in the cave. Windy had brought the pistol into the cave only due to the unprecedented circumstances. It was time to correct that. With the gun out of the way, he hoped they could focus on the schedule of intelligence gathering. How it would change now that they were a man down. They needed to maintain twenty-four-hour surveillance, and to do that they were all going to need to put in some extra hours. Maria retched again.

"Corned beef," said Logan, looking back over his shoulder towards the toilet. "She hasn't got the stomach for it." Carter poured the tea.

There was a morning sniffle, a couple of coughs, and a stretch or two before all four men were ready to talk.

"Where's Commander Gale's gun?" asked Logan point-blank.

Carter felt a cold sweat. "Safely put away."

"What does that mean?" The major's tone was argumentative.

"No firearms in the cave, orders from the Admiralty."

"So why did the commander bring it?" demanded Logan.

"Things didn't go to plan, as you know, but as the man responsible for all our health here in the cave, I've taken the liberty of securing the weapon."

"A liberty it is." Logan folded his arms. "What if Jerry comes knocking?"

"If Doc says we hide the gun, we hide the gun," said Bunny.

Logan didn't answer, just sat back in his chair, arms folded. Carter knew the conflict over the gun wasn't over but moved on.

He didn't want to say it himself, that he was now officially team leader. It felt too arrogant and he couldn't run things like Windy. It was better coming from one of them.

"So where do we go from here?" Carter said. "I suggest that we need to establish a new team leader right off the bat."

All three men nodded in agreement.

Bunny spoke. "Aye, it be you, Doc. That's right, hey, Albert?"

Young Albert spun his teacup once around and concurred.

Carter was happy it was out of the way. "I'll do my best. Thank you for your confidence in me. Can I suggest we start by establishing a new schedule, now with Windy gone?"

"Whoa! Just hold your horses there, chaps." Logan lifted both his hands in the air, palms up. "Before we promote the good doctor here to the team leader, let's discuss it for a moment."

Bunny turned in his chair to fully face Logan. His eyes shot a withering look. Carter saw another conflict brewing, just what he wanted to avoid. "We've discussed it, laddy, did you miss it?" Bunny said. "A decision's been made."

"Logan has a right to speak, Bunny," said Carter. It was the right thing to say.

Bunny reluctantly stood down and Logan took his chance.

"Well, it seems to me, as a major, that I outrank Doctor Carter," Logan said. "I also have more experience in leading a team. With the greatest of respect to you, Tom."

Everyone has more experience leading a team than I do, thought Carter, *short maybe of Young Albert.*

"And then there's that other thing," continued Logan.

"And what might that be?" asked Bunny, the tolerance in his tone stretched.

"Well, Young Albert and I are the only two, how do I put it..." Logan searched for the word.

Albert looked up with interest. "Chaps of the right stuff to lead," said Logan.

"By God, you're a toffee-nosed twat." Bunny was all but out of his seat and ready to punch Logan again but this time Logan appeared ready. Carter needed to act fast.

"He's right, Bunny," Carter said. His words drew both their attention and pulled the moment's teeth. "As a major, Logan outranks me. I've never led a team on a mission such as this or had men working under me other than in a medical role."

The delight on Logan's face was matched equally by the disbelief on Bunny's. "We can't put him in charge. He doesn't even want to be here."

"But I am here," Logan said, "and the only thing that matters now is executing the mission to the best of our abilities, is that not right, Doctor?"

Logan was clever. Carter could hear Windy in those words. It was true, nothing mattered more than the mission.

"Aye, and what do ya know of the mission? Nothing!" Bunny was incensed. "You've had no training. You were forced in here at gunpoint and almost got shot trying to leave."

"That was then," replied Logan.

"What, may I ask, will be your first order? Unblock the cave entrance, everyone out?" Bunny implored Carter. "It's ridiculous."

Carter said nothing. They both looked at Albert, who wanted to disappear into the wood of his seat.

"Say something, for God's sake!" Bunny commanded the boy.

Albert looked nervously at Logan, then back at Bunny. He stumbled but found some words. "You're right. Logan didn't do the training but he does outrank us all."

Bunny rolled his eyes. "Ya head's full of mince, lad."

Carter had done his best to bring Logan into the decision-making, to make him feel part of the team, but it was now time to end this. There was only one way to bring this situation to an outcome that everyone would accept.

"What say we put it to a vote?" said Carter. "A secret ballot. Everyone writes the name of the man they want to lead the team. We put all the votes into the teapot and whoever gets the most votes is the democratically elected team leader. Agreed?"

Carter looked for a consensus. He got an immediate agreement from Albert and Bunny, but Logan, stone-faced, sat legs crossed with his arms folded.

Maria stepped out of the toilet, wiping her mouth. Carter got up to meet her halfway as Young Albert and Bunny prepared the slips of paper for voting.

"Nothing from the other end?" whispered Carter, putting his hand delicately on Maria's forehead. She shook her head sorrowfully, eyelids heavy.

"Are you drinking enough water?" He knew she wasn't.

"I can't keep anything down. It's like morning sickness all over again. Everything smells awful," said Maria, "even the water."

"It'll pass, don't worry," Carter reassured her as Logan appeared at her side.

"We're voting for who will be team leader – *me* or Doctor Carter. I need your vote." His tone was dour but his intonation cast Maria's vote for her. She wrote Logan's name on the paper, folded it, dropped it into the teapot, and headed for her bunk. All four men did the same and the lid went on the pot. Bunny reached excitedly for the handle but Carter put his hand on top of the pot before Bunny could take it.

"Before we see the results," Carter said, "let's agree on one thing. We'll all abide by the outcome of this vote? We'll all accept the result and give one hundred percent support to the new team leader. Yes?" Carter looked at Logan. "Logan?"

Logan knew when he was being manipulated. "Agreed," he said half-heartedly.

Albert nodded and Bunny followed suit enthusiastically. Carter pushed the teapot across the table to Bunny, who reached in and pulled out the folded papers.

The first read *Logan*. They'd all seen it written by Maria. Bunny unfolded a second, which read *Doctor Carter*. The third Bunny unfolded simply read *Doc* and he laid the two votes together. Logan's name was next out of the pot, making it two votes each.

Carter recognised the handwriting of Bunny and Albert. The secret ballot had really only been that in name alone; they had been quite well exposed to each other's handwriting during their training for intelligence gathering and how to fill in the daily sheets of ship movements. The final piece of folded paper was obviously Carter's and Albert and Bunny knew it too, even if Logan didn't. Bunny unfolded it to see the name.

Logan was written in big letters at the centre of the paper. Confused, Bunny hurled an angry look at his doctor before thumping his fist on the table. It took a moment for Logan to register the result. He'd won the vote by three to two. When he finally caught on, he jumped from his seat. Logan stood tall and threw a small punch in the air.

Albert's look of confusion was full of questions while Bunny simply shook his head, unable to look Carter in the eye.

Albert spoke first. "But I don't understand."

"Logan outranks me, Albert. He's a major, as you said. He has the experience we need. He's the best man for the job and the mission must come first."

Bunny went to speak but stopped himself, remembering he'd given his word.

Carter knew the truth and it wasn't for the ears of his men. At least not yet. With Logan as team leader, he had hopefully achieved three of his most important targets in one go. Logan was not committed to the mission, that had been clear. Putting him in charge would surely focus his mind, get the best out of him. Logan's experience needed to work for them and not against them if the mission was to be a success. The most disruptive element within the group so far had been Bunny's relationship with Logan. The fighting among themselves had to stop or they were done for before they got started. Bunny had agreed to abide by the outcome. If he knew anything, he knew Bunny would keep his word. He'd just made it very difficult for the hot-headed Scotsman to hit Logan again.

Finally, if not most important, with Logan focused on administration and day-to-day logistics, Carter was free to view the bigger picture. Starting with the thief. One of them was stealing tins of corned beef. Had that same person stolen the radio receiver spare part? Carter desperately wanted to believe that Albert had just misplaced it and that the original part had been broken by accident. But wanting to believe it didn't make it true.

32

TRUE COLOURS

1942, January 9 (21:07h)

Angry Friar Public House, Rock of Gibraltar

Before the German-Spanish invasion, there were very few places left in Gibraltar for a candlelit dinner, but the Angry Friar pub was one of them. There were also no secrets on the Rock, particularly not for those few remaining Wren girls. Maria knew they all talked about her and not always in the most polite terms, but what could she expect? The Rock was full of men and they had a lot of testosterone. Her nickname was 'Virgin Maria' – she'd overheard a couple of RAF pilots discussing her while having a cigarette. She'd taken great pleasure in walking around the corner to their shock and surprise when her legs were mentioned. She knew that by dating Logan she would get tongues wagging. She didn't want that, but it was inevitable. Anyway, she needed somebody; God knows she'd spent her time selecting but couldn't find the right one. Out of all the men she knew, none of them fitted the bill. Then Logan suddenly arrived and she knew immediately that he was the one she wanted. Needed. She didn't even know how she knew, she just knew.

Logan sat down and moved the small vase of flowers that the bartender had placed on the table. The Friar had become known as the place to go for a date, and the barman had started adding those little touches, napkins and the like. Things that brought the few girls on the Rock to the Friar and the shillings of the men who wanted to see the girls. Logan laid his napkin on his knee and moved the flowers so he could get a clear view of Maria.

"What shall we drink to?" he asked. "The King? The end of the war? What about love?" Logan was cheeky and charming. He wasn't boring like so many of the others who had shown interest in her. He was confident and adventurous and almost certainly a cad.

"*Madre mía!* You are awful, Logan," replied Maria, lifting her glass. "Not the war or the King." She paused for thought.

"So love it is." Logan decided for her, clinking his glass against Maria's and taking a big sip.

He'd settled into his position on the Rock very quickly. Maria had watched him closely. She wasn't the only one Logan had charmed. The men under his command liked him too. Or at least they seemed to. He wasn't a stickler for the rules.

"How'd your family end up here in Gibraltar, Maria?"

She hadn't expected the question and didn't like to talk about her family, about the past. She didn't like to mention the bitterness she felt. She didn't want people to know those things about her. Tongues wagged on the Rock and even the smallest piece of gossip about her would get around. She knew that could do her real harm. But this Logan brought her out, even against her better judgement. She wanted to share with him. Tell him those things she'd bottled up. Tell him how she'd been transported in a trunk hundreds of miles during the Civil War.

"My father fought for General Franco in the Civil War. He was a member of the Falange movement. My mother left him and came here to Gibraltar as a refugee with me and my brother. I was seventeen and he was just twelve." She should have stopped, but the wine had gone straight to her head. She wanted to talk. She needed to. It had been so long.

"We lived in a tent where the airfield is today." She kept going, even though she knew she should stop. "There were hundreds, thousands of us. They didn't want us here, and why would they? So many people from the outside, the disease, the death." She remembered the smell;

it was a smell she'd forgotten but it just came rushing back. It was sweet but grotesque at the same time. The faces of the dead were grey and purple.

"The walking dead were sent back into Spain. We were the lucky ones." She stopped short of telling him what her mother had done to keep them on the Rock. She could never tell anyone that.

"Where's your brother now?"

It was an innocent question, but the answer raked up the pain. Maria felt the memory like touching a scar. She could see her brother's face. Clear as day, as if it was yesterday. Grey and purple. It felt good to finally talk about that stuff, but it was time to stop, before she made a mistake.

"What about you, Logan?" Maria turned the tables.

"Nothing to tell, just an everyday family." Logan took a drink.

"What was your father like?" She settled in for a story.

"Like any papa, you know."

She saw a shyness about her new boyfriend that she hadn't seen before.

"What are you hiding?" she poked him playfully.

"Can't you just leave it?!"

Logan's raised voice caught Maria off guard. His usual light-hearted demeanour had bounced. She felt the flowers on the table wilt with disappointment. The moment she'd hoped for was gone. She wasn't comfortable with the man sitting across from her. Maria stood up.

"Let's have another glass, hey?" Logan's voice was back to sweet.

"I want to go." Maria wouldn't look at him. They were being watched. There would be gossip, but this wouldn't work out as she'd hoped. She needed somebody that she could rely on. She needed somebody she could read and predict. Logan obviously had another side to him that might bubble over and surprise her later. She'd been wrong about him. He wasn't the one.

Maria waited for Logan to pick up her jacket. When he finally did, she slipped one arm into it and then the other. Logan paid the barman and they left the Angry Friar without another word. Logan offered her his arm as they walked back towards the barracks. She didn't take it.

"I'm sorry," said Logan.

Maria wasn't waiting for an explanation but she didn't cut him off either.

"My father was a magistrate," he said, stopping to face her. "My mother was a schoolteacher."

Maria waited for more. There had better be more or she'd keep walking. Logan's upper-class accent had left her believing he was born to the landed gentry. Clearly, that wasn't the case. *So where does it come from?*

"There's no harm in a man trying to better himself," said Logan, reading her mind. "My father was a bastard. He beat my mother. He wasn't a drinker, never touched a drop, but he had his own demons. I was fifteen when I packed a bag and walked out. I never went back."

Her stiffening resolve towards him softened. She could see the child in his eyes. She touched his cheek. "Oh, Logan." Like her, he'd a protection mechanism in place and she'd forced her way through it. She forgave him for his reaction, but she couldn't forget this unpredictable side of him. She'd need to manage that.

"It's late. We'd better call it a night," said Logan.

Maria took in every aspect of his vulnerability. The sudden hunch of shoulders, lowered chin, awkward stance, and the slight fidgeting of his hands. She'd never been more attracted to him than right then. She wanted him and she wanted him now. He wasn't going anywhere.

Maria was about to do something she'd never done. Taking Logan by the hand, she led him down Convent Ramp. It was quiet there except for the sound of a gramophone playing something far in the distance. She pulled him close and kissed him. She had a fire in her belly and it needed releasing. Once she'd started, she just couldn't stop the urge. She didn't want to stop it. Maria pushed Logan up against the dusty wall. She forced herself upon him, kissing him wildly as she wrestled with his belt, pulling it to and fro, trying to release the clasp. Caught off guard, Logan struggled to catch up with her. Only when she took him in hand did the fire she needed light within him. She gave herself to Logan in a back alley of a Gibraltar street. She'd be bruised the next morning, she knew it, Logan had grabbed her thighs so firmly. Even the damage to her jacket rubbed furiously up against the brick wall didn't matter to her at that moment. She'd get another jacket. Logan held her off the ground as they fought each other with grunts and tight grips. Another side to him she'd never seen. She took his hand in her hand and looked deep into his eyes. He'd tried to look away but she wouldn't let him. Her eyes penetrated his and he let go. He let go of everything at that moment. He gave himself to her and went weak at the knees. She was in charge. He *was* the one. She was sure of it.

As she made herself presentable again, Maria asked the question she already knew the answer to.

"Can you smuggle me some stockings across the frontier?"

"You know I can. What brand?"

"Lots of brands."

Logan stopped playing with his buttons. They were alone, but he checked the street, something he hadn't done before they'd had sex. He listened to the silence for a moment, then moved in close to Maria.

"Did somebody say something to you?" His tone was low, serious, and clandestine.

Maria continued, "You seem to know many Spanish people coming across the frontier. I know it's not allowed, but..." Maria shook her head. "Sorry. I shouldn't have asked, how rude of me. I just thought..."

Logan's face cracked a smile and he relaxed. "I'm your man. Stockings it is. As many as you like."

Yes, he was definitely the one.

33

ONE LIFE TOO MANY

1942, September 21 (10:23h)
Main Chamber, Stay Behind Cave, Rock of Gibraltar

Maria stepped gingerly out from behind the wall of boxes that secluded her bunk. Bunny and Logan were on duty, and Albert was in the radio room with a cup of tea. Carter and Maria were alone.

"Tea?" Carter couldn't think of anything else to say. She was having a hard time but there was nothing much he could medically do for her. Her breathing was shallow but that was probably just the uterus growing upwards. Her legs were swollen, with blue protruding varicose veins, she had heartburn, constipation, and headaches. She really had a full set of unfortunate thirty-two-week pregnancy symptoms and tea was the best he had for her.

Maria sat down at the table, taking the weight off her feet, but shook her head at the tea. She was pale, shoulders rounded, every movement seemed to be weighted.

"Will you help me kill it?" she said.

The words caught Carter off guard but more so the way they were delivered. Her eyes darted around. She seemed to be calculating the situation, and in a deeply clinical methodical manner. No histrionics, no tears or rambling questions. Her tone was steady. Difficulty focusing or making decisions would not have surprised him, that was common at the late stages of pregnancy.

"We both know I can't give birth here. Will you help me?"

Despite her apparent clear-headed pragmatism, she was moving too fast. Jumping ahead to action before the discussion and debate had taken place. He wasn't ready to kill the child. She wasn't thinking straight; hopelessness or feeling overwhelmed was normal, even if her current personal circumstances weren't. He needed to keep her steady. Even if she was right, and she probably was, she couldn't give birth to a screaming baby in there. She needed more time. He needed time. To his core, he was against the termination of a life. It wasn't just his Christian beliefs. To agree with Maria was to agree to do it and he wasn't ready to do that. Not yet.

Carter couldn't help but find the fortitude and control of her emotions extremely attractive. Logan didn't deserve her, that was for sure. He had seduced Maria and forced her into sex, but those thoughts weren't helpful right now.

"How do you kill it?" Maria pushed.

He needed to slow her down. A lack of energy or motivation would have been a more helpful symptom.

"Let's not get ahead of ourselves."

"I can't have a baby." Maria's tone was precise.

"Yes, I understand that."

"No, you don't." Maria paused. She was about to say something but changed it for something else.

"I'm not the motherly kind," was what came out of her mouth.

Motherly kind or not, that really had no bearing here. The mission was all that mattered; nothing was more important than the mission. Windy would have expected him to do whatever it took to protect the mission. The child was just one life against how many the mission could save. So what was his problem? *Why don't I want to kill the child for her?*

"One step at a time." Carter repeated the words out loud, more for himself than for Maria. She stood up and walked from the table with uncharacteristic mobility and obvious frustration with him.

"Fine. If you won't help me, I don't know what!" She just turned towards her bunk. The mood swings and irritability would pass and she'd have a different view in a few hours, Carter told himself.

"Promise me you're not going to do anything stupid before a decision is made?"

Maria didn't reply, she just glared at him.

Carter pushed for some reassurance. "Promise me?" Whatever needed to happen it had to be done as clinically as possible.

Maria looked back at him, drained of all expression.

"The decision has been made." On that, she slipped behind the boxes. Carter heard her climb onto her bunk.

34

RED CROSS

1942, September 21 (11:50h)
Outside Windmill Hill Prison, Rock of Gibraltar

Standartenführer Richter stepped out of his armoured car in the safety of cover behind the military prison below the Lathbury Barracks. There was silence across the Rock. He'd become used to the sporadic gunfire: his men and the British sniping at each other. Keeping bricks and mortar between him and a clear line of sight from the Rock had become second nature in recent days. The British snipers continued to prevent the free movement of his forces, killing indiscriminately from their vantage points high up inside.

His Spanish advisers had been correct. "Taking the Rock, without the tunnels inside it, wasn't taking the Rock at all." Streets open to a view from above were no-go areas, windows with a Rock-facing view were covered, and walking out in the open was an invitation to get shot.

He lit one of his Juno cigarettes and drew on it. Just three left in the packet; he'd been smoking more than usual. Back in Berlin he hardly touched them. The Führer was anti-smoking so as a career move he'd curbed his habit. Apparently, they were bad for the men's health. He needed to reduce his consumption. He'd run out of them at this rate and supplies from back home had all but halted.

The cigarettes had been a comfort. The high of taking the Rock by surprise had faded and the reality set in. The Berlin goodwill and accolades had dried up. His superiors wanted to hear that resistance on the Rock was at an end. Without gaining access to the tunnel systems, that wouldn't happen.

He was still unable to land aircraft on the runway safely. The first of those they had tried to land had been shot at from inside the Rock and crashed into the bay. They'd managed to shield a handful of planes and implemented a system of covering fire during take-off and landing but it wasn't safe. He needed to root out the British rats from their holes. How long could they last in the tunnels and caves inside the Rock anyway? A year? More? He had just weeks or he'd be commanding an assault unit at the Russian front.

Abwehr intelligence strongly suspected that there were secret access points into the Rock. Finding just one could be enough.

Major Haas had broken a handful of prisoners, but the intelligence obtained on tunnel access had been low-grade. Fundi was the best lead so far. He was prepared to take what he knew to the grave. *Why? Because he knows something worth dying for?* Richter had convinced himself that was the reason he was back at the prison again today. He didn't know how he knew but he sensed it. He'd interrogated enough men over the years for his intuition to tingle. Fundi made him tingle. He was impressive, certainly physically, and he'd survived Haas without a word; his resolve was remarkable, for a Negro.

The German took a deep breath of fresh air. He reminded himself, *There is no place for sentiment.* If access to the tunnel system wasn't discovered soon, he'd be forced to try something more dramatic. With Spain now allied with Berlin, a counterattack by the British would be difficult but not impossible. Rumours in Berlin that the Führer distrusted General Franco were rife. A look across the bay to see American ships refuelling in the Port of Algeciras, despite the Spanish dictator's agreement with Hitler, proved the point beyond doubt.

He dropped his cigarette, crushed it with his jackboot, straightened his tunic jacket, and entered the prison holding a Red Cross file, a pencil, and that bottle of whisky.

* * *

"What's this?" asked the Negro as he flipped through the pages of the Red Cross document. Wolfgang had deliberately left the cell door open and focused his guard. The pencil was a dangerous weapon in the hands of a passionate man.

The Negro had his shirt open, exposing his chest and stomach as Richter tossed him the bottle of whisky. He took the bottle this time without question: a good sign. A shower, clean uniform, starched sheets to sleep between, and a lampshade covering the previously bare light blub would all, he hoped, contribute to a more compliant Sergeant Fundi.

"Pure formality," replied Richter. "The Geneva Convention requires us to let you fill it in." He put his hands behind his back and crossed one leg over the other casually as he leaned against the cell wall. The front of the form had spaces for name, rank, and serial number. "Nothing we don't already know about you." Richter watched as the Negro continued to leaf through the pages. He needed a nudge. "Hubert Fundi, learnt your German from Captain Otto Beckerman, retired Reichsmarine naval officer, settled in Namibia. You volunteered to serve in the Royal West African Frontier Force in 1939. Transferred to a Somaliland Battalion July 1940 and distinguished yourself at the Battle of Tug Argan in British Somaliland." The Negro nodded his head, it appeared in recognition of the accurate information. Richter had Fundi's service record along with his medical file. He'd ordered a little research in Berlin and then joined the dots. The Negro's reaction to the mention of his home address in Namibia during their first meeting had confirmed at least one family member was in play, almost certainly his mother, whom he'd named on his medical file as next of kin. The name Captain Otto Beckerman appeared on Fundi's service record as the source of his German-language skills. He'd been quite forthcoming to his British masters in their questions. Richter was hoping for the same on the Red Cross form. Experience had proved the Red Cross form to be an important moment.

A prisoner decided whether or not they would engage, even on the smallest level. Those who filled in the form usually went on to relax into what he called 'the psychological approach'. If the prisoner believed that what was spoken about was known to the enemy already, then they would drop their guard. If the interrogator was able to tell a prisoner the details of his combat record, the name of his commander's dog, or his favourite English pub, then the prisoner might relax, and he would often slip valuable pieces of information into casual conversation. The Red Cross form had been revised for prisoners, of course. New pages had been added and mocked up to resemble the originals. The Negro picked up the pencil and began to write.

"I don't know where the secret accesses are into the Rock," he said, taking a sip of whisky as he wrote. "I don't know anything. And even if I did, I wouldn't tell you."

Richter denied himself a smile.

His prisoner took another swig before putting the bottle down by the side of his bunk. He focused on filling in the form.

Richter had seen questions of reliability and trust associated with Fundi's German-language skills mentioned in Fundi's service record. The British took great interest in personnel who spoke German but fought for the King. Hubert Fundi was held in high regard. With a well-above-average IQ of 140, the Negro had been considered for various appointments but apparently failed to be given any of them.

Richter caught a whiff of putridness about the cell, still present even after it had been cleaned.

"How's the food?" he asked. "Better, yes?"

"When do I get out of here?" replied his prisoner, not looking up from his work.

"That depends on you."

"I told you!" The Negro stopped what he was writing. "I don't know anything about secret access passages into the Rock." The intensity of his plea for release was not lost on Richter, but that wasn't what he took away from the statement.

Passages, he had never heard them called that before…

Safe in the back seat of his armoured car Wolfgang leafed through the information Fundi had entered into his Red Cross form. His home address in Namibia they already had, but his civilian profession 'Librarian', his unit and his commanding officer, a certain Colonel Cecil Drummond, was all new intelligence, on the first few lines. The Negro wasn't as clever as he thought he was.

Meanwhile, Hoop lay on his bunk staring at the ceiling. He'd begun to get a taste for the whisky. He knew the drinking was wrong, but it was easy to justify it right now after all he'd been through in that cell. He wanted out. He wanted out so badly. Anyway, he wasn't drinking that much, he had control of it. He didn't want to punish himself by taking away that pleasure; it was the only one he had right now. He'd stop drinking when he got out.

They must have my service record too. There was nothing relating to Operation Tracer in there, that was for sure. He had no idea what was in that file. A combination of information he provided at the time he'd joined up, probably. Had it been rewritten by Fleming's people to give credibility to his secondment to the Ordnance Survey Department of the Royal Engineers story maybe? Files were kept on all the men stationed on the Rock. It would have been suspicious for anyone to arrive for service without one.

Either way, they knew quite a lot about him. The Geneva Convention required him to provide basic information, he knew that to be true. That's what made the Red Cross ruse so clever, particularly the added pages, complete with matching serial numbers, but why would the Standartenführer single him out? He was sure he could have stuck the pencil in his throat, but getting himself killed was no longer his goal. Fail or succeed in killing the Standartenführer, attacks were out of the question – for now. He couldn't risk putting his mother in danger.

Hoop caught sight of the whisky bottle still on the floor by his bed. Deliberately left or not, he was taking another swig.

35

MIRROR MIRROR

The clock on the wall showed 13:00 hours, almost time for the shift changes at the east and west wall lookouts. The broken receiver hadn't prevented the team from transmitting to London, only receiving communications. Maria stood in front of the mirror. She had a rare moment alone in the main chamber, with the doctor in the toilet and Albert hidden away again in the radio room. She'd been looking at this woman in the mirror for a couple of minutes. She knew what she was capable of and what she wasn't. But there was something different about her. This pregnancy had thrown her from her own horse. Now she didn't know what to think. She was vulnerable for the first time since those days as a refugee, camped at the frontier. Was it heartburn, constipation, the protruding veins in her legs, or one of the other awful physical symptoms of her condition? She didn't think so. She'd managed physical hardships before, but they had never affected her confidence. Yes, she played the timid little girl for the men around her. It made life easy when she wanted an easy life, and she could play the hard-nosed woman too – those who'd crossed her had seen that. She was not to be messed with unless she wanted to be messed with. Well, she'd played with Logan. Look where that had got her. She had become everything she despised of womankind. Frightened, unsure, really tearful. Not the tears she'd turn on for effect when she needed to, but real tears, real emotions, real weakness.

Maria stroked her stomach thoughtfully. She had a life inside her. Something in her very make-up screamed, *Protect him-her at any cost*, but her head disagreed. *Remove this problem, there's way too much at stake.* She couldn't be a mother. *Me?* What, was she insane? What kind of a mother would she be? It was ridiculous. Absurd. In here, right now, with all that was going on, she was going to try to give birth? Even if they'd let her. No. She wanted it out of her. She wanted – rid of it. She'd been crazy to think that when this was all over they, she and Logan, could – could what? Be a family? Maria shook her head. She knew the woman in the mirror too well. No one would be making decisions for her. She was in charge of her body and she'd already made the decision. Maria removed her hand. She knew what she had to do. There. She looked deep into the reflection of her eyes. There she was.

Maria picked up a tin of corned beef from the table and threw it at the mirror. The tin cracked against her reflection and the glass split into multiple pieces, crashing to the floor. The cork tiles did their job of muffling but the sound of glass on glass brought Albert running from the radio room and moments later Carter behind him from the toilet.

Carter took in the scene. The broken mirror, Maria standing defiantly over it.

"What happened?" Albert said.

Carter knew immediately. Maria was falling apart. They needed to get out in front of this. She was breaking the furniture, enough was enough. Carter put his hand on Albert's shoulder.

"Fetch Logan and Bunny, please, Albert. Quick as you can, there's a good lad."

Albert shot out the door in the direction of the two lookout posts.

Maria dropped to her knees and began picking up the broken shards of mirror.

"Leave it. You'll cut yourself. We need to sit down and talk about it."

Albert, Logan, and Bunny stepped through the door and into the main chamber.

"Ria?" said Logan, walking up to her, stepping over the broken glass. He took Maria's shoulders in both hands with a firm grip and looked directly into her eyes. She burst into tears. Logan pulled her close and took her weight.

"Maria wants me to help her miscarry the child." Carter put it out there. He didn't want to, but what choice did he have?

Logan pushed Maria away, forcing her to almost stand again on her own two feet. The lines on his forehead became deeper.

"Maria?" His tone was firm, unlike his grip on her.

"It has to go. The lassie knows it too," said Bunny, thinking out loud.

Logan's calm cold monotone words were this time aimed at Bunny. "Say that again and I swear I will kill you."

Bunny moved towards Logan, but Carter stepped between them.

"Out!" Carter tried not to shout but raised his voice considerably. "You too, Albert."

"Kill me, will ya?" Bunny stretched his frame in all directions as he was backed out of the room by Carter.

"Out!" shouted Carter, pushing the Scotsman through the door towards the lookout posts, with Young Albert in tow. Carter took a last look at Logan and Maria before following Albert and Bunny out of the main chamber and closing the door behind him.

36

SUBHUMAN

1942, September 21 (14:22h)
Windmill Hill, Prisoner Cell, Rock of Gibraltar

Hoop took another swig from the whisky bottle; it was half empty. He pointed his finger confidently at Richter, who was sitting with his legs apart, leaning back on the chair in the middle of the cell, a smug look on his face. Hoop's king lay on its side at the centre of an almost empty chessboard, Richter's queen bearing down on it.

"Entitlement," Hoop said. "That's it, isn't it? You have an overblown opinion of yourselves, a huge ego, and a sense of entitlement. You're better than everybody else simply because you're German?" The words fell from Hoop's mouth as freely as the whisky was falling into it. He took another swig. He was tired of being afraid of what he said. *Screw the Nazi bastard.* Anything the Standartenführer was going to do, he was going to do either way, so what did it matter if he insulted him? It felt good. How often was he in a position to vent on a white man?

"Feels good to tell a white man what you think, hey?" Richter smiled.

The Nazi was reading his bloody mind, playing with him, but what the hell, he was on a roll.

"You're damn right it does," shouted Hoop, shaking the bottle to assess what was left. The carefree moment was addictive, the release brought elation. He lifted the bottle high in the air and the whisky crashed into his lips.

"Well? Is that it? Entitlement?" he continued. "You Nazis think" – Hoop changed his voice to mimic a German accent – "you have za-right to valk over everybody and take vhat you vant because you zink you are entitled to as the master race?"

Richter looked at the bottle in Hoop's hand. "I think we both know the answer to that."

"I don't," said Hoop indignantly. "I want to know, really, tell me what makes you think that the colour of your skin or being from your 'Fatherland' makes you special?"

"Ask yourself if you really want to have this conversation?" replied Richter.

"I do," said Hoop, moving slightly forward on his bunk and settling in for the Nazi's bullshit. "Tell me." He wanted the bastard to try to justify himself and every other German in his damn Third Reich. "You think you'll hurt my feelings? Or maybe you'll just shoot me for disagreeing with you." If he was shot for speaking his mind, so be it. Right now he wouldn't feel a thing.

* * *

Richter sat beyond the white king watching the drunk Negro with interest as he grew in whisky confidence. This was exactly where he wanted Fundi, basking in the freedom he was providing him. Freedom to speak as an equal. Of course, he wasn't equal. Had he been, he would have been aware of how he was being manipulated. Lured out of his shell into the light. Outside of his shell, he was exposed. Unprotected. Turning this Negro against his British masters was going to be easier than he'd expected.

The smartest of Negroes he'd encountered had been German mixed race. The children of white German women and Negro French troops left in the West of Germany after the Great War. They'd become known as 'Rhineland Bastards'. Growing national disdain towards them had resulted in the SS hierarchy branding them undesirables.

Sterilisation was Herr Himmler's preferred method for dealing with the problem. Preparation ahead of the forthcoming epoch's conflict between humans and subhumans.

"Okay, honestly, you're subhuman," said Richter matter-of-factly. "Your generic line is not the same as mine." The Negro stopped talking; the alcohol had slowed the communication between his ears, brain, and mouth. "Are you familiar with the works of Hans Günther?" Fundi's eyelids drooped and his shoulders swayed a little. "Of course you're not," Richter continued. "We have Dolichocephalic skulls and you clearly don't. It's simple anthropology. When I say 'we', I'm referring to my Aryan lineage. The vast majority of my Germanic people hail from Aryan-Nordic bloodlines. We are superior to you, mentally and physically." Richter paused. "Were you familiar with Günther, you would understand the clear scientifically proven strict hierarchy of the human race."

"You believe that?" Hoop shook his head. "You're more stupid than I originally thought."

Richter laughed. How the Negro was emboldened. He was stepping forward and he was going to be let to do so. Before he knew it, he would be his own man. He'd feel entitled to his opinion, exactly what Richter wanted him to feel.

"Wake up, my Bantu friend. Accept your reality."

* * *

The back-and-forth had been fun but Hoop didn't like the use of the word *friend*. He was enjoying talking to this deluded Nazi and drinking his whisky, but despite the fact that they were sharing an equality moment, they weren't friends. He'd been tortured in that cell and the Standartenführer had either ordered it or let it happen. Just the loose insinuation of the word *friend* bothered Hoop in a sobering manner, but the truth he told himself in that head-spinning moment hurt the most: they were becoming friends.

"It's a proven fact," the Standartenführer continued, leaning even further back in the chair. "The Nordic race is top of the food chain: Swedes, Danes, Norwegians, Germans of course, followed by the western Mediterraneans, Italians, the Spanish. There is only a small amount of Aryan blood, for example, in the Eastern Europeans but almost none in a Slav."

Hoop steadied himself and tried not to slur his words. "And me? Where are my Bantu people on your list?" Hoop knew the answer but just wanted the Nazi to say it.

"I told you, Negroes and Jews are subhuman – you have no Aryan blood."

"Nazi bastard." The words came out of Hoop's mouth before he knew it.

Richter's face was chiselled hard but his eyes smiled.

"You're deluded," Hoop continued.

"How so?" asked Richter open-handedly.

"Your science is pseudo. You rationalise the devaluation of human beings to justify your ideology. You need some justification for your actions and so you sell it as science." Hoop waved the bottle to help make his point.

"It's scientifically proven, you can't ignore science. Callous as you may find the truth, the truth it is, nonetheless."

"Bullshit," replied Hoop.

"Superiority is no sin. Take you, for example. I can see that you are exceptional. Highly intelligent, for your species, attractive, physically statuesque. A clear leader of your tribe. Do you deny it?" asked the Standartenführer with a wry smile.

Hoop liked to hear how he was special. He felt special, he wanted to be, although it sounded all wrong coming from this Nazi. His head continued to spin. He tried to focus, hold it together.

"What about the English?" he said. "They're more Aryan than you, according to your hierarchy. And the Japanese and the Chinese were writing on paper when your ancestors were living in caves and wiping their bums with their hands."

"I'll admit that the upper-class British boast some Nordic lines, but the lower classes are racially inferior. The Japanese and the Chinese are Aryans of the east."

Hoop felt the statement funny. It came out of the Standartenführer's mouth like a proclamation. "Aryans of the east? Wow. You really make this up as you go along, don't you?" He took off his shirt. Hoop felt sick, he was hot and uncomfortable. He wanted the Standartenführer to leave; he'd had enough of him and his racist conversation, but more than that, his head was now spinning like a Ferris wheel.

"You think because we play chess, chat, and you get me drunk that I'll tell you something you want to hear. Well, let me tell you this." Hoop steadied himself on the bed. "You'll get nothing from me. Nothing!" He heard nothing in reply. He tried to focus on the German's features but the alcohol had done its job on him. He'd been a fool to drink so much. He squinted, trying to get the Standartenführer back in focus. Still no sound. Not a word. Something was wrong. He was just sitting there silently. What was he doing? Did he have his hand on his chin?

"Guard?" shouted the Standartenführer. The raised voice snapped Hoop out of his drunken trance. The guard entered and picked up the chair. The Standartenführer turned to face Hoop.

"You'll be joining the rest of the British POWs tomorrow." He appeared to wait for a reaction, but Hoop was slow to register the words he'd been desperate to hear for so long.

"We've taken Harley Street and Little Bay tunnels from your British masters and it's just the beginning," said the Standartenführer.

Hoop knew both those networks. Harley Street was the bigger network that led to Beefsteak and Brewery Magazines; they must have fallen too. Without another word, the Standartenführer was gone. The cell door slammed and Hoop was alone.

I'm getting out. He dropped the bottle on the bed and looked up at the spinning ceiling.

"Thank you." He lay back on his bunk, took in a huge breath, lifted his chest high, and released the air slowly through puckered lips. It whistled slightly as it left his mouth mixed with whisky fumes. The news of the tunnel breaches was a shock, but he'd prayed for this moment and his prayers had finally been answered. He knew they would be; he knew, one way or another, his awful time, there in that cell, would come to an end. What he hadn't expected was what he also now knew: that Standartenführer Wolfgang Richter was attracted to men.

37

KING'S MEN

1942, September 22 (10:20h)
German Prisoner-of-War (POW) Camp,
Europa Point, Rock of Gibraltar

Flanked by two guards, Hoop walked towards the POW camp fencing. Two barbed-wire fences circled the wooden buildings, with a no man's land of twenty feet or so between them. Four watchtowers had been erected along each side of the fences, each complete with a machine-gun installation pointed at the camp. There were huts on the outside of the wire too now, inhabited by off-duty German guards.

He recognised the tables and deck chairs scattered under shaded areas and there was now even a plant pot or two. It looked a bit like a Romany caravan passing through on its way to the circus.

He had a small sack over his shoulder with the remainder of his lunch, cured ham, the whisky bottle, and an awful hangover. He, like everybody else, had become used to hanging on to anything of value during wartime. He left nothing behind for the guards.

After the interrogations, his claustrophobia, and then meetings with the Standartenführer, only the Standartenführer, he was delighted to see so many different faces. Even if the camp was spartan, at least he was back with the ranks. He could have a conversation, sit at a table, share a cup of tea and a laugh. He smiled as the German guards closed the camp gate behind him.

"Why's the Negro smiling?" he heard one of the guards say.

"I think he's simple," replied the other.

Hoop saw no reason to share his knowledge of their language – those who didn't know he spoke German might slip up one day. As the lock clicked into place, he had never felt more free.

He hadn't expected a greeting of any kind and he didn't get one. The men hanging around the main gate looked serious. They were clearly not being treated particularly well: their uniforms were tatty, their faces gaunt. The thirteen days since the German invasion had not been kind to some of the men. There was an air of tragedy inside the wire.

A game of football was taking place outside one of the huts and Hoop caught the eye of one of the players: it was Charlie. Everybody knew Private Charlie. A real joker, always a story to tell, never a serious ending. He had floppy hair, a long torso, and short little legs, with a permanent cheeky grin.

"Hoop!" Charlie waved. "Hut 10," he shouted. "Good luck!" Charlie might have been about to speak again but the ball was kicked at him rather than to him and the moment was lost.

The huts were numbered both on the ends and above the doors. Very German, Hoop thought as he walked between the two rows of constructions. The ground was dusty and the sun was hot, still hot enough to burn his dark skin. Some of the men were lobster red and others chocolate brown. He reached Hut 10. Three men he didn't recognise sat on the steps outside. They stood up as he reached them, more like delinquent gang members than fellow POWs. The largest of them folded his arms as Hoop approached.

"Hoop Fundi, just in, reporting, in need of a bunk." He smiled but none of the men showed a modicum of welcome.

"We know who you are," said one.

They reluctantly stepped aside to give Hoop a path up the short staircase into the hut. He was used to being treated disrespectfully, although usually not by the other men in the ranks. Never had he known the colour of a man's skin to be of less importance, socially, than since the outbreak of war. A sinking feeling crept up on him.

Hoop stepped onto the first run of the steps – he was given just enough space to pass and no more.

"Mind ya manners, boy," were the last words Hoop heard as he stepped inside Hut 10.

Two officers were inside. Hoop recognised one of them. He didn't know him personally but he knew his name to be Pip. Captain Pip Smith was built like an ant. Spindly but tough. He had a square jaw, thin moustache, and that air of superiority, the worst the upper-class English carry everywhere they go. The other was short, unshaven and uncannily hairy, with thick black hair growing out of the top of his collar and down the backs of his hands. Both men were seated behind the only table, in the centre of the room; both chairs were behind the same side of the desk and they were facing Hoop. Had he not known better, he'd have thought he just walked into a job interview.

Hoop heard the door open behind him and the largest of the unfriendly men outside stepped in, closing the door behind him. *Something is wrong.*

The room needed air; the windows were closed but the sun was streaming in. Why didn't they open the windows? The bunk beds pushed against three of the walls were all empty. The room had been given over to them. Hoop tried to normalise the moment.

"Hoop Fundi, reporting for duty, sir."

"We know who you are, my lad," said the hairy one.

"Sit," ordered Pip. It wasn't an invitation. Hoop put his bag down by his side and took up the empty seat on the other side of the table, opposite the officers.

"Group Captain Stern, the camp CO, has asked us to meet with you for" – the officer paused – "a debrief." Hoop shifted in his seat. The fat man standing behind him made him uncomfortable.

"How was your captivity, Sergeant Fundi?" The question struck him with trepidation. Hardly anyone called him Sergeant Fundi. He'd been Hoop ever since he'd arrived in Europe. From the nice lady who pressed his uniform to the only general he'd ever met, he was Hoop. Everybody knew it. Pip certainly did.

"Okay, thank you, sir," he lied, but the British never asked those kinds of questions looking for the real answer. It was small talk, like they did with the weather. No matter how bad things got, the British would play it down to show a 'stiff upper lip'.

"What's in the bag?" The fat man behind him picked up the bag and placed it on the table before Hoop had a chance to reach down.

"Food," replied Hoop.

The bag was emptied out onto the table in front of him, the bottle of whisky included. *I can explain the whisky.*

"That's nice," said Pip, picking up the bottle.

They distrusted him, that much was clear. What had he told the Germans to receive a bottle of whisky? Hoop could see what it looked like.

"Were you interrogated?"

Hoop knew he needed to be very careful in what he said from here on.

"Yes, sir."

"What did they want to know?"

He hadn't prepared for this or expected it, considering what he'd just gone through. Damn it, that wasn't fair, but that sort of reaction would get him into more trouble.

"They want to get inside the tunnels, they believe there are entrances to the tunnels, secret ones they haven't yet discovered."

"And what did you tell them?"

"I told them I don't know where any secret entrances are."

"So you admitted there are secret entrances?" The hairy one's retort was rapid.

Pip leaned back in his seat, his arms folded. He didn't speak, just looked at his hairy friend and back at Hoop.

"And they believed you, did they?" Pip said finally.

"No, sir." Hoop didn't elaborate; he didn't want to get himself accidentally into trouble.

"What else did they ask?"

"Basic information, sir, my name, rank, what I do here on the Rock."

"And you told them?"

"Yes, sir, if captured, under the Geneva Convention—"

Pip interrupted. "What language did these conversations take place in, Sergeant Fundi?"

They'd spoken German, almost the entire time he'd been held. That was the truth, to say anything else would have been a lie. Although he could see where this was heading.

"German, sir."

"Of course," replied Pip. "Why wouldn't you speak German to the Germans, makes sense; they speak German, you speak German."

Hoop didn't like the insinuation. Under normal circumstances, before the invasion, before his capture and torture, he would have just sat in the chair, said nothing silently, taken whatever was coming his way for having the wrong colour skin. But something had changed in him during his captivity; he couldn't put his finger on exactly what but something had changed. He'd spoken his mind to the Standartenführer. He'd found a new confidence. He'd come through the interrogations less afraid of the likes of Pip.

"What point are you making?" Hoop forgot the *sir* but added it. "Sir."

Pip unfolded his arms and leaned forward in his chair. There was indignation in his face. "We've been waiting for you to turn up, we heard that Standartenführer Richter had taken a liking to you. We heard that you were communicating with the Standartenführer in German. Playing chess too."

If you already know that, then why are you asking? Hoop wanted to yell. Instead, he bit his lip.

"What we don't know," Pip continued, "is what you've been speaking about, in German, all this time?"

"I told you, sir, they asked the same questions over and over."

"So you say, but riddle me this, Sergeant Fundi. Why has every interrogated man been returned to the camp here half-starved, beaten, and broken, some at death's door?"

"I was also beaten, sir."

Pip ignored Hoop. "Then you arrive, well-fed, smiling, swinging a bag of food and the remains of a bottle of whisky, given to you by the Germans? You walk in, not carried in on a stretcher, as if you're on a Sunday stroll. Can you explain that to us?"

Hoop had no idea that the others who had been interrogated had been sent to the camp in such a bad state.

"I can't say, sir."

"I bet you can't!" said the hairy officer.

"It doesn't seem right, sir,"

"No, it doesn't. Something is amiss. Are you sure there's nothing you'd like to tell us, Sergeant?"

"I didn't tell them anything, sir. Not a word. I swear it." Hoop watched Pip's eyes as they moved across him. He'd seen farmers look the same way at cattle as they decided to buy or pass.

"The Germans found one of those secret access points into the tunnels. One of those you didn't tell them about. Standartenführer Richter and his SS men breached the Rock defences. They took Harley Street and Little Bay tunnels, killing close to one hundred men in the process."

"Yes, he told me last night," replied Hoop seriously.

"Last night?" asked the hairy one, looking again at Pip. "Harley Street and Little Bay were taken at 0600 this morning.

Hoop's heart sank.

Pip leaned over the table as close as he could get to Hoop. "Can you explain to me why an SS Standartenführer is discussing German operations with you?" Pip waited for an answer, Hoop couldn't think of one.

"You're a liar," said Pip.

The words took Hoop by surprise. The accusation wasn't an insinuation anymore, it was direct. He was being accused of sharing information with the enemy, of being a traitor. For causing the death of a hundred men and profiting from it with a bottle of whisky and some cheese.

Pip said nothing more, just looked at Hoop, waiting for a reaction.

Hoop's indignation at the insult swirled like a smouldering volcano. He tried to keep it under control but he'd suffered so much, much more than this idiot could imagine. If only the prat knew what Hoop knew; if he knew about Stay Behind Cave and Operation Tracer; if he knew that he had accepted his fate, to die before revealing Admiralty secrets. Even now he couldn't defend himself because he couldn't tell Pip the truth. It was no use, he couldn't hold it in. Hoop looked across at this self-satisfied pompous British idiot and something inside him snapped. It was coming out and he couldn't stop it. He stood up, ejecting the chair backwards.

"I'm not going to listen to another word. How dare you call me a traitor?"

"The nigger doth protest," said the hairy one, now also on his feet. A nod and the fat man behind Hoop wrapped his arms around him, pulling them hard into his sides. Hoop felt pulled back to the door as the other two men from the welcoming committee entered. One held his arm, the other hit Hoop hard in the stomach, doubling him up. The punch to his stomach knocked the wind out of him and sent electric shocks through his recovering rib. Hit again this time in the face, he was let go. Hoop fell to the wooden floor of the hut and bounced slightly on the floorboards before reeling in more rib pain.

"You'll be treated as we see fit, boy."

Hoop gasped for air, curled up in a ball in front of Pip.

"You wear a white man's uniform, but don't mistake yourself for a white man."

Hoop breathed in the dust from the floor. It was different dust to the cell floor, he could taste the wood.

"I think you're a liar. I think you told the Germans everything you know to save your black skin from a beating." Pip sat down at the table again. "I think they found the entrance to the tunnel system of the Rock because of you. I think they're done with you because they have no further use for you. I think that's why we have you back in here with a packed lunch and a bottle of whisky."

Pip turned to the welcoming committee. "Get him out of my sight."

Hoop was lifted from the floor and dragged from the hut, out of the door, down the steps, and into the sunlight. He could feel his heartbeat on his rib. He didn't see the faces of the men on the outside of the hut, only their boots, but there were plenty of them. *Come to see the Negro traitor.* Hoop repeated the same phrase to himself over and over again. *They know not what they do,* he told himself, although it wasn't true. He knew that they did.

38

BABY COUNCIL

1942, September 22 (21:09h)
Main Chamber, Stay Behind Cave, Rock of Gibraltar

Carter, Logan, Bunny, and Albert had sat down at the table to discuss what to do about Maria's 'predicament'. Maria didn't want to hear their opinions. *Let them talk,* she told herself, closing the door to the main chamber behind her, then the toilet door again. *Why do they always leave the toilet door open?* The toilets smelt, she'd been allocated her own of the two, but one of them was a brute and continued to use it. When the door was open, that smell drifted throughout the main chamber. She could smell it as she lay in her bunk at night. How many times had she got up to close that door, each time swearing to herself that she would kill the next man who left it open? The truth was, they all did.

The smell of the toilet drifted away as she took the stairs up to the west wall lookout. It had become her go-to place for the fresh air she needed to curb her claustrophobia. She wasn't proud of herself for much right now, but she'd managed to control her panic attacks in the confined space. What choice did she have? The stairs were getting more of a challenge every day; she cradled the child to ease the strain as their voices faded. She liked it when men thought they were making decisions for her when in fact she had already made up her mind about what was going to happen. It made them feel important, it made them feel in control. When men felt in control, that was when they were at their weakest. The invasion had proved that if nothing else. Pulling off a surprise invasion of the Rock was impossible – that was what they said.

"Arrogant," she told herself. "Who do they think they are?" Logan didn't understand she couldn't have the child now. The moment they were hauled into this damn cave everything changed. Why hadn't he pushed harder to get her put back outside? He'd disappointed her, again. She reached the top of the second flight of steps leading to the west wall and walked towards the light of the letterbox-shaped lookout. Maria pushed her nose as far out as she could and took deep breaths of freedom. How she'd taken her liberty for granted in the past. Now it was gone and she was locked away; she'd do almost anything to get it back.

Maria could see the Spanish coast in the moonlight, no longer lit up like Christmas before the invasion. Spain was now at war with the Allies. Madrid must have also been blacked out, and every city in the country.

Could she still rely on Logan? Honestly, she wasn't sure. She'd trusted him enough to lie down with him. She'd needed him. Being a woman alone on the Rock had just become too much. She'd wanted a man. Every day she'd been surrounded by them. The smell of men was everywhere. Logan had come at the right time. "Well, you had him, and what did that get you?" Again she said the words out loud. A solitary gun fired somewhere off in the distance. How many had escaped into the tunnels inside the Rock? she wondered. How many were sitting at lookouts like this one? Sealed inside just like her but not like her. They wanted to be there.

Meanwhile, down in the main chamber:

"What's that supposed to mean?" Logan raised his voice.

"I'm just saying, speaking from a purely medical position, Maria might not carry the child to term." Carter put his palms up. It was just his honest appraisal of the situation, not a prediction. "Look, I've got a well-stocked medicine cabinet. I can amputate your arm and you'll probably make it, but I don't have the first thing to support a pregnant mother. Pregnancy just wasn't on our list of eventualities for this mission." Carter laid his hand palms open on the table. "We have food here, but it isn't the diet of a mother-to-be. Corned beef and sardines? Not to mention the stress level Maria is under. This is a stressful place and she's claustrophobic." Carter's body language was the opposite of Bunny's, who still had his arms and legs crossed. "So, you see the point I'm making? Maria might lose the child in the natural course of things."

Carter was telling the truth, but that wasn't really the point. Logan liked the idea of letting Maria and the child out of the cave after a successful birth. It wasn't an option. No one could leave the cave. He'd handed Logan the title of team leader hoping that he wouldn't have to wrestle it away from him again with Bunny and Albert's help so soon. He could see Bunny smouldering internally at the idea of Maria leaving but holding it together, for now. Training had done its job. Carter could read Bunny. He knew where Bunny was on this particular issue and was actually pretty impressed that he wasn't in open conflict with Logan, yet.

"Say Maria walks, what is she walking out into?" Carter tried a new approach. "They'll pick her up for sure. They'll ask her where she's been hiding, tell her to 'show them'. They'll see through any story pretty damn quick. So, she's lying. They'll try to make her talk. She won't. What will they do then? Think, Logan. Letting Maria out is a death sentence. Not to mention a terrible risk to the mission." Logan said nothing.

"And if the lassie carries the child to term, what then?" asked Bunny. Carter liked it better when Bunny wasn't speaking.

Albert stuttered the first words of his idea. "W-wha, what if we just put the child outside, in a box maybe?"

Silence followed. Carter filled it.

"It comes with some problems, that one too, Albert. Where would we put the child? We couldn't just leave the box outside the cave entrance, but the risk of one of us being caught taking the child further away would be even greater."

Bunny picked up. "Are ya off ya trolley, laddy? We can't open the cave again."

"But they'd look after it. Wouldn't they, Doc?" Albert looked to Carter for confirmation.

Carter gave it thought, although he knew Bunny was right: removing the bricks at the front entrance and anybody leaving was a huge threat to the mission. "If they were gentlemen, yes, lad. That's what they'd do."

"Better a crying baby out there than in here!" said Albert in support of his idea.

Bunny recrossed his arms. Carter could see his patience was running thin. They needed a consensus, of any kind.

"Do we all agree that if Maria has the child, here in the cave, we can't keep it here? Can we at least agree on that much?"

They all nodded.

"So, the child must go out with or without Maria, yes?" said Logan.

Carter saw Bunny's intake of breath. He knew what came next. The unmentionable. The Scotsman had held the idea back for as long as he could.

"Is nobody gonna to say it?" Bunny's words drew grave faces from them all.

"Be careful, Jock," Logan said, waiting for what Carter knew was coming.

"I'm not recommending it. I'm just saying we can't ignore the option. We have to talk about it."

"You want to talk about murder," Logan said.

Carter could see Logan wouldn't last long in this conversation.

"It wouldn't be murder. One life to save many others."

What Bunny was saying went against everything Carter believed in, but he couldn't deny it was the obvious solution. The least dangerous, albeit most traumatic, safest option for the mission. *So why don't I want to do it?*

"It would solve every issue." Bunny sat forward, his enthusiasm for the idea growing as he spoke about it.

Logan folded his arms, but Bunny pushed. "For God's sake, be realistic – how many lives will be saved if we complete our mission successfully? How many will be lost if we're discovered because of a baby?"

"Are you talking about killing my unborn child?" Logan's question to Bunny was direct.

Bunny had the answer but didn't use it. Thinking to kill a baby and saying it out loud was not the same thing. Saying it made it real.

Carter knew what Windy would have said but he wasn't Windy.

"Better now than when the poor bairn's born."

Logan jumped to his feet; Bunny followed suit.

"Nobody's killing anybody," said Carter "Can we all just take a step back?" He stayed seated deliberately, his arms spread and gesturing for calm. Logan needed to feel in charge of this situation, or all hell was about to be let loose again. "You're the team leader, Logan," he continued. "It's our job to give you your options. All your options."

Bunny's eyes flickered as he decided which way this would go. Finally, he sat down, eyes fixed on the wall in submission.

Logan cleared his throat. "We'll wait. See what happens. Let nature take its course."

The order came out like a proclamation. Carter knew that as the days rolled on it became more, not less, likely that Maria would carry her child to term.

"Agreed," said Carter.

Albert nodded. Bunny left the table without another word.

39

EPIPHANY

1942, September 24 (01:14h)
Hut 5, German Prisoner-of-War (POW) Camp,
Europa Point, Rock of Gibraltar

Hoop lay on his bunk. His rib was acutely painful, again. First the Germans, then the British; although it was his pride that occupied his mind. Everybody in the camp now considered him a traitor. Even those who knew him thought him to be a coward, at the very least. A man who would share information with the enemy to avoid a beating. He rolled over. What did he care, who were they anyway? Why was he fighting in this white man's war? To protect people who treated him like a slave? He wasn't one of them and never would be. They despised him. The British were no better than the Germans. What was the difference between them? The Standartenführer was right. Whoever won the white man's war, men of colour, like him, would always be considered slaves. He was putting his life on the line for what? He was keeping Admiralty secrets for whom? Pip? Hoop looked around the hut full of bunk beds with snoring white men, none of whom wanted to speak to him. For this lot? He spoke German and he wasn't white – that made him a traitor, did it? Even when they didn't believe him to be trading secrets with the enemy for whisky, he was hit by officers, paid less for his service because of his colour, forced to salute lower ranks, just like Richter had said. It was all true. How was his life worth less than a white man's? He'd given his word that he hadn't told the Germans anything and they didn't believe his word. His words meant nothing to these colonials. He was a lying Negro. That's it.

Hoop turned over again. He could taste the blood on his cut lip. They weren't his people. He had better treatment from the Standartenführer. With Richter, he could speak his mind without being beaten for insolence. This Nazi was at least honest with him, even if he disagreed with almost everything he said. Maybe he'd been wrong. Maybe he had to do what everybody else was doing: look after himself. Maybe he shouldn't close the door on the Standartenführer's offer too quickly but reconsider it.

Both sides treated him the same. The idea that the British were different, that they respected him, valued him, was naive; he was just another Negro to them all. If they were going to treat him the same, maybe he should treat them the same too. Play both sides of the fence? *Can the Standartenführer really get to my mother?* He couldn't say for sure, so he needed an insurance policy. Yes, he was a Nazi but he'd been straight with him, hadn't he? He could do a deal. He actually quite liked the man; he was better than Pip.

Hoop turned over in his bunk. The rib just wouldn't settle, it throbbed constantly. He closed his eyes trying to sleep but it was no good. His eyes were alive and active behind the closed lids. Were they coming to beat him in his sleep, if he could even get to sleep? They thought he was a traitor, why wouldn't they? He tried deep breaths to relax; he wanted to sleep, he needed to sleep. The camp had been worse than the prison cell so far. He couldn't believe it was true but it was. He was safer with the Standartenführer right now for sure. Richter 'liked him', he could use that. If he took him up on his offer, it would get him back out of here. If he shared some information, the Standartenführer would improve his conditions; he said as much.

The revelation hit Hoop like lightning; he sat bolt-upright in his bunk then froze. The epiphany sent a cold shiver down his back. His memory was electrified. Why had they beaten everybody else? Tortured them, starved them, and sent them back to the camp barely alive but he'd been singled out and fattened? Because he spoke German? Because the Standartenführer liked him? Because he was a

Negro? How could he have been so stupid? Why had he not seen it?

He had seriously underestimated Standartenführer Richter.

Hoop was lying there, contemplating switching sides. He was actually considering becoming a traitor and he could justify it to himself. Of course he could, because that's exactly what the Standartenführer wanted. Richter had stopped the Haas beatings; he'd been well treated, fed, the man the Standartenführer believed had detailed knowledge of the tunnel accesses. He'd been sent back to the camp with a bag of presents the day after they'd broken into the Rock. The threat to his mother, the drinks, chess, and friendship building – it had all been planned to the finest detail. He told him about Harley Street and Little Bay tunnels before they'd been taken! He'd wanted him to slip up. It was brilliant and he'd played along unaware, a willing participant in a plot to turn him and it had worked. It all fell into place. It was suddenly clear, clear as day.

Hoop dropped his legs down over the edge of his bunk and stood up, despite the pain that for some reason now felt more like a badge of honour. He made his way to the door of the hut and opened it, just enough to talk to the sergeant outside who had been placed there specially on his account, and never let him forget it.

"I need to see Group Captain Stern."

"I need to see Mae West." The sergeant smirked at the corporal next to him.

"It's important!"

The sergeant's smile faded and he moved towards the door. "Listen, darky. You're confined to this hut, on Group Captain Stern's orders, which means you stay in the hut. If he wants to see you, he'll come and see you. If he doesn't, then he won't. Now piss off."

The door slammed in Hoop's face. His way back to his bunk was punctuated with expletive requests to be quiet and one questioning why they were forced to share a hut with a traitor. Hoop reached his bunk and lay down again. He had to respect what the Standartenführer had done to him. It was quite brilliant.

40

NOT TO BE TOUCHED

1942, September 24 (01:20h)
Guardhouse, German Prisoner-of-War (POW) Camp,
Europa Point, Rock of Gibraltar

Richter stepped out of his armoured car between two guard huts just outside the perimeter fence of his new POW camp. He looked inside his packet of Juno cigarettes: one was left. He put the packet back in his pocket. He wanted to enjoy the last one. He wouldn't, here.

Major Haas stood in the vehicle's headlights, waiting for him. He saluted but not with the enthusiasm that Richter was used to from his subordinate officers.

"Two more escapes today? You assured me the escapes would stop, Major." Haas lifted his chin and grimaced, either to suppress his immediate response or reformulate his thoughts. Finally, he spoke.

"The British have outside help." He pushed his shoulders back before carrying on. "I've doubled the guard and stationed men outside the perimeter fence on night duty to watch for intruders approaching."

Richter nodded but was asking himself why such measures hadn't already been undertaken. "Berlin expects the escapes to stop. A few British here and there might be tolerated, but that's three escapes this week. Not acceptable."

"Yes, Herr Standartenführer."

Richter heard the yes, but the smouldering irritation of the major was what he saw. "Your failure to establish authority in this camp discredits me with my superiors in Berlin and discredits you with me,

Major. I don't care how you achieve it but the escapes stop, now!"

"Yes, Standartenführer."

"Do whatever is necessary but put an end to them or I'll be signing papers for your transfer to the Russian front. Have I made myself clear?" The threat of transfer off the Rock was an empty one, he knew. They were stretched for experienced officers. Haas was already overseeing the POW camp on top of his other duties. He was a talented assault unit commander but lacked the skills required for Camp Commandant. It was the reason he'd forced the position upon him.

Letting Haas go right now just wasn't an option, although maybe the major didn't know it.

"Yes, Standartenführer!" There was fear in the major's reply this time. Enough to satisfy Richter. He knew, without a doubt, the one really in danger of being relieved of command and sent to the Russian front was he himself. The escapes raised questions in Berlin but also some for him. Where were the British escaping to and who was helping them? Was there a plan for a counterattack that his intelligence gatherers had so far missed? He needed to get inside the Rock at all costs as soon as possible.

"And the Negro?" he asked now.

"You were correct, Herr Standartenführer." The words forced their way through the major's gritted teeth. Richter could see the bitter taste they left.

"Dragged from Hut 10, unable to walk. Currently confined to Hut 5."

"Good." Richter tried to contain his delight. His plan was working perfectly.

"I would like the opportunity to finish my interrogation of the Negro, Herr Standartenführer," said the major.

Richter didn't like being played with. The major knew the answer before he asked the question.

"The Negro is not to be touched. I'm not finished with him."

Haas nodded but with a thin insubordinate smile.

"How can you stomach it speaking our language, and he knows

nothing?" The comment from the major was a veiled challenge to Richter's authority; they both knew it. The SS man couldn't let it go.

"You will follow my orders, Major, or you will end up in Russian snow."

The major pulled himself rigid, slammed his boots together, and saluted while staring off into the distance. Richter didn't wait to see the theatrical recognition of his rank.

41

MISSING A PIECE

1942, September 25 (20:01h)
Main Chamber, Stay Behind Cave, Rock of Gibraltar

Back inside the cave, Carter was enjoying the silence. Maria was finally sleeping. Albert was in the radio room probably fiddling with wires and plugs. He was a little worried about Albert. His light-heartedness and humour had all but abandoned him; after the nightly transmissions to the Admiralty in London, the boy had taken to squirrelling himself away alone in the radio room for long periods with only tea for sustenance, usually after talking with Maria. They'd struck up a friendship. They'd shared common suffering, and both of them were taking the sudden incarceration badly. Despite, or maybe because of her own troubles, Maria had tried to take him under her wing, but his strange behaviour had grown worse rather than better. It wasn't healthy for any of them to withdraw to the degree that Albert did to the radio room. After completing his shift on the bicycle to charge the batteries, or intelligence gathering at the lookout, his answer to a game of cards or drafts was always the same. "The equipment needs maintenance." It was wearing thin as his excuse to disappear with a tea. God knows what he was actually doing there. Carter was afraid to go in when the door was closed. He couldn't help but notice the embarrassed looks the boy had developed. Had the radio room become a personal retreat for the youngster for onanism? He'd asked Commander Fleming to address the issue with the men, being that they were to be locked up together for such a long time, but the commander had only laughed and told him that it was a 'medical issue' and that he and Doctor Milburn had his 'fullsupport' to address the issue publicly or privately with the men. They'd decided not to, being that they didn't expect an 'epidemic'. He and Syd had laughed full belly laughs. It was hard to believe that Syd, Windy and Hoop were all gone.

The box of broken shards of mirror sat in the corner of the chamber on top of the corned beef. Now was a good time to piece it back together. Carter seemed to be the only one interested in having the mirror back, which was surprising because Logan was the one who used it the most. Logan spent more time in front of a mirror than a man should but that was just his opinion. That said, looking after his appearance had obviously helped him attract Maria. Carter didn't have a great deal of respect for Logan so far, but he did for Maria. If she saw something in him then maybe they all needed to look a little harder and they would too. It couldn't just be the Brylcreemed hair. Bunny said to leave the broken bits in the box and Albert had become irritated just by hearing of the plan. Anyway, it was the only mirror they had and everybody used it. He liked to pluck the hairs in his nose; without the mirror, they'd probably grow wild but his greatest incentive, if he was being honest with himself, was that he thought Maria would like it back.

Carter picked up the box of broken pieces and placed it on the table. So he was putting it back together to please Maria. *Be honest with yourself, Doctor,* thought Carter as he began to lay the pieces out on the table. He started with the large pieces first, placing them face down with the reflective mirror side out of view and the grey-painted back showing. He picked up a large yellow tin of Samuel Jones butterfly brand air raid precaution sealing tape and placed it on the table. The specially coated adhesive was designed for securing windows to prevent them from shattering and spreading glass everywhere during a blast, but he had found the stuff handy for all sorts of little jobs in surgery. Fishing through the box of broken glass trying not to cut his hand, Carter remembered the moment the Tracer mission was activated. A moment he would never forget.

1942 September 10 (13:03h)
Doctor Carter's Surgery, British Military Hospital,
Europa Road, Rock of Gibraltar

"Streptococcal," he'd said, looking beyond the tongue of the patient in his surgery. There was gunfire in the distance, something was happening, and he wondered what.

"You have tonsillitis," he told the young soldier sitting on the table looking blankly at him. "It should clear up in a couple of days on its own. Gargle salt water, and stay hydrated. Come back and see me immediately if you develop a fever, joint pain, muscle spasms, that sort of thing."

The boy smiled. "So I'm not dying then, Doc?"

"Not today," joked Carter as sirens rang out. His first thought was a drill.

"Air raid, sir?" asked the young man in uniform. Carter didn't answer because he didn't know. The sound was new to him. He stepped out of his surgery and into the small waiting room. His next patient was on his feet looking out of the window. The outer door opened and Commander Knott leaned in.

That was the moment he knew something was seriously wrong. Knott had never been in surgery. He was an extremely healthy man for his forty-five years of age. He was also the Tracer mission supervising officer on the Rock. At their only meeting, on arrival, Knott had told him that Windy and the rest of the Tracer team members would not be speaking again unless...

Knott said one word only.

"Tracer."

A shiver ran down Carter's back and goose bumps along his arm. Nothing had gone well from that moment.

Main Chamber, Stay Behind Cave, Rock of Gibraltar

He had all the pieces of the broken mirror laid out on the table and back in their original positions. A piece was missing. Just one. A large shard shape. He checked the box to see if it had become lodged in the folds. It hadn't. He checked the floor area where the mirror had fallen and all the surrounding area on his hands and knees, but the missing piece was nowhere to be found. About the size of his palm and triangular in shape, the piece couldn't just have vanished into thin air.

"You're missing a piece," observed Maria, coming out from behind her wall of boxes.

"Can't find the bugger anywhere," replied Carter.

"I'm sure it will turn up." Maria sat down at the table. She had a sprightliness about her which he was happy to see. She moved with greater purpose and dexterity, her shoulders back and chest out. Carter tried to focus on the job at hand.

He filled the space the missing piece had left with a cardboard cutout of the same shape. It completed the puzzle and he gave a small cheer and a little applause. Maria smiled. It was good to see. Carter opened the yellow tin of air raid precaution sealing tape. He tore off a strip.

"Hold the end?" With Maria's help, Carter began to secure the pieces in place, laying line by line of tape on the back of the broken mirror. Placing the original rectangular wooden back down on the taped glass, Carter held the two together, flipped the mirror over and began to tape the edges to keep the glass on the board. The smashed collage he had created reflected his and Maria's faces, side by side, like a Picasso splintered painting, piece by broken piece rather than a whole. Looking at them in the broken mirror, Carter saw their mutated reflections sliced into segments and put back together again in a gruesome Frankenstein form. Maria was looking at him, staring even. *Wasn't she?* She didn't blink, just held eye contact with him in the mirror. Carter looked away. He was uncomfortable but had no idea why. She made him nervous. Carter flipped the mirror back around and hung it back on the bolt protruding through the wall.

Maria wasn't as pleased as he'd hoped. As Carter put the tape, scissors and leftover cardboard away, he told himself to think less about Maria. She was his patient and nothing more. Although he knew that wasn't true.

42

CUBICLE THREE

1942, September 26 (06:20h)
Hut 5, German Prisoner-of-War (POW) Camp,
Europa Point, Rock of Gibraltar

Hoop had been waking progressively earlier every morning. He was finding it harder and harder to sleep and just lying on his bunk had become painful to his back. The men in the hut had perfected the art of living with him but not talking to him. They'd walk right by him and not one of them looked at him. He was invisible. It was known as being sent to Coventry. Coventry was apparently a city in England. He'd never heard of it and the current experience wasn't an advert for a visit. A trip to the 'shitter' shadowed by his sergeant guard was both the highlight and lowlight of his day. At least it had him out of Hut 5.

The two men exiting the makeshift toilet building averted their eyes while a third, a union flag tattooed across his pumped forearm, stood in his way forcing Hoop to walk around the man. Being confined to Hut 5 was, in some ways, worse than the German cell. The Standartenführer's plan was working. He couldn't take it much longer, something had to give. He wasn't going to be living like this until the end of the war. That wasn't going to happen. One way or another he was getting out. He knew what he had to do but nothing would be possible until he met Group Captain Stern.

The shitter was worse than going in a hole in the ground back home. At least back home a hundred men hadn't been there before you. A plank of wood with a hole cut into it. He was as quick as he could, the smell was terrible. As he left the cubicle the wooden flap opened at the back of the makeshift construction, light filled the small dark space, and he wished it hadn't. A hand grabbed the barrel he'd just relieved himself into, dragging it out. Cleaning the shitter was the worst job in the camp, served up to those who broke the rules. Given the option, he'd have taken the job rather than be locked up again. Anything to get him out, into the open air, was preferable to confinement, even if that air wasn't fresh.

The sergeant was waiting for him outside, picking his teeth.

"You can't deny my request to see the camp CO, you don't have the authority. So I ask you again. I want to see Group Captain Stern! Please pass my request up the chain of command." The sergeant continued to pick his teeth. Hoop waited for an answer. Finally one came.

"If you ask me again, I'm going to punch you in the face." The sergeant's facial expression remained perfectly blank, he never took his eyes off Hoop and he never stopped picking his teeth. It was a promise, not a threat.

Hoop climbed back into his bunk and pulled the blanket over his head. There was only one thing for it, but it was going to get messy.

1942, September 27 (04:05h)

Hoop tossed his blanket and swung his legs down to the floor. Moonlit Hut 5 was quiet, less the usual snoring and farting. As he slipped his stockinged feet into his boots, the voice he expected was right on cue.

"Going somewhere?" His shadow never slept; the sergeant was a machine.

Hoop didn't like the man but he had to respect him. Apart from the four hours or so every afternoon, when different faces would stand in for him, the sergeant was always there. Looking over his shoulder, watching his every move like a hawk. Hoop didn't make trips to the toilet in the middle of the night. It was cold for one, dark for another, and he'd rather stay under his blanket but tonight was different. He needed to go.

"Make it quick," said the sergeant, buttoning up his tunic and tying his shoelaces.

"Keep it down, won't you!" came a voice from the darkness as Hoop exited Hut 5, wearing his boxer shorts, a vest, and his uniform shirt for extra warmth. The sergeant tailed Hoop the short distance to the shitter door and lit a cigarette.

Hoop closed the door of cubicle three. The usual stench hit the back of his throat, but he'd chosen cubicle three deliberately. Cubicle three had a broken wooden shelf. There'd been talk in the hut about getting it fixed before somebody fell into the barrel of shit below. The jokes had flown at the prospect of one of them getting covered in shit. Hoop had laughed silently to himself at the time but he wasn't laughing now.

He didn't have much time. The sergeant would quiz him after a couple of minutes and when he didn't answer, he'd enter. He needed the head start to make it to Stern's hut before they caught up with him. Trips to the shitter at night were allowed but roaming the camp wasn't. He'd have to walk to Stern's hut; if the German guards saw anyone run they'd bring the camp lights up very quickly. He didn't want that. Stern might listen to him if he arrived in his hut covered in shit but if he woke the whole camp up and had them out on parade in the middle of the night he'd be further from an audience with the Group Captain than he currently was. Convincing the Camp CO to listen to him was going to be tough enough.

Sitting on the wooden plank, Hoop dropped both legs into the toilet hole, gripped both sides of the broken piece and pulled. The space opened up large enough for him to slip through, down into the barrel full of shit. The barrels were emptied in the morning at 11:00 hours and then again at 18:30. He'd expected the barrel to be almost empty. It wasn't. His boots splashed down through the urine and he was almost up to his knees in faeces. It was a tight squeeze under the plank with only just enough space for him to slip between the top of the barrel and the underside of the plank seat. The smell of shit consumed his nostrils and his throat. It lay on his tongue. He could taste it. Hoop tried not to vomit. The sound of him vomiting would surely bring the sergeant his way. He retched silently, multiple times, puked and swallowed it. He needed to get out of the barrel as quickly as he could, but quietly.

Hoop slid his body between the barrel and the plank but the edges of the barrel were sharp. Adrenaline prevented pain but he felt the cut to his hand and thigh as he climbed over, coming to rest on the outside of the barrel next to the retrieval flap. Hoop touched his wounds. He thanked God that they weren't serious. His boots were wet and sludgy, slurping with something he never wanted to see. There was no time to waste, everything in his very being said get out of there. Hoop rolled onto his knees and gently pushed the flap on the backside of the simple wooden construction and peered out. There wasn't a minute to lose, Stern was in Hut 11. He'd formulate what he was going to say on the way – he'd make the rest up as he went along. Hoop leaned on the hinged flap and pushed, rolling out into the moonlit dust, right into the boots of the waiting sergeant, Pip standing next to him, a knowing look on his arrogant skinny face.

43

IN THE SHIT

Hoop tried to get to his feet. There was no explaining to do. What could he say?

"Don't get up." The sergeant used his boot to push Hoop back down onto his backside.

"What was the plan?" asked Pip, sarcastically. Hoop didn't want a conversation. He'd been caught, okay, but he wasn't going to help this awful man humiliate him. "Really, what exactly were you planning, or were you taking a bath?"

"Shall we take him to the showers, sir?" inquired the sergeant, turning his nose up at Hoop's new smell.

"No. Put him back," replied Pip with a sadistic grin.

The sergeant, who Hoop had seen take orders better than anyone, clearly didn't understand.

"Sir?" said the sergeant, squinting his request for a repeat of the order.

"Put him back in the shitter," replied Pip.

The sergeant connected the dots at the same time as Hoop.

He couldn't mean it. *What for?* The sergeant was as slow to move as Hoop.

"Now, Sergeant." Pip raised his voice.

The sergeant grabbed Hoop by his collar but he wasn't going. *No way.* Pip didn't have the authority to lock him in with that barrel. *I'm not going.* Hoop tried to wrestle himself free but the sergeant had a firm grip and help. Three, maybe four others came out of the darkness and laid hands on him. Struggling and screaming as he did, he was back inside the flap next to the barrel, his hands pried from the edges of the entrance. The flap slammed shut.

"How long?" asked the sergeant on the other side of the flap.

"Until I say otherwise," came the order from Pip.

The searchlight hit the shitter and Hoop heard German boots and voices. The commotion he'd caused had brought the guards into the camp. He heard the questions shouted, then the flap was thrown open again.

Pip, the sergeant and several other men were standing hands in the air. Never had he been so happy to see Germans holding weapons. The torch shone in his face blinded him momentarily but he could see the gun barrel and face of the guard behind it.

"I want to see Stanhdartenführer Richter," Hoop requested in German. The guard swung his torch around the inside of the shitter and as he did so Hoop got a glimpse of his pursed lips and contorted expression.

"Tell the Standartenführer. He'll want to see me!" pleaded Hoop again in German. The torch blinded him a second time before the flap began to close. Hoop saw a smile on the face of the guard as the flap closed out the light once more.

"I demand to see Standartenführer Richter!" Hoop shouted this time into the darkness. His voice hoarse and his throat full of shit, he kicked out at the wooden flap multiple times and demanded to see both Stern and Richter.

At that moment Hoop couldn't decide who he hated more, his British masters who wanted him to spend the rest of the night in a rancid toilet, or the Nazis who defined him as subhuman and wanted the same. They were both just cruel white people.

"Even his Nazi friends have no more use for him," Hoop heard Pip say outside. He kicked the flap again in frustration. It was inhumane.

Even for Pip. Hoop sat in the darkness as they nailed the flap shut. How would he make it to the morning? He vomited at the thought and lay in his vomit. It smelt better than the shit.

* * *

1942, September 27 (08:05h)

Hoop woke to the splash of urine hitting the barrel. He'd drifted in and out of consciousness. The space was cramped, with barely enough to lie down. The first user of cubicle three seemed unaware of his presence although by full daylight he'd become the camp attraction. He could hear the conversations on the other side of the flap. "Nigger traitor, getting what he deserves" to "ghastly, the whole affair, unbecoming of the British Army." One comment stuck with Hoop all morning. "What's to be done when dealing with his kind?"

Hoop couldn't get the words out of his head, 'his kind' – who were his kind? Traitors? People from Namibia? Christians? Or simply people who didn't have white British skin? Sitting there with human faeces dried to his legs, he remembered the Standartenführer's words. No matter the outcome of this white man's war, the world for people like him, people of colour, would go on the same.

It was midday before Hoop heard what he'd been waiting for – the opinion of Group Captain Stern. It came in the shape of gossip, orders passed down the ranks. Hoop pushed his ear to the wall of the shitter.

"The punishment was Captain Pip Smith's and would end when the captain said it would." Hoop's heart sank. "Sergeant Fundi was to be given food and water three times a day. The barrel was to be removed" – which it was – "cubicle three was to be labelled 'Out of Service' until further notice and the men were to disperse and get on with their daily routines. Anyone found loitering in the vicinity of the toilets better have a bloody good reason for being there or they too might find themselves confined."

The orders floored Hoop. How could Camp CO Stern go along with such treatment? The removal of the barrel helped Hoop stop vomiting and gave him proper space to lie down but lunch was one of the worst experiences of his life. He was hungry but the bread, ham and cheese put through the patched-up hole above his head were inedible. Nothing was clean inside the shitter. Nothing. It didn't matter that the barrel was gone, it was filthy under the plank. Everything was contaminated. He could taste the urine and faeces in his mouth; he couldn't put food in there no matter how hungry he was. He washed his mouth and face with the water every time they brought it but even the water tasted putrid.

By dinner time Hoop ate the food. He had to. Every mouthful he chewed tasted of human faeces. He was being treated worse than a dog.

As he ate, Hoop made a decision. The British were no longer his friends. He would never forgive them for this. Never. When they finally let him out, he would do whatever it took, to better his circumstances. Whatever it took. The Tracer mission was now a bargaining chip, as and when he deemed it so, to get what he wanted. As God was his witness, he had justification.

44

ROOM 502

1942, September 10 (14:11h)
Room 502, The Rock Hotel, Rock of Gibraltar

On the day of the invasion Doctor Carter sat nervously with his small rucksack on the bed in room 502 of the Rock Hotel, his pistol pointed at the door. There was a sound missing. The big guns? They should be dominating the moment. The enemy was at the gates but only one or two of the big gun defences seemed to be firing. Something had gone wrong.

He'd trained for this moment but felt unprepared. Sitting alone, and waiting for the others wasn't part of the plan. Small-arms fire was audible somewhere close by, inside the hotel he was sure of it. *Where were the others?* What if no one came? What then? Should he leave without them, go on his own? The idea was bonkers. They were coming, they couldn't be killed, not all of them. Carter paced the room. The frayed rug on the floor was turned back on itself. He flipped it flat to the floor again nervously. He'd executed his departure perfectly in line with protocol. Done everything right. Damn it, why hadn't the others! What if they'd skipped the hotel and headed directly up the Rock? *Was he sitting there like an idiot while they were already in the cave?*

He snatched another nervous look at his watch. He'd been there less than fifteen minutes but it seemed like an hour. The goat herder looked down on him from the painting of the whitewashed Spanish town on a hill, a peaceful image far from the reality of distant gunfire.

He noticed the brush strokes on the painting for the first time. He'd been in that room so many times and looked at that same painting, but never noticed those brush strokes. The crack of gunfire on the floor above snapped him back to reality: the invaders were inside the hotel. The handle of the door turned and he nearly shot Young Albert as he entered followed by Bunny.

"The others?" said Bunny.

Carter shook his head.

"We can't wait, we have to go, no?" said Albert, white as a sheet. Five more minutes, thought Carter. If they could just hang on until they got there, until Windy got there. Bunny waited for him to make a decision, and give an order. Albert too. *Damn it, where was Windy?* That was his job. He was the team leader. If they left now without the rest of them, without Windy, would they live to regret it? If they didn't would they live at all? Where was bloody Syd? He was off duty today! Syd was supposed to take the reins if anything happened to Windy. Gunfire rattled the door. The invaders were in the corridor.

"Doc, we gotta go!" Bunny gripped his machine gun and Albert his rifle; their weapons were shaking in their hands, and pointed at the door.

Shit, they had no choice. Carter tossed his pistol onto the bed and picked up his rucksack, Bunny and Albert followed suit. Carter locked the door to room 502 as Bunny opened the small walk-in closet. They heard a shout of *'Schnell'* – the Germans were in the room next door.

Their procedure was simple. It went like clockwork in training but now it felt like moving in slow motion. The rant of a German-made machine gun next door shook Young Albert as Bunny pulled open the small doorway at the back of the walk-in closet. Albert and Carter ran through into the darkness and Bunny pulled the door closed behind them. The next step was to slide the large bolts to secure the secret entrance. Somebody burst into room 502 and Carter put his hand on Bunny's hand, holding the bolt, and squeezed. They were too late to lock it, the sound might give their position away.

The secret door into the tunnel system was well concealed; the first time he'd entered the little closet space looking for the doorway, knowing it was in there somewhere, he couldn't find it. The entrance had been extremely well camouflaged into the natural architecture and interior design of the small space. They needed to sit tight. The only way they would be discovered was by making a noise. The bolts would have to wait. Bunny held the small door closed with his fingertips as the three of them sat in the darkness. The protocol had been to lock the door. The team not being there, all together, had never been discussed. If they locked the entrance now and Windy came later with the others they wouldn't get in but if they left it open, the Germans might find it. The jackboots left room 502 as quickly as they entered. There was more gunfire in the distance but room 502 was quiet.

"Lock it up," whispered Carter finally. Bunny gently slid the bolt closed.

"Done," whispered Bunny.

"Let's go," replied Carter. It appeared he was now in charge.

45

PRIVATE CHARLIE

1942, September 29 (05:39h)
Shitter, German Prisoner-of-War (POW) Camp,
Europa Point, Rock of Gibraltar

Hoop was drifting, the seagulls screeching high above him. *Gulls meant land was close, didn't they?* His head rolled on its neck like a ball on a string, and it woke him up. His lips were dry and cracked. The shitter had lost its potent smell and become the norm to him.

The camp siren screeched again. It wasn't seagulls. He was pulled back to reality in cubicle three.

He had no idea what time it was. The siren squealed again, this time louder. The flap to the shitter was pried open at one corner. The sound of nails being wrenched from bedded wood brought him wide-eyed awake and the sergeant appeared on the other side.

"Fundi, out! You stick to me like fly paper, hear me, boy? I don't want to see you more than two feet from my side. Got it?"

"What's happening?" asked Hoop, pulled from the shitter.

"Never you mind, just know I've got my eye on you." Out of the flap into the night sky, Hoop tried to find his feet.

The searchlights were up, full and blinding as Hoop and the sergeant followed the crowd. The atmosphere was upbeat and many of the men were laughing and joking as if they were on an evening jolly but the mood changed as the parade ground came into view. Three men, on their knees, held at gunpoint. Hoop recognised one of them, it was Private Charlie.

Hoop followed the sergeant as he moved through the crowd. The shock of seeing him out of the shitter or the smell of the toilet he'd brought with him cut a clear channel for them up to the prisoners' line, the line of wire that ran all around the camp. There were ten feet between the wire and the fence. Cross it and you were in danger of being shot. Hoop stood next to the sergeant in earshot of the guards pointing their guns at Charlie and his two friends. The watchtowers on both sides had the crowd of British POWs in their sights. The jovial walk to the parade ground had been replaced by serious faces and a low murmur of disdain. No one in the parade ground liked having a loaded weapon pointed at them.

"Calm down," Hoop heard one German guard tell another. The guards were pale-faced and nervous. The crowd was large enough to overpower them but the machine guns in the watchtowers would be capable of killing many in the process. The atmosphere was a tinderbox.

Beyond Charlie, the guards and his two friends on their knees was a hole in the fence. Beyond that hole, another in the outer fence. Charlie and his friends had almost made it out of the camp and one had got clean away.

Group Captain Stern came into view. Hoop had thought so much about getting an audience with the camp CO, the man had become more of a target than a person, so when he walked into view he wasn't what Hoop had expected. Firstly, he was in his boxer shorts, service-issue boots and a vest. Only his walk gave his credentials away as he strode through the crowd, which opened for him as if he were Moses parting the waves. Six foot tall, at least, with salt-and-pepper-coloured hair, he had the air of a man in charge, with the camp medic, who had treated him in the cell, Pip and the hairy one in tow.

Stern ignored the prisoners' line that had held the trespass of the rest of the crowd, striding out into no man's land as if it wasn't there and right up to the guards, Charlie and his two friends.

Action at the guard house on the other side of the fence drew everyone's attention. Six to eight guards boarded a truck driving off into the darkness of the early morning while another three German guards rushed to the main gate trying to keep up with black-toothed Major Haas as he entered and approached Stern.

"May I remind you, Major," Stern began, "that under the Geneva Convention—"

"Silence!" The dishevelled morning-faced major was briefed in German on the missing, 'fourth man'. He turned to face Stern.

"You were warned, Commander, and you've chosen to ignore that warning." Major Haas addressed the crowd behind the prisoners' line. "For those of you who are still under the illusion that you are prisoners of war, with the obligation to try and escape, let me make one thing clear. You are not! Your commanding officer has been informed of this. If he has taken it upon himself not to tell you, for your safety I am now doing so." The POWs stood silently. "Not one man here is classified as a prisoner of war. As of yesterday, you are all now being held for the crime of spying. This new classification has been placed upon you by your Spanish neighbours, allies of the Third Reich. The Rock of Gibraltar is now and has always been Spanish territory, ceded to Britain illegally. By inhabiting the Rock, with the express purpose of spying on your Spanish neighbours, and as captured spies in a foreign land, you are no longer afforded the protections of the Geneva Convention." Haas paused and Group Captain Stern squared up to the Nazi.

"Article 5 of the Convention states that, spy or not, every individual has the right to a fair trial. Before such a trial, the letter of the Convention must be applied. Detainees must be treated with humanity. Escapees or otherwise."

"A trial was held this morning and you were all found guilty," said Major Haas, nonchalantly pulling his pistol from its holster.

"Escapes will end from this camp tonight. Know this. If a prisoner leaves this camp, he will be gaining his freedom but taking the life of a fellow prisoner with him. One of your lives. From now on, if one man escapes, one of you men left behind will pay the price with your life."

Haas primed his Luger pistol ready for firing. "If two men escape, two men will be shot and so on. You're all then reliant upon each other. Next time you plan an escape, remember that you are also planning the execution of one of your friends."

Stern approached the Nazi and the guards turned their guns on him. "If you shoot my men you will be committing a war crime. A war crime that will be punished – you and all your men here will pay the price for that crime, I assure you."

Hoop knew the Group Captain's threat would fall on deaf ears. Like a beetle threatening the foot about to tread on it. Hoop had first-hand close-up experience of black-toothed Major Haas, he knew what came next – unless? Hoop decided in an instant. One he wasn't sure he'd live to regret. Hoop stepped across the line into no man's land and walked directly towards Haas.

"Stop!" The guards turned their guns on Hoop.

"Halt!" But Hoop just kept walking. The sound of a discharged rifle made Hoop flinch and duck for a moment but no round connected with him so he kept on going.

"The Lord is my shepherd, I shall not want," he whispered under his breath.

"Get back!" he heard the German shout but Hoop walked on, straight for Major Haas. His actions hadn't just caught him by surprise but everyone else. Haas lowered his pistol as he watched, what felt to Hoop like slow motion progress towards him. One foot in front of the next, arms swinging to keep forward momentum. His knees had been weak the first few steps but the closer he got to Haas and Charlie the more stable they became. He was still alive and almost upon them. The guards had stopped shouting and firing. Hoop continued to whisper the words of the Lord as he walked on.

Group Captain Stern and Major Haas shared a silent wide-eyed surprise, but by the time Hoop was finally upon them Haas had reverted to furious indignation, and if he wasn't mistaken, a little fear. *It was working.*

Hoop's legs stiffened as he reached Charlie and the other two men on their knees. They looked at him like children caught stealing apples. The guards swung the barrels of their guns nervously, from Hoop to the prisoners and on to the line of POWs close enough to rush them. Hoop stood within touching distance of Major Haas. The man who had beaten him, all times of day and night, with a black-toothed smile.

The silence from so many men in the parade ground was deafening, broken only, ironically considering the location, by the chirping of a cricket.

Doubt and confusion had replaced the previous confidence of Major Haas and it spread through the faces of his men like wildfire.

Everybody waited for Hoop to speak, but he didn't. He just stood there looking at Haas. The major lifted his pistol and pointed it directly at Hoop's head. Hoop waited to hear the click of the trigger and for it all to be over. Freedom from the shitter, from this godless white man's war, no more secrets to keep and no one believing he was a coward.

The major's eyes were dark and full of hate. He wanted to pull the trigger. Hoop could see the hate but he didn't. Hoop stepped towards the barrel of the gun and the Nazi, rather than fire his weapon, took a step backwards, lowering it and then raising it again. A deep murmur came from amongst the British holding their ground behind the prisoners' line. Hoop stepped again toward Major Haas, who continued to backpedal.

"*Nein!*" he shouted, finally getting a hold of himself and striking Hoop with the butt of the pistol's handle. Hoop felt the blow at the front of his forehead. It was followed swiftly by another and then another. As Hoop went down on one knee, the final blow sent him into the dust. What followed Hoop couldn't say but he heard the discharge of a pistol and the rattle of larger calibre weapons from the lookout towers above them. Blood ran down his cheek.

When Hoop came to it was the sergeant's face and voice that replaced the ringing in his ears.

"You're a tricky customer if ever I've seen one," said the sergeant. Hoop wasn't sure what that meant.

"Hut 10, 09:00 hours. You wanted to see the commander, well you've got your appointment." The sergeant lifted Hoop to his feet. "Shower first."

The men were making their way back to the huts, plenty of them looking over their shoulders in his direction while medics lifted Charlie's body onto a stretcher. He hadn't saved Charlie, but he'd proved his theory. Standartenführer Richter had made him untouchable.

46

CARPE DIEM

1942, September 29 (09:00h)
Hut 10, German Prisoner-of-War (POW) Camp,
Europa Point, Rock of Gibraltar

Hoop stood outside Hut 10, showered and wearing a clean uniform. The lavender soap smell was better than the shit but it reminded him of Haas. The image of the major backing away from him in fear returned to make him smile. The sergeant's smile seemed odd on his face, he wasn't used to seeing it. Maybe he'd warmed to him since the parade ground incident. The killing in the yard had resulted in a major meeting. Senior members of the camp filed out of Hut 10 past Hoop. Three greeted him politely while the other two scowled. Several men had introduced themselves to him on his arrival back in Hut 5. One had even made him a cup of tea. He had split camp opinion, that much was clear. *Was he a hero or a traitor?* Honestly, he wasn't sure himself.

The last out was the hairy officer. He closed the door to the hut and stood in front of Hoop.

"If you think we're all convinced by that piece of theatre, think again. I don't know what your game is but I know you're still a liar. No one trusts you here." Hoop walked around the hairy officer who stood his ground and glared. The parade ground incident had given him this chance to meet Stern face to face and proved he had leverage with Standartenführer Richter. Haas didn't shoot him and that could only be on the SS man's order. He couldn't waste that power. His life depended on it.

He knocked on the door of Hut 10. Pip opened and reluctantly invited him in.

"Sergeant Fundi, as requested, sir." Pip's introduction was audibly laced with distrust.

Group Captain Stern stood by the small table in the hut. His uniform was cleaned and pressed, his hair combed and his boots polished. There were blemishes here and there in his presentation but he was head and shoulders the best turned-out POW in the camp.

"Hoop, isn't it?"

"Yes, sir," replied Hoop.

"You're causing a lot of trouble in this camp, you know that, don't you, Hoop?"

"Yes, sir."

"I don't mind telling you that your whisky-fuelled meetings with Standartenführer Richter were known to us before you arrived so spritely with a bag of German tuck. As for today's debacle, quite frankly I'm dumbfounded as to what to make of you. Are you one of our chaps or not?"

"Begging your pardon, sir, but what I have to tell you is for your ears only."

Pip behind him scoffed. "I can deal with this for you, sir."

"You need to hear this, Group Captain," Hoop added.

"You have a full schedule, sir," continued Pip. "Why don't I listen to what Sergeant Fundi has for you and bring you up to date after squaddies?" Hoop couldn't take the risk of sharing what he knew with anyone but Stern. Anyway, he now had a personal agenda and that required Stern too.

"I wouldn't make such a request without it being a matter of life and death, sir." Hoop searched for a demeanour of gravitas. *Without Stern nothing was possible.*

"A man may have died due to your antics this morning, Sergeant Fundi. You're aware of that, I assume?" Stern's tone matched his name.

"Yes, sir." Hoop agreed but he felt blaming Charlie's death on him was unfair. He'd risked his life, on a wild theory, to try and save him. So what if he had ulterior motives, saving Charlie had also been in his thinking.

"That's right," snapped Pip. "You're a bloody traitor, and when this is over you'll be damn well shot for it." He softened his tone after a glance towards his CO. "Can't expect a negro to act like a gentleman, sir. Never did. Never will."

Hoop ignored Pip, never taking his eyes off Stern until the camp CO turned his back and looked out of the window.

Pip seized upon the nonverbal cue, opening the hut door. "Confine Sergeant Fundi to the barracks until further notice."

"Wait," said Stern without turning back around. "Give us the room please, Captain Smith."

Pip appeared to hate every syllable of his commanding officer's request with every fibre of his being but the use of Pip's rank made clear the order wasn't up for debate.

"Right you are, sir." The words coming out of Pip's mouth were regulation but his eyes spat venom at Hoop. "We'll be watching from the window, boy. No funny business." The door closed and a furious Pip appeared outside at the window.

"Coloured," is a better word," said Stern, turning from the window, hands behind his back. "You have two minutes, and it better be good. Carpe diem, Sergeant Fundi…"

Hoop began to speak.

Pip watched through the window of Hut 10. After the first minute, Stern took a seat. Two minutes later, Hoop was offered one. The next half an hour slipped by slowly at the window for Pip as the two men could be seen exchanging thoughts as close, physically, as a courting couple on a park bench. Finally, Hoop and Stern stood up. The Group Captain put out his hand. Hoop took it. The short shake confirmed an agreement. Pip, exasperated at the window, couldn't for the life of him imagine what agreement had been made.

47

HAY'S LEVEL

1942, September 29 (10:20h)
Hay's Level Tunnel Entrance, Rock of Gibraltar

The bullet ricocheted off the wall, and fragments dusted Richter and two SS guards crouched beside him. Daily updates on the progress of various tunnel entrance sieges were no substitute for seeing first-hand how the British were keeping him from reporting total control of Gibraltar. He needed something positive to share with his superiors in Berlin, anything at all, to illustrate progress. Friends in the SS had warned him he was running out of time. There had already been talk of replacing him. He'd been advised that taking the Rock was the easy part but British resistance from inside the network of tunnels would always prevent him from claiming to have fully secured Gibraltar. He hated to admit it, even to himself, but that's exactly what had happened. *Why hadn't he listened to the warning? He'd put himself in this position.*

Movement around the Rock for his men was more of a challenge than ever. They were being picked off by British snipers systematically. It had been hard to determine exactly where those snipers were firing from although his men had narrowed it down to 'danger areas' mostly thanks to the bodies mounting up at those locations. He'd ordered the Spanish under his command to take up guard duty, rather than use his men whose morale was being seriously affected. He'd been informed too of 'talk', some of his officers wanted off the Rock. "Leave the damn thing to the British,", was the popular opinion. Jokes about getting shot on the way back to the barracks were too true to be funny anymore. There was real fear. He'd ordered Major Haas to punish those men spreading dissent amongst the ranks but either Haas was ignoring the order or it wasn't working. Desertions would follow, he was sure of it.

Unhappy men on the Rock, irritated superiors in Berlin. He felt the hairs on the back of his neck lift at the thought of soon sitting on a Panzer tank, north of Stalingrad.

The entrance to Hay's Level tunnel perfectly illustrated the Germans' problem. Sealed by a double set of metal doors, it had lookouts cut into the wall on either side. Major Haas had blown through the doors but beyond them was a bend in the entrance and another set of doors. The opening was too small for a tank; numerous attacks had ended in failure. The British had a contingency defence in place for every type of assault his men had so far undertaken. They needed a new approach.

Another series of British bullets hit the wall above Richter. He'd seen enough. Hanging around here he might get shot by accident. Ducking low, he scampered back to the safety of the Moorish Castle walls.

He pulled a piece of paper from his pocket. The printed words were pale and the paper thin, trace-like, as were all the communications he received from Berlin. This one was heavily creased and crumpled having been rolled up into a ball and tossed into his waste paper basket. He'd retrieved it having come to terms with its contents.

New orders from Berlin: *'Disrupting British intelligence gathering was now his number one priority on the Rock.'* He'd rolled it up and thrown it at the corner of his office in frustration. They had no idea in Berlin of the problems he was facing in Gibraltar. He was doing his best.

It was easy to write an order from a chair in the Fatherland but executing it here on the Rock was something else altogether.

Somehow the British still knew about every aeroplane that landed on Gibraltar's runway and the name of every Axis ship that passed through the strait. The Abwehr military intelligence service had confirmed the unbroken stream of information the British had maintained despite him having taken most of the Rock. They were spying on the airfield and the waterways for sure but from where? All the apparent locations of observation from inside the Rock, those areas held by the British as vantage points, had been obscured or blocked up where possible. The north-facing Rock didn't have views of the Strait so they weren't getting their ship movements from there. Every letterbox opening carved into the Rock that his men had discovered, received SS snipers and grenades when important convoys made their way past Gibraltar. So where was British intelligence getting its detailed information from?

A Spanish resistance movement, backed by the Americans, had developed quickly after the Führer's deal with the Spanish leader and they'd made their headquarters the port of Algeciras just across the bay, but British intelligence was also operating somewhere inside the Rock, he was sure of it. He called a pale freckle-faced junior SS officer forward.

"Get a stethoscope," he ordered. The officer looked blankly at him.

"Take three of your best men and listen to the walls at the top of the Rock." The officer nodded without question.

"Where exactly, Herr Standartenführer?" The question was reasonable and Richter knew his answer wasn't.

"Everywhere. The British are up there somewhere, they're looking and they're transmitting what they see, find them." The freckle-faced officer marched confidently away and Richter was impressed. It seemed a hopeless task. His chances of succeeding looked extremely limited.

Standing next to his armoured car Richter reached inside his jacket pocket for his pack of Juno cigarettes. The pocket was empty. He'd forgotten again that he'd smoked his last. His craving for tobacco was overwhelming. It was killing him. *When would the damn things arrive?* Yanking heavily on the vehicle door handle, Richter climbed back in.

His thoughts turned to Hubert and the secret entrances the map-drawing negro, apparently, *"knew nothing about."* The British had softened him up, it was time to grant his request for another meeting. He wasn't going to end up at the Russian front because the *Schweinehund* British wouldn't turn on their comrades. The thought stopped Richter in his tracks. He had an idea. He rolled down his window and called over a guard.

"Tell Major Haas to select three British POWs from the camp. Three we can do without."

48

GET BACK TO YOUR POST

1942, September 29 (18:30h)
Main Chamber, Stay Behind Cave, Rock of Gibraltar

Carter left Logan on the bicycle in the main chamber peddling furiously to charge one of the 12-volt batteries and headed out past the toilet and radio room, up the steps towards the east wall lookout. Time on the bicycle was doing them all good, it was relieving tensions, like nothing else in the cave was.

He didn't feel well but the sight of Maria sitting with her back to him, binoculars held high up to her eyes, was a tonic. He was quiet enough for her not to hear him in the dark. With both her arms lifted the army-issue slacks were pulled tight around her buttocks. Carter shook off the image, turned right and headed up the next flight of stairs. He didn't want to think about her in that way. He had no right to do so but it was impossible not to. He'd caught Bunny watching her, Logan must have seen them both. It was only a matter of time before the looking was going to cause a problem.

He headed down the tunnel. There was churning in his stomach, *nausea, brought on by nerves maybe?* Albert was silhouetted at the west wall lookout. The light entered the dark tunnel beyond him. Albert was focused on his hands. Carter was upon him before Albert heard him coming and he did the strangest thing. An unnatural thing. He straightened his head, directed his ear to the tunnel, confirmed he was being approached and put one hand quickly into his pocket. Only then did he turn around.

"Thought I'd relieve you early." Carter looked at the boy's hand in his pocket. He wanted to address the strange behaviour light-heartedly but the stiffness of the boy's demeanour persuaded him otherwise. It was a secret, whatever it might be. *Was Albert allowed a secret?* They all had their secrets.

"Great, thanks," said Albert as if he had nothing to hide except whatever was in his pocket.

"Everything all right, lad?" Albert wasn't biting. "You know that you can tell me anything that's on your mind, don't you? I'm your doctor, anything you tell me would be in complete confidence." Carter's look at Albert's pocket confirmed the invitation.

"I'll certainly do that, sir," and off down the tunnel into the darkness went Albert. Carter picked up the binoculars and looked out over the bay. Young people were complicated. Way more than in his day.

The air was fresh on the other side of the slit in the rock. There was a clean honesty about the breeze that made him take a deep breath. He'd tried to normalise the living experience after early chaos, bring some stability to the group, and put them at ease with each other, but it hadn't worked. Even Albert was hiding things now.

"There is one thing, sir." Albert's voice came out of the darkness. It made the hair stand up on the back of Carter's neck. "Christ, Albert!" The boy stepped slowly back into the light.

"What is it?" Carter's brow furrowed from the startling and his heart was up to double time. Hand still in one pocket and glancing nervously over his shoulder Albert took another step towards his doctor. He whispered.

"Before Commander Gale..." The boy paused. The word finally came: "Died." Albert took a breath and carried on more confidently, "The commander asked me to send a message, to the Admiralty. He requested..." The boy paused again and lowered his voice further, "background checks on Maria and Major Warlock, sir. I just thought you should know," continued Albert.

Standard security procedure on Windy's part, thought Carter.

Suddenly landed with a couple of strangers he knew nothing about. As they were unable to receive communications, the results wouldn't be offering any kind of answer anytime soon, but Carter nodded in appreciation of Albert's confidence in the matter.

Although he'd finished speaking Carter could see from the look on the lad's face that there was something else. The hand, still in his pocket, began to fidget and he snatched a glance at it.

"What is it, Albert?" Carter softened his tone to coax Albert out of his shell.

"It's just…" The boy took another look over his shoulder and lowered his voice.

"What's the point, sir? We stand here for hours but what's the point? I saw just a single tanker yesterday. That's it. How is my intelligence gathering sheet with one unknown tanker on it helping the war effort?" Albert's tone was deeply disillusioned.

"Albert. The Admiralty needs every piece of information we can give them. Everything. No matter how small or insignificant it might seem." Carter tried to sound upbeat although Albert's shoulders sank, and he shook his head in bewilderment.

"I couldn't even be sure it was a tanker. How does that help?" In truth, Carter felt it too. Pushing that bloody aerial out of the rock religiously they were transmitting what they'd seen but without the ability to receive transmissions they had no idea if the Admiralty was getting their intelligence, let alone utilising it. A fear he wasn't about to share with Albert.

"Let's say it was a tanker and the Admiralty sees your intelligence sheet. A single tanker might mean the Navy sank the other five it was travelling with." Carter added a little more optimism to his tone and kept going. "Or it might mean the Jerries are planning some operation that needs extra fuel. We don't know. It's not our job to know but someone at the Admiralty does. It's our job to make sure London has as much information as we can give them. We just focus on doing our bit." Albert finally nodded. It was the best Carter could hope for. "The

Admiralty couldn't have gathered what we've sent to them so far in any other way." Carter decided to quit while he was ahead.

Without another word the boy walked away.

Carter took a deep breath and scanned the vessels docked in the harbour below. Windy's death had hit them all hard but none of them more than Albert. The boy had idolised Windy. Albert had deferred to Windy for not just what to do but how to act and what to think. Windy's death had set Albert adrift. He'd turn inward. The only one he seemed to relate to now was Maria. *Maria and Albert, what on earth did they have in common?* The thought of Maria led Carter back to the shard of missing glass. Did she have it to cut her wrists? He had no reason to think that Albert had the missing piece. Why would he want it? So why was he placing the glass now in Albert's pocket? What would Albert be doing at the lookout with a broken shard of glass? He looked out across the bay of Algeciras as the last rays of sunlight streamed through the lookout. They reflected momentarily off the glass of the binoculars and a thought occurred to Carter. It was ridiculous. It added to his nausea.

Carter heard voices!

He stood perfectly still. He couldn't quite make out where they were coming from. *Outside?* He pushed his ear up against the lookout slit but all he could hear was the wind. He leaned away from the lookout. *There!* He heard them again. Carter walked a few feet back up the tunnel. It couldn't be coming from downstairs.

This time it sounded like a shout. He quickened his pace back towards the staircase.

"Let go of me." It was Maria's voice. Carter ran, almost falling as he leapt down the tunnel steps.

"Get off me!" Maria's shout was loud enough to wake the dead.

Carter bounced off the wall, stumbling back into the spot he'd seen Maria. She stood on the steps, Logan holding both her arms, Albert, wide-eyed, gripping one of Logan's. Bunny arrived at the same moment from the main chamber, the same dumbfounded look on his face.

"What the hell's going on?" whispered Carter as a shout. Logan released his hold over Maria. All four of them stood on the staircase, eyes blazing in a silent Mexican standoff. Bizarre, thought Carter, but not funny. Not funny at all. *The whole bloody mission was at stake!*

"Logan?" Carter's raspy whisper hissed at him for an answer.

"Get back to your posts," replied Logan. His eyes were red and flaming.

"Bloody pushed her against the wall didn't he?" Albert sprang to Maria's defence.

"I could hear you from the west wall lookout, for God's sake." Carter felt sick. "Are you out of your damn minds?" His voice was strained with muted emotion.

"Get back to your posts, all of you. That's an order," repeated Logan. His tone told Carter he'd made a mistake trying to give Logan command. Albert and Bunny ignored it too.

"If I can hear you, all the way up there, the Germans can hear you too. Are you trying to get us all killed?" said Carter. He could see Albert and Bunny preparing to physically restrain their commanding officer, all he needed to do was say the word. But relieving Logan from the imaginary command he's given him would only make things in the cave worse. *Wouldn't it?* Logan let go of Maria and took a step away. His demeanour changed in an instant. Another personality inhabited his frame and even his voice was different. Polite. Kind.

"You're right of course, old chap. What was I thinking?" Maria rubbed her wrist and Carter saw Logan's backpedal visibly ease Bunny and Albert's body language. Carter, still feeling sick to his stomach, lifted his palms in a silent plea, an invitation for Logan to recognise that he was correct. He wanted to strangle Logan, right there on the stairs, but he also needed to get hold of himself. *Had the Germans on the outside heard Maria?* Continuing to give Logan a hard time wouldn't save them either way.

Then, without warning Carter vomited on the staircase. He was about to speak, something about a pot of tea, but the thought of tea caused him to retch. The trajectory of his vomit missed the others but only thanks to his last-minute turn towards the main chamber. Half-digested powered egg slapped against the stone steps and splashed the lower tunnel walls. He retched a second time, and more contents from his stomach hit the steps. His second retch also released his rectum, and Carter soiled himself. Then came the sound of another, Bunny was also puking. His embarrassment turned suddenly to fear.

49

WRETCHED

1942, September 30 (09:16h)
Toilets, Stay Behind Cave, Rock of Gibraltar

Carter retched again, his head in the toilet. A long drawn-out retch that pulled on his arse like a string was attached to it. Nothing came out of his mouth again but he could taste the bile. He lifted his forehead from the toilet bowl. 'Elson Manufacturing Company Limited, Sanitary Engineers, 21 Clapham Road, London' read the porcelain. *The toilets came from London.* How many more times would he vomit? He'd lost count. He was exhausted. He just wanted it over. The bowl was cool on his forehead. It was nice but the feeling wouldn't last. Nausea would return soon. Logan retched and his foot kicked Carter. They were side by side. Logan had his head down the other toilet but unlike Carter, he was still managing to bring solids up. In just a few hours they had all fallen foul of it. Whatever 'it' was... Logan, Bunny, he and Maria were all in and out of the toilet. Only Albert wasn't sick at both ends. Carter wiped his mouth on his sleeve and stood up. The smell in that small room wasn't helping. He had to get out of there. He pumped the flush system three times until he could no longer see what had come out of him.

"Water?" The question brought a sorry nod from Logan before he retched again. Carter stepped out of the toilet and closed the door. No sooner had he done so than Bunny pushed past him to enter, vomiting before arriving at the toilet bowl. Probably over Logan, he wasn't going back to check, he'd be back there soon enough.

He made his way slowly across the main chamber. The cup of water he'd poured Maria was still on the table. She hadn't got up to drink it as she'd agreed. Carter picked up the cup and took it around the wall of boxes that secluded Maria's bunk.

"You have to hydrate, Maria," he said but there was silence, no reply. Stretched out on her bunk, Maria was wrapped tightly in two blankets. She appeared to be shivering. Carter put his hand on her forehead. "You'll be fine," he said, although the truth was he had no idea what had made them all so sick and Maria's condition didn't help. *Would they both be fine? Maybe.* Carter handed Maria the cup. She reached her arm out of the cocoon she'd created for herself, sat up, and took the handle of the cup but wouldn't sip.

"I'll drink some later, I promise."

Maria was young and strong and gastroenteritis was strangely common during pregnancy.

"Any cramps or abdominal pain?" he asked. Maria shook her head. She looked like a sausage roll wrapped up in all those blankets. "Can I have a quick look just to be sure?" Maria began to unwrap herself from the twisted warmth. She pulled the army-issue shirt up to expose the pale smooth skin on her stomach and legs. Carter put his hands on her lower abdominals and pushed.

"Pain?" Maria shook her head. He moved his hands and tried the same again. He wanted to be thorough. That was why he was trying it again. Maria's skin was soft and warm. Her smell rose from inside the cocoon she'd created and he noticed scratches on her knee. She'd fallen over and not mentioned it. *He was her doctor and he needed to examine her fully. There was nothing immoral or untoward in that!*

"All good," said Carter, finally. He tucked Maria's blanket firmly under her mattress and caught her eye in doing so. She was worried, he could see that.

The baby was fine, so far. It was his instinct to feel pleased that the pregnancy was not in danger but he knew what everybody was thinking because it had crossed his mind too. *Would Maria's child be stillborn?* Was this the moment that the problem of the baby was about to, 'go away on its own'?

Hoping for a child to die was wrong. Under any circumstance. He couldn't get past that and he was glad of it.

Carter poured Logan and Bunny two tin cups of water and left them outside the toilet door. Albert was still in the radio room fiddling with cables. He could see his back through the almost closed door. *Why wasn't he sick?* Young Albert seemed to have some sort of immunity. Living in such close quarters he'd been exposed to the same bacteria. *Why hadn't it had the same effect? His youth?* Either way, Carter was disappointed in the boy. Not for staying healthy but for failing to step up. He had neither taken on the extra lookout shifts to cover his sick team members not being on duty nor offered any medical assistance. Albert had shrunk in the face of difficulty, continuing to hide away in the radio room. Not even Maria, who'd gone in to talk to him when she was well enough, was able to inspire the lad. If he didn't know better he'd have thought the boy wanted them all to suffer.

Carter felt the nausea return. It wouldn't be long before he'd be back in the toilet. He poured himself another water and sat down at the table. They looked to him to make them better but the truth was he had no idea where this gastroenteritis had come from. They were eating tinned food. *A bad tin?* One tin wouldn't have affected them all so devastatingly. Treating the sick while being sick himself was becoming impossible. He struggled to think straight. All he wanted to do was lie on his bunk and sleep.

Logan came out of the toilet leaving Bunny retching alone. He looked awful. Pale, gaunt, thin-lipped. He paused to glance at his reflection in the broken mirror before taking a seat at the table.

"We need to keep the head clean. I know it's difficult but the mess in there could lead to something worse."

"Worse?!" replied Logan indignantly.

"You need to stay hydrated." Carter poured him water.

"That's all you've got for us? More water!" Logan raised his voice.

Carter wondered when somebody was going to break, mentally. They'd been vomiting all night his patients were worn out. They couldn't take it anymore and honestly neither could he.

"You're the doctor. What good are you to us if you can't do what you were put in here to do?" Logan's tone was angry and resentful.

Carter's nausea rose in line with his frustration. It hurt because it was true. He hadn't yet tracked the source of the sickness. He couldn't just wave a magic wand and make them all well again. It wasn't fair to blame him.

There were no 'magic bullets' in his medical kit, what the Americans were calling these new antibiotics. They were sure to be available by the time they made it out of the cave. *If* they made it out. *Until then, well...*

"I'm doing everything I can." Carter tried to remain calm. Losing it with Logan now wasn't going to help.

"Well, it's not enough. Whatever it is you say you're doing isn't working, is it?" Carter had tiptoed around Logan ever since he'd arrived, for the good of the mission, for the morale of the team; that was his job too. Keep the boat from rocking. His head told him Logan wasn't thinking straight, he was sick. But they were all sick, including him... What gave Logan the right to spew his frustration? He'd had just about all he was going to take from the selfish upper-class twit. He'd tolerated his childish behaviour long enough and he wasn't going to roll over this time. The morale of the team was in the toilet anyway, so what did it matter?

"I've had just about enough from you," Carter said, squaring up to Logan.

The radio room door slammed shut, as Albert sealed himself off from the conflict.

"Who the hell do you think you are?" Carter went on. It was too late to stop himself. It had stuck in his craw. He was letting go, he knew it would all come out now. He'd opened the floodgates and he couldn't close them again. He didn't want to.

"He's right, Tommy, you have to do something. We can't go on like this." Bunny's voice stopped Carter in his tracks. Bunny came slowly towards them across the cork floor. Carter couldn't quite believe his ears – Bunny was siding with Logan, against him!

"We could all die here." Maria's voice was weak but devastating as it came from behind her wall of boxes. It cut him like a knife. All of them. They had all turned against him. Despite everything he'd done for them and was trying to do. He wanted to vomit but not from the sickness.

Bunny sat down at the table and poured himself another water.

"Screw you all!" That was it, thought Carter. He'd done everything he could think of. He didn't know why they were sick, and if he did, didn't they think he would do something about it? He'd expect as much from Logan but Bunny and Maria? His anger mixed with his nausea and Carter's usual calm exterior cracked. He stood up abruptly, knocking two cups of water over the table.

"Treat your bloody selves!" Carter knew he would regret what he was about to say but he'd reached the end of his tether. As the first words of his rant formed on his tongue, his eye watched the spilt water run off the table and onto the cork floor. The table was pretty clean and they did their best to keep the floor that way too but the floor collected dust easily and so you couldn't eat off it. Carter had all the body posture of a man about to lose his temper but he was just standing there looking down at the water dripping off the table onto the floor. When he finally looked back at Bunny and Logan they all shared bewilderment. They must have thought he'd lost his mind. Maria, obviously confused by the long silence, stepped out from behind her boxes to see what was going on.

"The floor," said Carter. He knew he had to say something and those were the words that came out. The revelation dropped the first domino of a theory, his mind was still trying to catch up. Questions and answers completely replaced frustration and anger.

"The water," he said calmly, stepping forward and running his fingers across the wet table. Bunny put his tin cup down and pushed it away with a new look of understanding and disdain.

50

WON'T TAKE A MINUTE

It had to be the water, what else could it be? Renewed in spirit, Carter walked quickly to the radio room. He opened the door hoping not to find Albert in a personal moment. Luckily he wasn't. Carter felt like he was trespassing. Albert's ownership of the space was going to have to come to an end.

"Do you have a screwdriver?" Carter asked from the doorway, impatiently.

Albert turned just enough in his chair to show interest. "What size?"

"The large one," replied Carter.

"Maria has it," said Albert turning his focus back to the cables in front of him. Carter saw what he wanted at the back of the desk, stepped forward, reached over Albert's shoulder, took it and left the radio room. Albert followed, somewhat reluctantly. Carter crossed the main chamber, walked straight past Bunny, Logan and Maria, rounded the corner of Maria's box wall and grabbed the leg of her bunk bed. He pulled the frame away from the wall, and it slid silently with ease over the cork floor. He pushed it sideways until they could all see a square-shaped metal inspection door hatch, painted the same off-white colour as the walls. Carter put the screwdriver into the seam between the wall and the door and levered the door open enough to get his fingers inside and pulled. Hinged on one side, it swung open. There was nothing but darkness on the other side of the hatch hole in the wall.

"Torch please, Bunny?" Bunny ran to the radio room. There was a cool dampness coming from the darkness on the other side of the hatch.

"Shall I go?" asked Logan. Carter was surprised by the offer. It was the first time Logan had seemed keen to suffer hardship for the good of the mission. It would be a difficult crawl in the darkness. *Maybe he'd been too hard on Logan?*

"Hold on, we better get Commander Gale's revolver, just in case. Where is it?"

Carter's optimism towards Logan faded at the question.

"Won't take me a minute," replied Carter as Bunny returned with the flashlight. Logan, Bunny and a shocked-looking Maria were standing just a few feet behind Carter as he crawled through the square hatch into the darkness beyond.

The rectangular-shaped construction they called home was just a sleeve inside a raw carved-out cave. The space between their flat walls and the jagged rock beyond was almost a metre. Carter's torch illuminated the narrow space with its uneven floor. With one hand holding the torch and the other sliding along the cool rock, Carter edged his way to the corner. He'd seen the construction plans and knew that the main chamber had a pitched roof. The trusses were visible on the inside. The rock being porous, it rained on the inside: that's what filled the water tank and the roof kept them dry. Ten thousand imperial gallons could be captured and refilled by mother nature when it rained.

At the corner, the narrow channel turned at a right angle. Carter pointed his torch down the back wall of their cave construction, and both walls disappeared into the darkness. Both walls were flat, and one of them was made of steel. The water tank. Carter ran his hand along the tank. It was cold to the touch. A pipe protruded out of the bottom of the metal sheet and ran directly to the main chamber's sleeve wall. On the other side was the wash pit faucet he knew so well.

"Need some help?" Logan's voice filled the chamber, startling Carter. Its echo reverberated off the hard rock walls. *For God's sake, man, keep it down,* thought Carter as he shushed Logan with a long-drawn exasperated hush. He felt sick again. Emotion had kept nausea at bay but it was back. The tank wall was fifteen feet high, minimum. Beyond the pipe that fed water to them was a ladder fixed to the side of the tank. Stepping over the pipe he made his way to the ladder. The torch dropped into his breast pocket, he started to climb. The light swayed from side to side as he made his way up. He was careful not to slip his footing in the darkness. He wanted to vomit, either from the exertion or the fast-moving light, but he held it in. If he puked on the ladder he might fall. It was far enough down to cause him a serious injury.

He felt the coolness of open space and a large volume of water before he saw the final rung of the ladder in the low light. Pulling the torch from his breast pocket he shined it out in front of him. Square in shape, about ten feet across and almost full, the tank was completely open at its top. *Of course, it had to catch the rain.* The light from his torch reflected off a black cable, high above the tank. One end disappeared into their roof, the other, through a hole in the wall in the direction of Lord Airey's Shelter. *Their electricity supply.* The water surface, stretched out in front of him in the low light, was like a sheet of black glass, a vat of oil. He dipped his hand, breaking the surface and causing ripples to run in small waves to all four corners. Shining the torch corner to corner he couldn't see anything amiss. *Had he been wrong? Was the water fine?* If it wasn't the water then what the hell was it? The water was the only link between them. Albert drank a lot of tea but very little plain water. He didn't like cold water. It had to be the water. Carter scanned the top of the tank again with his torch. Nothing. Below the surface maybe? Something sunk at the bottom? But what? If there was, how would he get it out? Climb in and swim to the bottom? Even if he could hold his breath to get down there. There'd be no light and the tank was huge; he'd never find it. If it was there at all.

What if they emptied the tank? Ran the water out of the wash pit faucet until it was almost empty then maybe he could jump in and wade around looking? But how would he get out after? A rope tied to the ladder maybe? What about the wasted water? Did he really want to wade around their drinking water looking for something that probably wasn't there anyway? Carter dropped his head to the rim of the tank and rested it in disappointment. It was then that he smelt it. Putrid, he knew the smell all too well. Methane. The smell of death. Just a whiff, nothing more. It made him want to vomit. There was no mistaking that smell. Carter ran his torch along the edge of the tank, more slowly this time. *There!* Something floating, almost completely submerged, just a little hump resting against the side of the tank no more than six feet from him on the ladder. He undid the lace of his right boot, slipped it off and dropped it to the floor. The sock followed. Climbing to the top of the ladder he perched on the edge of the tank, rolled up his trouser leg, swung his right leg over and dropped it into the cold water. With the torch back in his breast pocket, Carter shunted himself slowly along the edge of the tank. There it was again, the putrid smell stronger now. He reached for the torch and shone it down into the tank. There it was. About the size of his shoe, silky smooth from the water matting its hair. A dead rat. Carter reached down and grabbed it. He retched as the rodent came up and out of the water. The methane was overpowering, thick in the air, rancid. It raced up his nostrils and he could taste it, dry and putrid on his tongue. He tossed the rat over the side and down into the channel, vomiting after it.

He tried not to vomit into the water. That was his mistake. He knew it the moment he made it. Balance was lost and with it the torch into the tank as he grabbed furiously for the edge. The space plunged into darkness, his hand missed its target and he fell. The wrong side. An involuntary sound of surprise came out of his mouth. Down into the channel between the tank and their hut wall fell Doctor Carter.

The impact knocked the wind out of him in a guttural moan. Adrenaline removed most of the pain but he couldn't breathe, couldn't catch a breath. He rolled around on the uneven surface trying to get his bearings. His ankle, his knee, his ribs, his wrist, they'd all taken a hit. Finally oxygen returned to his lungs and he lay there gasping in the pitch darkness, vomit still in his mouth and nose.

"Doc!?" It was Bunny's voice.

He was coming. Carter could see the light flickering as Bunny approached the corner with another torch. He put his hand in front of his face and found there was blood on it. He had no idea how serious his injuries were, although the fingers and thumb on his right hand were still where they should be. He lay his head back down on the hard surface. Something hairy touched his cheek. The rat. This time there was the smell of sulphur dioxide, worse than the methane, and he vomited again as Bunny's torch blinded him.

"Jesus!" said Bunny, straddling him. Carter reached for the rat and tossed it as far as he could but the smell had filled every one of his cavities and it wasn't going away anytime soon. "Can ya stand, man?" Bunny's voice echoed throughout the chamber. Carter just moaned in reply, looking for the words. *Was he okay? He had no idea. No, he wasn't okay.*

"Bunny?" Albert came around the corner with another lamp, panic in his voice.

They wrapped their arms around Carter and lifted him to his feet. He couldn't put his right foot down, it was too painful.

"Dead rat," said Carter, "dead rat in the tank." Bunny and Albert didn't answer as they dragged Carter. His bare foot hurt almost as much as his knee, ankle and ribs as they rounded the corner of the brick sleeve wall and edged towards the light of the hatch and Logan's head pushed through it.

"What happened?"

"He's hurt," replied Bunny, irritated.

Pulled through the hatch, Carter lay on his back looking up at the whitewashed ceiling and the iron beams that stretched across it, as his eyes readjusted to the light in the main chamber.

"It's the water!" Never had he been prouder to give a diagnosis. They doubted him and he'd proved them all wrong. *He'd found the source of the sickness, hadn't he?* His wet right leg dripped water onto the cork floor, and his right knee dripped blood.

51

FETCH A BEAKER

1942, September 30 (09:56h)
Main Chamber, Stay Behind Cave, Rock of Gibraltar

Carter yelped in his chair as Maria turned the bandage around his ankle.

"Too tight." This time Carter was irritated. She'd made the same mistake on his knee and wrist already. She wasn't listening. "Too tight will cut off the circulation, too loose and it won't support." Maria released some tension as Bunny, Albert and Logan looked on. He could still smell the stench of the dead rat in his nostrils and taste it on his tongue. Adrenaline was replaced by the pain. He'd broken a rib maybe, and his wrist and ankle were more likely strained. He'd been lucky. Cut and swollen but hopefully no long-term damage. He'd cleaned and dressed everything and prescribed himself rest. That was the good news; the bad news was the water.

"So what have we got from the water?" Logan asked.

"Leptospirosis, maybe Weil's disease," replied Carter. The men looked blankly at him.

"Bacteria in the water, leptospira?" Maria surprised him.

"That's right. The symptoms are flu-like." He wanted to say that's what confused him but he knew they didn't want excuses, only answers.

"Now you know what it is, can you treat it?" Logan got to the point.

"We can empty the tank and replace the water," replied Carter.

"That's not what I asked. Do you have anything in that medicine cabinet to make us feel better?" Carter wasn't going to lie to them.

"We don't have antibiotics," he said.

"Anti what?" replied Logan.

"Never mind." Carter started again. "Not drinking any more of the water is our way forward." The answer was honest but it wasn't what they wanted to hear.

"Will that stop the vomiting?" Bunny's question was more of a plea.

"Eventually."

"How do we replace the water in the tank?" asked Albert, although Carter sensed he knew the answer.

"The same way we filled it. Rainwater." Bunny answered for him.

"You're saying we're without clean water until it rains?" Logan's question came with the tone of the team leader. Carter nodded.

"Well, that's it isn't it?" Logan walked into the middle of the room. "This mission is over. We can't survive here without water."

"We'll need to boil all the water we drink." Bunny and Albert stayed silent. "At least until the tank is refilled." Bunny knew better than anyone what that meant. He'd trained them all in the use of the Benghazi stove; it ran on Flimsy fuel. Four gallons in each Flimsy. Albert's hot tea-drinking habit had been the greatest strain on their supply so far. When they ran out of fuel there would be no more hot food or worse, for Albert, tea, for the rest of the mission. Boiling any more water would go through the fuel pretty quickly.

"How many Flimsys do we have?" Logan was doing the maths too.

"Five," Bunny answered, looking at Carter.

"How long will they last?" Nobody answered Maria.

"It might not rain for another month or more!" Logan provided the worst-case scenario.

"It will." Carter's answer was for reassurance purposes only.

They all sat silently. He agreed with Logan but he couldn't say out loud that it was over. They couldn't survive there without water. They could survive on what they could boil, for a while, but if it didn't rain soon, Operation Tracer was over.

* * *

By midnight the same day the cave was full of receptacles holding water. Every cup, can, bucket, or anything at all that would hold water was filled, covered and laid out along the north wall of the main chamber. Albert had pulled pieces of the radio equipment that were shaped well enough to hold water and filled them, some not much larger than a thimble. Carter had done the same with his medical store. Bunny had lit the Benghazi stove and Maria had started the process of boiling every drop they could hold. Some of the receptacles still emanated steam in the corner of the hut, cooling. Carter stood by the wash pit faucet looking back at the ramshackle store of purified water and containers. That was it. Once they'd drunk them, the condensed milk and tinned juices they would be out of consumable fluid until it rained.

They all watched as Carter turned the faucet and the water began to run, out of the faucet, into the square-spaced wash pit and down the waste pipe. It sounded like the fountain of a small stream.

Too agitated and nervous to sit, Carter walked over to the table.

"How long can we last with what we have?" asked Maria.

"On average we would each lose about two pints of water from urination, sweat glands and breathing over twenty hours." Carter looked at what they had stacked against the wall and pondered. "We'll need to ration and so let's say we replenish a pint per day rather than two, to start with."

"So, we're going to drink half as much as we need." Logan sounded sceptical.

"Yes. Except for Maria. I suggest she gets a pint and a half, considering her condition. She's drinking for two. Okay with everybody?" They all agreed although Bunny did not wholeheartedly.

"You're going to be dehydrated. That means you'll pee less, find it hard to focus and concentrate, might suffer headaches, and you'll

221

certainly feel weak and tired. We'll need to keep exercise to a minimum, so no long sessions on the bicycle. Let's revise the roster, and split up the usual rotation to reduce the time we each peddle. Albert, please make the adjustments." The boy nodded and Carter continued.

"I'll pour out the rations three times daily, breakfast, lunch and dinner, and we'll all drink together. Give us something to look forward to."

"How much water do you think we have?" Albert's voice was worried. Carter didn't know the answer, but Bunny hazarded a guess.

"Five or six gallons? So we'll have a little over a week. Unless we drink less." Bunny looked at Carter for a reaction. "So if you don't need to, don't drink?"

Carter was against the idea. "No. We have to drink our rations. I need to keep track of what water we each have in our bodies. We don't want any surprises. We'll leave a little in the tank for washing." Maria's smile was a 'small mercies' one.

There was nothing else to say as the Operation Tracer team listened to their water supply splash a peaceful relaxing sound down the waste pipe and away, an irony not lost on Carter with the suffering he knew was to come.

52

THIS TIME WITH A PLAN

1942, September 30 (10:12h)
Hut 5, German Prisoner-of-War (POW) Camp,
Europa Point, Rock of Gibraltar

Back in the POW camp, Hoop was on his bunk when the German guards came for him.

The walk, at gunpoint, from Hut 5 to the main gate of the camp left Hoop as confused as the faces of those who watched it. Were they removing the negro to punish him for the parade ground incident, or was it more Nazi theatre to protect the identity of their spy from reprisals? Every eye Hoop caught on the way out offered a differing opinion but it was clear which way Captain Pip Smith saw it. Smith and his hairy friend were at the main gate as Hoop passed through it. Pip never spoke, just pointed at his eye and held his finger there. Group Captain Stern had been true to his word. Pip was still in the dark.

Hoop walked back into the cell block building he knew so well, flanked by the same two guards who had now lowered their weapons and were casual in manner. A shiver ran down his back as he reached his old cell door and remembered being carried out, dragging his toes over the stone floor. He steadied himself and focused, taking a deep breath. The smell was unnervingly familiar, and he pushed it out through his nose in slow motion. He told himself this time it was different. This time he was sober, this time he knew who and what he was dealing with. This time, he had a plan, something to trade.

* * *

Richter heard the boots approaching the cell door before the door itself swung open. He was excited to see Fundi, not just to assess the results of him having suffered at the hands of his comrades but something else. He pushed those feelings to the back of his mind. *Focus on the job at hand,* he told himself. Tunnel access could solve all his problems, the right piece of information could change everything on the Rock.

The chessboard was set up with Richter's chair placed on the other side of the board from Hoop's bunk, ready for a game. The German stood up to politely welcome his prisoner.

"Hubert." He pointed at the chessboard. "I trust your move to the camp went well?"

Hoop tentatively entered the cell and looked long and hard at the bunk bed before moving in behind the board to sit on it. He looked uncomfortable but his voice was confident.

"Very good thank you, Standartenführfer." He moved the first pawn forward. Richter was white and so should have gone first but he let it go and played on; he wasn't here for lessons in chess etiquette.

"Glad to hear it," said Richter, picking up a pawn. Of course, he knew exactly how the negro's return to the camp had gone. "So what can I do for you?"

"The camp CO, Group Captain Stern, thought I might be a helpful translator, a conduit between you and him."

"Good idea," replied Richter, taking one of Hoop's pawns from the board. Stern knew he spoke excellent English, well enough to communicate with him directly if he wanted to, and he hadn't, but that wasn't the point. Richter was intrigued by the negro's strategy.

"He's a Jew you know, Stern," said Richter.

"Yes," replied Fundi.

Richter's peripheral vision could see the negro looking at him but he didn't offer eye contact.

"Be careful, a Jew will lie to you as quickly as look at you." Richter had experienced negroes who didn't like Jews and vice versa. *Where did Hubert stand?*

"Our Lord Jesus Christ was a Jew. I'm guessing you're an atheist?" replied Fundi. It was a clear verbal rebuff. It only intrigued Richter to a tingle.

"Not at all. Atheists are egotistic." Richter tried to prevent his tone from sounding playful. "An atheist places himself at the centre of the universe."

Fundi tipped his head ever so slightly and raised an eyebrow. "You don't think the SS does that?" There was something different about the negro's tone. It was light, almost flirtatious.

"The SS is a collective, we thrive by working together. I'm Christian." Richter brought his knight into play on the board and began a double attack.

"So how do you justify praying to a Jew?" Richter liked the question. The negro was clever. Albeit, naive.

"You've been taught that Jesus Christ was a Jew but he was not. The institutions that protect your Catholic faith have lied to you, Hubert. Jesus Christ was never a Jew," said Richter.

"So what was he, German?" Fundi's tone was full of ridicule.

"Your Catholic doctrine is antiquated." Richter was enjoying himself. "It's 1942, not 1842, Hubert. Christianity has moved on and your church has been left behind."

"I believe in one God, the Father Almighty, maker of heaven and earth, of all things visible and invisible, there is no moving on." Fundi leaned back.

"Isn't there?" Richter scoffed. "Take your principles of Christian mercy for example. All men are not created equal and thus all men do not deserve the same treatment under God."

"I can see how that might get in the way of the Führer's plans," replied Fundi. Richter moved his queen right across the board and took Hubert's knight. "Don't believe me?" Richter flicked a piece of dirt from one of his boots and waited for an answer.

"We're all sinners but we can all atone for those sins equally if we ask God for forgiveness." Richter saw a simple negro in front of him but he heard the words of manipulative white missionary men flow out of his mouth.

"Your church is against abortion but what if a woman has a child inside her that she doesn't want? Should she be forced to bring an unwanted child into this world? Abortion, contraception and sometimes sterilisation are necessary. Without them, the world will continue to be overrun by subhumans."

"Like me?" said Fundi.

Richter stopped. The air in the room thickened with palatable anticipation. The moment gave Richter his way in. He knew in an instant how he would break his negro prisoner.

"Yes." He wasn't going to lie to the negro. The truth would do the job for him. "The British see you as inferior too. It's just not cricket to say so." Richter waited for a retort but none came. Fundi sat on the bunk bed looking at him. Richter could see the thought processes taking place behind Hoop's eyes. The silence and posture of a decision maker. Or was he flirting with him? This was his moment to strike.

"Enough of the chit-chat. Tell me, why are you here?" Richter leaned slightly over the chessboard for dramatic effect.

He saw Fundi mirror him.

"I've been thinking about what you said, your 'offer'." *There. There it was.* Richter turned his attention back to the chessboard, forcing an expression of indifference.

"Oh really?" His tone was uninterested, and he tried not to make it absurdly so.

"I'd like to improve my circumstances," continued Fundi. "Maybe you and I can help each other after all."

53

06:00 HOURS

1942, October 1 (05:58h)
Room 502, Rock Hotel, Rock of Gibraltar

The secret doorway in the closet of room 502 of the Rock Hotel was there, just like Fundi said it would be. Richter had requisitioned a packet of Junos from one of his men in celebration. Pulling a cigarette out of the packet, he lit it and looked at his watch.

Two minutes to six. The timing of the assault was critical. It had to begin at the same time as their full-frontal attack on all the known access points into the Rock, including the Hay's Level tunnel access. He wanted the British focused on his men outside. If, as Hubert had said, the secret access to the Rock via room 502 led directly towards the British command centre and what was known as the Great North Road, then he wanted to approach the enemy with the element of surprise. If they were firing at his men outside they wouldn't hear those SS coming up behind them on the inside.

Richter walked the line of sleepy-eyed and nervous men lined up outside the doorway of room 502, and down the corridor. He offered a few reassuring nods to those he recognised, although if he was honest he felt the nerves himself. He had nine hundred of his men ready to enter via Hubert's secret passage and a thousand more in support if they were successful. The negro's information had the access tunnel running fifty feet from room 502, opening out into a larger chamber before splitting into two, one tunnel leading east and the other west.

The channel was too narrow for heavy-duty artillery beyond their portable MG42 machine guns. He'd assembled three independent assault units, one to hold the main chamber and the others to exploit the two access points. All three units were extremely well supported. They had the element of surprise and wanted to move fast through the Rock, to claim and hold as much territory as possible.

He'd arranged for hand-, stick- and anti-tank grenades but the use of explosives had been a contentious issue in the planning. There was always the danger of the tunnels falling in on both them and the British. A report to Berlin that he'd killed a large number of his men due to overzealous use of explosives would be the end of his career for sure.

He had no idea how many men he'd lose today but whatever the number, if they took even fifty per cent of the tunnel networks back inside the Rock, Berlin was sure to accept the loss. Time was of the essence. His men needed to move fast, take as much ground as they could on entry and keep moving. The plan was to reinforce the assault teams as quickly as possible. That meant replacing the fallen on the front line to maintain the attack's forward motion but also to have enough forces inside to secure and hold every position they took. He caught the eye of a medic waiting patiently with dread. It was going to get raw and ugly.

Major Haas had been the ideal man to lead the assault but he had no option but to take the job on himself. If it was a success he didn't want Haas claiming credit for the manoeuvre. Haas had friends in Berlin and back channels to some very important people. He knew these contacts were already being used to undermine his position in charge of the Rock. He wasn't going to let Haas take credit for this one.

He was back at the closet entrance in room 502. The second hand on his timepiece lurched past the top of the hour and then he heard it. The first salvos outside. The battle had begun. The British would be making for their vantage points and priming their weapons in preparation to repel.

Perfect. It was time to go in.

Richter stepped aside for the battering ram. With the small door now hanging from its hinges the first team ran into the dark tunnel, followed by reinforcements. They decided to send in the heaviest weapons the squad could carry: MG42 machine guns, rocket launchers, S18 anti-tank rifles and even a couple of flame throwers, although the debate if they could be used in a confined space had also been a contentious one. Richter had only sent them along just to annoy Haas, who was vehemently against using them.

He watched his men file past him into the dark tunnel. Less than fifty had disappeared through the secret entrance of room 502 before the echo of the first gunfire reverberated back down the tunnel to the closet door entrance. The sound filled Richter with dread. *His men had met resistance already?* It was small-arms fire, which might mean just a few British taken out as the surge forward proceeded. The men in front of him continued to enter so those on point must be still making headway, *right?* With no radio signal possible he'd have to wait for messengers to relay the mission's status. If his men kept entering the closet he could be optimistic that things were going well. As the thought crossed his mind, the line in front of him halted. Richter peered into the darkness in frustration but could see nothing but bodies queuing. Heavily armed bodies stalled in a confined space. The gunfire coming from the distance grew louder. *Something was wrong.*

"*Scheisse*," shouted Richter. The two junior officers flanking him clearly only knew what he knew. Richter summoned the short one, whose name he could never remember.

"Go," he said, pointing up the tunnel to where the battle was raging. "Find out what the problem is." The boy didn't move, he simply looked at Richter in fear. "Now," Richter ordered loudly. He peered after the youngster as he fought his way past the queue of Waffen and SS uniforms. The men let him pass, although some couldn't resist poking fun at their youthful superior officer rushing up to the front line.

Insubordination was going unpunished all around him but it wasn't the time to address it. Singling out one of his men would backfire on him. The atmosphere was charged, he felt it too.

Richter paced as he waited.

Some of his men avoided eye contact. Others watched him, unblinking. Some of them viewed him with distrust and even, in some cases, dislike. Haas had turned many of his men against him since the invasion with lies and rumours, he was sure of it. With long guard duties, shortness of food and alcohol, and restricted visits to local girls on the Spanish mainland, Haas was telling the men that he, 'the Standartenführer', was to blame.

Sounds of battle from the tunnel grew louder as he paced.

He'd heard from men he trusted, men still loyal to him, what Haas was doing. Winning back the approval of those men corrupted by Haas would be difficult. He needed a win today, damn it. Richter took a seat. He didn't like being confined in close quarters with his men for this period of time. He didn't have the rapport with them that Major Haas did.

Outside of Major Haas, who the men saw as indestructible and some kind of champion, he and his officers weren't popular. Those officers who had taken up residence there at the Rock Hotel had been publicly living it up. Importing local girls from across the border and drinking Schnapps excessively. He looked across at the young officer in front of him.

He understood that they needed to let their hair down, but rumours of wild nights here at the hotel had reached the ears of the junior ranks and enlisted men, those without such privileges who were out in the streets dodging British sniper bullets night and day. They'd taken a dim view of course. *So had he.* Morale was low enough without his officers lowering it further. He'd set the date of October 8th for some rest and relaxation for all the men, but leading a successful assault on the British in their tunnels would also help him restore his reputation.

Richter stood up abruptly. It was no good, he couldn't wait any longer. He dipped his head under the low closet doorway and pushed his way up along the line of men.

It was dark inside the tunnel, cramped and hot.

"*Schweinehund*," shouted one of the men over the increasing sound of gunfire as Richter pushed him out of the way and headed towards the front line. Apology after apology came to Richter as his men realised who was shoving them in the low light. Finally, he could go no further. The tunnel was filled with flashing lights and the echoes of the battle taking place fifty feet up ahead, but the men in the tight space were jammed. *It was a mess.* Richter's throat was suddenly full of dust. He wretched and coughed to clear it. The dust entered his eyes too and he closed and squeezed them. He had the mission update he came for.

"The British have fortified the entrance on two sides, Herr Standartenführer," said a thin-faced, confident boy in front of him before leaning against his friend to hear more information being passed down the line of trapped Waffen infantrymen. "It's too dangerous to use explosives without the risk of bringing the tunnel ceiling in on us," the boy added, "sir." More dust descended on Richter and his men, floating down the tunnels like smoke trapped in a bottle.

"Out," shouted Richter. There was nothing else for it. Even the order to retreat out of the tunnel didn't move the men in front of him. There were too many behind waiting to get up towards the battle. Richter leaned against the tunnel wall. The darkness was somewhat of a relief. It hid his embarrassment.

"They should have sent Haas," he heard a whispered voice say.

"The British would all already be captured and we'd be back in the Fatherland tomorrow," replied another. Richter wanted to disappear.

Sitting there, stuck in the darkness, unable to move one way or the other, Richter experienced something he hadn't felt in a long time. He felt just like one of the men. They were right. He should have sent Major Haas.

54

THE KNOTT DEAL

1942, October 1 (17:15h)
Third Reich Army Corps & SS Headquarters,
The Governor's Residence, Rock of Gibraltar

Hoop walked out in front. He didn't recognise the guard behind him. They took guard duty in shifts and a new batch had arrived. This one had dark patches under his tired red eyes and, even younger than the other, he was Gibraltar-weary already. The German guards all had different-shaped faces and bodies. Short, tall, fat, thin, blond hair, black, brown, big noses, small ones, bushy eyebrows and various degrees of white skin, but despite all the differences Hoop had noticed one strong commonality in the times he'd been their prisoner, something to a man that was the same – they were all worn down by their twenty days on the Rock.

How they'd changed. The arrogance of taking it had gone. Their uniforms had been clean, their chins up, shoulders back, they walked with purpose, confidence, with a crystal belief in each eye. That had all gone. Hiding from British snipers, to avoid being shot in the head as they returned to duty each day, had demoralised them. Their uniforms were weather-worn and generally scruffy, the triumph had sunk into the reality of daily truth. They hadn't taken it at all. They were just walking around it as sitting targets. Their shoulders had rounded, backs bent, confidence had turned to endurance, purpose to indifference and as for the eyes – the German guards' eyes, to a man, said the same thing to Hoop. Get me off this Rock.

The guard behind him today looked nervously up each street that had even the smallest view of the Rock, quickening his pace to cross the road junctions and slowing in the protection of the building that shielded him from exposure to British line of sight. Hoop knew exactly where and how to overpower the guard escorting him to the Standartenführer. It would be easy. Although where would he run? What would he do once he was free? Hide? Swim for it? Try to get across the frontier into Spain? The Rock was small; without help, he'd be recaptured a few streets from there, he didn't have the anonymity that came gifted with a white face. No, he and his guard were more alike than maybe they'd care to admit. They were both destined to stay prisoners on the Rock. The only difference between them, he had a plan to get off the Rock alive and his guard didn't.

Hoop was led across the courtyard up to the Governor's residence. He knew the two-storey large red brick building well, although the porch, made of white stone, now had large red flags with swastikas at their centre draped on either side, and two machine gun positions set up beyond them. The men on duty viewed Hoop curiously as he and the guard passed the small armoured vehicle parked in the square.

Inside the residence, Hoop peered through the open doors of an office on the ground floor at a hub of activity. It was the heart of German central command on the Rock. The Germans had made the building their own, moved the furniture, removed the British decor, and replaced it with filing cabinets, typewriters and pictures of the Führer.

Sitting at the desks, typing, were two German women, one blonde with artistically shaped hair, the other pale with almost jet-black hair. Both were in uniform, typing furiously, and clean, how clean they were. Hoop hadn't seen German women on the Rock before. He'd heard the men in Hut 5 make jokes about them. He looked in with interest as he waited in the hallway flanked by his guard. One of the girls stopped typing, looked up, caught his eye and smiled. A hello smile. The same smile white women often gave him. It always came with cat's eyes. Hoop was sucked back in time to a world before the war when people didn't wear uniforms or hold guns but exchanged pleasantries, real or otherwise. He smiled back before the door was closed on him by a frowning officer in the middle of dictating.

As one door closed, another opened. The guard ushered Hoop inside.

Hoop knew of the room, it was the office of the Vice Admiral although he'd never actually been in here. The room had wooden floorboards, a thick patterned carpet, British racing green-coloured walls, and aged wooden panels, shelved with bound books. A speckled marble clock stood above a wrought-iron fireplace, complete with a statue and four gold-coloured legs in the shape of lion heads. Next to the clock was a large white paper calendar, unceremoniously taped to the wall. At the centre of the room was a table, surrounded by ornate chairs, some covered in leather, others made of carved wood, stained and shining from years of cleaning. Between two of the chairs was a leather-clad chessboard.

Richter stood up from behind a heavily polished oak desk. He was jacketless, with his shirt sleeves rolled up. Hoop smiled, with the eye of a cat.

"Thanks for coming," the German said. *Like he had a choice,* thought Hoop but the theatre Richter preferred them to live in was alluring. It was better than his reality. Unlike the men under his command, the Standartenführer had a smile, a real one, backed up with a tone of optimism. He genuinely believed he would prevail in all his endeavours, believing it to his core. Hoop hated the Standartenführer, and loathed his opinions and everything he stood for, but he couldn't help but respect him. When he asked politely for something, he made you want to oblige.

If the Standartenführer would maintain his current treatment and keep him out of the British camp, he was prepared to share some of what he knew. Chess games, the clean sheets, open door cell policy, four square meals and regular showers were his now, and Hoop wanted to keep it that way.

Richter opened the top of a small drinks cabinet designed in the shape of a globe. The bottles in the bar clicked together as they came into view. Hoop hadn't seen ice for a while, and the sound of it dropping into a glass was an unexpected pleasure on its own. He wanted to rub the ice around his face but he wouldn't. Although he couldn't for the life of him understand why not. Richter's love of theatre was rubbing off on him, somehow it seemed rude.

"It's not allowed you know," said the Standartenführer. Hoop took the glass offered to him, and could smell the whisky lapping against the ice inside it.

"Alcohol," the German continued, pouring himself an identical drink. "Herr Himmler doesn't approve and the Führer says smoking is bad for us." The Standartenführer picked up a packet of Lucky Strike cigarettes. "Not my brand but it's the best our Spanish friends have to offer at the moment I'm afraid." He opened the packet with the red target at its centre, took out a small white cigarette and lit it. "God knows where they're getting them from!"

The Standartenführer closed the bottle and the globe bar lid as Hoop took a sip. The ice burnt his lip and the whisky his throat. It was heaven. "Alcohol reduces a man's ability to perform his duties." The Standartenführer walked towards him. The glass was cold and thick, heavy crystal. Hoop couldn't remember ever having a heavier glass in his hand. So thick was the base, it took up a quarter of the mass of the little glass. The whisky and the ice slipped playfully around the smooth interior like dancing partners.

"*Prost.*" The Standartenführer tapped his crystal against Hoop's and the sound was a light high-pitched ring of opulence. After so much suffering the moment was more intoxicating than the liquor. The Standartenführer was in touching distance, almost too close for comfort. In the light of day, away from the darkness of the cell, Hoop noticed how young he was to have been made Standartenführer. His cap removed and his shirt unbuttoned, Hoop could see the young Nazi's pale white skin, hardly a blemish. Nothing like his skin or that of the men in the camp, red like lobsters from the sun or dark leathery tanned. The Standartenführer looked like he'd never spent a day exposed to the elements in his life. His skin was tight across his face, rubbery in youth. The smell of the whisky mixed with some other fragrance. The Standartenführer was doused with toilet water. There was almost something feminine about him. Hoop's stomach turned but he smiled again.

"I won't tell if you don't," said the German, turning his back on Hoop.

That thought that never left him came back again. It would have been so easy to break his glass and stick it into the Standartenführer's throat, or subdue him and kill him some other way without alerting those on the other side of the door. It would be justice for all those he'd made to suffer, but that wasn't the new plan. Not even close to it. This Nazi was worth much more to him alive than dead. He was showered, clean-shaven and safe, drinking whisky with ice. Out of Pip's reach. Anyway, it would be a shame to break such beautiful glass.

* * *

"I should be very angry with you," said the Standartenführer. "Room 502 was a dead end. Well fortified and defended just a short distance inside." Richter studied the whites of the negro's eyes carefully as he spoke.

"I'm sorry, I didn't know." There was surprise in Fundi's voice, even if Richter couldn't see any on his prisoner's face. It was difficult to tell with the brown skin and dark eyes.

"Didn't you?" His words were full of accusation but he deliberately maintained a conciliatory tone. "No. It's the only reason you're here today and not escorted back to your bunk in Hut 5." Richter gestured to the leather chessboard.

The pieces on the board were black and white, made of ivory and some deep, shiny stone. The chessboard, like the room, was all part of the proposition. He was going to enjoy playing with him.

Richter picked up a pawn and placed it forward towards Hubert on the board.

"Some battles are fought for no prize, only honour." Richter wanted to beat his visitor on merit. Not because he was his prisoner. "You may have forgotten so let me remind you, I'm white, I go first." The Standartenführer's words lacked even a hint of irony. He could see it was all Hubert needed to inspire him.

"Aren't you afraid that I might overpower you, kill you and escape?" Fundi picked up a pawn of his own and determinedly forced it down onto the board, directly in front of the Standartenführer's.

"Chess holds its master in its own bonds, shackling the mind. You're going nowhere." Richter didn't look up from the board but heard a light laugh from Fundi as he brought his knight into play.

"Does my double attack amuse you?" he asked.

The negro didn't answer but were he planning an attack, which Richter very much doubted, he certainly wouldn't do it during one of their games of chess, Hoop clearly enjoyed them too much.

"It's a shame," continued Richter, "your intelligence on room 502 came to nothing." The Standartenführer moved his bishop to knight four. "I'll have to send you back to the POW camp of course. I can't justify your luxury cell accommodation without something to show for it." Richter watched his guest all but ignore his threat.

"I like you, Hubert, so I'll be straight with you. You have a window of opportunity to share everything you know and reap the reward for doing so. That window of opportunity, however, is rapidly closing. Other avenues of intelligence gathering are opening up for me. If you have something of value to share, I suggest you share it now. Secure your preferential treatment. Before it's too late.

"Electricity, lighting and heat inside the tunnels are provided by four power stations. Generators run on diesel fuel. Extractor fans carry fumes out of the Rock. There's a hospital near the southeastern corner." Richter sat back in his chair and listened. Hubert kept going.

"All the communication tunnels can be traversed by jeep. Brigade headquarters is just off what they call the Great North Road. They have supplies for a garrison of men." There was a long silence. Richter took a sip of his whisky. Had he made a mistake, did the negro map maker know something of value or not? Or was he just playing with him?

"That's it?" said Richter disappointedly. "Is there talk in the POW camp of a British counterattack to try and take back the Rock?"

"Group Captain Stern is encouraging escapes because there is no plan for rescue. They say a counterattack would be doomed to failure." Richter didn't doubt that. He'd studied it from every angle.

"What about entrances into the Rock? I need more secret entrances."

"There are none that I know of." His prisoner was looking directly at him, shoulders firm, straight-backed, unflinching. He was very convincing. The negro was lying.

"Then what use are you to me?" Richter put his glass down.

"Commander Knott," said Hubert. "Knott is the officer responsible for all British Naval Intelligence operations here on the Rock." Richter put his hand back on his glass. If Hubert knew of such a name, he knew much more but there would be no more rewards for dead ends.

"Is Commander Knott in the POW camp?"

"No," replied Hubert.

"Dead?" suggested Richter.

"I don't know." It wasn't what he wanted to hear but Hubert was talking. Richter glanced at the clock. There were matters of urgency he needed to attend to, reports on his desk to read about American ship movements.

"I need secret entrances to the tunnel system!" he repeated.

In truth, he knew that dead or alive, Knott's name would be useful to his superiors in Berlin.

"Tomorrow at noon is your deadline. Get my men inside the Rock!" He tried to generate a tone of finality. "So long as the British hold the

tunnels inside the Rock there is a risk of successful counterattack."
Richter stood up.

"There's no British infrastructure in place for a counterattack."
Fundi's tone was adamant but it didn't change his ultimatum.

"If you have nothing of value for me by tomorrow noon, then,
Hubert, you'll be returning to the POW camp."

"The British have a purpose-built spy cave inside the Rock. They're
observing the movement of your forces twenty-four hours a day and
reporting every detail back to London. I'll give you the location of the
cave but I want more than a shower, clean sheets and a cell with a lamp
shade." Richter sat back down. The Americans could wait.

55

TURN THE OTHER CHEEK

1942, October 2 (09:08h)
Hay's Level Tunnel Entrance, Rock of Gibraltar

It was time to see how loyal the British were to each other, thought Richter as he walked through the old Moorish Castle off Willis's Road on his way back to the Hay's Level tunnel entrance. There was silence on the other side of the wall, even the usual sporadic shots had stopped. Stalemate. They couldn't root the British out of their tunnel hiding places and he had lost more men, time and most importantly, hardware, trying. He had no idea what supplies the British had, although Hubert had suggested maybe enough for a year. He'd be dead in a frozen tank in Russia by then.

Just thinking about Hubert frustrated him. He wanted to shoot the negro in the head one moment and then embrace him the next. He knew the location of the British spies inside the Rock but his price to tell was high. He wanted off this Rock. Passage back to Namibia. His negro friend was evolving, thought Richter. Ending British naval and aircraft intelligence somehow making its way to London would show Berlin real progress. In the meantime, he'd start upsetting British morale.

Richter kept low and ran to the last line of defence, the low wall. The two sides were exchanging odd bits of sniper fire and that was that. Something had to change the status quo. Maybe this was it? His idea was going to be frowned upon by some of his men and maybe outlying voices in Berlin: the very reason Richter had selected Major Haas to run the operation.

He was handed the trench mirror. It was a simple mirror, about the size of a book, affixed into a metal casing with a flip, a bracket at the back that sat on the top of a bayonet knife, the knife clipped to a rifle. Richter lifted the rifle above the low wall to evaluate progress. The view was wobbly so he took a tighter grip on the butt of the weapon and steadied the image. There. He could see the remains of the armoured car, most of it blown away, crushed and recrushed by Tiger tank treads on their way to and from unsuccessful assaults on the Hay's Level entrance. Two heads poked above the wreckage, one with red hair, the other dark in complexion. He couldn't see the third.

The idea was simple: if they couldn't fight their way in, get the British to fight each other. He didn't expect them to surrender their tunnel positions, not outright, but he could undermine their resolve. For all he knew they could already be at each other's throats.

The British weakness was their care, their compassion for their '*mates*'. He had no idea what the chain of command was inside the Rock or if the tunnels were all linked up, although Hubert said they were. Maybe there was no command centre and they were just pockets of individual resistance. If that were the case maybe those pockets could be broken down individually.

The three British POWs, selected from the British camp by Major Haas's men and now shackled to the wreckage of the armoured car in no man's land, would stay there exposed to the elements, with no food, no water until they either died of starvation, were shot by their friends, or the British surrendered their tunnel positions.

Wolfgang tipped the mirror up to get a better view. He could see the heads of two British POWs and beyond them the British lookouts. He could see movement inside the deep slits cut into the rock. The ultimatum had been repeatedly broadcast to them, in their language. It would have started its work by splitting their ranks for sure. If they were going to stay inside there frustrating him, they weren't going to be happy in doing so. The broadcasting needed to continue. The narrative was aimed at the men inside the tunnels, but also, the three shackled to the wreckage. He needed to break the POWs too. If they died well in front of their comrades the plan would backfire and generate a greater determination to hold out. He needed the three men to beg to be put out of their suffering. Only then would their comrades inside be left with the moral dilemma that would create the conflict he wanted. There was no downside. Unlike room 502, if things went wrong he'd hang the whole idea around the neck of Major Haas. It was he who had selected the men from the camp after all.

He'd seen all he needed to see. It would take a while for the British to die, if they weren't shot before then. Richter took a last look at the armoured car. He finally saw the third man. A negro.

He fumbled the handle of the rifle. His eyes were deceiving him. He can't have seen a negro. There was only one negro he knew of on the Rock and he wasn't chained to the armoured car out there. Major Haas was given strict instructions that the negro was not to be harmed. Richter steadied the rifle and tilted the mirror, which was shaking in his hand. He knew what he'd seen, even though he didn't want to believe his eyes. There. It was Hubert Fundi, no doubt about it. Chained up with the other two British POWs. The hairs lifted on Richter's back and he felt cold. He looked again. He'd given orders! He'd been clear. The negro was his. He hadn't finished with him. Haas and his men knew it. Everybody knew it. Hubert was one step from providing him with what he wanted, secret access to the British tunnels.

Richter sensed he was being watched. His SS men were looking at him. He avoided eye contact with them, he needed time to think.

Give the order to retrieve the negro. Only the negro? *Undermine his own plan to destabilise the British watching from their tunnel lookouts? Undermine Haas, publicly? Hubert had crucial information and he was about to tell. Wasn't he?* Or was the negro playing him? What would it look like? What would those SS men still loyal to him say? What could they say? *Nothing.* He'd have them shot! No, he wouldn't. He would seriously damage his reputation if he were to save the negro so publicly, again. There was already talk. He couldn't do that. *Could he? No.* He wouldn't. He was going to have to leave Hoop where he was. Leave him, along with the other two British POWs to die. There was nothing else for it.

Richter knew Hubert hadn't been selected, as one of the three British to die, by accident.

Haas had done it deliberately.

* * *

Major Haas had gone too far this time. Overlooking his insolent attitude was one thing but not following orders and the chain of command was another.

Richter strode into the corner of Town Range and Convent Place on his way back to the Governor's residence flanked by two guards. He was out in the open and there was a real chance of getting shot by a British sniper but the rage was building inside of him. *Don't touch the negro.* He'd been very clear with Major Haas. If they'd been in Berlin he'd have brought the major up on charges but they weren't. Here, right now, the Rock unsecured, his options were limited to deal with such insubordination. He needed Major Haas and his expertise right now, and the major knew it. His threats were beginning to sound empty. Transferring the major off the Rock to the Russian front wouldn't be as simple as all that. He had powerful friends in Berlin. Arrogant as he was, Haas was also the most experienced assault commander he had, replacing him would not be possible right now. Those men loyal to Haas, under his command, would also be a problem. They were a large and tight-knit group. Demoting the major would also cause trouble in the ranks, something he had enough of already. The truth was, he was stuck with the swine, at least until the Rock was fully theirs. Richter rounded the corner and came into the courtyard. Major Haas was waiting for him, flanked by two of his own men.

"Were my orders for the negro unclear?" Richter raised his voice as he closed in on the major who pushed his chest out and lifted his chin.

Three men sitting on a tank in the square turned to view the encounter. One jumped down onto the ground and stepped forward to get a better view. The guards outside the Governor's residence exchanged quizzical glances without breaking guard duty stance and the two British POWs mixing concrete at the barrel of a gun, paused, as did their captors. All eyes were on the Standartenführer as he reached Major Haas.

"Not to be touched. THAT WAS MY ORDER!" Richter shouted in the major's face. Haas kept his chin high in the air, his back upright, his shoulders square, and hands down by his sides.

Richter removed his leather gloves and walked up and down in front of the major, unsure how to proceed. The man was a swine. He knew what he'd done. He'd done it deliberately and he was waiting here for this very confrontation, flanked by his witnesses.

"Why is the negro so important to you, Herr Standartenführer?" The major's question was impertinent but what could he do? Richter felt his face warm with blood. How dare he? Was there no end to the man's disobedience?

"That is none of your concern," he replied as Haas physically grew in confidence. "I hadn't finished interrogating him." Richter straightened his jacket. That was it. The interrogation wasn't over, he told himself. The information Hubert was about to give up, if correct, was extremely valuable. *Damn it! He didn't have to explain himself to a major under his command.*

"Removing him will show weakness to the British," stated Major Haas, appearing to take glee in pointing out, to his superior officer, the folly of overriding him.

Richter squeezed both hands into fists of rage and bit down hard. They were being watched.

"When I give an order I expect it to be followed. Is that

understood?" The major adjusted his posture, eyes, legs and shoulders front, although Richter was sure he could detect the faintest sign of a snide grin on the major's lips.

The major had completely outflanked him and they both knew it. Haas wanted him to show weakness in front of the men, and rescue the negro. Berlin would hear of it and he'd be undermined. Maybe he'd be recalled and who'd replace him? 'Colonel' Haas of course! Well, it wouldn't work. He wouldn't play along.

"There're plenty of other young men of a more appropriate colour," said Haas. Richter couldn't believe his ears. Had an officer under his command just accused him of something? He had. Richter lost it. He took a firm grip on his leather gloves and slapped them across the face of Major Haas.

The attack caught the major by surprise. His eyes widened and flamed red like both cheeks. His previous smirk converted to a grimace and his thin lips quivered. Haas squeezed his lips together, sealing them from the inside. The courtyard was silent. Nobody moved. Richter could hear the breeze gently blow. He'd publicly hit an officer under his command. He knew there would be fallout over his actions but it was too late. He'd done it.

Major Haas brought his jackboots together firmly. The leather-on-leather sound culminated in a dramatic heel-to-cobblestone clash. Haas saluted his commanding officer and marched away.

56

LORD TAVISTOCK

1942, October 6 (19:32h)
Main Chamber, Stay Behind Cave, Rock of Gibraltar

"As kids, we spent quite a lot of time at Woburn Abbey. Do you know it, sir?" Albert placed a jack of hearts down on the table and picked another card up from the deck.

Carter had managed to coax Albert out of the radio room for a game of hearts. He wanted to keep a closer eye on him. He'd allowed him to monopolise the radio room long enough, he was clearly in there with whatever he was hiding. He also needed to see him drink his quota of water. The youngster was still the healthiest of the team, not having suffered the effects of the putrid water. The mood swings were beyond his medical help.

The vomiting and diarrhoea they'd suffered before the discovery of the rat in the tank had been replaced by the effects of dehydration. Dry mouth, cracked lips, light-headedness and a real sense of tiredness throughout the group had so far been the effects. His own urine illustrated the problem the others were also having. It was a dark yellow colour with a very strong scent, when he passed it, which wasn't often now.

The containers of boiled and cooled clean water against the hut wall were already depleted. They were each taking their quota for the day but it wasn't enough. Maria had cried on his shoulder the night before but there had been no actual tears. A stillborn child looked certain.

He didn't want to think about the next stage, for any of them; seizures and coma. Surrender, opening the wall and leaving, would have to become an option. If they all died in there the mission was over anyway.

Maria and Bunny were on shift up at the lookouts while Logan lay on his bunk reading a copy of Bulldog Drummond.

Albert was looking at him quizzically. *The boy had asked him a question.* He hadn't answered.

"Woburn Abbey! No, Albert. Can't say I know it." Carter tried to focus. With his rib, ankle and wrist all bandaged and aching from the water tank fall, the card game was a welcome distraction. He turned over a six of hearts and followed suit. "I know of it. Not far from Bletchley?"

"That's right, sir," replied Albert, and Logan put his book down. He had dry skin around his mouth and on his forehead.

"Recently inherited by Lord Tavistock?" Logan's question was aimed at Albert.

"Yes, sir. Hasty, I mean, Lord Tavistock" – Albert appeared to formalise the name of his family friend – "is an old school chum of my father's."

"The 12th Duke of Bedford, yes?" Logan dropped the book and swung his legs over the edge of his bunk.

"Yes." Carter saw Albert's upbeat demeanour shrink as he looked to leave his own conversation. "As I said," he addressed Carter only, "we spent tons of time at the Abbey when we were kids." Logan interrupted.

"Lord Tavistock the pacifist?" It was Logan now who had energy in his voice. Carter didn't know who Lord Tavistock was.

Logan hopped off his bunk and came towards the table. "Parrot collector and close friend of Oswald Mosley?"

Albert folded his arms and crossed his legs. "I believe they know each other, yes."

"The same Oswald Mosley who leads the British Union of

Fascists?" Logan was now standing over Albert. The boy's brow was furrowed and a little paler than before.

Carter knew of Mosley, everybody did. So what if Albert's father knew somebody who was friends with Mosley?

"Exactly how well do you know Uncle Hasty?" Logan accentuated the word 'uncle', although his question went unanswered. "I asked you a question, Corporal."

"Steady on, Logan, give the boy a chance," said Carter.

There was a long pause. They weren't in some military tribunal. Logan's personality shift took Carter back to the staircase. Logan was becoming unpredictable, irrational. Sickness could bring out the best and the worst in people. It often stripped away the facades.

Albert had sunk into the chair. He was grinding his teeth and sucking his dry lip. Carter could see the blood rushing to his face. Pumped in, the boy coloured a beetroot shade of red.

Logan was waiting for an answer. Honestly? He now wanted to hear it too.

"It's not a difficult question, Corporal, how well do you know Tavistock?" Logan was almost shouting.

"He's my godfather!" Albert shouted back.

Carter dropped his cards on the table exposing his hand. "Christ, Albert."

"He's not the man they say he is, sir. Hasty's a good chap. Really he is." Albert stood up for a more solid defence.

"Oh, he's a great chap, your godfather, in favour of doing deals with the Nazis. Quite public about it too!"

"You don't know him as I do." Albert's intake of breath was short and dramatic.

"Does the Admiralty know of your connection to this man, Albert?" Carter asked the question because he couldn't quite believe that this had escaped the Naval Intelligence background checks. *Did Fleming and Godfrey know?* The Admiralty had researched all the team members. They'd each been interviewed, so many questions had been asked. Had they missed Albert's connection to a known Nazi sympathiser?

"No, sir. It never came up," replied Albert. He snatched some oxygen to continue. "With the greatest of respect, I'm not responsible for my godfather, sir."

Carter didn't disagree with the boy but the youngster was missing the point. "Albert, your godfather is a close friend of the leader of the British Nazi party and you didn't think to mention that?"

"No, sir." Albert's body language mirrored that of his schooldays. He made to leave but Logan's heavy hand pushed him back into the chair.

"What else haven't you told us, Corporal?" Logan's tone was thick with innuendo. "You haven't explained how you stayed in 'tip top' health while the rest of us all got sick."

Carter was forced to agree with Logan. It had been unusually fortunate that Albert didn't like the taste of cold water. He was suddenly seeing Albert in a new light. Hidden away, day and night, in the radio room. What had he been hiding in his pocket up at the west wall lookout, a broken shard of mirror perhaps, to send signals? Had he been blind to the boy? When they lost their ability to receive communications from London, who had brought the broken radio part to everybody's attention? Albert. Who was in charge of the spare part? Albert. He'd complained so emotionally about the broken receiver. Had he broken it and tried to deflect attention away from himself? Was the boy masturbating in the radio room or was something more sinister going on?

Carter couldn't help searching his memory for more proof of Albert's guilt. The missing corned beef – *Stop it,* he told himself. *Guilt of what?* Trying to sabotage the mission? Young Albert? It was ridiculous.

"Your accent slips now and again. I haven't told you that, have I, Major Warlock?" said Albert.

Logan's approach to the boy convinced Carter he was about to hit the lad when Maria stepped into the main chamber. All three men looked at her in silence. Maria scanned their faces. "What's going on?" she asked.

Carter and Albert looked at Logan to answer.

So did Maria.

"It appears Albert here is a close personal friend of a well-known Nazi traitor and we want answers."

Albert went to speak but was beaten to it by Maria.

"Hey! Leave him alone, Logan." Maria began to shuffle forward. Before her boyfriend could use the breath he'd drawn, Maria cut him off. "I mean it, Logan." Logan took a breath to speak for a second time but stopped as Maria reached Albert and put her hand on his shoulder. They both looked at Logan. The Operation Tracer team leader picked up his book and returned to his bunk.

57

CORNED BEEF

1942, October 7, (01:30h)
Main Chamber, Stay Behind Cave, Rock of Gibraltar

It wasn't just Carter's rib that had kept him from a good night sleep – it throbbed, no matter which side he lay on – but his thoughts of Albert and what he might be up to just wouldn't go away. It seemed impossible that the youngster could be sabotaging the mission deliberately, but Carter couldn't ignore the circumstantial evidence against him.

Dreams, random cognitive signals had been absent since arriving in the cave but tonight Carter's sleep was alive with colours, shapes and sounds. He was high up in the corner of the room in a canoe and it was sinking.

Carter frantically bailed the water out of the boat, with a soup ladle. Maria sitting opposite did the same but with a teaspoon in slow motion, almost unaware the boat was sinking. Bunny, Logan and Albert were there too, watching the canoe and the chaos engulfing it. Sat at the table they watched but just played hearts.

The faster Carter bailed the water out, the faster boat filled again. Maria smiled as they began to sink. Her bare neck was swan-like, long and elegant, she blew a kiss at him then returned to her teaspoon. The rushing water came over the edge of the vessel and consumed it. Carter tried to shout at Bunny but no sound came out of his mouth. Maria was now almost underwater but her demeanour was unchanged; she just kept smiling at him. Water in his eyes blurred the scene. He ran his sleeve across them trying to restore vision. Maria was gone. She was on her hands and knees crawling through the water towards him, like a cat, her head steady while her body approached in elegant motion, wobbling through the water in womanly places. She reached his legs and was still coming. She crawled across his groin.

Carter woke up, sweat on his brow. He opened his eyes. *Damn it,* he couldn't afford to lose valuable body fluid that way. He was cold. The canoe was gone, no water, he wasn't in the corner of the room, he was lying on his bunk under a blanket. The main chamber was silent. The lights were out, the others had clearly decided not to disturb him and made for their bunks. He dropped his head back down on the pillow. He had a headache. He ran his finger along his cracked lips. The dream had been so vivid. Looking at the blotchy, poorly painted ceiling he told himself to be calm. The mission would all fall back into place. *It will rain soon.* Just give it time. He had to believe it or he was lost. Something moved on his bed! He was wide awake in an instant. It had a hairy face and dark eyes. The size of a small child but with teeth. Very long teeth. He smelt it before he saw it. It smelt like a donkey. A mixture of faeces and coarse hair. An ape. There was an ape on his bed.

"*Yarp!*" Carter made an unconscious noise, something between a yelp, a cry and a deep-throated roar. The ape leapt off the bed and was by the table leg in a flash. The shot of adrenaline removed the pain from his rib. Bunny and Logan were out of their bunks quicker than Carter. Both stood wide-eyed in front of him. Carter tried to speak but what came out was gibberish. His pointed finger did the job. The ape, less frightened than them, looked out from behind the table leg, almost daring them to come for him.

"Jesus!" said Albert as Logan launched a pillow. The three-foot-high interloper was across the room, running on all fours, out the door and racing up the stairs shrieking before the soft furnishing landed by the table leg. Bunny came dashing out of the toilet, his trousers around his ankles, holding Logan's copy of *Bulldog Drummond.* The intruder reached the east wall lookout at the top of the stair. The ape turned back for a final look, showed its teeth at the four men in the doorway, and Maria now peered around the west wall tunnel steps holding her stomach. Slinging one arm out through the lookout space, a moment later the ape had squeezed back out into the darkness on the other side.

"Crikey!" said Bunny...

"Friend of yours?" said Albert, looking directly at Bunny's manhood swinging slightly in the low light. Carter laughed first, Maria followed and then even Logan.

Bunny turned sideways to shield his private parts from Maria's view. The twist of his trousers resulted in a loss of balance, and Bunny fell backwards hitting the toilet floor. Carter felt it. The camaraderie that had been missing.

For a split second, the old Albert was back and they were a team, for the first time since entering the cave. While he and the others tried to suppress the sound of their laughter, Carter felt the world lift from his shoulders. He'd been wrong about everything. There was no thief amongst them stealing tins of corned beef. The apes had been taking them. Albert hadn't broken the radio receiver and stolen the replacement part in an attempt to sabotage the mission. It had been the apes all along. The realisation and relief caused him to laugh even more. There was nothing sinister about Albert, he was just an awkward young man, with an unfortunate family friend.

"Shh." Team leader Logan hushed the exuberance. As the laughter faded, like the light of a firefly, Logan, gaunt and dry-skinned as he was, then surprised them all. Carter could tell by the silence that followed.

"Why don't we sit down for a fruit juice together?" Logan's voice was soft, even friendly, all-inclusive.

"What about the rest of the lookout shift?" asked Maria.

"We all need a treat and a good night's sleep. Let's sip some juice, have a chat and lie in tomorrow. We'll start afresh."

Nobody wanted to argue with that, least of all Carter. Logan finally leading the team was music to his ears.

"You know it's raining," said Maria. She was right. Carter thought all his Christmases had come at once as he and the team stood at the east wall lookout and watched a few drops grow into a deluge. Carter had no words as water dripped off the stone above their lookout hole in the rock and splashed continually onto the small shelved space they spent so many hours peering out from. They each took turns running their hands along the surface and rubbing cold wet hands across their dry lips and around their dusty faces. Maria's eyes were mad with pleasure. Carter tried not to stare. The sound of the rain outside was therapeutic, almost musical. *They'd turned a corner. Everything was going to be okay.*

* * *

Outside the Stay Behind Cave, hundreds of feet below Carter and the team enjoying the rain, was a tin of corned beef resting where it had landed, on a ledge above the track known as Dudley Ward Way. The tin was dented considerably but the fall had not broken the integrity of the container, only misshapen it. Wrapped tightly with grey string around the tin was a tracer mission intelligence gathering sheet. An almost identical second tin of corned beef, the same damp paper and puffed wet string, dented in a new way, lay thirty feet along the ridge. Beyond the second tin was a third, but this time the paper had torn and turned back on itself revealing a signature at the bottom of a handwritten note. It read, 'A-54'.

58

JUST A NEGRO

1942, October 7 (09:45h)
Third Reich Army Corps & SS Headquarters,
The Governor's Residence, Rock of Gibraltar

Standartenführer Richter sat at his desk staring at the chessboard in his office, chain-smoking Lucky Strike. He topped up his glass of whisky. There was a knock at the door and a guard entered.

"Out!" shouted Richter. The guard stepped straight back out, closing the door behind him.

He's just a negro, he told himself. What's wrong with you? He's not worthy of your attention, your admiration. *Pull yourself together.*

His eyes wandered around the room. Everything in it screamed power and influence. How far he'd come to be sitting there. Richter thought back to his time as a boy. His enrolment into the SS-Junker school in the town of Bad Tölz in 1934. His father had not approved but his mother had her way. His family had been considered Aryan back to 1798 and they'd presented evidence to support that claim. Proving lineage was a requirement but family status and class hadn't taken him to his current rank. His SS promotions had come via commitment and political reliability. He would not have been able to rise at the same rate in the Wehrmacht. He wasn't going to put all that at risk by rescuing one subhuman he'd become fond of. He took another sip of whisky and picked up one of the fifteen reconnaissance reports scattered across the highly polished wooden surface. He hadn't read any of them.

He'd insisted on reading all reconnaissance reports, just in case there was something important that had been missed. Those under his command would sometimes overlook details in the intelligence gathering – a pattern, or just that one piece of information that gave away the intentions of the enemy. He'd neglected the reports, like everything else since Hubert… *damn the man!* Wolfgang read the words on the page: 'list of newly arrived American ships in the Bay of Algeciras'. He dropped the paper back on the desk. It was no good. He couldn't concentrate.

Saving Fundi would be a terrible mistake. His men were watching, those loyal to Major Haas, who already hated him, wanted him to do it. There had already been 'talk'.

Richter knew the consequences of dishonour in the SS. Prohibition to wearing the uniform, detention, demotion, suspension, and potential expulsion. His SS had its own courts to deal with crimes within the ranks. *Although he hadn't actually done anything! Nothing anyone could prove.* He couldn't be punished for what he felt. He was the perfect SS officer and dared anybody to say differently.

He pulled another cigarette from his packet of Lucky Strikes. There was only one thing he wouldn't – or couldn't – do for Herr Himmler and the Fatherland: get married, have children, extend the Aryan bloodline. He finished his glass of whisky in a single shot, threw his jackboots up on the desk, leaned back in his chair and took a long draw on the cigarette. He'd met several girls who had been deemed 'racially fit' to bear his offspring. He blew the smoke out slowly. It drifted up to the ceiling. SS marriages had to be approved through official channels. 'Racial hygiene' had to be maintained; there was no sustaining the 'Thousand Year Reich' if SS men didn't procreate. He agreed, but they would have to do without his seed.

He had his feet on the desk at the very heart of Gibraltar. The Overseas Territory the British had held for so long and were so proud of. He'd taken it from them. Him. In the name of the Fatherland. He had no place caring for a negro. One more dead negro was just that, one more, and if he was fighting for the British, all the better.

Richter spun his feet back onto the floor and put out his cigarette.

Although he wasn't that was he? *Just a negro.* Hubert had given him the location of room 502 in exchange for protection; he was about to divulge everything he knew about British spies on the Rock. They had an agreement. He'd given his word. *Did his 'word' mean nothing?* He poured another shot of whisky into his thick crystal glass, picked it up and walked over to the leather chessboard. He could smell the leather. He'd never noticed that before.

When Hubert died it would be on Major Haas not on him, he hadn't chained him out there.

Richter lifted his thick scotch glass and eyed the liquid inside. He'd made a huge success of his career in the SS, gone further than everyone he knew thought possible for a man of his humble beginnings, and he'd achieved that by making calculated intuitive decisions. He followed his gut and his gut had brought him to the attention of Herr Himmler himself. His gut had never let him down.

His gut said it would be a terrible mistake to rescue Hubert. His negro was going to have to die.

59

COLEOPTERA BEETLE

1942, October 7 (10:50h)

Hay's Level Tunnel Entrance, Rock of Gibraltar

Hoop couldn't remember the name. It was red with black spots on its back, waddling across the small stones, gravel and dust. Boundless energy. He watched the beetle climb the small vertical smashed brickwork wall, defying gravity and marching on to wherever it had a mind to go. If it had nothing else, it had freedom. Freedom to go where it wanted, something Hoop didn't have. He lifted his head from the dusty concrete ground and the beetle was no longer defying gravity but simply scuttling across in front of him. He knew the name once, he was sure he knew the name of the beetle, but it was gone. He searched for a reference, an experience to link the memory so the name would come back to him, but the effort to concentrate was just too much. He'd do it later.

He and aircraftmen James and George were as sharp as needles that first day. He'd noticed everything around him, they had lots of ideas and plans they could implement to save themselves, although none of them was realistic. That sharpness of mind had slipped away from them in recent hours. James was first to withdraw, as far as he could. He'd become irritable, nothing was right that he or George said or did, they squabbled, and he'd called him a nigger. It was the strain they were under, he felt it too. He wanted them to pray with him but neither of his fellow captives was 'religious', and both declined. How things had changed. He could hear them whispering for the Lord to save them, help them, forgive them. Not to release them from their chains, they knew that was not going to happen, but to save them from themselves. They were broken.

This wasn't the end he had expected either. Everything had been going to plan. He'd said all the right things to Richter. They had a deal. What went wrong? His agreement with Stern, had it been discovered? *What does it matter now?* It was over and he was too weak to care. Hoop's muscles had withered in recent days. The weight had simply fallen off them all. At night they'd huddle close together, like animals in the wild for warmth, but they could never quite get warm, not even in the sun. Hoop had chills all day but George had them worse. He pretty much shook permanently now.

The beetle stopped a moment and seemed to pamper itself with one leg rubbing on another before continuing on his way. Coleoptera! It was a Coleoptera beetle. The name came back to Hoop in an instant. Almost as quick as James's hand that slammed down to kill the beetle. Hoop watched in horror as James took the corpse up in three fingers and put it on his tongue. Hoop screamed inside, not in defence of the creature but out of frustration. He hadn't thought of it first. He'd seen the beetle before James and that made it his. *Didn't it?*

The wheel of the armoured car cut out the sun and Hoop shivered. A moment later his entire body was lifted from the ground and hauled aboard a German armoured car. God had finally come for him, thought Hoop. He was ready, ready to meet his maker.

60

JAMES AND GEORGE

1942, October 8 (09:53h)
Windmill Hill, Prisoner Cell, Rock of Gibraltar

"I don't believe you. I don't believe anything you say." Propped up by a pillow, Hubert Fundi glared at Wolfgang Richter standing over his bunk back in the cell. "You're in charge."

Retrieving this situation wasn't going to be easy, Richter knew, but after the histrionics Hubert would still be in the same predicament as before, reliant on him for his future. He'd come around again and share what he knew.

The cell door was open, the sheets were clean, and a breakfast tray lay by the bed. There was colour back in the negro's cheeks and that sparkle had returned to his dark eyes. Although happy to see both, Richter was now on the clock. He needed to justify the rescue of the negro before Berlin got wind of it.

Hubert had been treated for mild anaemia by the young British medic. The paralysed creature dropped on the bed had 'fight' back in his voice. He was well enough to tell Richter what he wanted to hear.

"You need to release James and George," said Hubert. That wasn't it. Richter didn't expect the man to be grateful for the rescue, not until he regained some perspective, but he needed him to quickly understand what was required.

"Please concentrate on our agreement. I need to know the location of the British spies and I need to know it now."

"James and George," replied Hubert, unwavering.

"Forgive me, Hubert, but you need to focus. Your rescue comes at a price."

"Rescue? You put us out there!" Hubert folded his arms.

"It was Major Haas's mission. Not mine. There are things that you don't understand, you need to trust me. I've taken a great risk protecting you."

"You want my thanks?!"

"I want what we agreed. The British intelligence gathering location, and access points to the main tunnel system inside the Rock. You know what I want. The deal is the same. I'll keep you out of the British camp until transport arrives. You will return safely to Namibia." Richter was stretching his voice box with frustration. "Help me, help you out of this white man's war," he shouted. There was silence.

"James." Hoop's reply was slow, articulate and methodical. "And George."

"They're dead!" Richter could hide it no longer. Hubert would find out later anyway.

Pulling him out of harm's way had resulted in the unexpected. A conflict had ensued between the two men left behind, causing one to attack the other. The British had shot the assailant themselves; apparently the other died from the trauma of the attack. Not what Richter had expected, but the outcome would certainly have unsettled the British rats in their tunnels.

"What have you done?" Hubert's shoulders sank at his words. "Murderer. A violation." He shook his head.

"I murdered no one." Richter paced the room in frustration. The conversation wasn't going where he wanted it to. *There was no time for this.* "Your British friends killed each other."

"They're not my friends." Hoop adjusted his pillow. "Not anymore, but what you did was a sin."

"Why do you care?" asked Richter bluntly.

"James and George were innocent men, prisoners of war. They

should have been treated in line with the Geneva Convention. Not tortured." The two men were expendable and insignificant, that was the truth, but if Richter tried to point that out it wouldn't help right now.

"General Franco defined you all as spies," he said, "hiding on Spanish territory."

Hubert interrupted. "Rubbish. You'll pay a price, you know that don't you?"

Richter ignored him.

"There'll be a reckoning, if not in this life then in the next. You've committed a mortal sin," Hubert went on. "Maybe God can give you absolution, I can't."

The negro had no idea what he was talking about.

"You'll be held accountable." The negro's voice began to sound like that of a priest. It was all so ridiculous, thought Richter. They were at war.

"Accountable?" He couldn't contain himself. "You're not the intelligent negro I thought you were. I'll be dead long before anyone can hold me accountable." It felt good to speak his mind. He'd bottled it all up for so long, the pressure on him had been immense. "Saving you alone could have me sent to the Russian front if we're not careful." He took a seat. "You forget yourself, Sergeant Fundi. I have my reasons for saving you but don't run away with the idea it's because I want a chess partner. I want much more than chess from you!" Hubert glared at him for a long period. Richter waited for him to speak but he didn't. They just looked at each other. Richter's brow furrowed in confusion but he didn't break the spell. It was intimate. The eye contact. Then something unexpected happened. Hubert's dark glare softened. They were the eyes of a friend. There was no hate or animosity in them but deep warmth. Hubert's whole demeanour had shifted. The impact on Richter was immediate. He relaxed, the muscles in his face, the tension in his back and shoulders, slipped away, all of it. Hubert could see past his SS uniform. He'd stopped pretending. The negro was never more alluring than at that moment.

When Hubert finally spoke his tone matched his soft eyes.

"What do you really want from me, Wolfgang?" It was the first time he'd heard Hubert use his Christian name.

Richter looked at the open door. He knew there were no guards outside, he'd sent them away and would have heard the old clanky door at the end of the corridor open if any of them had returned. He'd learnt to be over-cautious, with so much to lose. He couldn't afford to make a mistake, ever. He couldn't afford to get it wrong. To misread situations. *Was he misreading this one?*

The negro never had him more confused.

He wanted to ask Hubert if he'd been to Bavaria, but of course he hadn't. He wanted to suggest that one day after all this was over, they might see it together. The idea was bizarre, even to him. They weren't friends and never would be. He'd never be walking the Bavarian hills with a negro in lederhosen. Richter listened to the silence in the room. It had a tone, a pitch, a sound we all overlook when people are speaking. The truth of any conversation exists in empty spaces, not in the words. It's there deep in what isn't said. Richter listened. Then stiffened, his tone clear, his words precise.

"Every hour that passes, the risk of a British counterattack grows and my recall to Berlin becomes more likely. You're a traitor to the British and just another negro to my successor. We need each other. Don't you get it?" He stood up.

"I want you to tell me how to get into the tunnels and where the British spies are hiding. In return, you will get a ticket home, but I need you to tell me what I want to know and I need you to tell me now." Hubert's answer was quick as a flash.

"Gold." Richter thought he'd misheard the negro until he said it again. "I want gold. Safe passage to Namibia and enough gold to sit out the war." He mimicked Richter as he articulated every syllable of the words that followed. "That is what I want."

Gold? Richter found himself repeating the word. It was the last thing he'd expected Hubert to say.

"Give me gold and I'll give you the British spies and four secret accesses to the tunnel system." It was exactly what Richter wanted. He'd offered paper money for information on taking the Rock but gold? Could he even do that without approval from Berlin? *They'd never give it.* They expected him to torture information out of the British, not buy them off with Third Reich riches. He'd never get away with it.

"The British know your spies frequent Hotel Reina Cristina across the bay in Algeciras and have done for years." Hubert adjusted his pillow confidently. "It's the perfect location. It has excellent vantage points." The negro continued, "They also know about your spy houses along the coast." Hubert had Richter's full attention. "Villas Leon, San Luis, Villa Isabel and Haus Keller. The British call the road from Algeciras to Gibraltar, Spy Row."

"Okay. Gold. It's a deal," said Richter unblinking, reaching out his hand. "Now tell me, where are the spies?"

Hubert gave Richter's hand a light shake and let it go again. "Gold first."

"You have my word," said Richter. Hubert's withering silent reply questioned Richter's honour. Any other negro he'd have shot just for the look but somehow, Hubert had got under his skin, and he hated him for it.

"When then?" Richter's irritation was only outweighed by his frustration.

"When the gold is loaded aboard a plane and I'm on it with the engine running," replied Hubert confidently.

Richter headed for the door, blood rushing to his cheeks. He was ready to shoot this man. He needed to get out of the room before he did.

The guards outside the cold stone building were smoking. Richter lit one himself to calm his nerves and he watched the young British medic getting searched on his way in to see Hubert. If he gave gold to the negro, Haas would be the problem. Major Haas could never know. Richter blew smoke into the darkness of the evening and watched it float up the silhouette of the Rock beyond. *Why was everything so difficult?* A little gold, he told himself, and a seat on a plane to Casablanca, just that and he'd be inside the tunnels. He could arrange that. Saturday morning would work. Haas and his men, like the rest of the Rock, would be too hungover from their Thursday night parties to care. By the time they'd sobered up, he'd have captured the British spies and justified Hubert's flight home.

Richter blew a slow steady stream of smoke out into the cool Gibraltar evening air. If nothing else, he finally had his answer to that burning question that had so bothered him. Why was there only one negro on the Rock and how did he know so much about British intelligence? It was so simple. *Hubert Fundi was a spy.*

61

SCREWDRIVER

1942, October 8 (10:00h)
Main Chamber, Stay Behind Cave, Rock of Gibraltar

Carter turned the faucet closed and the water stopped running from the wash pit. He wasn't sure he'd ever get used to the free-flowing stream that had returned to change everything in the cave. A simple downpour of rain had saved the mission and maybe even their lives. Water back in the system dramatically improved the atmosphere amongst the team along with their health. Carter made sure that everybody replenished their missing body fluids, and the psychological and physical improvements had been fast and obvious at a glance. Maria's skin was radiant again, her hair glossy and rich. Somehow she'd managed to avoid a miscarriage; she really was a remarkably resilient woman, on all fronts. That said, the elephant in the room, the baby on its way, was an issue they could no longer ignore.

Maria would give birth any day now. They were about to be faced with a screaming child. Barring a nasty fall or some other unforeseen circumstances, they needed an immediate plan and Logan hadn't made one. Was Maria going to be put out of the cave? It was against all protocol but it seemed the most sensible option now. It was the one he would argue for. He'd gambled that the pregnancy wouldn't run its course but it had. They were in the worst possible position, the one Bunny had warned of. He had every right to say 'told you so' but he hadn't. Even Bunny had cooled on the idea of hurting the child in any way.

Albert had soundproofed the radio room as best he could with cardboard boxes. It was where Maria would give birth although it wasn't a long-term solution. The cardboard would muffle the sounds of a crying baby, but that was all. In preparing the room Albert and Maria had become inseparable. The two were almost clandestine in their long stays together in the radio room. He could see Logan's jealousy of the boy, he too felt a little of it, but their team leader was no fool. Public shows of resentment towards Young Albert wouldn't curry any favour for him with Maria, quite the contrary.

Carter pulled on the tea leaves tin lid. It was stuck again. He gave it two knocks on the tabletop but this time it didn't release the cover. It was time to fix the damn thing once and for all. Bunny had already powered one of the team's three batteries and was on the bicycle peddling amps into the other. Carter left through the door towards the radio room. He could see Logan at the top of the flight of stairs gazing out of the east wall lookout. He was about to open the radio room door when he knocked on it instead. It came as a surprise to him that he'd done so. There wasn't much privacy in the cave for any of them and the radio room certainly wasn't a place to look for it, but he knocked all the same. There was no answer. Carter entered.

Neither Albert nor Maria was inside. They must have been up at the west wall getting some air. Carter scanned the shelves for that same screwdriver, the flathead one he'd used to open the hatch. Just a bend of the top of the tin should permanently loosen the lid for good. There were tools scattered around the room. Albert appeared to be working on something but the screwdriver was nowhere in sight. Carter opened two of the cupboards under the desk looking for Albert's toolbox, then finally behind the third door, at the back next to the wall, stacked on top of a large pile of intelligence gathering log sheets, he saw the toolbox he was looking for. He pulled it out. Carter was just thinking how the box was way lighter than he expected when Albert arrived in the doorway.

"Don't touch that!" The boy rushed forward and snatched the toolbox. The assault caught Carter by surprise.

"Woah! Albert. What are you doing?"

"You can't come in here just taking things." Carter wasn't sure exactly what the problem was but he'd had enough of Albert's childish antics. The radio room wasn't his private preserve. He needed to make that clear, right here and now.

"First of all, calm down," said Carter. The commotion brought Bunny and Logan to the doorway. "This radio room is NOT your personal space."

"What's in the box, Albert?" asked Logan. Albert had both hands around the toolbox, pulling it tight to his chest.

"You have no right," repeated Albert. There was a whine in his tone.

"Give me the toolbox, Corporal Hamilton." Logan put his hand out. It wasn't a request but a clear order.

Albert took a step back, the only space left in the small room, but Logan was upon him. It took very little of Logan's brute strength to rip the box from Albert's grasp.

Logan handed it to Carter who opened the lid.

There was nothing but ripped-up toilet paper on the inside, then Carter saw it scuttle. He almost dropped the box in shock. A mouse. *There was a mouse in the toolbox.* Carter put the box down on the radio room table as gently as he could. He now knew what Albert had been hiding. Carter had allowed his imagination to run wild, now came the truth. Albert had a pet mouse. Carter felt like an idiot.

Albert moved quickly to comfort the frightened creature which was now cowering in the corner of his toolbox home. Albert picked up his pet, cupping the mouse in his hands, and holding it close. Carter suddenly saw the real Albert: the frightened child who had been put in uniform without the opportunity to grow up first.

"What's its name?" asked Carter in the softest voice he could muster. Albert's posture, hurt look and silence mirrored Carter's new view of the boy.

"His name's Bertie," said Albert finally.

"How long have you had Bertie, Albert?" Carter's medical mind kicked in. Bertie had been running around urinating in the radio room and at the west wall lookout for how long? The last thing they needed was another sickness.

"I rescued him after the first few days." Albert stroked the head of the rodent who seemed much more relaxed now in the hand of his friend.

"Christ, Albert. You know they transmit disease, don't you?" Carter couldn't believe the boy could be so stupid.

"I knew that would be your attitude! That's why I had to keep him a secret. Bertie's very clean." Carter shook his head.

"Albert, there's a chance that Bertie could make us all sick again. You understand that don't you?"

Logan stepped forward again. His frame stood tall, his chest pushed out as he grabbed at the mouse. Albert screamed, the pitch was high, like Maria's. The boy twisted to avoid Logan and protect Bertie but fell backwards in the small space and against the table. Bertie didn't wait for his defender to right himself but shot out of Albert's hand, down his leg in the direction of the radio room door. Logan was quick to act, and his boot came down on Bertie, hard enough to kill the mouse in one stamp.

Albert's knees gave way and he fell to the radio room floor with the distraught hopeless sound of a grieving widow. He crawled the short distance to his dead friend bleeding out on the cork tiles.

"Nooo…" An anguished moan escaped his quivering lips. "What have you done, what have you done?" And the boy began to cry.

62

TEARS OF BLOOD

1942, October 8 (23:10h)
Main Chamber, Stay Behind Cave, Rock of Gibraltar

It was Maria who finally managed to extract Bertie's dead body from Albert's hand. Carter didn't ask what she did with the mouse and in truth he would have rather she didn't handle the creature in her current condition, but she'd insisted. Maria also spent the next two hours alone with Albert in the radio room. When she finally did come out, leaving Albert on his own to grieve, she pointedly ignored Logan, despite his multiple attempts to explain his actions and how they were for 'the safety of the mission'. The truth was, Carter agreed with his team leader. Bertie couldn't live with them as a pet, the outcome was for the best, even if Logan's route to get to it was questionable.

The main chamber was finally quiet again. Logan and Bunny were asleep after transmitting the day's intelligence gathering to London while Albert hadn't been seen for hours; he and Maria were still awake, neither of them seemed to be having much luck getting shut-eye. Carter lay staring at the ceiling. Logan had a knack for dismantling any progress they made in building positivity within the team. It was almost as if he wanted the mission to be full of turmoil. Killing Bertie was unnecessary and his own relationship with Albert would probably never heal. He was trying but failing to hold together what they called a 'Team' at the start of the mission. It didn't feel like a team anymore. Just a group of people who were tolerating each other while suffering their own personal demons silently or otherwise. Including him.

Maria was on the move.

Carter watched her cross the cork floor quietly on her way to the toilet. Her hair looked like she'd been dragged through a hedge backwards, and she used her hand to push it from her face – an inconsequential mannerism now etched on the back of his eye. She disappeared through the door. Carter rolled over. He was going to struggle to function in the morning if he didn't get at least five hours' shut-eye but seeing Maria play with her hair in the low light wasn't going to help him sleep. He sighed and gave the wall a little tap with his fist. He closed his eyes as Maria closed the toilet door.

Had they all been too hard on Albert? If he hadn't suggested the mouse was a health hazard maybe Logan wouldn't have stamped on it. The boy had obviously had Bertie for weeks and he hadn't fallen sick. *No. It wasn't his fault.* They couldn't have a mouse peeing around the place, God knows the next time they got sick somebody might never recover. Albert wasn't a child, they couldn't make decisions based on the boy's feelings, they weren't running a nursery. He'd get over it. *He'd talk to him in the morning.*

Carter spun again in his bunk, positioning himself for a good view of Maria as she walked back. Maybe she'd toss her hair again or perform some new action he hadn't seen before. What did she see in Logan? He would never understand that. They weren't well matched, anyone could see it. She was smart and kind; he was vain and cruel.

Carter heard the toilet pump and then the door open. What did it matter anyway, she didn't think of him in that way, and never would. Maria screamed!

Carter leapt from his bunk so fast that his rib electrified his nervous system and his ankle, still wrapped in a bandage, barely held his weight.

It wasn't a light scream but a full-blooded shriek and she gave another. Bunny was at the toilet door before Carter.

Maria was standing in the radio room doorway and screamed again. This time louder. Bunny grabbed her from behind, putting his hand over her mouth and dragging her backwards.

Then Carter saw him. Albert, lying on the floor of the radio room in a thick puddle of blood. His face white, lips black, eyes staring back at them. Maria was hyperventilating behind Bunny's hand. The boy had been dead for hours. The fatal wound was a long cut with a sharp instrument from his wrist to his bicep.

The muted sound of a scuffle behind him drew Carter's glance. Logan was grappling with Bunny to release Maria who was trying to catch her breath. Whispering abuse at each other, Logan held Bunny's wrist, their arms tangled, like Greco-Roman wrestlers, connecting and releasing continuously. Carter shut the radio room door but Maria, having stood in Albert's pool of blood, painted the corridor in footprints. She was frantic, trying to wipe the red stuff from her foot but getting nowhere in panic. Logan and Bunny stood over her trying to disconnect their hands from one another, which were one step away from turning into fists. Carter knelt in front of Maria. She was shaking all over.

"Maria!" he said as loud as he dared. She ignored him. The panic contorted her face. Her mouth was twisted, and her nose flared as the nostrils continuously reached for clean air. Her eyes were full of fear.

Carter put both hands on Maria's cheeks and held her head and vision. He slapped Maria's face, then again, a second time. Logan and Bunny stopped grappling as Maria focused.

"Breathe," said Carter. Maria looked into his eyes. "Deep breaths." Carter pulled off his shirt and, taking hold of her bloody foot, wrapped it so the blood was out of sight. "We'll get it off. Breathe!" Maria nodded a short fast nod as Logan put his arms around her. Maria released all her weight onto Logan and began to sob quietly.

* * *

Meanwhile, outside a cave at the top of the Rock, in one of the pedestrian tunnels, a pale freckle-faced junior SS officer with a stethoscope plugged into both ears crept along the wall. He stopped momentarily to listen before moving on again. His chin was up in the air and his eyes were full of interest.

63

DAMN WAR

1942, October 9 (11:00h)
Radio Room, Stay Behind Cave, Rock of Gibraltar

Carter and Bunny hadn't said a word to each other as they crawled the cork floor mopping, dabbing and drying the large pool that had leaked out of Albert. The stain on the cork tiles would never come out; it was black, in the low light, a permanent reminder of how they'd failed the boy.

Carter had helped Maria, still tearful, up to the west wall lookout, as far away from the scene as she could get. Logan had offered to escort her but she'd refused his arm. Defending Logan didn't come naturally to Carter but if Albert had snapped over the death of his pet mouse he'd have snapped over something else down the line. Logan didn't kill Albert.

Carter stirred his tea at the radio room table. He'd prepared the corpse, while Bunny dug a second space in the corridor next to Windy. Albert lay on the floor of the radio room next to his feet. It upset Maria to look at his body in the main chamber.

Wrapping up Windy had been bad enough but Albert had been worse. He hadn't failed Windy. He also hadn't suspected Windy of being a traitor. He'd tried not to look at the boy's face as he'd worked, his pale young skin, so young. *Damn war,* he told himself, but he knew the blame lay closer to home.

Maria, Maria, Maria. She was now always on his mind. If it wasn't the pregnancy, it was watching her, just be her. He should probably give her a full medical before the birth. Carter took a sip of his tea and looked up at Albert's poster of Ingrid Bergman. It was going to be difficult to convince Maria to give birth, here, in the radio room. Although it was the best place. Albert's work soundproofing with the cardboard boxes shouldn't go to waste. The irony of a birth and a death in that same little space had surely not been lost on any of them. Albert's body was putting him off tea.

Carter stacked the completed intelligence gathering sheets in individual team member name order, Logan's on top, and took hold of the chain to turn the radio room lamp off when something on one of the sheets caught his eye. He let go of the chain, picked up a sheet and compared it to another. Rifling through the sheets he compared two more, then three. His brow furrowed. Pulling out another box of older intelligence gathering log sheets Carter began to rummage through them looking for something specific. Finding it, he stopped. He held two sheets up to the lamp, side by side, and switched his eyes between them until he was sure.

Bunny opened the door to the radio room, a worried look on his face.

"You'd better come quick!"

"Maria?" asked Carter, stuffing a sheet in his pocket.

"Yes. She's bleeding," said Bunny.

64

MISSING PIECE

What he'd found would have to wait. Carter had dreaded this moment, despite having prepared for it in every way he could. Even if the birth went well, they were entering new territory. They needed to get Albert's body out of the radio room and pillows and bedding in for Maria.

"Boil some water, Bunny!" said Carter. A baby was about to arrive in their very unstable environment. A baby none of them wanted here, least of all Bunny. If the child died today, in the process, it wouldn't be a bad thing. *My God, man!* He shook off the thought. It went against everything he believed as a doctor and a human being.

Stepping through into the main chamber Carter tried to take in the scene. Logan's mattress was on its side half off his bunk. Maria was back from the west wall lookout, sat with her legs apart, her hand on her knee covered in blood and Logan, what was he doing standing over on the other side of the room?

"I told you. I didn't put it there." Logan's voice, frustrated, but low in tone, was aimed at Maria. *Didn't put what where? What the hell was going on?*

As Carter reached Maria she drew his eye to the table. There it was. The missing shard of glass from the mirror. He recognised it immediately. Maria put out her hand, her palm was cut. A thin slice.

Blood on the shard of the mirror, blood on the table and Maria's hand. Maria had cut herself with the shard. Carter ran to his medicine cabinet.

"Take her to the wash pit." Carter grabbed a bottle of sulfa powder and a bandage.

Bunny led heavily pregnant Maria slowly behind the row of boxes to the wash pit faucet as Logan looked on.

"How, Maria?" Carter took her hand and held it under the water. Maria winced with pain. The cut was minor, just a nick, the blood was making it look much worse than it was. She didn't answer so Carter looked at Bunny. In turn, he looked at Logan a few feet behind them now, getting a better view of Maria's injury. Patting the wound dry, Carter sprinkled some yellow sulfa powder onto the still slightly bleeding wound. Maria winced again. Carter took a piece of gauze and pressed it down hard.

"Keep the pressure up." Maria closed her hand around the gauze and made a fist.

"What happened?" Carter asked again while wrapping a small bandage around the gauze. He ripped the end and tied it tightly. Maria looked at Logan for permission to speak. She didn't need it. Logan spoke for her.

"She cut her hand on the shard of the mirror."

"I can see that," said Carter. Bunny chimed in with venom.

"The lassie was making Logan's bed. The shard was hidden under his mattress." Bunny's tone convicted Logan of every crime he'd ever assigned to him. "She cut her hand tucking in this blanket." His intonation of the word *blanket* was the final nail in the coffin. "Why did you have the shard of the mirror under your mattress, sir?" Bunny seemed to enjoy the word 'sir', as never before.

"I told you! I didn't put it there."

"Then how did it get there, the fucking tooth fairy?" Bunny's body language illustrated his mental state, he was on edge, ready to snap.

"What would I want with a piece of broken mirror?"

Bunny was quick to reply. "Been signalling to your German friends, haven't you?" The words came out of his mouth like water finally released from a dam.

"You really are a stupid Scotsman. Are you hearing this?" Logan looked to Carter for some support.

Carter knew he hadn't put the shard of the mirror under Logan's mattress, Maria cut her hand on it, so that only left Bunny. Was Bunny trying to frame Logan? For what? And then there were the intelligence gathering sheets.

"I've been looking at your log sheets, Logan." This wasn't how he wanted to question Logan about the sheets. He hadn't expected a confrontation, but he couldn't have this conversation without addressing the sheets.

"Why?" replied Logan, putting his hands on his hips.

"Your sheets, unlike the rest of ours, show almost no German Kriegsmarine naval movement through the Straits. Your sheets fail to distinguish the type of vessel observed on almost every occasion, and despite multiple battleships spotted by the rest of us, you appear not to have seen a battleship. Not one. Not since the mission started. Can you explain that, Logan?" Logan simply shook his head.

"Poppycock, you're mistaken, I know what I wrote." Now Carter knew Logan was lying. He'd seen the sheets with his own eyes. "Fetch a sheet and show me!" demanded his team leader. Carter pulled the crumpled one from his pocket and tossed it at Logan. He and Bunny watched as Logan flattened out the paper and read it.

Logan's brow furrowed with confusion. He was almost apologetic with an innocent frown when he finally looked up and spoke. "I didn't write this." Carter knew everybody's handwriting, and that was Logan's.

"I knew it!" shouted Bunny. "I bloody knew it."

"That's my handwriting but I didn't write those words, somebody has forged this sheet." Logan looked at Bunny and the accusation was clear.

Damn, he was good, thought Carter. He had to hand it to Logan; he'd fooled them all. All except Bunny. Even now, having been caught, Logan was convincingly earnest, sticking to his guns.

It all came together. The apes had been innocent after all. Everything now pointed to Logan. If Logan was lying about the intelligence log sheets, what else was he lying about? The shard of mirror under his mattress, for sure. Logan was a saboteur if not a spy, just like Bunny said he was.

He'd suspected Albert because of Logan. Logan had pointed him at the youngster, planting that seed of doubt with the whole Tavistock debacle. His casualness over the nightly transmissions to the Admiralty in London. All the while Logan, their team leader, the man Carter himself had put in charge of the mission, was trying to sabotage it. *Why would he do that?*

"The game's up, Logan, quit the act." Bunny moved towards Logan. Carter could see Bunny had made up his mind about what happened next.

"It's the Scotsman." There was a panic in Logan's voice Carter hadn't heard before as he looked at Maria. Her eyes were red and wet, her cheeks pale.

"Admit it, you bastard. We're on to you." Carter couldn't disagree with Bunny this time. He didn't want to believe it but the evidence was clear. The intelligence sheets in his handwriting, the shard under his mattress. Maria must have thought it too or why wasn't she defending him? He'd been disruptive from the start. Had he broken the radio receiver, too? Stolen the spare part? He'd wanted to end the mission when the water was polluted. He'd wanted out from the very start. If he wasn't a spy, what was he? A danger to the mission at the very least. He could no longer be trusted.

* * *

Logan implored Carter with every wrinkle of his face. *What did he expect?* To argue a case for him. He would if there was a case to argue but there wasn't, not this time. The three men eyed each other, unsure of what to do next. They'd all made up their minds about where they stood and what they believed. The time for debate was over.

The atmosphere changed in the room. Carter could see from the body language, they all felt it. They were entering the point of no return. The moment things got physical they couldn't be taken back. The Rubicon would have been crossed, but what was the alternative? They were accusing Logan of spying, of treason. They couldn't just sit down and have a cup of tea now. Logan took a step back from Bunny and widened his peripheral vision. He looked like a man who knew what was coming. He would defend himself. His back to the corner of the wall, trapped by Carter and Bunny on both sides. Logan clenched his fists.

"No, stop it," said Maria with panic in her voice but it was too late. Carter knew what had to happen. They all did. Bunny moved first, running at Logan, wrapping an arm around his waist and rugby-tackling him, sending them both crashing into the wall. Carter saw Bunny hit his head, which would need attention when this was over but right now the goal was restraining Logan. He ran forward and grabbed Logan's arm. "Stop it, leave him alone!" Maria held her belly in one hand and leaned against the wall with the other. Logan released his hand from Bunny's shirt, grabbed Carter and pulled him hard forward, trying to head butt him. Logan's head hit Carter's shoulder but Bunny's attempt to do the same landed on Logan's nose, breaking it. Carter was out of his depth. His experience of fighting had been limited to his schooldays; none of those experiences had prepared him for this. Bunny and Logan were ferocious, like wild animals fighting for their lives. There was nothing gentlemanly about it. Logan brought his clenched fist down onto Bunny's face multiple times in succession. Blood burst from Bunny's nose but the Scotsman smiled at Logan. Who smiled when they were punched in the face? Carter felt he didn't know Bunny, not that Bunny. The Scotsman's teeth were covered in blood. Logan fell forward with his head against Bunny's chest.

Opening his mouth, he tried to bite him but only managed to clamp down on the shirt. Carter threw two punches, the first glanced off the side of Logan's head and the second caught him squarely, hurting Carter's knuckles more than Logan's head. Bunny brought his knee up into Logan's groin. Logan yelped as the rest of his oxygen was stolen from his lungs. Carter and Bunny stepped away. Logan lay gasping for breath on the cork floor, saliva popping from his wet mouth like the exhaust of a poorly tuned engine. Bunny stepped forward and kicked Logan in the back. Carter couldn't believe his eyes.

"Leave him alone," Maria pleaded weakly through her wet mouth of salty tears.

"Bunny, no!" The Scotsman kicked him again, harder, ignoring Carter who pulled him away from Logan on the floor.

"What are you doing, man?" Carter didn't recognise Bunny, the man he thought he knew was gone.

"Traitor!" hissed Bunny at Logan still squirming on the floor.

"Pull yourself together, man." Carter pushed Bunny against the wall. It got his attention. The Scotsman's wild eyes gave Carter the impression he was next. Blood trickled down Bunny's forehead and dripped from above his eye onto his bright red cheek.

"We need to patch your head." The words took the fight out of the Scotsman. His taut shoulders dropped and his face lost its sharpness. He slid down the wall to a seated position on the cork floor. *Concussed?* thought Carter.

There was silence in the main chamber, only the panting sound of men trying to catch their breath and the light sobbing of Maria as she made her way to Logan. Carter ran for rope, as many short pieces as he could find, grabbed a chair and carried it over to Logan. Maria was on her knees by his side, stroking his head, still crying. There was no lifting him onto the chair without Bunny's help, he was too heavy but he needed to act fast or Logan would recover, *then what?* Carter laid the chair on its side behind Logan and started to tie the chair to him. Legs first to the bottom of the chair then Carter adjusted Logan on his side, pulled his arms to the back of the chair and started to tie his hands.

Bunny was on his feet. The Scotsman stumbled over to the table and tried to sit. Carter quickly finished tying Logan's hands to the back of the chair, left him on the floor tended by Maria, and made for Bunny.

* * *

1942, October 9 (11:17h)
Tunnel, Top of the Rock of Gibraltar

Meanwhile, a pale freckle-faced junior SS officer held a stethoscope to the tunnel wall and listened intently. He nodded silent confirmation of his findings to the Wehrmacht uniformed men flanking him. Pulling gently on a corrugated iron panel, the SS officer watched it come away from the rock and reveal a crudely bricked-up entrance.

65

NO MORE GAMES

1942, October 9 (11:19h)
Third Reich Army Corps & SS Headquarters,
The Governor's Residence, Rock of Gibraltar

Richter's tired eyes watched Hubert approach the Governor's residence through this window onto the square. He loved and hated the negro in equal measure. One part of him wanted to shoot the bastard for not having helped him avoid this outcome. The other wanted to protect him, keep him hidden away somewhere so he could continue to see him, speak with him and who knew what else.

Major Haas caught Richter's eye on the other side of the square. The major was looking directly at him. So were the three men with him. Their posture reflected their intentions. Aggressive, poised. Haas saw Hubert being led towards the main entrance of the residence. *A vulture,* thought Richter, *circling, waiting for the moment of death before moving in to feed.*

Richter had been summoned to Berlin. They all knew what that meant. He wouldn't be coming back to the Rock. Major Haas was earmarked for a promotion to colonel. He would take charge of Gibraltar. Richter's friends in Berlin had told him as much.

It had all happened so quickly, he'd been given no notice. The transport he'd planned for Hubert had been cancelled by one of his superiors in Berlin. The gold he'd arranged, loaded aboard the plane, had 'gone missing'. Then came the news of his recall. His plan to buy Hubert's information had got out. It was the final ammunition his enemies needed to bring him down. Haas, the swine, had surely played his part. Berlin had had enough.

Richter hadn't slept a wink, while the rest of his men had partied late into the night – surely another nail in his coffin, unauthorised parties! The bags under his eyes weighed heavy as did his heart for the loss to follow. He checked the clip of his Luger pistol and put the weapon in his pocket. Hubert had given him no other choice. He'd waited and waited for the negro's help to get the information he desperately needed but Hubert had decided to play games with him, to ask for too much. He'd allowed his emotions for Hubert to cloud his judgement. He'd saved the negro's life. *How many times?* What had he received in return? Richter's time had run out and that meant Hubert's had too.

The door to his office opened and Hubert was shown in. Richter watched as his negro prisoner dared to judge his own appearance. He wasn't his usual groomed self and it was obvious to Hubert too. His hair was uncombed, he was unshaven with light wisps of facial growth patching his chin and cheeks. His uniform was dishevelled and his jackboots were scarred and scuffed. He looked like he felt, so didn't bother with pleasantries. Reaching into the drawer of his desk Richter pulled out a gold bar and dropped it on the table with a thud.

"Tell me what you know and do it now!" he demanded.

Hubert stepped forward and with both hands picked up the heavy gold bar on the desk. He turned it over, studying it. Weighing it with little lifts. He ran his fingers over the swastika, gently and thoughtfully, as if to formulate some grand assumption about war itself.

"And the rest?" said Hubert. The image of a negro holding a bar of Third Reich gold in his office was bizarre even to Richter.

"On the plane waiting for you as we speak." Richter's lip twitched. There was no going out to the waiting aircraft, there WAS no waiting aircraft.

Hubert looked at the clock on the mantelpiece. "I'll tell you at the airfield." He turned to lead Richter out of his own office.

"No," shouted Richter. His tone was adamant. "I've kept my word. Now you keep yours. Where are the British spies hiding and how do my men access the Rock? Tell me now and I'll send you home." Hubert looked again at the mantelpiece before turning his back on Richter, walking across the room and surveying the walls and their paintings. Richter's blood boiled. His transfer to the Russian front was probably being signed as they spoke and he was still being led a merry dance.

"What more can I do for you? There's a plane loaded with gold waiting for you on the runway. Take it. In God's name take it and give me what I want!"

Hubert looked up at a painting of the Rock with galleons approaching under full sail. "I don't trust you, Wolfgang," was his reply.

The negro was now insulting his honour. He'd had enough. Richter pulled his Luger pistol from his pocket. His head was hot, his face red. The vein in his neck pulsated. He didn't want to escalate the situation in this manner but he had no choice. Richter marched towards Hubert as the door to his office opened.

"A call for you from Berlin, Herr Standartenführer. It's SS Headquarters." The guard's words only hastened Richter's approach to Hubert and the painting.

It was now or never to provide him with the British spies and access to the Rock. It was now or never that Hubert could save him from the Russian front and save himself.

"Tell them I'll call them back." He grabbed Hubert by the neck and pushed him up against the ornate gold frame of the painting. He saw Hubert's eyes blink in surprise as he gripped his throat and squeezed, making it hard for him to breathe. Richter put the barrel of his pistol on Hubert's forehead and pushed it into his skull.

"Last chance, Hubert." Richter had never been this close to his negro friend. He could smell his breath, some kind of meat, although not unpleasant. He could see the dimples on his brown skin, which was oily, not dry. His stubble hair was black above his lip and on his chin but it was his eyes that unsettled Richter. He was choking Hubert, his grip was restricting the air he needed to fill his lungs. The negro was one trigger-pull away from his life being snatched from him but Hubert's eyes weren't blazing with fear or wide with dilated pupils, not at all. They were soft, calm, serene, and even kind. What was worse, they weren't even looking at him. Hubert was looking over Richter's shoulder. He had the negro's life in his hands, he would decide if Hubert lived or died at that moment, but it was Hubert who was somehow in control, not him.

"I'm sorry, Standartenführer," came the nervous voice still in the doorway, "but SS Headquarters don't want to speak with you. There's a transport aircraft bound for Berlin on the runway, ready for take-off." The guard's voice dried up, and he swallowed as he looked for saliva to lubricate it. "They're ordering you to board the plane." He paused again. "Now, Herr Standartenführer."

Richter's grip eased on Hubert's throat. He looked at the messenger in the doorway whose gaze dropped to the floor to avoid eye contact. It was too late. It was over. He was as good as dead. He might as well turn the pistol on himself and blow his own brains out. He looked back at Hubert. This time the negro was looking directly at him, maybe even through him. He was smiling too. Not a big smile with teeth but it was there behind the negro's eyes. Not inviting, caring or playful, but a twisted one. A liar's smile. Richter's heart had been pumping fast on adrenaline but it slowed at the revelation. A plane was waiting. He'd lost his command and his reputation, lost to Haas, lost to the British. There was only one game left that he could still win. Richter looked deep into Hubert's laughing eyes, adjusted his index finger on the pistol's trigger and squeezed hard.

66

SAFETY FIRST

As Richter squeezed the pistol's trigger nothing happened. Harder and harder he pulled on the trigger but the weapon failed to discharge its bullet and splatter Hubert's skull across the painting of approaching galleons. *Safety catch,* Richter remembered. He flicked it from on, to off.

"We've found them, Herr Standartenführer." The voice in the doorway was different, deeper in tone and more confident. Richter looked over in a trance-like state. His focal length took a moment to adjust. He saw the stethoscope before the man. "The British spies, Herr Standartenführer, we've found them," said the pale freckle-faced junior SS officer. Richter dithered as he tried to comprehend the words he was hearing. He looked again at Hubert. The smile he was sure he could see was gone, replaced by something resembling doubt. Richter watched as doubt turned to insecurity before the fear he'd hoped for.

It wasn't over, maybe he could still turn it all around. He let go of Hubert and walked, pistol still in hand, towards the doorway. *Focus,* he told himself. Hold it together. There's a way back if you hold it together.

As he reached the doorway a third guard appeared, this one holding a dented tin of corned beef in one hand and a handwritten note in the other.

Wolfgang read the first sentence of the handwritten note, then the signature 'A-54'. He stuffed it into his pocket. He didn't need to see any more.

"Have Sergeant Fundi escorted back to the POW camp." Richter never looked back at his friend. He followed the freckle-faced stethoscope-carrying junior SS officer out of the building. "Goodbye, Hubert," were his final words.

1942, October 9 (11:27h)
Main Chamber, Stay Behind Cave, Rock of Gibraltar

"You stupid bastards," hissed Logan from the floor, kicking wildly at his restraints and trying to release himself from the chair. Carter and Bunny waited for Logan to calm down before righting the chair.

"What now? You can't keep me tied up here forever." Logan spat blood onto the cork floor before continuing, "I'm your superior officer. This is mutiny. You'll both hang for it."

"You're the one who'll hang. You're a traitor," replied Bunny.

"You have no proof of me sabotaging anything,"

Bunny pushed out a laugh.

"Ah but that's where you're wrong. You faked your intelligence reports, proof in your own handwriting."

"You're accusing me of sabotage because you say I didn't note down a ship you say I should have seen and you say I put a piece of the broken mirror under my mattress? That's your proof, is it? You're an idiot."

"You broke the radio receiver and stole the spare part too," said Bunny.

"Did I?"

"Who are you working for, the Germans?" demanded Bunny. Logan laughed out loud and then addressed Carter.

"I'm surprised at you, Doctor Carter, a physician such as yourself, a man of letters and facts."

"Your intelligence gathering sheets are a problem, Logan. I didn't put the shard under your mattress and Maria cut herself on it so unless you're accusing Bunny of putting it there, how did it get there?"

"I'm accusing the Scotsman."

Carter could no longer take Logan seriously. "You wanted out of here on day one and have called for an end to the mission more times than I can remember."

"And that's your proof of wrongdoing is it?" Logan's tone was indignant.

He was right. The missing piece of the mirror would be the perfect tool to signal passing ships although nobody had actually caught Logan using it. The intelligence gathering sheets were all incorrect but Logan could say he wrote down what he thought he saw. Logan was right. Nothing they had on him would constitute proof at a military tribunal. The fact that they'd attacked their commanding officer and tied him to a chair, would not reflect well on them.

"I'm not saying you're a saboteur, but considering everything since you've been here in the cave, your behaviour, your desire to get out, I'll admit I don't trust you."

"I suppose I put the rat in the water tank too, did I?" It had crossed Carter's mind, despite Logan having been sick. Neither he nor Bunny said anything.

"Really!? That's what you think, I poisoned myself to sabotage the mission? Okay, you couple of geniuses, what do you plan to do with me? Are you going to keep me tied up for the next, what, a year maybe three?" Carter didn't have the first idea of what happened next. He was beginning to wish Bunny hadn't acted in such haste. *What if they were wrong?*

"We could drug him, what drugs do you have, Doc?" They couldn't drug him permanently, they didn't have enough morphine for that even if they wanted to.

"Just let us out, let us go," pleaded Maria.

"After what your boyfriend's done in here, no way. He'll run straight to his German friends."

"He's not a spy." It was the first time Maria had given her opinion on the matter and it only added to Carter's misgiving.

"Let me tell you what's going to happen here." Logan adjusted himself in the seat. "You're going to untie your commanding officer." Bunny laughed. "I'm going to accept that you both lost your minds for a moment due to solitary confinement. I'm not going to report the matter to the Admiralty and we are going to go on as normal. We'll complete the mission or stay as long as we can, trying." Carter liked the sound of the plan. Make it all go away. But he knew it was naive.

"We have to kill him," said Bunny. Maria made a guttural sound of shock.

"Nobody's killing anyone, Bunny." A shiver ran down Carter's back. Could he even control Bunny now? Would the Scotsman listen to him or were they on the edge of the abyss?

"There's no other way, Doc," insisted Bunny. "We can't trust him, we can't keep him tied up and we can't let him go." Carter desperately needed an alternative but nothing came to mind.

"I'll do it." Bunny nodded. He'd asked himself if he would, could, and answered, yes.

"You will, will you?" Logan replied angrily.

"Take Maria up to the west wall, I'll do it and get the body under the rubble before you come back down." Bunny spoke as if Logan wasn't even there. "Think of the mission, Tommy."

Carter didn't want to hear what he was hearing and the fact that Bunny believed his murderous plan was reasonable, deeply worried him.

"We can't complete the mission with two, Bunny." Carter decided to challenge logic rather than morality. He couldn't be a party to murdering a man and simply tell himself it was for the greater good. For King and country. *Could he?*

"We can't trust his intel so what good is he now?"

"And when the baby comes?" Logan's teeth were gritted. His eyes were dark and deeper set into his skull than Carter remembered them being. "It will cry. What then? You're going to send the doctor away and kill our baby too?"

Bunny didn't answer. Maria was looking at him.

"We're not killing anyone, for God's sake, listen to yourselves," shouted Carter.

"What then?" demanded Bunny. "If you're so bloody clever, what's your plan to preserve the mission?"

"Let me think!" insisted Carter. Everything was out of control, he was out of control. Logan's idea of just going back to normal and releasing him was sensible. Maria had a fearful look on her face. They all looked at Carter waiting for him to take charge of himself, of them, of the mission.

"We have to kill him, Doc, it's the only way." Bunny's tone was final.

"Let him murder me, why don't you?" Logan growled.

Carter put his head in his hands. They'd finally got to where he'd feared they would after Windy died. They'd descended into chaos no matter how he'd tried to prevent it. In the darkness of his hands, he wanted out of this god-awful place as much as anybody. His sanity was stretched, he couldn't take it anymore.

"Doc!" Bunny's voice was guttural, like a reflex. Carter came out from behind his hands just in time to see Logan swing the chair that he'd been tied to. It hit Bunny on the shoulder and the side of his head, sending him spinning off into the wall for a second time. Logan had slipped the ropes. Carter couldn't believe his eyes. Logan walked slowly up to the table. Carter didn't move, he just watched. He wasn't sure if it was the fear, his knowledge that he was no match for Logan in a fight or his desire for restored calm. Whatever it was he stayed seated in his chair and Logan stood in front of him. Logan's eyes were bloodshot and unblinking. He picked up the shard of the mirror. He was in touching distance but Carter could do nothing. He did nothing.

Logan turned back towards Bunny, still stunned and reeling from the blow of the chair.

"Logan, no." Maria read her boyfriend's thoughts first. Carter and

Maria watched in horror as Logan knelt beside Bunny. The first thrust of the sharp end of the shard grazed Bunny's face, and the second embedded itself in the Scotsman's throat.

"Logan!" Maria's voice echoed Carter's emotions. She called her boyfriend's name but the man she knew had left the room. Carter jumped to his feet but by the time he'd stepped out from behind the table Logan had driven three, four, five frenzied thrusts of the glass shard into Bunny's neck. Bunny's heart pumped blood clear across the chamber but Logan didn't stop, he just kept stabbing the Scotsman as fast as he could. In the face, in the ribs, wherever the shard would bury itself.

Logan looked around at Carter to see if he was coming. Wild-eyed, he never stopped stabbing, his face daring the doctor to try and stop him. Logan's hand was dripping with blood; his own, his hand lacerated from the assault, mixed with Bunny's. Carter could hear Maria hyperventilating, but he couldn't take his eyes off the murder or the murderer. Frozen by the spectacle, Carter did nothing. Maria vomited where she stood. Bunny, drenched in blood, was shaking on the floor, and finally he stopped gasping and lay still but Logan didn't stop. Like a crazed animal caught feeding on the flesh of its prey Logan continued to drive the shard into the dead body. The crazed individual in front of him, who was he? Carter didn't know him, but he knew he and Maria were next.

The gun, thought Carter, he needed Windy's revolver.

67

IT BETTER GO OFF

Carter ran for the cave entrance channel. Logan seemed to ignore him as he passed by, continuing to stab Bunny for every insult he'd uttered in the time they'd been locked up together. Like a fox in a chicken house, Logan watched Carter run aimlessly with no way out. His eyes lit, Logan appeared to enjoy ending Bunny's life, and he wasn't rushing it. Carter ran out onto the uneven rubble between the main chamber and the tunnel's bricked-up entrance. *Where was the revolver?* He couldn't remember. He scanned Windy's shallow grave. Yanking up the bricks and stones he cut his fingers, trapping them between the rubble, but adrenaline dulled the pain. At any moment he expected to see a blood-covered mad Logan in the doorway. He snatched at the bricks, dropping them in panic.

It was all happening in slow motion. His hands pulled at the bricks, his eyes trying to focus, his mind trying to think, to concentrate on what he was doing but the fear was paralysing. Carter's heart beat like it was trying to break out of his chest. He'd been afraid before but never like this.

Logan stepped into the open doorway. He was calm for a man who had just committed murder. Covered in blood he just stood there. Carter lifted a brick ready to throw it at Logan and there it was, the pistol wrapped in the cloth he'd covered it in. Logan's frame filled the doorway. He was larger than Carter remembered but he wasn't looking at him. Logan's blood-splattered body was shaped directly towards him but his head was turned, looking back inside the main chamber. Carter could hear Maria's voice. She was speaking to him but *what was she saying?* Carter unwrapped the cloth, and it took an age. Over and under, over and under. Finally, the handle.

Carter was sent flying off his feet. Logan was upon him. He dropped the revolver and came crashing down onto the uneven surface behind him. Even with the adrenaline pumping, Carter felt terrible pain as a brick cut his back. Logan was lying on top of him, *did he have the shard?* Expecting to be stabbed at any moment, Carter wrapped his hand around a brick and without thinking, he hit Logan as hard as he could on the side of his head. Like a boxer stunned for a moment by a punch Logan leaned against him. He was heavy, too heavy to roll aside. As Carter pushed to get free, Logan headbutted him. Carter's head bounced backwards hitting the bricks. His eyes rolled back into his head. The tunnel spun, he couldn't focus, and then he was back, albeit dizzy, waiting for Logan to hit him again but he didn't. Logan rolled to the side. Maria was in the doorway. She spoke but he was confused, his ears were ringing.

Logan would surely hit him again at any moment but nothing came. His head throbbed. Logan stumbled to his feet.

"Wait." Carter knew what was coming. Logan stood holding a brick of his own, the blood from his hand dripped down it and onto Windy's resting place beneath them. Logan steadied himself then stepped towards Carter. This time he heard Maria loud and clear.

"Logan!" Maria shouted. Logan heard it too. It snapped him from his bloodthirsty daze. His heavily pregnant girlfriend, one hand holding up his unborn child, the other Windy's revolver. It was pointed at Carter.

Logan dropped the brick. The frenzied madman was gone in an instant. He inspected his bloody hand. Carter could see at least one cut was deep, it would need stitches. His head throbbed and he felt the blood run down his back beneath his shirt.

Was it over? It seemed like it. Logan made his way across the rubble to Maria but stopped before he reached her. Touching his head he inspected the blood still seeping from Carter's attack. He looked back at Carter and weighed the situation with obvious thought.

"Don't, Logan, we need him," said Maria, still pointing the gun at Carter. She was trying to keep him alive, Carter knew it.

"Let's save the bullets. Might as well be hanged for a sheep as a lamb. Sorry, Doc, but what was it you said? I just don't trust you anymore." Carter saw the madman reinhabit Logan as he walked back towards him. Nowhere to run, he'd have to fight again. He picked up a brick but he knew. He knew the outcome of this before it began. This was a fight he couldn't win. He didn't have what it would take to beat Logan to death. There was no crazed killer inside him to protect him. He only knew how to save lives, not take them. He hadn't saved Bunny and he couldn't save himself. His hand gripped the brick a little tighter. Die he might but he would die trying. He wasn't going to make it easy. Carter ran at Logan and the gun went off.

The sound of the discharged weapon in the enclosed space echoed off the hard rock surfaces and rang in Carter's ears. He closed his eyes and shook his head. There was a thud in his eardrums, the smell of sulphur from the discharged weapon in his nostrils. He squinted but couldn't shake off the thumping sound.

Maria had shot Logan, the father of her unborn child.

Leaning against the doorway, she dropped the revolver, both hands now clutching her stomach.

Logan lay sprawled face down across the uneven rubble, a hole in the back of his head. Carter's ears finally heard the atmosphere in the cave again but the thumping noise continued. It wasn't coming from inside his ears. Three or four seconds apart, the blows were coming from the bricked-up wall. The entrance to the cave. Somebody was breaking in.

68

YOU'RE STILL TALKING

1942, October 9 (11:47h)
Tunnel, Top of the Rock of Gibraltar

Sledgehammers were being swung at the bricked-up wall behind the corrugated iron panels as Richter walked up the tunnel with two men holding a large drill. Major Haas followed close behind. He was still talking.

"You have been relieved of your command, Herr Standartenführer. Your orders are clear. Return to Berlin. The British are no longer your concern." Richter continued to ignore the major, striding out down the tunnel with purpose. He was still in command of operations on the Rock until he boarded that plane. Capturing the British spies, bringing an end to the British intelligence gathering on the Rock, removing that thorn in the side of his superiors in Berlin, the steady stream of British intelligence which they knew had been somehow maintained. Haas was right, this last mission probably wouldn't save him. If headquarters had decided to replace him, he was going to be replaced, but if he could take some news to Berlin of a successful last mission on the Rock, a late commendation just might save him from the Russian front.

"Herr Standartenführer, your transport is waiting. My men will take charge of this." Richter liked the tone of frustration in the major's voice. He wasn't giving this to him. Over his dead body would Haas claim credit for this.

The tunnel was packed, as many as forty SS uniforms waiting to enter the bricked-up secret cave. They stepped aside to let Richter, Haas and their entourage pass.

"Standartenführer!" Haas continued to demand Richter's attention but didn't get it.

Richter had no idea how many British were sealed inside the secret cave but there surely couldn't be more than ten of them. Would they put up a fight or would they lay down their arms and give themselves up? They surely knew a fight was futile but that hadn't always been enough to get these British to surrender.

"Shoot on sight?" asked the pale freckle-faced junior SS officer. They were British spies: wearing a uniform or not, spies should be shot on sight. So why was he hesitating? The answer was a plain yes.

"Only shoot to return fire. If they come peacefully we'll take them alive."

"Stop!" shouted Major Haas. "No more." Haas pulled his pistol on Richter. The action set in motion a string of loud-voiced exchanges between Richter's men and those of Major Haas. The small group, with differing loyalties, primed their weapons and pointed them at each other to the astonishment of the larger body of SS men in waiting.

Richter calmly lifted his hand to bring quiet. He and Haas agreed on little but neither wanted to get shot by their own men. Haas copied Richter, his hand went up and the tunnel fell silent. A sticky heavy quiet.

"You won't make colonel if you kill your superior officer." Richter's voice was steady. He knew Haas. He knew what he wanted. "If you think you will, you don't know Berlin."

Haas adjusted the handle of his pistol to get a firmer grip. "You disgust them, they know about your dirty little secret, your negro lover. They'll thank me."

"You think?" Richter knew he'd never make it to his pistol before Haas pulled the trigger. "Because the SS high command has a history of allowing junior officers to get away with killing those senior to them without punishment. If you believe that, pull the trigger." The tunnel was dark, lit only by handheld torches and those few lanterns needed for the assault. "Pull it!" shouted Richter.

So many witnesses. Haas had miscalculated. Richter couldn't see the major's face but his pistol went back into the leather holster on his hip, and his men lowered their weapons too.

"It's too late to save yourself, Standartenführer." Haas's words were laced with disdain as he took a step back away from the cave entrance.

Richter signalled to his men to start drilling.

69

SLEDGEHAMMERS

1942, October 9 (11:51h)
Entrance Tunnel, Stay Behind Cave, Rock of Gibraltar

"Maria?" Carter was holding her shoulders but Maria wasn't listening, her eyes fixed on Logan's body. Her legs gave way and she slipped to the doorway floor. A large pneumatic drill was added to the sound of the sledgehammers on the other side of the wall and Carter heard bricks drop to the floor as he ran across the main chamber. Opening box after box, Carter threw everything from biscuits, corned beef, a tin opener, a blanket, woolly hats and gloves, into a hold-all. He couldn't stop glancing at the gruesome sight of Bunny lying now in a large pool of blood. He could see his pale face from clear across the cave. Grabbing the screwdriver, he shoved Maria's bunk out of the way of the hatch to the water tank, opened it, and ran back for Maria.

She was still slumped in the doorway staring at Logan. Carter tried to lift her to her feet but she was heavy and he needed her help. The drill and the hammering made it hard for Maria to hear him.

"You have to get up, Maria." Carter's face was right up against hers. He could smell her. He tried to ignore her smell but he couldn't.

"He was going to kill you." She looked at Carter. "I had to." Carter put his hand on her cheek.

"We have to go." This time Maria helped and he had her on her feet. "They're coming in." Carter led Maria back into the cave, closing the main door behind them.

"It's over." Maria's tone sounded relieved, almost happy to be caught. She was physically and mentally exhausted, Carter could see that. It wouldn't be long before she would go into labour and that would be the end of the hiding, but there was a small chance, just a small one, that they could remain undetected. They weren't going to just stand there and wait for Jerry, who might shoot on sight. He needed to keep her safe until the baby came.

"Give it up, Doc. We did everything we could." He wasn't going to let her give up. Carter grabbed a torch and killed the lamp in the cave.

"We're leaving." Carter guided a reluctant Maria to the hatch.

"I can't get down there!" Maria was indignant. He could tell she was irritated with him but he wasn't taking no for an answer. It would be a struggle considering her size and condition, not to mention uncomfortable, Carter was well aware of that. But she needed to get in. Maria climbed down to her knees. The distant sound of drilling and deep thuds of hammers were still audible at the entrance. They weren't in yet but it wouldn't be long. There was a good chance the Germans wouldn't see the hatch, if they weren't looking for it. Even if they saw it would they go to the trouble of searching behind the walls? Maybe they wouldn't be that thorough.

"I can't do it, I'm too tired." Maria's will gave out at the hatch entrance and she collapsed. They'd be in at any moment. *Damn it, get in!* He needed her to get in. He needed her to believe, or at least trust him. Climbing in wasn't the problem. Carter could see she simply had nothing left to give, killing Logan had broken her spirit. Almost. They sat by the open hatch listening to the drilling and thumping, looking into each other's eyes. Despite all that had happened, her eyes were still sharp and bright. The windows to Maria's world were active. That shine only mothers-to-be have. Radiance.

Carter put his hand on her lump.

"What about him or her?" He had Maria's attention. "Maybe they'll take us prisoner, maybe they'll take us outside and shoot us as spies. What if they have orders to shoot us on sight? Are you giving up for the both of you?" Maria looked over at Bunny. Her demeanour changed and Carter took his chance. "We're gonna hide, we're gonna do everything we can to stay alive. Damn it, Maria, don't give up. You're fighting for two now." Carter could see Maria assessing his words. She rolled back onto all fours and crawled towards the hatch. It was dark, only the light from the cave illuminated the inside. Lifting the lump of her child over the edge of the hatch and almost toppling forward, Maria crawled into the darkness. Carter tossed the hold-all bag in after her and climbed in behind. Putting his shoulder against the inside of the sleeve wall, Carter reached back through the hatch with both hands, grabbed the leg of Maria's bunk and pulled. The bunk moved an inch. He tried again. It moved another inch. Sweating and panting for breath Carter inched Maria's bunk back towards the wall, finally closing the hatch, and jamming the screwdriver between the door and the frame, leaving it there to hold the hatch closed.

If they weren't looking for it they might not notice the bunk out of position and the hatch behind it, *right?* Fumbling in the darkness for the torch, Carter crushed the biscuits which crumbled in their packet. *There.* The rubber handle. He pulled out the torch and switched it on. Maria had inched her way in the darkness along the channel between the wall and the cave rock. She was waiting for him at the corner, leaning against the water tank. No drill or the sound of sledgehammers. They were inside.

70

RUN AND HIDE

"You're bloody crazy, I can't get up there!" whispered Maria standing at the bottom of the cast-iron ladder. They'd be safe in the tank, Carter was sure of it. The Germans would check the space around the wall when they finally found the hatch but not the tank. Who in their right mind would climb into the tank? Into the water? No, they'd check the cavity space and leave. There was only one way in and out. Why would they come back for a second look? They had to get in the tank and they had to do it now.

"They'll shoot us." The torch illuminated Maria's face on one side. She was more than irritated.

"You don't know that."

"Do you want to climb a ladder and get wet or do you want to take that risk?"

"I'll fall, I can't."

"You won't fall and you can. I'll be right behind you." The look on her face. If she had the revolver in her hand right then she would have pulled the trigger on him too but he wasn't taking no for an answer. She was going up that ladder and into the water.

She looked like she wanted to scream but Carter settled in under Maria as she began her accent. Step by step Maria moved slowly up the ladder. His shoulder under her behind to secure her weight, Carter tried not to push. He heard her whispering under her breath, and she swore several times at him for rushing her. Maria's complaints were loud enough to lead the Germans right to them but they finally reached the top, the edge of the tank, where Maria stopped. Carter gripped the ladder and stood up behind her. He shone the torch out over the water. The tank had filled again, almost to the top. The rainwater had done its job.

"Keep climbing." Maria didn't move.

"I can't."

"One more rung and ease yourself over the edge."

"Damn it, Carter, I told you I can't, I'm coming back down." There was nothing else for it. Carter put his shoulder firmly under Maria's backside and eased her up. "Stop!" There was panic in her whispered protest. Against her will, Maria went over the edge of the tank and lolloped into the water on the other side. In, behind her, the torch went out quickly after Carter hit the water. Reaching out to find Maria in the pitch darkness, he grabbed her arm and pulled her close. He could feel her breath on his neck as she tried to catch it.

"Arsehole." The first word to come out of her mouth through chattering teeth.

Light streamed back into the blackness. Carter could see Maria's cold frightened face close to his shoulder. The light could only have come from one place. The hatch. They were coming.

"Carter?" whispered Maria. He put his finger up to his lips to silence her. It didn't.

"I've got contractions."

Carter felt a shiver and it wasn't from the cold water. Nothing Maria had said in opposition to hiding had penetrated his determination to get them where they needed to be but *contractions,* that was different. She was going into labour and that was a problem.

"How far apart?"

"Ten minutes, maybe less."

"Why didn't you say something before!?" His plan was backfiring.

Damn it, he needed to know that. Would they shoot? A woman giving birth? She was a spy either way.

"I wasn't sure, I thought…" Maria didn't finish. Carter silenced her. There were boots inside the sleeve wall and they were coming their way.

Had her waters broken? He could hear boots below them. Carter wrapped his legs around her. He could feel her struggling to hold onto the edge. The sounds were at the bottom of the ladder. As the torch swung around, Maria's face came in and out of view. Her shaking lips, chattering teeth. Her eyes were full of fear. Carter couldn't tell if it was fear of being discovered by the enemy or fear of giving birth in the pitch darkness. He could feel the child moving inside her, it was preparing itself, with no idea of what the world outside held. If the child knew what was waiting on the outside it would opt to stay in there. *Please stay in there,* was Carter's next thought. Maria was shaking all over. *Why were they still there? Why weren't they moving on?* He could hear the sound of ripples in the water every time they moved. They were small sounds but right now, deafening. He could smell and feel Maria's breath against his face. It smelt of corned beef. When it came mixed with Maria's breath it smelled better than out of the tin.

They moved. The torch light and the boots. Back towards the hatch. They were leaving. As the light disappeared, so did Maria's face. Her body contorted in a contraction. He heard her teeth crack together as she bit down and breathed through her nose. Maria's body tensed like she was being electrically shocked and the water moved with her, the lapping sound against the edge of the tank rang in Carter's ears. *Stay still, she had to stay still.* He gripped her with a plea to remain still, take the pain. Carter could hear her nostrils flare as she kept her mouth closed and tried to breathe deeply. He was glad of the pitch darkness. He didn't want to see her face right now. The contraction stopped as quickly as it came. Maria's body went limp. Had the contraction been thirty seconds or longer? It had felt like minutes. He listened in the darkness. No sounds. They'd gone.

The relief was overwhelming. The water didn't feel so cold. How long would they have to stay there? He'd need to go first. Getting Maria out of the tank safely was going to be a job of its own but one thing at a time. She'd need to stay while he checked the coast was clear. If it wasn't? If he was captured, killed? He couldn't leave her. She wouldn't get out on her own, she'd give birth, in there without him, they'd both drown. No, he couldn't leave her. They had to wait together until it was safe for both of them to leave. Together. How long? Would the Germans leave a guard? Inside the cave or out? What did it matter, Maria wasn't going to give birth quietly.

"Ya okay in there, mac?"

The voice came before the light. Carter's heart missed a beat and he felt Maria jolt in shock. The blinding light was in touching distance. "Sorry, sir." The torch holder, at the top of the ladder, turned the blinding light off them and onto his own face. A face Carter didn't know but there was no mistaking the helmet with the pack of cigarettes strapped to it. He was an American.

Maria began to cry.

71

HÄNDE HOCH

1942, October 9 (12:20h)
Airfield Surveillance Cave, top of the Rock of Gibraltar

Commander Knott and five British servicemen stood in the central living area of an almost identical cave to the one Carter and Maria were in. The bunk beds were arranged against different walls, the wash pit and faucet were located on the other side of the room, but the cork floor and doorways on each side of the chamber were identical. Knott and his men were unarmed, wearing their British uniforms and looking worried.

There was nowhere to run. Commander Knott knew it and had dreaded this moment. There was no contingency plan for being caught. If either cave at the top of the Rock was discovered there was little else for it but to surrender. His men were wearing their uniforms but they were spies. At least as far as the Germans were concerned.

What had given them away? Had they been heard from the outside, seen watching the airfield through their narrow slits in the Rock, or had somebody talked? That was the least likely since so few men had been privy to the operation and none of those were there on the Rock. His five men were unaware of Windy's team and vice versa. Commander Fleming had wanted it that way and with the Germans at the door, what a sensible decision it had proved to be. He trusted his men but what they didn't know couldn't be tortured out of them. Was Windy's operation still undiscovered?

The drill and the sledgehammers stopped, replaced by the sound of multiple bricks tumbling inward. Knott listened intently; he could hear his heart thumping in his chest and what he thought were explosions in the distance. This was it. He stood to attention, along with his men. If they were to be murdered they would die as the best of bloody Englishmen, with honour.

Commander Knott watched the door to the main chamber, waiting for the Germans to come crashing through, but nothing happened. One of the big guns was being fired outside. *What the hell was going on?* The door opened, slowly and only a couple of inches. A smoke canister rolled in onto the cork floor releasing a stream of thick white smoke. Then another followed it and another. Commander Knott and his men crouched low, still expecting the door to be flung open at any moment. Knott led his men out of the main chamber, away from the smoke, past the toilet and up a flight of stairs to the lookout with a view of the airfield. The smoke followed them, exiting via the lookout hole, out and away like smoke from a chimney. A dark blue F6F Hellcat American fighter plane came tearing through the white stream of smoke, banked hard down towards the Gibraltar airfield and began firing indiscriminately at the Messerschmitt and Stuka planes and German ground crew now running for cover in all directions.

The Rock of Gibraltar was a hive of activity. Multiple and continuous explosions echoed and reverberated across the Rock. The blue skies were as full of movement as the land below them. American marines dropped in their thousands from slow-moving aircraft circling above. A blanket of parachutists covered every corner of the Rock. The sound of propellers approaching and departing and the smell of aviation fuel mixed with black smoke and pungent sulphur laced the air around Gibraltar. An Armada of US battleships also approached the Rock from the bay of Algeciras, horns signalling their unstoppable intent like the battle cries of a band of mad-eyed warriors. British forces, previously sealed inside the Rock and unassailable, finally burst free from their tunnel hiding places forcing their German enemy to break for cover and protection. British tanks, armoured cars and artillery rolled in convoy back out into the daylight, peppering predetermined targets with great accuracy as they went. Surprised, the German occupiers scattered, grabbing only what they could carry to defend themselves. German ships in the port began to explode, one after the other. Flames burst forth from the heart of the vessels as some listed while others sank in situ thanks to the mines of British frogmen.

72

DRY MOUTH

1942, October 9 (12:33h)
Tunnel, Top of the Rock of Gibraltar

Richter, heading for the exit, intuitively knew the Rock was under attack before the guard reached him in the tunnel. Although the sounds he could hear, when the drill and sledgehammers went quiet, were muted and low in the distance they were also distinctive and unmistakable.

"The Americans, Herr Standartenführer," said the worried-looking guard, his chest rising and falling, desperate to catch his breath.

"Why wasn't I informed sooner!" shouted Richter striding past the guard.

"We couldn't find you, Herr Standartenführer." The guard's reply faded as Richter ran down the tunnel towards the exit. His intelligence had assured him this could not happen and Hubert had backed that up from word inside the POW camp.

There'd been whispers and he'd ignored them, the potential of a counterattack from the day after they'd taken the Rock. He couldn't put a contingency plan in place individually tailored to every whisper that was reported to him. The Americans were a threat but the orders from Berlin were clear: "Hold the Rock at all costs." They had a basic plan in place, they were as ready as they could be for this moment, but without the luxury of being able to retreat into the Rock's tunnel systems they all knew the likelihood of holding the Rock from a full-blown attack was zero. As Richter ran down the dark tunnel towards the light at the end. He had feared this moment would come, and the longer the British had kept him out of the tunnels the more likely it was. He knew it and so did his superiors in Berlin. They had warned him to be ready but what more could he have done?

He needed to get down to the command centre as quickly as possible. Hubert's intelligence had been wrong. *No invasion planned,* he'd said. *Chaos inside the tunnel systems, only a matter of time before his British friends ran out of food and gave themselves up.* How could Hubert have been so spectacularly wrong? *Why had he listened to Hubert!?*

Focus, he told himself. *Repel the initial attack.* He hadn't taken the Rock to give it up easily. There was no way he was going to allow that. Over his dead body.

Major Haas appeared in front of him. Richter felt the discharged round enter his gut before he heard the sound of the weapon. He fell back against the entrance to the tunnel wall and slumped to the concrete floor.

The smell of sulphur mixed with the damp raced past his nostrils as a light breeze wafted through the tunnel entrance. The pain was excruciating. He wriggled trying to evade it but it was inescapable.

Haas was waving his arms but everything was now in slow motion. The sounds were muted. Haas was giving orders but the major's shouts were blended with the gunfire outside, large and small calibre. Richter's head was on its side and his breath sucked dust into his mouth and nostrils and then blew it out again. He could finally taste the Rock he'd tried so hard to claim.

He'd seen so many lives end but never really thought about the actual moment that his would. Better than the Russian front. He coughed, it hurt, he could taste blood in his mouth. He reached for his Lugar but it was gone. He felt light-headed and tired. The tunnel came alive with repetitive flashes. His head shook with the vibrations but he was still half deaf. He closed his eyes as the battle raged around him. His mouth was dry.

73

HEAD BLOWN OFF

1942, October 9 (12:42h)
Top of the Rock of Gibraltar

Hoop tried not to lose his footing as he ran as fast as he could along the uneven surface of the rough track that joined one side of the top of the Rock with the other. His SS guard was still breathing when he left him. Not that it mattered.

If he had any sense he'd hide, wait out the battle, but he didn't. He was risking his life trying to save the Nazi who just tried to kill him. His plan had blown up spectacularly. Richter was supposed to be in his office when the Americans arrived.

Another explosion and the crack of gunfire failed to bring Hoop to his senses. Richter had saved his life *how many times?* Three, four, that he was aware of, how many more that he wasn't? He had to do what he could for him. He couldn't go to his grave knowing that he didn't lift a finger to help a man who'd saved his life so many times, no matter what he thought of him. He owed him that much if nothing else.

Hoop looked out over the bay. He'd known what to expect but he hadn't planned to be there, so high up the Rock, in such a vantage point to witness it first-hand. The Americans had dropped from the sky like leaves and their armada of ships approaching from Algeciras was a sight to behold. The camp medics had been the perfect messengers between him and Group Captain Stern. Stern said his communication channels with the Americans and the British inside the Rock were cast-iron and he'd clearly been right. The date and time of the invasion had been crucial. The British were to exit their tunnels and target the big guns, the key to the invasion's success. Stern's plan had clearly worked, only one large calibre gun installation was still firing but that was it. He could only imagine the Germans' surprise when they were hit from behind. Sweet revenge for what the Falange saboteurs had done. Those secret entrances Richter had so desperately wanted to find had been his undoing. The irony of it. He almost felt sorry for Richter, almost.

Hoop ducked down behind a small wall to avoid a company of marines trotting down the path. He watched as they passed his position. There were coloured faces alongside the white ones. Plenty of them. He wasn't the only negro on the Rock anymore. Men he would like to meet but right now he needed to avoid unnecessary engagements.

Hoop had lost sight of Richter and Haas as they'd made their way up the Rock, although it didn't make sense: if they had discovered the Tracer cave *what were they doing down this end of the Rock?*

Hoop leapt back over the wall and back out onto the path. He rounded the bend.

"Halt!" came the call, in a loud voice. It stopped Hoop in his tracks. Two marines stepped out into the open. It took Hoop a moment to see the ten or more gun barrels pointing at him from the cover of the trees. He threw his hands in the air.

"British!" It was the first thing that came to mind. "King's African Rifles, Sergeant Hubert Fundi."

"Lucky ya didn't get ya head blown off, mac." The voice came from behind him. Two more marines stepped out of nowhere and were within touching distance of him.

"Now you're an eager beaver, what's cooking, ace?" Hoop didn't understand the question. He was just happy to be hearing the accent and to still have his head.

"I'm looking for Germans," he said.

"Aren't we all?" replied a cocky marine.

"A Standartenführer Wolfgang Richter. Or his body." Hoop tagged the corpse hunt at the end. It just sounded right. If he told them the truth, that he wanted to save his life, they might shoot him on principle.

"There're some dead ones at the end of the road, maybe he's one of those?" Hoop slowly lowered his hands and continued up the road. The scene of the ambush came into view. He was too late.

Walking along the track Hoop nodded at the marines stepping out of their hiding places. The sheer number of Americans had clearly been the deciding factor. Stern had said as much. Thirty thousand was the number Stern had suggested, way more than was needed. The Spanish had also walked away, just as Stern said they would. 'A deal had been done' with General Franco. The Americans had pulled it off.

Hoop walked weaponless down the path to inquisitive looks. He seemed more like a man out for an afternoon stroll than a soldier on a battlefield. Would they have shot first and asked questions later if he'd appeared with a rifle? Richter's men had been ordered not to shoot him but if he held a gun, that might have been different. He was safer without one.

The German dead scattered the path, still lying where they'd fallen, arms and legs twisted, marines delving through their pockets. There was that hint of urine in the air. Hoop caught sight of a dead freckle-faced junior SS officer with a stethoscope around his neck. He was in the right place. He walked the path checking the bodies, hoping to see Major Haas but not Richter.

"What y'all doing, boy?" asked a marine with his sleeves rolled high up his biceps. "They're all dead." *Richter wasn't there.*

"Is that all of them?"

"Not enough for you?" said the marine. Hoop smiled to be polite.

"Like I told ya lieutenant, the live ones are beyond the trees. Two o'clock." The marine pointed like the hands of a timepiece. Hoop took off down the hill.

Get your story straight, he told himself. *What are you going to say if quizzed?* "Standartenführer Richter had intelligence crucial to the war effort and he was taking him prisoner on the orders of the Admiralty." It was surely true too. Richter must have been worth more to British intelligence alive than dead. Although he knew Wolfgang would never co-operate. Either way, he just needed to rescue the man. Save his life, just once, then he could sleep soundly. His motives were personal, not patriotic.

Hoop stepped out of the trees and into a small clearing. He recognised the prisoners immediately, they were Richter's men. Torn, blackened uniforms but the same faces he'd come to know. The same but broken, sat calmly observing him. Them now prisoners and him a free man. Richter wasn't among them. Beyond the prisoners were the wounded, some sitting up, two lying on stretchers. It was the heels of Richter's boots he saw first.

74

SALVATION

Hoop walked up on Richter taking in his gut wound. The British guards didn't bother to ask questions; they were too interested in the action down in the harbour. German ships were on fire, clearly victims of British frogmen and their limpet mines. The British medic had provided Richter with a field bandage but that was it. The man with the red cross on his helmet was lighting a cigarette and moving off to take in the show as Hoop came up on him.

"Will he live?" asked Hoop, gesturing at the German as casually as possible.

"He's lost too much blood," replied the medic matter-of-factly, dropping his match with a large portion of nonchalance and a small amount of interest. "What's it to you?"

Hoop didn't answer and the medic didn't care. Richter was still and pale, barely breathing. Hoop knelt down and put his hand on the German's chest.

"Wolfgang?" he murmured. Richter opened his eyes, looked for focus and smiled. His teeth were red with blood, his eyes were glazed, the smile nostalgic but fleeting.

"Got yourself shot then?" said Hoop, in German. "Bloody idiot."

Richter looked at his pocket. Hoop knew what he wanted without thinking. A cigarette. He pulled the crumpled packet of Lucky Strikes from the pocket, put one in the man's mouth and lit it. Richter took the longest draw he could before letting it fall from his mouth. He blew the smoke out slowly.

"American…" Richter nodded in defeat. "Checkmate." Hoop could barely hear his voice over the battle. "Well played," Richter said in a whisper.

"The medic says you'll make it." It sounded like the right thing to say until he'd said it.

"More lies?" asked Richter, reaching for Hoop's hand. Their relationship had only consisted of misinformation and manipulation. Maybe it was finally time for some truth.

"I'll pray for you." Richter shook his head.

"It's never too late," continued Hoop. "Repent, there's salvation through Jesus Christ." Richter beckoned Hoop closer. He tried to speak but couldn't find his breath. Hoop lowered his ear to Richter's mouth and the Nazi kissed him on the cheek.

"Too late." Hoop heard the words pushed slowly out of Richter's lungs before a sharp object electrified Hoop's nervous system. The point of the knife entered his shirt around his hip. The tip of a blade. The shock wrenched him from Richter's light grip. He could see the knife in the Standartenführer's hand. Blood on the end of it. His blood. The blade fell from Richter's hand as he smiled through blood-stained teeth a final time, a final smile that faded along with the life from his eyes.

"What the bloody hell's going on?" shouted a British officer at the top of his voice.

Hoop looked up at the medic standing over them with a very red-faced British officer. He put his hand on Richter's eyes and closed them without answering. "Is that bloody German you're speaking?" The officer, a second lieutenant, had a small cane under his arm and stood straighter than seemed humanly possible, arms and legs pulled in together.

"This is Standartenführer Wolfgang Richter." Hoop stood up. "Commanding officer of German forces here on the Rock."

"I don't care who the damn Kraut is. Did he kiss you, boy?"

"Yes, sir." The medic laughed but the second lieutenant's face quickly shifted from red into a deeper shade of purple. He slipped the cane from under his armpit and lifted it over his head. Hoop reached out and grasped the cane before the second lieutenant had a chance to swing it down towards him, pulling it from the officer's hand. *He'd had enough.* He wasn't going to be hit today, not now, not here, over Richter's dead body. He knew that if he knew nothing else. Hoop stood tall and pulled his shoulders back, although the wound in his side forced him to grimace.

"I'm Sergeant Hubert Fundi, King's African Rifles, seconded to British Naval Intelligence, enacting my orders for the Admiralty and more specifically the Director of Naval Intelligence Admiral John Godfrey, and I tell you this: your actions are unbecoming of an officer in the British Army. You will not be hitting me today, or any other day. Sir!" The red-faced second lieutenant shrank in stature, popped and shuddered a few inexplicable compliant sounds, like a car trying to find ignition. Hoop handed back his cane. The officer mumbled on, took it and turned to the smirking medic.

"Don't just stand there, man," were the British officer's last embarrassed words before spinning on his heels and taking off with as much pride as he could muster. The small group of British guards and German prisoners who witnessed the incident each found something else to look at as Hoop caught their eyes.

75

MOTHER SUPERIOR

1942, October 9 (13:05h)

Main Chamber, Stay Behind Cave, Rock of Gibraltar

"Almost there. One last push," encouraged Carter.

"I can't do it anymore," Maria panted.

"You can!" She was being held upright by an American she'd never met, on the thin mattress. The Yanks had moved the bunk beds and draped blankets over the sides of them to give her some privacy. Ridiculous. There were so many men. The indignity of it all. The medical assistant Carter had commandeered couldn't take his eyes off her private parts, and the other was looking away, having lost all the colour in his cheeks. Some medic he was. *Just don't be sick on me,* thought Maria followed by *please God make it stop. How long is this going to take? I can't do it anymore, I've got nothing left, get it out of me.* Keep calm, she told herself, but how could she? It was happening here, in this awful dirty place. *Please be healthy, I don't want to kill you too.* The image of Logan wouldn't leave her mind, the look on his face, the shape of his fall. If she lost her baby she'd deserve that.

Without warning the child was out. Into the hands of Carter.

"You have a son, Maria," he said and Maria dropped her head back. *A boy.* She addressed the skies beyond the roof of the cave, above the Rock and through those few lingering clouds. *Dear God, thank you,* but she knew the words would fall on deaf ears. God knew what she'd done and he wasn't happy with her. That she could be sure. She was a killer, they both knew it. A cold-blooded killer and no amount of prayer would forgive what she'd done. *Where's the cry? Why isn't he crying? Stillborn? Had his vengeance been that swift?* The child cried. Maria's relief was visual as Carter dropped the baby on her chest. Covered in something white, with scarlet red skin, Logan junior opened his mouth wide and screamed at his mother.

"Well done, Maria," said Carter. *Well done? For what? Killing his father?* She'd given birth but she couldn't be a mother. It was hard to even look at her perfect son. He was finally clear of her and he needed to stay that way. God knows he deserved better than this. Better than her.

* * *

Exhausted, and aching all over, Maria was back on her feet. Just standing was painful, and walking was worse. The two marines felt firm to the touch as she rested her weight and shuffled towards the main entrance. She was finally getting out. How she'd wanted this moment. Carter rocked her crying son in his arms. There was something natural about Carter holding him. Most men looked uncomfortable with babies in their arms but not Carter, he was completely at home and even enjoying it. Her next step sent a sharp pain up through the centre of her core and she cried out a little.

"We can wait here rather than in the outer chamber if you would be more comfortable, Maria?" The marines paused on Carter's suggestion. "You're going to be sore until well into tomorrow. Maybe you'd be better just staying here for a while?"

"No! Really I'm fine, I want to get out of here. I need to get out of here." Knowing the entrance to the tunnel was now open she couldn't just go and lie on her bunk. No matter how painful it was she was getting out of this godforsaken cave. Carter nodded his understanding; he wanted out of the cave too.

Logan's body had been moved to the wall and covered with a blanket in the ante-chamber as she entered. He was on his back now, although his pale hand protruded from the covering. Her son, his son, had no idea what she had just done. She went limp at the memory of him falling, face down. She'd never forget that, or the blood as it seeped out onto the rubble.

She wanted to vomit but held it back. What choice had he given her? She had no choice. Carter knew that if nobody else ever did. She'd saved his life. He'd always fight her corner and protect her for that. He was a reliable and honest man. A good man.

Logan's blood stained the bricks where he'd fallen. She closed her eyes, She didn't want to see Logan's blood; it made what she'd done all too real. The stain would never go away. She'd killed the father of her baby, what kind of a woman was she? She'd done some things that she was not proud of, things she could never speak of and lies she could never share, but nothing came close to murdering the father of her son. Nothing she could ever do in her life now would wipe that stain from her. How was she going to live with that? The pain, she felt it again but this time she knew she deserved it, and worse.

The mound that was Albert's shallow grave caught her eye. Then she remembered. She'd forgotten all about it. So much had happened in the last few hours so quickly, she hadn't been prepared to leave the cave and never return.

"Wait." She removed her arms from the two marines and turned gingerly, on her own, back through the main chamber doorway. Carter stopped rocking the child in surprise.

"What is it?"

"I promised Albert, I need a moment." Maria waddled like a duck across the cork floor, trying to avoid painful positions. She faltered but refused assistance. She needed to do this on her own.

She reached the exit to the lookouts, pulled herself up the small step, entered the radio room and closed the door behind her. Logan's intelligence-gathering sheets, the cause of so much trouble, were piled on the desk in front of her. Those few sheets had been the cause of his death. She ran her finger slowly along the handwritten letters of his name at the top of the first sheet. It had taken her so many hours, hidden behind the boxes, to learn Logan's writing style, to perfect the swirl of his letter 'L'. The squiggle of his letter 'W'. Not to mention all those quirky lowercase letters that ran into each other like a train wreck. Faking Logan's handwriting had been a real challenge for her.

76

PREY

Maria picked up Logan's log sheets, folded them over and stuffed them in her pocket. She didn't need her sheets, they were all correct, legitimate intelligence. She'd decided on day one that it was Logan's intelligence sheets that she needed to falsify.

She couldn't take the risk of her own being discovered as incorrect and if she needed to discredit Logan, they'd work perfectly, as indeed they had done. Tom had discovered it all on his own. Clever old Tom.

Removing them now was probably over-cautious, as it would take a handwriting expert to expose them as forgeries if they even had cause to check, and they didn't. It was an open and shut case, Logan was a traitor.

She'd trained herself to cover her tracks, as she hated loose ends no matter how unlikely they were to be discovered. If Logan's sheets were 'missing', even if they wanted to follow up with an investigation at a later date, they'd have nothing to work with. Just Carter's word, if he could even remember what the sheets said. She was in the clear. There was nothing else in the cave that could incriminate her.

She looked around the radio room one last time. The broken radio receiver sat forgotten on the shelf. She'd snapped it in seconds and was out of the room before anybody saw her. She'd tossed the spare out of the east wall lookout.

That little room held a lot of memories of Albert. She hadn't expected him to take his own life. At least that's what she'd convinced herself. She'd chipped away at his confidence night after night. She'd sowed the seeds of doubt in his mind that he wasn't strong enough to make it through the mission. A broken Albert destabilised the team and their communications with London. Talking him down into a dark place had been easier than she'd expected, the melancholia was already there in the boy, waiting for the poor lad through all his jokes and bravado; he wasn't emotionally stable. Discovering his body, however, had been a shock. Her first scream had been real. He was just a boy in the wrong place at the wrong time. A casualty of war, the moment he put the uniform on.

A sharp pain shot down her leg. *Sciatica?* She held the wall and grimaced. The sound of her newborn crying was ever present in her mind. She wanted him close to comfort him. The thought surprised her. She'd heard babies cry before, it had just been annoying but this one was hers. *Primeval?* The burden of motherhood. His fear mattered to her, she didn't like to hear him cry, she was going to need to get used to that.

Maria left the radio room and stepped back down into the main chamber. Carter was waiting for her but the two GIs were gone or milling around with the rest of the unknown faces. The Americans. She hadn't accounted for them.

"Don't even ask," she answered Carter's inquiry before he made it. He had no idea. None. And he never would. Keeping men in the dark was her speciality.

Maria waddled across the cork floor. She hated everything about the cave so why was she strangely nervous to leave? No more damp smell, permanent whiff of cork mixed with shit from the toilet and the body odour of dirty men. No more wash pit, never having clean clothes and that bed, God how she hated that thin mattress. An American GI was lying down on Windy's bunk. It brought back the memory. It had been the biggest risk she'd taken, killing commander Gale. Had she been seen lifting his head to sip from the tin cup, the cup she had specially prepared for him, then it would have all been over. The cyanide sewn into her lapel was enough to kill all of them but a trace in his water, once a day, was her plan for Commander Gale. She hadn't expected it to work so quickly. Cut the head off the chicken and the body will run wild, exactly what happened. She'd managed to reduce the intelligence gathering considerably with Windy out of the way. As it turned out, she'd been right not to poison them all, it would have been a costly mistake. Polluting the water supply had almost worked as an alternative to force them all out, had it not rained. Carter had seen the scratches on her knees – the crawl through the hatch while they were all asleep had also been a big risk. She'd just got plain old lucky finding the rat. Carter smiled at her. He'd accepted the retching sounds from the toilet as confirmation of the sickness she never had. Thank God for the fruit juice and tins of condensed milk.

"Don't want to leave?" asked Carter. "I know what you're thinking." She doubted that. "You'll miss the old place."

Maria smiled. "I will. Strangely." *She wouldn't.* She paused to share the moment with Tom, holding her son. She needed to get used to thinking of him as Tom. The boy would need a father and she couldn't call him Doc or Carter.

She caught her reflection in the broken mirror over Tom's shoulder. She remembered the day she broke it. It felt good, but it was the shard she wanted. She'd been looking for a way to smash it. Her public mental breakdown got the job done nicely. She's tried signalling with the shard from both lookouts, multiple times, but without success. Ironic, but it had been Carter who had given her the idea to plant the shard under Logan's mattress. The doctor had been lucky not to cut himself while tucking in her blanket. It had been the perfect way to put herself out of suspicion. *Who would cut their own hand?* Just a little nick, large enough to draw blood but not deep or long enough to cause her a serious problem.

How disappointed she'd been in Logan. He'd accepted their

imprisonment too easily. Gifted the role of team leader, did he get her out? Did he hell! She'd pleaded with him on the stairs, begged him to put her and the baby out. *He couldn't compromise the mission as team leader,* his words. She couldn't bloody believe it! In the end, she'd hit him.

Logan knew too many pieces of the puzzle. Enough to put them together, if not then, later maybe. All the names she'd given him. People he needed to allow across the frontier border without checks. The contraband he thought they were carrying. The money he thought they were making. Sure, Standartenführer Richter could have provided funds, cash to support the lie, to protect her identity, but this way was cleaner.

He was a loose end, a liability. She'd done the right thing. *Hadn't she?* Anyway, there was a savageness about him she feared. Christ, he was going to kill the doctor, just before she was about to give birth. How selfish was that!

He'd have been caught for contraband smuggling eventually. Cigarettes, stockings and alcohol across the frontier. Having helped her Falange saboteurs across the border, unwittingly or otherwise the trail through him would have led back to her. Undoubtedly. It wasn't going to end well for Logan. She had to do it.

That said, she was going to miss him. *How handsome he was!* The Brycreem, the manicured moustache, his trousers pulled high up that muscular waist. Better he died not knowing the truth. He'd played the army's system to make a few quid but he wasn't a traitor.

She stood in the doorway with Carter. He put his hand on her shoulder as they looked over at Logan. His body hadn't moved but somebody had placed his pale hand back under the blanket.

"You have to let it go, Maria," Carter said, trying to help her to move on. They began to traverse the rubble towards the cave entrance.

Two GIs passed them carrying Bunny in a bag. What would she have done without Bunny? He gave her everything she needed to pump Logan. She had him so wound up that when the opportunity came she knew Logan would take it. The weak knot she'd tied at the chair helped too, he'd worked it free easily.

Logan had it in him to kill but she hadn't predicted the viciousness. He had a demon, and he was far more violent than she could have imagined. He was frightening at the end, even to her. Would he have killed her too? He certainly would have killed Carter. She'd told him to stop as he stood at the doorway, to incapacitate Carter only. To take the gun from him. To keep him alive. He didn't listen. Logan killed himself when he stopped doing as he was told. *It wasn't her fault.* The thought eased her conscience. She was protecting their son.

She stumbled on the rubble and two GIs took a firm grip on her.

"Steady there, ma'am." She'd never been called ma'am before. She'd met very few Americans. This one had kind eyes and broad shoulders. She allowed him to take her weight.

"Hungry?" One of the GIs had his arms full of corned beef and started tossing the tins to his friends. Another of her plans had failed. Tossing the cans had been a silly idea. Although eating them was worse. If she never ate corned beef again in her life it would be too soon.

Maria stepped through the newly knocked hole in the wall and out into the tunnel. The claustrophobia she'd suffered so terribly in the early days was completely gone. *Ironic,* she thought, because she was free at last.

77

REUNITED

1942, October 9(13:10h)
Top of the Rock of Gibraltar

The sounds of war became fewer as Hoop walked slowly back along the top of the Rock, the small hole in his side that Richter had managed with his last breath, patched up by a confused medic.

Hoop could see a level of calm descending upon Gibraltar below. Sporadic gunfire continued, although most of it seemed to be coming from the area beyond the frontier, somewhere in Spain. American ships were still arriving, he'd never seen so many in one place, and their aircraft dominated the skies. Burning German planes littered the runway and those that weren't shot down, had long made a run for it. The Germans had simply been overwhelmed by numbers on every level, land, sea and air. The Rock was America's now. There were British faces he recognised on the path back towards the Tracer cave but every corner was guarded by US marines, laughing, and telling stories of a remarkably short and successful battle.

Who was in the cave? Now it was over, that was the big question. Richter had all but confirmed somebody was. The Tracer team intelligence gathering had drawn the attention of Berlin and become a thorn in the German's side. The thought of Richter led Hoop to rest his hand on his wound. Had the Standartenführer only stuck the tip of his knife in deliberately? Had he tried to kill him or had he just wanted to prove a point?

Hoop reached the bottom of the hill that led up to Lord Airey's Battery and the Tracer cave entrance. Despite his wound, uniform and lack of weapon the attitude of the marines guarding the way up to the big gun at O'Hara's Battery was quizzical. Did the Americans know about the cave? Had Group Captain Stern informed them of the mission? If not, were Windy, Doctor Carter and the others still hiding? Maybe the Admiralty had given them orders to stay put? They'd have seen very little from the lookouts of the actual battle but the sounds would have informed them it was over, if London and the Admiralty hadn't.

He needed to be careful not to expose them. Just in case. Even if he was able to get right up to the cave entrance tunnel he couldn't communicate with them behind the wall but a walk past would at least confirm if they were still sealed inside.

Hoop picked up speed. If the cave entrance was still sealed up he would just walk on. He'd keep his story simple. He was there looking for Commander Gale, that's it. How surprised they'd be to see him. They must have thought he was dead. *What had it been like in the cave?* They'd had a less eventful time than him, that was for sure.

Hoop reached the entrance to Lord Airey's Shelter as Carter walked out into the sunlight right in front of him holding a baby.

4 YEARS LATER

78

ADMIRALTY HOUSE

1946, November 10 (13:35h)
The Cenotaph, Whitehall, London, United Kingdom

Hoop stood reading his newspaper. Dotted across the pages were pictures of Victory in Europe Day, the street parties, the smiles on the children's faces, the long tables filled with food and the waving of the union jack flags. He couldn't see enough of them. He remembered the day like everybody else although he'd been in Burma, the King's African Rifles had been disbanded and he'd been given a promotion to command men in the India Corp down the Irrawaddy River. They'd celebrated all right but there had still been work to do. Japanese resistance had been fierce.

He counted himself lucky to have seen what he'd seen today: the Cenotaph, and the remembrance of so many fallen men, many of whom he'd known. He'd seen King George, in the flesh. He'd expected him to have been a larger man, although he had no idea why. Pushing his way closer to the front of the Remembrance Sunday crowd to get a better look, he'd seen the King laying a wreath on the steps of the monument. There'd been a small group of men who had taken offence to him being pushed up against their families so he'd made his way back out towards the buildings. Out of uniform, he'd noticed a change in how he was being treated. More people had looked past his colour in a uniform. He didn't want any trouble. Not on this day and not wearing his new suit and tie. The crowds having left, the street was populated by those cleaning up the mess and a few stragglers like himself, there for other reasons.

"Hoop!" He didn't notice Carter and his new wife Maria until the doctor called his name. It was good to see a friendly face.

Carter greeted him with a hug and slapped him on the back with a big smile. Maria held the hand of her son Antonio. How he'd grown from the baby he'd met in Gibraltar. Carter had earnt some happiness after what he'd gone through. The Tracer mission they'd all trained for wasn't the one they got but it was a success all the same. The war was won.

Although they kept in touch after Tracer, it had been difficult, what with him in Burma. They'd corresponded via mail as soon as he'd been demobilised, only then had they found out that they had both, independently, been invited to the Admiralty.

"Ready?" asked Carter. Hoop didn't like surprises.

"Do you know any more?" Carter pulled the invitation letter out of his pocket and it matched the one Hoop had in his hand.

'Dear Doctor and Mrs Carter, You are cordially invited to attend a memorial gathering etc.' The time, the date, the location, the Admiralty building, a short distance from the Cenotaph monument and number 10 Downing Street. This was Hoop's first time at both.

As they walked Carter talked of hope for the future and political stability in Europe but Hoop couldn't help but think of Wolfgang Richter. He'd shared some of what had happened to him after he was captured, although he'd been embarrassed to confide some of the more personal details and been sworn to secrecy with others. Carter's new wife Maria had surprised him, she'd been particularly interested. Gripped by his tales of life on the Rock under German occupation, she clearly had an inquisitive mind.

The Admiralty building was the grandest construction Hoop had ever been invited to. Set back from the road in a small courtyard under an arch with classical columns everywhere, the brown brick four-storey building was intimidating. White stone steps led up to a set of polished stained wooden double doors.

Carter gave the door a knock and took Antonio's hand. The door was opened by a man in a naval uniform. Carter was about to introduce himself when the man spoke.

"Doctor Carter! Delighted that you and Mrs Carter could make it." The man looked down at the child, smiled and put out his hand. "And you must be Antonio." Antonio stood up straight, looked at his father and then shook the man's hand.

"Mr Fundi, it's an honour, sir." The uniformed man saluted Hoop. The action caught him by surprise; he hadn't expected such a formal welcome, or any welcome at all for that matter.

The floor on the inside was stone-tiled and heavily polished. The uniformed man led them down some corridors with thick runner carpets and large paintings in grand frames, past an ornate narrow staircase with thick red carpet pinned to steps rising one flight to a small landing where it split in different directions left and right. The uniformed man opened a set of doors to a drawing room with a window looking back out onto the courtyard. Closing the thick cream-patterned fabric curtains he lit the room with the crystal chandelier high above them. The room had bright yellow patterned walls with huge oil paintings of naval battles. An Indian silk carpet clashed with the wallpaper but it was the dark wood sideboard, at the far end of the room, that grabbed all their attention, along with the row on row of empty seats. Four large framed photographs, each with a small red leather box placed in front of it, adorned the sideboard equally spaced out. The photographs were recognisable to them all. They were head and shoulder images of Windy, Bunny, Albert and Doctor Milburn. Hoop remembered the day they were taken at training before the Tracer mission had started. Picking up the little red box in front of Windy's photo, Hoop put it down again quickly when the door behind them opened. A man in his thirties, wearing black-rimmed glasses and a youthful smile, stepped in.

"I'm guessing those photographs bring back some memories." The man made his way confidently across the room. "We're delighted that you could all make it. I trust you all enjoyed today's remembrance parade?"

"Yes thank you, sir," replied Carter.

"You're not in the service anymore, Tom, we can dispense with formalities, except those we're here for of course. Let me introduce myself. John Bradley." He put out his hand, taking time to greet each one of them individually, with eye contact. "Assistant to the Director of Naval Intelligence, Commander Fleming's replacement. Demobbed last year." Bradley answered the Fleming question before it was asked and was over by the photographs with a short march. "I hope that your deployments post-mission were to your liking?" Hoop listened as the doctor and Maria small-talked with Bradley. For him the answer was no, he hadn't wanted the posting to Burma. It had been ugly, although he'd appreciated the promotion. It didn't matter now and would have been rude to bring it up.

"Recognition." Bradley paused, clearly starting official proceedings, then spoke as if prepared. "Today, being a day of remembrance, we here at the Admiralty believe it's high time we recognised your extraordinary commitment. Operation Tracer, despite its challenges, was a great success. The intelligence provided by the team, I can assure you, contributed in no small part to crucial decisions made in the war rooms here in Whitehall. Your accounts of the mission and its unspeakable difficulties set you all aside for commendation. Those not with us today, who made the ultimate sacrifice, must and should be recognised along with you." Commander Bradley moved swiftly on without missing a beat. "Four good men were lost to Operation Tracer. Commander Frederick Gale, a man who…"

Carter drifted. He heard Bradley's words as he honoured Windy, Bunny, Albert and Syd. They, more than anyone, deserved recognition but there were two elephants in the room, neither of which Carter could ignore. The first was the event itself. The room was large enough for fifty or more guests and there were chairs for almost that number placed row-on-row, so where were all the guests? Windy's family? Bunny's family? Were they at a pre-event to the main event with people arriving later? Carter watched Antonio as he listened to Bradley speak. The other elephant was the missing photograph of Antonio's father. He'd never asked Maria what account she had given to the Admiralty when they'd been debriefed. She wouldn't talk about Logan, ever, although he told her that wasn't healthy. He assumed that she'd told them what he'd told them – that Logan had cracked, it had all been too much for him, but also that they suspected him of acting to frustrate the mission. He'd never actually used the word sabotage, although he'd quoted Bunny's accusations. Carter looked at Maria. He was sure that she knew he was looking at her but she kept her eyes fixed on Bradley and the photographs. She was thinking of Logan too, she must have been. A tear welled up under her long eyelashes and he watched it trickle down her cheek as the commander opened one of the red boxes to expose a medal.

"Finally," said Bradley, producing three more red boxes, "the War Office is delighted to award you, the surviving three members of the Operation Tracer mission, with the George Cross." Commander Bradley placed the three red boxes on the sideboard next to those of the posthumously awarded ones. Maria stepped forward first and shook Bradley's hand although the commander left the medal where it was. Carter suddenly realised why the room was empty.

"The medals stay here don't they?" Commander Bradley clasped his thin lips tightly together and his brow slightly furrowed. Carter could see he didn't want to disappoint but they'd got to the real meaning for the visit.

"Yes, I'm afraid so."

"Is there something else we need to know, Commander?" Hoop's question came before his handshake.

"Well, now that you mention it, yes actually there is one thing. A decision has been made to keep Operation Tracer off the books. Permanently." Bradley paused before his next request. "We'd also ask that you never mention it again, even amongst yourselves. You know how it is."

"Thank you for the invitation, Commander Bradley," said Hoop as he stood up. Carter could see Hoop had had enough of the spy game. The truth was so had he. "And the recognition." Hoop smiled at Carter.

"You're welcome," replied the commander, exposing hundreds of years of Admiralty lack of irony. Hoop shook Carter's hand and then Maria's, patted Antonio on the head and walked out of the room. The man who welcomed him into the building closed the front door of Admiralty House behind him, and he was back in the fresh air. He crossed the courtyard the way he'd come and stepped back down onto the Whitehall pavement and looked up at the sky. It was a beautiful day. Hoop turned right, walked, and left the war behind him.

79

UP THE STAIRS

1946, November (13:56h)
Admiralty House, Whitehall, London, United Kingdom

Carter listened as Commander Bradley justified the decisions of the Admiralty to Maria. Antonio walked along the sideboard looking at the red boxes. He wanted to pick one up and play with it. He looked back to see if he was being watched. Carter shook his head, playing with the boxes or touching anything on the table wasn't allowed. Antonio reached the picture of Bunny and peered in to get a better look at the man. Carter's mind shot back to Logan, frantically stabbing Bunny as he lay on the cork floor.

Antonio could never know about his biological father. They'd protect him from that. Sometimes the truth should be permanently hidden. What good would it do to share such horrors with a boy or even the man later? Forgetting Operation Tracer would be easier than they knew. Maria already acted as if it had never happened. The truth was he had some questions, things he couldn't quite understand, stuff that didn't quite fit together. He thought if Maria talked about Albert's suicide, the murder of Bunny and, most importantly, the shooting of Logan, it would help her come to terms with all of them. She wouldn't have to carry them around with her, the nightmares would stop, and the guilt he was sure she harboured would ease. His wife had a certain sadness about her and she just couldn't shake it. It was always there creeping back to remove her smiles, telling her she had no right to be happy. He'd given up asking questions trying to get her to talk. She simply got angry with him and, *'Seeing a professional?'* That was, *'Ridiculous. What would she share exactly? Details of the mission?'* He had to admit it might be difficult trying to explain the issues without exposing national security secrets. Commander Bradley had just, unwittingly, given her the weapon she needed against him to end any further talk of discussing what happened.

It was time they were leaving. They didn't want to be on the bus too late, it would get chilly later and they hadn't brought their warmer coats.

The uniformed man from the front door removed the photographs and the little red boxes that contained their medals, the military awards no one would ever know existed. Antonio watched as the same man opened the thick curtains allowing light to stream in.

Carter was about to thank Commander Bradley when he turned the tables on him.

"Thank you for coming in today, both of you, it was a great pleasure to meet you and Antonio of course." He smiled the briefest of smiles.

"Just one last thing." There was always one last thing when it came to the Admiralty. "The Director would like a quick word on the first floor."

Bradley lifted his eyes to the ceiling. The way he mentioned the Director's title, it was as if he was referring to some divine being. *Why hadn't the Director come down if he wanted to meet with them?* Carter wondered if John Godfrey had also been demobbed or if he was still in charge.

"We'd be delighted wouldn't we, dear?" replied Carter politely. Maria didn't answer him and he could see that she, like him, had thought about the coat situation and the weather and would rather leave as soon as possible. Commander Bradley's tone was direct.

"With Mrs Carter." Carter thought he'd misheard but the commander continued. "Mrs Carter alone."

Maria flashed a worried look at him, enough to set him off.

"What the bloody hell is going on, damn it!" Carter's usual calm eluded him for a moment. What did they want with Maria?

"Apologies, old chap, nothing untoward I assure you, but it is rather important and a bit hush-hush." Carter could see Maria didn't want to go and would have objected further had there not been a knock at the door. A woman in her late forties entered. A face like a bulldog, her hair on top of her head in a tight bun, she wore a white shirt with a high collar buttoned up to her throat, tight enough to choke her. A sag in her cheeks hid something Far Eastern about her. She carried a stern look the short distance between the door and Commander Bradley, and whispered something in his ear, before taking up a seat and ignoring them all. "We very much appreciate your patience in this matter. Please let me assure you both that I wouldn't be making such a request were it not of the utmost importance to the Admiralty, King and country." The mention of the King pulled the teeth that Carter was slowly growing against having Maria taken upstairs alone. Maria looked even more nervous than before but what choice did they have? "Anything you need, anything at all," Bradley looked over at the stern woman still not making eye contact. She looked more like a prison guard than a waitress to Carter.

Maria implored him with her eyes to object further but what else could he say? Whatever it was she just needed to get it over with so they could go home. They'd left the service and everything that went with it but the navy was still making demands on them. It stuck in his craw as Commander Bradley held the door for Maria.

"You'll wait for me won't you, Tom?" Silly question thought Carter. Of course he'd wait, she was only going upstairs. The door closed and Maria was gone.

The fierce-looking woman, being choked by her collar, was yet to make eye contact. Carter didn't like her. She was rude.

"Can I make a den with the chairs, Daddy?" Under normal circumstances the answer would have been no, but if Antonio damaged a chair or inconvenienced the Admiralty in moving them today that was okay with him.

Carter stood at the window looking out onto the courtyard. The street beyond was busy with people going about their lives without fear of an air raid. How different life had been just over a year ago. All recognisable references to the war had been removed, the sandbags that had become permanent fixtures, the tape on the windows, so many people in military uniform, and that look, the look people had during the war, that was gone too.

A black Vauxhall pulled into the Admiralty courtyard and a man got out. He spoke through the window to the driver, who joined him outside the vehicle. Both men were thick-set, one blond, the other swarthy with black hair. The blond man lit a cigarette and leaned against the car. Carter could see his misshapen nose from the window. The driver had been in the services; Carter could tell by the way he stood and moved, he was regimented. So many of the army boys had that same demeanour, it was drilled into them. He knew the feeling. He still made his bed every morning before breakfast.

"Look, Daddy." Carter turned his attention back to his son. Antonio had created a space with four chairs. Carter played with his son to the displeasure of their only audience member. Finally the door opened and Commander Bradley stepped back in and the woman took her leave.

"Sorry to have kept you waiting, Doctor Carter." Bradley sounded official. "I have a bit of bad news."

Where was Maria?

"Your wife won't be going home with you."

There was a long pause as Carter tried to assimilate the words. Had he just heard what he'd thought he heard? Commander Bradley's very serious face cracked a smirk as Maria stepped out from behind him, beaming. He hadn't seen her smile like that since their wedding day.

Maria took his hand.

"Maria?" Carter addressed his wife. An explanation was very much in order.

The commander looked at his watch.

"Quick as you can please, Mrs Carter, your car is waiting." With that, Bradley left the room.

"Say you won't be angry, Tom, promise me?" Maria's excitement was off the scale.

"Angry about what?"

"They want me to go to Madrid, tonight, now!" There was a light in her eyes powered by adventure. "It's a diplomatic mission" – she looked over her shoulder – "that's all I can say, it being hush-hush and all." Her voice lowered with secrets. "Three days at most, they'll drop me directly home. There's a car waiting to take me to the airport."

Carter didn't like it one bit. That was the truth but he held his feelings down. Antonio was watching them and already a little confused. *No! You bloody can't!* That was what he wanted to say but he'd never raised his voice at Maria in front of Antonio and wasn't about to start. He felt 'railroaded' as he heard an American once say, and she was so happy about it.

"Of course, Maria, if that's what you want." The words stuck in his throat.

"You're a darling, it's terribly important stuff, you know." Carter didn't know but she kissed him and took Antonio's head in both her hands.

"Mummy has to go away for a couple of days but Mummy loves you very much and I'll be back very soon, okay my darling?" Antonio looked to his father for reassurance as tears welled. The door opened and Commander Bradley leaned in.

"Sorry to interrupt but we'll need to get a wriggle on."

"Right you are, sir," replied Maria with a spring in her step. She kissed her husband and listed various Antonio-related bits of advice that Carter didn't listen to with so many unanswered questions running around his head. Maria, handed a new hat, coat, gloves and briefcase by the bulldog, followed Commander Bradley out the front door of the Admiralty building and into the back of the black Vauxhall car. Maria waved as she was whisked away.

Carter thanked the man in uniform who helped him and Antonio back out into the courtyard. Carter took a tighter grip than usual on his son's hand, although he couldn't say why. *They needed to catch the bus home.* That much was clear to him.

As they walked away from Admiralty House Carter glanced back. He was sure he could see the silhouette of a man in uniform, standing at a first-floor window, watching them.

29 YEARS LATER

80

BROKEN CUP

1975, November 20 (13:00h)
*The home of Tom and Marie Carter,
Kent, England, United Kingdom*

Midday had a crispness about it. The sun had dried the morning dew but a dampness hung in the air outside Carter and Maria's thatched cottage. The musky smell emanated from the rot that had taken hold in one small quarter of the north-facing roof. Carter had been meaning to get a man in, he'd ignored the problem for too long. Outside of the rot Maria and Carter's home was perfect.

Heavy draped and embroidered curtains, sun-warmed through the leaded living room windows, lay softly on the thick pile fitted carpet. The Georgian antique server with gold-plated drawer handles was adorned with framed photographs that presented a permanent reminder to the framer that she should be happy. The wedding photos had faded along with those of the three christenings, first days at school, family skiing in the Pyrenees, their children's university graduation cloaks and an assortment of other moments marking the Carter family life together. One particular photograph stood out from the others, it had a dark wood frame and an age-faded image. It also seemed deliberately placed slightly off to one side. It depicted a teenage Maria standing in front of the Rock of Gibraltar. Behind the framed photograph on the hard polished varnish lay two passports, both Maria's, and on top of them was a Walther PPK British secret service-issue revolver.

Removing her jacket and placing it on the back of a dark elm wooden carver chair, 50-year-old Maria, mother of three and wife to retired neurosurgeon Doctor Tom Carter, picked up the passports and gun and carried them to the open door of a wall safe built low to the ground behind the antique server sideboard and single-seater comfortable chair. Maria closed the safe door with practised ease and spun the dial securing the tools of her intelligence-gathering trade inside.

Maria left the living room, crossed the corridor and entered the kitchen at the front of the house. After wrapping the strings of a pinafore around her waist twice, tying them in a bow at the back, she reached into the sink. *When would these children learn to wash up?* Maria released the water into the deep ceramic sink, pulled on a set of Marigold rubber gloves and hit the radio on button. Adding washing-up liquid to a kitchen cloth, she picked up a teacup and began to rub in time to the top-of-the-hour BBC news jingle.

"Spanish dictator Franco dies," came the voice. "General Francisco Franco, who ruled Spain with an authoritarian hand for thirty-nine years, has died at the age of 82," said the announcer. The teacup slipped from Maria's hand and broke in the bottom of the sink. "Hopes for democracy run high as Prince Juan Carlos prepares to take the reins of power." Maria turned pale, steadying herself on the draining board as a black Jaguar car pulled into the driveway. Maria watched through the kitchen window as its tyres crackled on the gravel. She didn't see the two men exit the vehicle; she was already back in the living room.

A salt-and-pepper-haired Commander Bradley, now with black-rimmed glasses, sporting a moustache and carrying a few extra pounds, followed a much younger, black-suited, well-built man across the threshold of the family's open door without ringing the doorbell or signalling their arrival. A rubber glove lay on the floor of the corridor. The younger man, one hand permanently in his pocket, eyes alive, dark hair pushed flat with cream to the side of a square head, peered into the living room, before more confidently entering.

Maria, still in her pinafore, watched him silently, sitting bolt upright in the wood carver chair. Bradley also made his entrance. Maria spoke first.

"John. Come in. Should I be expecting you?" Her tone was inquisitively honest but her eyes sharp and cat-like.

Bradley looked around the room and then back out into the corridor. "Anyone else home?" Bradley spoke and moved with caution.

Maria stayed seated, looking at the younger man. "A business call rather than a pleasure one I'm guessing?" She smiled, although there was an unnatural twist to her mouth and the upbeat tone of her voice was out of sync with the rigidness of her posture.

Maria's intelligence handler took up a comfortable chair next to the family photos with a deep sigh, almost the sound of regret. Almost.

"You must have known this day would come." Maria ignored the comment. "If it's any consolation, I assure you I won't enjoy this. We've been a good team you and me."

"Enjoy what, John?" Maria's nervous laugh had no effect on her visitor whose face remained serious. Bradley and Maria sat silently looking at each other. Maria's eyes never blinked; they rarely did.

"It's over, Maria. Or should I say, Agent-54?"

"Agent who?" Maria's bewilderment was very convincing.

Bradley reached inside his jacket pocket, pulled out a plastic sleeve and tossed it onto the coffee table a few feet from Maria. Maria bent forward to get a better look. Although it was heavily faded, damaged, torn up and sellotaped back together, the piece of paper on the inside of the plastic protector was unmistakable: the note Maria had wrapped around a tin of corned beef and tossed from the east wall lookout of the Stay Behind Cave all those years ago. She recognised it instantly.

"What's that?" she said flatly.

"Come now, Maria, it's late in the day for both of us." Maria adjusted in her seat.

"If you thought that I was…" Maria paused. The words got stuck in her mouth. She swallowed them before dragging them out. "…some kind of agent – 54 you say? – then why haven't you arrested me?" Maria leaned back in her chair this time and awaited an answer. Her hands were still deep in the front pocket of her pinny.

"Simple. We knew your allegiances lay with the Falangist movement. With General Franco. Your secondment to the Nazi party had ended. We simply let the bird fly home." Maria shifted again in her seat.

"You presented us with a direct line of communication with the Franco regime of course. We shared with you what we wanted them to know." The realisation that she'd been, 'had', used, played, manipulated, controlled, flooded into Maria's demeanour. She began to fidget uncontrollably in her seat.

"The Six-Day War in Israel, the Egyptians. All your work, Maria. Indirectly." Maria's eyes narrowed and the left one twitched.

Maria shaped her face for another act of innocence but then stopped. She sat staring into nothing. A featureless face in deep thought. Finally, she rejoined the two men in her living room and in an instant her demeanour shifted seismically. Her shoulders softened but her eyelids seemed to stiffen, the features of her face visibly hardened, to that of a whole other person. Her legs crossed; her hands tucked into her pinafore.

"It took us a while after the liberation of Gibraltar, but the pieces finally came together," continued Bradley. "We couldn't just forget about Agent-54, not having found the note." Bradley picked up the dark-framed photograph of Maria at the Rock. "We only suspected you at first, just before the end of the war. It was only after you were recruited and the misinformation we were feeding you began to surface through intelligence channels that we were sure you were 54." Maria gave a small nod and Bradley placed the framed photograph of her back where he found it. He interlocked his fingers, crossed his legs and rested them on the top of his knee. "The game's up. Things are done differently these days."

He shifted himself forward in the chair, shaping to stand. "Franco's death brings change for both of us. I'm being 'promoted' out of the way. The Foreign Office. I'm sorry, Maria." Bradley looked at his watch and then at the younger man who had stood silently throughout. The younger man's hand came out of his pocket holding a revolver. He stepped forward towards Maria. "It's time to go." Commander Bradley stood up but something caught his eye, something behind the chair he'd been sitting in. It was low down and against the wall, a little door, and it was wide open.

The first shot came through the pinafore front pocket and hit the young man just above the groin. He doubled up in pain. The second, fired from outside her kitchen protector, arm stretched, was aimed at the young man's head. It hit his shoulder, exiting his back, splattering blood over the marble fireplace wood shelves and the French clock on the mantelpiece. The young man managed to get off a shot of his own but only into the floor as the third and deadly bullet hit his head. Back and left it forced him before a moment of inertia. There was a surprised look on his face as his large frame dropped, dead-weight, hitting the side of the coffee table hard. He rolled to a standstill and began leaking blood onto Maria's heavy pile carpet.

81

SPILT MILK

Carter was thinking about beef wellington as he pulled his silver Rover into the driveway. His hair was almost totally white, his skin paper-like having lost much of its elasticity over the years, but the doctor's eyes were still sharp. Fillet of beef covered with pâté and puff pastry; he'd been threatening to make it for Maria. Just the ticket to impress her and he'd done his homework, he wanted the meal to be a surprise with all three kids back in the house this evening.

With a newspaper and a bottle of milk on the passenger's seat, he pulled up to the side of the unknown car parked outside his home. Maria had promised, barring a national emergency, she'd be home before midday for 'Family Day'. She'd agreed but the unknown car had all the hallmarks of officialdom. Carter felt a tinge of pending disappointment. That same feeling he'd grown to accept being married to a 'diplomat'. Wellington might have to wait. They'd all got used to Mum leaving at a moment's notice. Today might be another one of those days. Pulling on the hand brake and stepping out of the car, with milk and newspaper in hand, Carter smelt the damp thatch. It was time to fix that. The sound of gunfire came from inside the cottage.

He hadn't heard that sound for as long as he could remember. He knew exactly what it was but had he really just heard it? There in his driveway? It was so out of place, but the second shot confirmed it. He wasn't daydreaming or hearing things. The adrenaline pumped in an instant, slowing down the world around him, and his vision glazed. Unsure if the milk bottle had broken as he dropped it and the paper on the gravel, Carter's foot slipped as he tried to move quickly across the small stones, his eyes fixed on the front door alcove. He crossed the short distance and rounded the corner into the house and onto the hallway carpet. His peripheral vision was at its peak, unsure of what he might encounter. The surreal smell of sulphur from the discharged weapon was the last confirmation he needed to be sure he wasn't hearing things. A gun had just gone off in his home.

Carter stepped over Maria's discarded rubber glove as he entered the living room, expecting to see his wife in mortal peril.

Standing in the middle of the carpet, wearing one rubber glove, she looked back at him in shock.

"Thank God." Carter scanned the room. One dead with a hole in his head, obviously the assailant. John Bradley was alive but in considerable pain. Carter's medical training kicked in without a thought. Assessment? Two entrance wounds, one in the gut and one in the shoulder.

"Call for an ambulance." The order was for Maria as he set to work. He had to stop the bleeding: two wounds, which one first? The gut. Carter found the hole leaking John Bradley's blood and plugged it with his finger. The pool already pumped from Bradley's pale body had seeped into the pile carpet and Carter could see plenty of it. He replaced his finger with the corner of a small cushion, the bull-embroidered one, and pushed it hard against the leaking hole. Bradley winced in pain.

"I'm sorry, Tom." John looked up at Carter with tired eyes. Maria hadn't moved an inch.

"Ambulance, now!" This time Carter raised his voice, something he rarely did to his wife. "Maria!" Maria snapped out of her daze and walked out of the living room without a word. "At least you got the blighter, hey? Hang on, John. Help's on the way."

Bradley shook his head. "Maria."

"She's fine, don't worry." Carter had dealt with plenty of gunshot wounds in those early days and he could recognise the fatal ones. Bradley tried to capture breath but his lung was collapsing.

"Couldn't tell." Four holes. He couldn't plug them all.

"Tell what? Maria!" shouted Carter again, although he knew there was nothing to be done, there was no reply. Bradley pointed at the coffee table before running out of life. Carter felt his body weight increase and saw his bladder release. Dead on the living room carpet. He closed the eyelids.

What the hell's going on? Carter stood up. The smell of sulphur had been replaced by urine and faeces. Commander Bradley, a man he'd known for nearly thirty years, was dead in his living room. He needed answers but something intuitively told him he didn't want to hear them. Carter caught sight of the plastic sleeve on the coffee table, the paper inside was familiar to him, but *where was Maria?*

Out of the living room, up the stairs, he could hear Maria in their bedroom. She had a suitcase open on the bed.

82

NO MORE LIES

"What the hell's going on, Maria?" Maria ignored him and continued to add items to her small suitcase. He waited for an answer but the sight of his wife packing forewarned him he wasn't going to like the answers.

"Where are you going? Why didn't you call the ambulance? Maria?" She paused but wouldn't look at her husband. "MARIA!" yelled Carter at the top of his voice. She stopped her fumbled packing and turned to face him, her eyes full of tears, her face contorted. Carter realised in an instant that Maria had shot John Bradley. He knew his wife, she didn't need to say a word, he simply knew and she knew he knew. "You? Why? For God's sake what's going on, Maria?"

She didn't answer but sat down on the bed and started to speak. Carter listened. After the first few minutes of Maria's confession, his knees became weak and he slumped to the floor, propped up by the bedroom wall. As he listened, words stuck in his head and he repeated them to himself: *'misinfirormation', 'state secrets'.* He wanted to roll into a ball and die, right there and then. His life, the life he thought was his life, was being pulled from under him. Shattered, by every word, into a million pieces. *What had she done?* His life had been a lie. Everything. Their marriage? The children? What would he tell the children? They'd be home at any moment.

Maria admitted to killing Windy. He couldn't believe his ears, it wasn't possible. She was lying, but the detail, how could it not be true, the web of detail, so elaborate. The missing tins, Maria had tossed them? The note on the table, that's why he recognised the paper. It was a Tracer intel sheet. He began to feel sick, sick to his stomach. She'd pumped Logan to kill Bunny then murdered her lover and taken up with him.

Carter vomited over himself.

He wanted her to stop speaking but she didn't, and he puked again, this time just bile.

"Sorry," he heard this woman say, whoever she was. She was 'sorry'. How dare she? Anger took hold of his thoughts towards her, anger like he'd never felt before. He'd stopped listening as his blood boiled.

"Take care of them for me," were the next words he registered as Maria closed the suitcase. Carter lost it. He was no longer himself. He was somebody he didn't know running at Maria. He caught her by surprise, and she yelped as his shoulder crashed into her ribs. Carter knocked her off her feet and they both tumbled down the side of the bed. His mouth was dripping with vomit-tasting saliva. His nose was blocked with vomit or tears. He could taste the bile. Carter had his hands around his wife's neck and he was holding her hard to the floor. Maria's face was red and getting redder but she didn't kick or fight for release, just lay there looking up at him as he choked the life out of her. His vomit-ridden saliva dripped onto her face, he could see she couldn't breathe but her eyes were calm, defiant, almost daring him to finish the job. They bulged and Carter knew that at any moment she would lose consciousness. Who was she, this woman beneath him? Who was he? A man about to kill her? He wanted to.

Carter let go.

Maria opened her mouth like a fish out of water, straining for what she needed to stay alive. Somewhere in her third choke, she managed an intake of air. Then another. She lay on her side coughing, trying to fill her lungs with the oxygen her husband had denied her.

Carter put his head between his knees, pursed his lips and cupped his hands over his mouth, he was hyperventilating. He held his breath as Maria choked through the silence between heavy breathing. Could he have done it? Who would he have killed anyway? It wasn't the woman he's spent his life with, not the woman he knew and loved. She wasn't capable of murder, she wasn't a traitor to her country. A cold-blooded killer. She was a loving mother of their three children.

His memory kicked in and set fire to his imagination. The nightmares, the mood swings, the sad distant gaze, the trauma from the war years and her resistance to talking about the cave. The revelation sent a cold shiver down his back. A killer, that's exactly what she was. He watched her shoot Logan, the father of her unborn child, she'd murdered Logan right in front of him. How could he not have seen it until now? How had he been so blind? Did she ever love him? She was the mother of his children. Did she love them?

"Was anything real? Anything at all?" Carter couldn't bear to look at her.

"How can you ask that?"

"I don't know you," replied Carter.

"Yes you do. It was war." Maria coughed again but she was breathing steadily now. "I was killing the enemy."

Carter slammed his hand against the bedroom floor. "You killed our friends!"

"Your friends."

"And Logan?" Carter shook his head. "What about Logan?"

"It was him or you. Would you rather I'd shot you?" said Maria.

Right then Carter's answer was yes.

"I defended my country, just like you did." Maria's chin lifted in belief.

"No! This is your country and you've betrayed it. You betrayed me. Our family. Our children." Carter stood and left the bedroom.

Walking through his home nothing felt the same. All the familiar things weren't familiar anymore. Fifteen minutes of his life had changed everything. Nothing would be the same again. Nothing mattered anymore. It was over. Life in that house was over.

Carter sat down on the chair next to the telephone in the hallway. He stared at his feet. There was lint on the thick pile carpet, dust and dirt along the skirting boards. He'd never noticed it before. It was time to call the police. Maria came down the stairs wearing her raincoat and carrying the suitcase. She placed the revolver on the table next to the telephone and turned her back on her husband.

She knew he wouldn't shoot? Was that it? The arrogance angered him. After a life together she was just going to walk out the door. He had meant nothing. She'd used him up and was moving on? Just like Logan. Well, he wasn't Logan. No. She was going to be held accountable for her actions. For murder.

"You don't just get to walk away." Carter picked up the gun and pointed it at Maria. "I'm sorry, I can't allow that."

"Then shoot." She stood in the hallway looking at him. Waiting for him to shoot her. After twenty-seven years of marriage, Carter didn't know the woman standing in front of him.

"Why, Maria?"

"You know why."

He didn't. "Money?"

"Please." Her tone, full of indignation. "I'm a patriot." Then stoic, that voice she always had when she spoke of Spain.

"You could have stopped. After the war, you could have stopped, walked away."

"You don't walk away from your country."

"No. Only from your family." She shook her head. He'd been such a fool.

"My God, Maria, what about the children? They deserve an explanation."

"They're not children anymore." Carter reached for a reply but there was nothing left to say. Maria had already left. The woman who stood before him was rotten to the core with lies, years of deceit, manipulation and secrets, awful secrets.

"Goodbye, Tom." Carter stood, the gun at his hip. "You're not going anywhere."

Maria smiled in sympathy. The smile only doubled his resolve. She was going to be held to account for what she'd done. Two men were lying dead in the living room. What kind of a man would he be to let her leave? She had to pay for his pain if nothing else.

"Let me tell you what's going to happen. I'm going to call the police. You're going to be taken into custody. You're going to confess so that our children can understand why they can't love you anymore. You're going to spend the rest of your life in prison for what you've done." Something changed in Maria's stature at the mention of a prison cell. She took a step towards Carter who tightened his grip on the revolver.

"You think because you hold that gun you're in charge here?" Maria's demeanour also changed, even her voice became unrecognisable as if a personality he'd never met before had suddenly possessed her. Taken over her body. "You've never been in charge." A sinisterness, deep behind her eyes, chiselled her features. "In the cave, in the tank, when they found us. Remember?" He remembered it like it was yesterday. "I was ready to cut your throat." Maria moved toward him. "I was so disappointed they weren't German." She moved like a cat, her head and eyes perfectly still. "I had a knife in my pocket. You didn't know of course. You'd been useful up until that point. If it hadn't been an American who came over the edge, do you think I would have thought twice about slitting your throat?" What was she doing? Goading him? Did she want him to pull the trigger? Christ, she wanted to be shot.

"Stop it, or I swear I'll shoot." Carter was sweating profusely, beads ran down his cheek, his palms were wet, slippery.

"Truth is I'd had enough of you. In that cave twenty-four hours a day. Your pathetic attempts to *keep the morale of the troops up*." She mimicked him. "Your incessant questions, how was I feeling. Appearing to stay professional while all the time lusting after me. Even while I'm pregnant with another man's child." Maria was upon him.

Touching distance. The revolver slipped in the sweat of his hand.

"I saw a use for you. I spared you. You're only here because I gave you your life. I needed cover and you were desperate to give it to me." Maria pushed her coat up against the barrel of the gun and her face up to his. Her eyes were darker than usual, her stare, cold. He could smell her. Joy. She was wearing Joy. She'd been leaving the house after killing two men and walking out on him and the children and she'd had a mind to perfume herself. He didn't know the woman pressed against him. He was seeing her for the first time, the real Maria.

"I never wanted the children." She really didn't fear him at all. Not in the slightest. He knew those eyes so well and she knew his, better than he did. "But they completed the perfect cover and I rather liked them in the end."

The gun slipped. He thought he could pull the trigger but now the moment was upon him, he just couldn't do it. She had betrayed everything he held dear. She'd murdered Windy, Albert and Bunny, lied and deceived him, used him. He'd lived a lie with her his whole life but he still couldn't hurt her. Carter felt weak, helpless. Maria took the revolver from his sweaty hand.

"If you walk out that door I'll spend the rest of my life looking for you. I will find you and you will face justice for what you've done. I promise you that." He couldn't pull the trigger but he would have her looking over her shoulder for the rest of her miserable life. Maria's face softened. She put her hand on his cheek sensitively.

"I know you will." Her words were laced with a deep sense of pity.

Outside the house, the sun kissed the chrysanthemums in the front garden and tears of dew trickled down the lily turf stalks in the shade. Carter had planted black-stem purple echinacea along the fence that bordered the farmer's field next door. They were yet to flower.

The last of the day disappeared behind the corner of rotted thatch.

The sound of the revolver was only heard as a dull muffle in the garden. Autumn's silence indifferently consumed it. Only the wind and chirping starlings remained.

Maria walked confidently out of the front door with her small suitcase, past the newspaper and unbroken bottle of milk. She didn't appear to notice the small amount of blood splatter on the bottom of her coat. Climbing into the Rover 2000 she turned the key in the ignition, adjusted the mirror and addressed the tear in her eye before it had a chance to roll down her cheek. Taking a last look at her home Maria put everything into reverse. On exiting the driveway she pushed hard on the cassette, and the silver Rover pulled away from the house to the emotional cries of Spanish flamenco song.

A Volkswagen beetle pulled into the driveway moments later, Maria's son, the spitting image of his biological father Logan Warlock, behind the wheel, laughing. The children of Maria and Carter climbed out of the car. The youngest had Carter's eyes, his sister, the image of her mother thirty years previous. Home for 'family day', they made their way in through the front door of the house.

The End

ACKNOWLEDGEMENTS

I was lucky to meet Gibraltar police officer and *SUR In English* journalist Ashley James Maer back in 2019. Ash shared the story of the Stay Behind Cave with me. I knew immediately that I would write this novel.

I am also very grateful to Gibraltar Historian and Researcher Ralph Capurro. Ralph allowed me to pick his brains and generously responded to my many questions. The maps, letters and diagrams Ralph shared with me in the early stages formed the backbone of my Tracer mission research.

Philip Smith, Senior Guide and Site Manager for the Gibraltar National Museum gave me a memorable tour of the Stay Behind Cave. Philip's insights on what life would have been like in the cave for the Tracer team were priceless. My visit to the cave, I hope, helped bring the space alive on the page.

I'm indebted to the children of Dr William Albert Bruce Cooper, the last surviving member of the Tracer team who died at the age of 96 on the 3rd of December 2010. Ann, Graham and Heather shared their father's memories from an illustrious career as a Surgeon Lieutenant in the Royal Navy Volunteer Reserves. The character Tom Carter is, however, a complete fiction of my own invention and not based at all on the life of Dr William Albert Bruce Cooper.

Although some of the records that pertain to Operation Tracer still remain classified under the United Kingdom Official Secrets Act, Arthur Milner's part in the planned mission, as the second doctor, is publicly acknowledged and worthy of recognition here. The mission was supervised by Commander Pyke-Nott, Petty Officer Harry Brown is rumoured to have been one of the three radio operators, while the Tracer team leader is said to have been one 'Windy' Gale, a native of Kent. The audaciousness of the Tracer mission is less surprising when the name Ian Fleming becomes attached to it. Real-life spy and future James Bond author, Commander Fleming was Assistant to the Director of Naval Intelligence Admiral John Godfrey in 1941. Fleming and Godfrey were the masterminds behind Operation Tracer.

The declassification of sealed British Naval Intelligence files in the future will hopefully one day correct and complete the picture of the World War II planned Tracer mission and confirm the names of the full Tracer team.

Numerous others helped in the research process for this novel, either because they knew something of Gibraltar at the time of my story, or had military, medical or other experience enabling them to offer advice or spot technical errors.

A final big thank you goes to my editor Robin Seavill. Robin's wisdom, experience, advice and eagle-eyed knack for not just spotting errors and inconsistencies but uncovering new ways to deepen characters and give clarity to the plot helped make the novel more than it might have been otherwise.

9 781838 485368